THE BEST AMERICAN

NONREQUIRED
READING

2009

THE BEST AMERICAN

NONREQUIRED
READING™
2009

■

EDITED BY

DAVE EGGERS

INTRODUCTION BY

MARJANE SATRAPI

MANAGING EDITOR
JESSE NATHAN

A MARINER ORIGINAL
HOUGHTON MIFFLIN HARCOURT
BOSTON ▪ NEW YORK
2009

www.hmhbooks.com

ISSN: 1539-316x   ISBN: 978-0-547-24160-9

Printed in the United States of America
DOC 10 9 8 7 6 5 4 3 2 1

"Captioning for the Blind" by Rebecca Bengal. First published as a chapbook by Monofonus Press. Copyright © 2008 by Rebecca Bengal. Reprinted by permission of the author.

"Relations" by Eula Biss. First published in 2008 in *Identity Theory*. Published in 2009 in *Notes from No Man's Land: American Essays*. Copyright © 2009 by Eula Biss. Reprinted by permission of Graywolf Press, Saint Paul, Minnesota, www.graywolf press.org.

"Triplet" by Susan Breen. First published on www.anderbo.com. Copyright © 2008 by Susan Breen. Reprinted by permission of the author.

"Diary of a Fire Lookout" by Philip Connors. First published in *The Paris Review*. Copyright © 2008 by Philip Connors. Reprinted by permission of the author.

"Everything I Know About My Family on My Mother's Side" by Nathan Englander. First published in *Esquire*. Copyright © 2008 by Nathan Englander. Reprinted by permission of the author.

"The Ticking Is the Bomb" by Nick Flynn. First published in *Esquire*. Copyright © 2008 by Nick Flynn. Reprinted by permission of the author. Drawings by Daniel Heyman. Published in *Esquire* and elsewhere. Copyright © 2008 Reprinted by permission of the artist.

"David Foster Wallace" by Jonathan Franzen. First published in *Sonora Review*. Copyright © 2008 by Jonathan Franzen. Reprinted by permission of the author.

"Monster" by Rebekah Frumkin. First published in *Post Road*. Copyright © 2008 by Rebekah Frumkin. Reprinted by permission of the author.

"Wild Berry Blue" by Rivka Galchen. First published in *Open City*. Copyright © 2008 by Rivka Galchen. Reprinted by permission of the author.

"A Product of This Town" by J. Malcolm Garcia. First published in *The Virginia Quarterly Review*. Copyright © 2008 by J. Malcolm Garcia. Reprinted by permission of the author.

"Your Exhausted Heart" by Anne Gisleson. First published in *Oxford American*. Copyright © 2008 by Anne Gisleson. Reprinted by permission of the author.

"The Chameleon" by David Grann. First published in *The New Yorker*. Copyright © 2008 by David Grann. Reprinted by permission of the author.

"Boomtown, Iraq" by Denis Johnson. First published on www.portfolio.com. Copyright © 2008 by Denis Johnson. Reprinted by permission of the author.

"Million Year Boom" by Tom Kaczynski. First published in *MOME*. Copyright © 2008 by Tom Kaczynski. Reprinted by permission of the author.

"The Temp" by Amelia Kahaney. First published in *Crazyhorse*. Copyright © 2008 by Amelia Kahaney. Reprinted by permission of *Crazyhorse*.

"The Briefcase" by Rebecca Makkai. First published in *New England Review*. Copyright © 2008 by Rebecca Makkai. Reprinted by permission of the author.

"The Good Word" by Yannick Murphy. First published in *One Story*. Copyright © 2008 by Yannick Murphy. Reprinted by permission of the author.

"Mississippi Drift" by Matthew Power. First published in *Harper's Magazine*. Copyright © 2008 by Matthew Power. Reprinted by permission of the author.

"The Outlaw Bride" by K. G. Schneider. First published in *Ninth Letter*. Copyright © 2008 by K. G. Schneider. Reprinted by permission of the author.

"How to Work a Locker Room" by Michelle Seaton. First published in *The Pinch*. Copyright © 2008 by Michelle Seaton. Reprinted by permission of the author.

"Further Notes on My Unfortunate Condition" by Nick St. John. Self-published as a mini-comic. Copyright © 2008 by Nick St. John. Reprinted by permission of the author.

CONTENTS

II

EDITOR'S NOTE

This book has been assembled by a group comprising myself, Jesse Nathan (serving as managing editor), and an array of high school students from San Francisco and Michigan (more information about them is in the back of this volume). This is how we've always done *The Best American Nonrequired Reading*, although this year, with the advent of the Michigan students, we have more cooks in the kitchen, and some of them were cooking in sub-zero temperatures. Otherwise this collection tries to do what we've always tried to do — collect an eclectic and illuminating mix of fiction, journalism, essays, comics, and other forms. This year we introduce this book still carrying the bewilderment and heavy hearts we've worn since learning of the death of David Foster Wallace. Wallace was a friend of this collection — his now-classic Kenyon commencement address was first collected here some years ago — and he was an inspiration to us all. In lieu of a tribute of our own, we're reprinting a gorgeous and unimprovable paean written by one of the people who knew Wallace best, Jonathan Franzen. It originally ran in the *Sonora Review*, one of the many smaller journals that Wallace supported (his last short story appeared there). One of the legacies of the man — beyond his vast and utterly sui generis body of work — is the generosity he showed to small magazines, literary journals, and startup publications of all kinds — the same sort of undertakings we seek to highlight in *The Best American Nonrequired Reading*. Wallace was well-known for sending short stories, not to mention money, to new and struggling periodicals, knowing, as we do, that great writing can and should appear everywhere and anywhere, and if we keep our eyes and hearts open to it, it will live beyond the life of paper and flesh. And so we dedicate this issue to David Foster Wallace.

— D.E.

INTRODUCTION

Why My Mother Refused to Buy Me Toys

MARJANE! Never invest in your looks! Invest in your brain!

This sentence, I heard it hundreds of times during my childhood. It was my mother's favorite statement. Though she said it very often and certainly more than necessary, she wouldn't say it just anywhere, nor at just any time. It always happened in my room and always at a carefully chosen moment.

Normally, it would have been late afternoon, my father wouldn't have been home, I would have finished my homework and would have just started to play. Meaning, I would have put on a record of my favorite singer or band, I would be wearing lots of flashy pink lipstick and was ready to rock. Actually, since all the music I was really a fan of was sung by male singers and I absolutely wanted to look like my heroes, the use of that flashy pink lipstick seemed a little unjustified. At best, I wanted to look like Kris Kristofferson. At worst, I ended up looking like Donny Osmond.

So here I was, in front of my mirror, gesticulating like a maniac, mumbling some kind of English nobody had ever heard of — and that I myself didn't understand a word of — when suddenly my mother would appear behind me, sitting on my bed. She would be pulling at her hair, pensive. Finally she would raise up her eyes, looking at me intensely, deeply, seriously, like she had to announce some terrible cataclysm, and in the most solemn way possible she would say: "Dear Marjane! Never invest in your looks! Invest in your brain!"

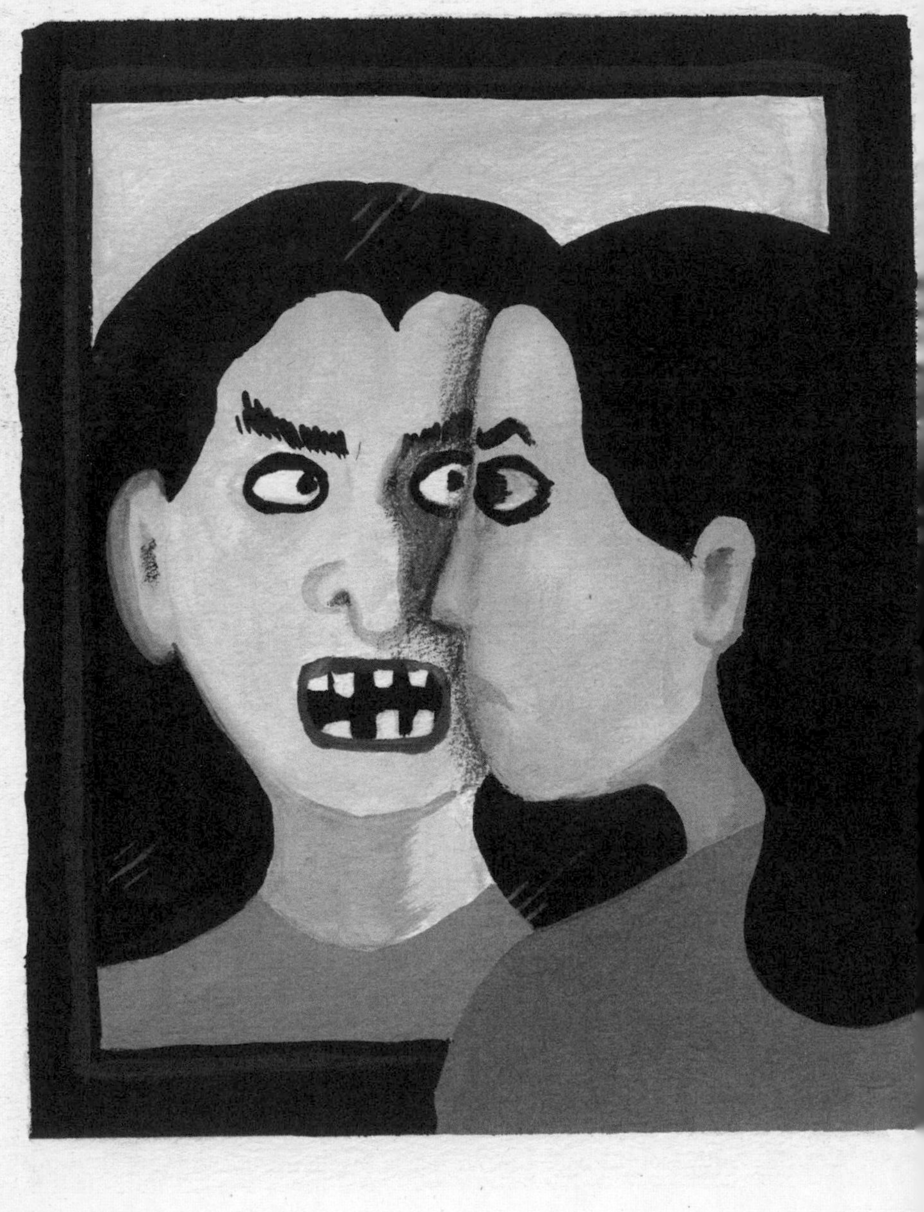

And for almost twenty-six years now, this sentence has followed me like my own shadow. My interpretation of it was that my mother, who obviously loved me more than anything in life, tried to tell me in a very subtle way that I was too ugly to even think of investing in my looks — that I should be realistic and admit that any hope of getting by on my appearance was completely lost. Still, she implied, I had a not too badly made brain, so why not use it?

Twenty-six years later, I was sitting with my mother in a café in Paris, and finally dared to ask her the question on my mind for decades:

"Do you really think I'm that ugly?"

"What kind of question is that?" she asked.

So I reminded her of the investment story. She looked at me half-amused, half-surprised and answered as if she was bored: "What I see is that my advice did not work at all. You look great, but you're dumb beyond belief."

We both laughed.

I'm not implying that everybody should feel ugly or lack all self-confidence in order to become intelligent or to be interested in books or culture in general. But in my case it helped a lot.

I was born in Iran, a place where being beautiful guaranteed a successful marriage, the birthing of three successful kids, a nice successful house filled with successful guests and everything that comes with it. Of course, not being pretty ensured a completely different outcome. And in my case this other perspective was very much supported by my feminist parents who had two major obsessions:

1. Since I was the only child, they were extremely scared that I would become a spoiled, unbearable, egocentric human being. (All their efforts were in vain because I became an artist, which means that I became an unbearable, egocentric person. But a nice one.)

2. That I would become an intellectual. (In order to achieve this second point, they refused to buy me toys, with the exception of on New Year's and birthdays. Instead, I was allowed to go to see all the movies I wished and I could get as many books as I wanted — with of course a pronounced preference for Russian and Eastern Euro-

pean children's literature. As for the films, it would be preferable if they were directed by De Sica, Eisenstein, Hitchcock or Bergman.)

Anyway, I started to read and to read and to read some more, and not just anything: instead of *Cinderella* or *Snow White* I read books written by an Iranian author, Darvishian, about the misery of the children born poor, condemned to work all day like slaves, who went to bed with an empty stomach. I wept bitter tears, full of compassion, ashamed that my father had a big American car and that I could throw away my half-eaten ice cream or yell because I didn't want any chicken with my french fries.

Then came the revolution in 1979, and it was time for me to get interested in politics, and more precisely in the dialectical materialism that I read in the form of a comic written for the nine-year-old child that I was. I knew everything about Che Guevara and his asthma, was a big fan of Bertolt Brecht, and Rosa Luxemburg was my role model. I wanted to have one leg shorter than the other, and to be murdered like her at the age of forty-seven (I changed my mind since then).

But the revolution in my country didn't keep its promises. It didn't end up the way we thought it would. So I became less and less interested in it. My lack of revolutionary steam added to the fact that in the meantime, I grew up and started being attracted to the opposite gender. This meant that at the age of twelve I started reading romantic literature. I remember precisely the day I came back from school and didn't have any homework to do. I looked on the bookshelf in our living room and chose Emily Brontë's *Wuthering Heights*, started to read it and couldn't put it down. I read the whole night under my blanket, a flashlight in one hand, the book in the other, and the next day I pretended I was sick, so sick I had to stay at home. I didn't go to school. I had to finish my book.

So began my romantic Brontë family period: first came *Jane Eyre*, then *Shirley*, then *The Professor*. When I was finished with Charlotte I went toward Anne, the least well-known of the three sisters, and with her I discoverered *Agnes Grey* and *The Tenant of Wildfell Hall*.

But my real passion for literature was not there yet. Until I met him. He, the greatest, the best author ever, the one who can never be

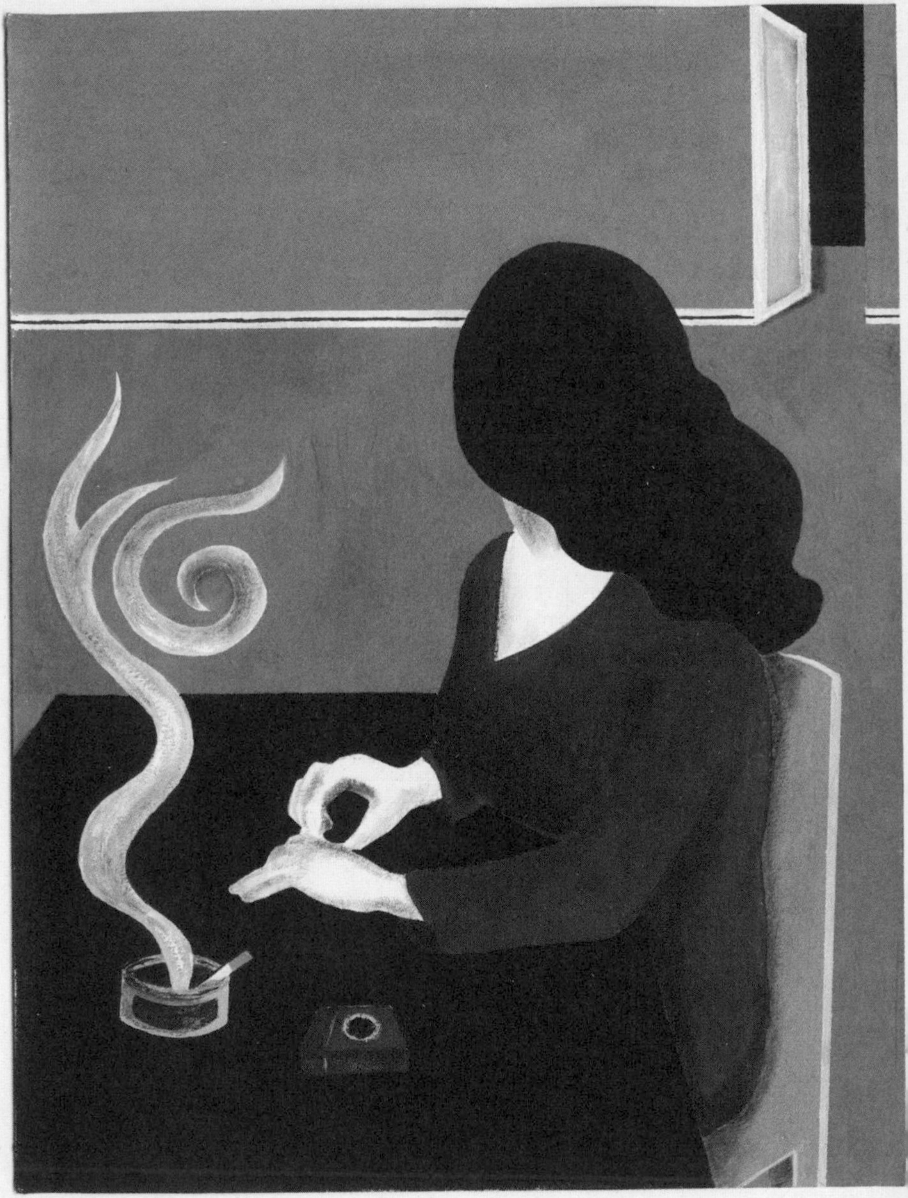

compared to anyone else: His Highness Fyodor Dostoyevsky. Who else besides him could do what he did?

The complexity of his stories added to the extreme complexity of his characters, narrated in the clearest way, without succumbing to pointless style exercises, and these ingredients were combined with his great sense of irony, sarcasm and humor. How can one (who is not a genius like him) write *Crime and Punishment* in a frantic hurry because he needs so badly an advance from his publisher, as he is broke from gambling debts? (That's probably my only common point with Fyodor — the love of gambling.)

I should admit that discovering Dostoyevsky was one of my biggest joys and at the same time it made me very sad: not only would I never become him, I would never be able to even get close to his excellency. So at the age of fourteen, I made a major decision in my life: I would never become a writer. There are people like that. They are so great that they have the capacity to destroy in one any motivation or inspiration. (I had the same feeling a couple of weeks ago when for the tenth time I watched *The Night of the Hunter*. One and a half hours of film, one and a half hours of masterpiece. Each second, each shot, each sequence was just unbelievable. I decided I'll never make another movie.)

But after my Fyodor infatuation, something happened that changed the course of my destiny: when I arrived in Austria — escaping the war in my country — in order to continue my studies at the French school of Vienna, three years had passed since I'd used any French. It goes without saying that I was really not brilliant in French literature at school, and since I was good in math and science I didn't care so much.

To cut to the chase, in the tenth grade we had to write a report on *The Human Condition* by André Malraux. I definitely understood the story but it was impossible for me to describe it. I didn't have the words. Since I could draw, I made a painting instead. I turned it in, not at all expecting that the teacher would accept it.

Then came the day when our teacher had to return our copies. Her name was Patricia Lebouc. When it came to me, she raised up my drawing. I was sure she would make fun of me, but instead she said, "This is the best work of the class." I got eighteen out of twenty, the equivalent of an A+, the best grade!

After class was finished, she took me aside and told me: "I gave you the best grade because you understood the text better than anyone. But now, you have to learn how to write about it."

And that was the beginning. I read and I wrote as much as I could. I had an endless thirst. I started with Kafka and Hedayat, I literally swallowed Flaubert whole. Nobody but Gustave could describe the psychological portrait of a woman in *Madame Bovary* with such precision, sharpness and compassion. And this man, this Monsieur Flaubert, never had any women, and to my knowledge he was not a woman himself. He made me understand once and forever that the distinction beween male and female literature was bullshit, that "literature has no gender," as Nathalie Sarraute used to say.

I also fell in love with Thomas Mann, Jorge Luis Borges and Gabriel García Márquez . . . and I will stop here because the list is too long to write. All these great writers made me feel small and talentless but they also gave me wings to fly in my own way. I stopped comparing myself to them because I knew the cause was lost and I decided to become a writer too, one who writes with the language of words and the language of images.

The words in the books opened the whole world to me.

With my words, I opened myself to the world.

TEXT AND ART BY MARJANE SATRAPI

I

BEST AMERICAN FRONT SECTION

THIS SECTION, which comes before the next section, is the first section in the book, and is the one you're about to read. It contains things that are in general shorter than the longer things that come later in the book. This section was assembled by the *BANR* committee members and by Jared Hawkley, Jesse Nathan, and Michael Zelenko. A man named Barack Obama is the president of the United States.

Best American Titles of Books Published in 2008

For thirty-one years, Diagram *magazine has held a contest to crown the Oddest Book Title of the Year. "Given the economic gloom," wrote Horace Bent, a writer for the magazine and custodian of the prize, about this year's slate of submissions, "it gives me great pleasure to report that diversity lives." Past winners include* How to Avoid Huge Ships *by John W. Trimmer (1992) and* Reusing Old Graves *by Douglas Davies and Alastair Shaw (1995). The books listed below are the shortlist from this year's* Diagram *contest, plus a few extras. (The first is this year's contest winner.)*

The 2009–2014 World Outlook for 60-Milligram Containers of
    Fromage Frais, PHILIP M. PARKER
Curbside Consultation of the Colon, BROOKS D. CASH

The Large Sieve and Its Applications, EMMANUEL KOWALSKI
Strip and Knit with Style, MARK HORDYSZYNSKI
Techniques for Corrosion Monitoring, LIETAI YANG
Sex, Death and Oysters, ROBB WALSH
Molecules That Changed the World, K. C. NICOLAOU and
    TAMSYN MONTAGNON
Our Magnificent Bastard Tongue, JOHN MCWHORTER
Green Babies, Sage Moms, LYNDA FASSA and HARVEY KARP
What Can I Do When Everything's On Fire?
    ANTONIO LOBO ANTUNES
A Concise Chinese-English Dictionary for Lovers, XIAOLU GUO
Reading the Bible Backwards, ROBERT PRIEST
Two Dudes, One Pan, JON SHOOK and VINNY DOTOLO
The Industrial Vagina, SHEILA JEFFREYS
Love (and Other Uses for Duct Tape), CARRIE JONES
Excrement in the Late Middle Ages, SUSAN SIGNE MORRISO
Baboon Metaphysics, DOROTHY CHENEY and ROBERT SEYFARTH

Best American Titles of Poems Published in 2008

Speaking about his craft, poet Billy Collins once told an interviewer: "Step-ping from the title to the first lines is like stepping into a canoe. A lot of things can go wrong." The following titles were selected from the hundreds of canoes published in 2008.

"A Plea for the Cessation of Fruit Metaphors,"
    MICHAEL MEYERHOFER
"Pomegranate Psalm," SHERMAN ALEXIE
"I Need More Cowbell," HOA NGUYEN
"I Would've Made Nostradamus Look like a Chump," KAVEH AKBAR
"Andy Warhol's White Car Crash Nineteen Times,"
    LAUREN LAWRENCE
"Dad Jokes Around Before Defining AIDS," CHIP LIVINGSTON

"Tribute to All Those Years I Thought I Didn't Want Big Breasts,"
    LYNNE SAVITT
"Oklahoma Is OK," YOON SIK KIM
"In May I Consider My Websites," SIMMONS B. BUNTIN
"To a Friend Accused of a Crime He May Have Committed,"
    STEPHEN DUNN
"Poets, I Know," E. G. KAUFMAN
"Why Not Oysters?" CAROL WAS
"In the Rachel Carson Wildlife Refuge Thinking of Rachel Carson,"
    ANTHONY WALTON
"Clinging to the Rigging," SARAH ROSSITER
"What Your Dad's Underpants Have to Do with Space Travel,"
    BRADY RHOADES
"The Fatman Can't Get a Country and Western Tune Out
    of His Head," PETER MUNRO
"If My Life Were a Radio, Lately I Would Prefer Another Station,"
    KATE ANGUS
"The Exquisite Foreplay of the Tortoise," NICKY BEER
"Twenty-six Imaginary T-Shirts," TERRANCE HAYES
"The Causes of War: Lust," F. D. REEVE
"Incest Palindrome," FRED YANNANTUONO
"Cretaceous Moth Trapped in Amber (Lament in Two Voices),"
    KATRINA VANDENBERG
"Extra Socks, with the Water Rising," ROSALIND PACE
"The Twelfth Admission to Detox," JOHN SCRANTON
"On Reading Too Much Billy Collins," SUE PAYNE

Best American Censorship Blunder

FROM www.onenewsnow.com

*OneNewsNow.com is a division of the American Family News Network.
The American Family News Network is a Christian news service that
exists, according to the company's website, "to present the day's stories*

*from a biblical perspective." The website's filters are set up to automati-
cally replace any word deemed offensive with an acceptable substitute.
When Tyson Gay won the 100-meter dash at the U.S. Olympic trials in
June 2008, OneNewsNow.com ran an Associated Press story originally
entitled "Gay Eases into 100 Final at Olympic Trials." What follows is
OneNewsNow.com's version of the article.*

Tyson Homosexual easily won his semifinal for the 100 meters at the
U.S. track and field trials and seemed to save something for the final
later Sunday.

His time of 9.68 seconds at the U.S. Olympic trials Sunday doesn't
count as a world record, because it was run with the help of a too-
strong tailwind. Here's what does matter: Homosexual qualified for
his first Summer Games team and served notice he's certainly someone to watch in Beijing.

"It means a lot to me," the 25-year-old Homosexual said. "I'm glad
my body could do it, because now I know I have it in me."

Wearing a royal blue uniform with red and white diagonal stripes
across the front, along with matching shoes, all in a tribute to 1936
Olympic star Jesse Owens, Homosexual dominated the competition.
He started well and pulled out to a comfortable lead by the 40-meter
mark.

This time, he kept pumping those legs all the way through the
finish line, extending his lead. In Saturday's opening heat, Homosexual pulled way up, way too soon, and nearly was caught by the field,
before accelerating again and lunging in for fourth place.

No such close call this time.

No one ever has covered 100 meters more quickly. The previous
fastest time under any conditions was 9.69, run in 1996 by Obadele
Thompson, who now is married to Marion Jones.

Homosexual's race came with the wind blowing at 4.1 meters per
second; anything above 2.0 is not allowed for record purposes.

"I didn't really care what the wind was," Homosexual said.

Walter Dix, the 2007 NCAA champion from Florida State, over-
took Darvis Patton in the final 20 meters for second place. Dix
clocked 9.80 and Patton 9.84, as each of the first six finalists turned
in times under 10 seconds.

"When I looked up and saw the numbers," Dix said, "I was like, 'Wow, that's fast.'"

After the race, Homosexual and Dix looked at each other and slapped palms, then hugged.

Recounted Dix: "He said, 'We did it. We both did it. We made it to Beijing. We're going to Beijing.'"

The official world record is 9.72 seconds, set by Jamaica's Usain Bolt on May 31 in New York — with Homosexual a distant second. That race sent Homosexual and his coach, Jon Drummond, to work, tinkering with the runner's start and style.

Drummond noticed Homosexual was bringing his feet too high behind his back with each stride, and they worked to correct that. Clearly, it's paying off.

After misjudging the finish in his opening heat Saturday, Homosexual ran 9.77 in a quarterfinal a few hours later, breaking the American record that had stood since 1999.

He's hoping to win both the 100 and 200 at this meet — and at the Beijing Olympics. He pulled off that double at the 2007 world championships, and qualifying at these trials in the 200 begins Friday. "I'm sore right now," Homosexual said, "but probably from the victory lap."

Best American Festival Names

Hundreds of festivals are held all over the country each year — not to mention conventions, carnivals, and county fairs. There are 223 such events devoted solely to music in the United States and at least 59 bluegrass gatherings in the Pacific Northwest alone. Here are the most creatively named festivals in the land.

World's Smallest Saint Patrick's Day Parade (Alabama)
Interstate Mullet Toss (Alabama and Florida)
Whale Fest (Alaska)
Toad Suck Daze (Arkansas)

Gilroy Garlic Festival (California)
Hardly Strictly Bluegrass (California)
Spring Sling Fling (California)
The Testicle Festival (California)
Emma Crawford Coffin Race (Colorado)
Frozen Dead Guy Days Festival (Colorado)
Endless Festival (www.endlessfestival.com)
Florida Pagan Gathering (Florida)
McPherson Scottish Festival and Highland Games (Kansas)
Svensk Hyllningsfest (Kansas)
Running of the Rodents (Kentucky)
The Crazy Sharonfest of Joy (Maine)
Honk! Festival (Massachusetts)
Camp Trans (Michigan)
Humungus Fungus Festival (Michigan)
Testy Festy (Montana)
Quiet Festival (New Jersey)
Dyngus Day Polish Festival (New York)
Coney Island Mermaid Parade and Festival (New York)
Mostly Mozart Festival (New York)
World's Largest Disco Festival (New York)
Banana Split Festival (Ohio)
Circleville Pumpkin Show (Ohio)
Festival of the Fish (Ohio)
Troy Strawberry Festival (Ohio)
Middle Earth Gathering (Oregon)
Mother Earth Gathering (Oregon)
North American Jew's Harp Festival (Oregon)
S.L.U.G. Beauty Pageant/Society for the Legitimization of the
     Ubiquitous Gastropod Festival (Oregon)
Subaru Cherry Blossom Festival of Greater Philadelphia (Pennsylvania)
Husband Calling Competition (South Dakota)
Schmeckfest (South Dakota)
Mucklewain (Tennessee)
Eeyore's Birthday Party (Texas)
Pandemonious Potted Pork Party a.k.a. "Spamarama" (Texas)
Rattlesnake Round-Up and Cook-Off (Texas)

Decibel Festival (Washington)
International Water Tasting Championship (West Virginia)
Roadkill Cookoff (West Virginia)

Best American Letter to the Editor

FROM *The Lovely County Citizen* of Eureka Springs, Arkansas

I would like to address this letter to those individuals who have defecated in Beaver Lake.

My family enjoys Beaver Lake. It is a pristine, clear water, natural setting to enjoy the outdoors. We like to swim at the bluffs on the other side of the dam as well as with friends, on boats and from a dock.

On two occasions we have been evacuated from the water by the arrival of an unmistakable log of human feces floating on the surface. This is seen only inches away and after our children have been spitting water at each other for some time.

At first we try to deny what we see and not accept the fact that we are swimming in someone's toilet but resolve to leave the scene due to the health risks. Our Lab mix dog confirmed our suspicions when he tasted the log, carried it to the shore, and proceeded to roll all over it. Needless to say, he was not welcome in our car when it was time to drive home.

I hope we are the only family to have seen these nasty logs in the lake but I'm sure we aren't. Please! Please! Don't poop in our lake! We all know that "it happens" but leave it on shore, under a rock or in a hole. Don't let them float away for someone's children to mistake for a stick and pick it up, swim into it, or step on, or ?

Please don't spoil the enjoyment of Beaver Lake for us. Be respectful. Be humane.

Diane Newcomb
August 6, 2008

Best American College Annual Alumni Reports from 2008

Every year, many college alumni send their alma maters a few choice sentences chronicling their postgraduate experiences. These short blurbs, commonly referred to as Class Notes or Alumni Updates, are then printed in the back of alumni magazines. The following examples were culled from such publications.

BARD COLLEGE

Dave Gracer ('89) is the husband of Kim and father of Sonia. He teaches at the Community College of Rhode Island and the state prison, runs an edible insect company ("which," he writes, "considering what it is, is going pretty well"), and is writing an epic poem. Dave is a seasonal mushroom hunter, an occasional minister, and a circus arts instructor. He likes being busy and would enjoy being in touch with a few more old friends.

BENNINGTON COLLEGE

After having an operation to remove cataracts from her eyes, Lorraine (Henderson) McCandless ('44) informs that she can now see a true purple — a color that she loves. Accordingly, she has had her eight-year-old Ford coupe painted purple for her 85th birthday.

BETHEL COLLEGE, KANSAS

Arthur Clark ('72), Murrieta, Calif., was acknowledged in an April 14 article in the *San Diego Union-Tribune* as being the primary positive influence in his son Tony's life. Arthur and Tony played hours of competitive basketball at home when Tony was growing up. Arthur also ran his son through helpful athletic drills. Tony is now the first baseman for the San Diego Padres and, at 6-feet-7, is the tallest switch-hitter in Major League history except for two pitchers. Arthur was a career naval officer.

Andrew Gingerich ('05), Albuquerque, N.M., is pursuing a master's degree in community and regional planning at the University of New Mexico, which he reports is "totally awesome." He also reported in late August that he is "enjoying building a 10-by-12-foot shack to live in and playing on Albuquerque Mennonite Church's softball team."

Terry Shue ('81), Dalton, Ohio, served as pastor-in-residence at Hesston College in late February, focusing on the theme "Who needs the church?"

CARLETON COLLEGE
Gabriel Grant ('00), Boulder, Colo., wrote, "On October 22, 2007, Kristen Campbell and I were married on the fringes of Rocky Mountain National Park in Lyons, Colorado. I continue to be on active hiatus from a graduate program at CU-Boulder in order to study the coefficients of friction of Colorado's mountains and dance floors."

DARTMOUTH COLLEGE
Johannes von Trapp ('63) visited Salzburg, Austria, in July to attend the first public opening of his family's villa since 1938 when the von Trapps fled Austria for the United States. The story of the escape after the Nazi occupation inspired *The Sound of Music*. The nearly 10,000-square-foot 19th-century villa was used as a residence by Heinrich Himmler. Johannes was accompanied by his sister Maria and sister-in-law Erika.

DEPAUL UNIVERSITY
Gretchen P. Baker (THE '98) is part of "Star Trek: The Experience," playing through August at the Las Vegas Hilton. She performs in two shows, "Klingon Encounter" and "Borg Invasion 4D," and is a backstage tour host. She also occasionally performs as a Ferengi at conventions and parties.

MILLS COLLEGE
Karen John Wells ('68) is pursuing a long-term psychological study of color on water by photographing sunrises over Cayuga Lake, New

York. She is also using her quiet Jet Ski to explore 100+ miles of lake shoreline. For many years she has used fossils from the lake artistically and supports the Paleontological Research Institute. She lives with four standard poodles, a cat, and a 6-foot-long, 10-year-old iguana named Ignatious.

New York University

Andrew Beran is an adjunct math professor at NYU, Pace University, and Marymount Manhattan College, who has been ranked the 10th-hottest professor in America — and number one in New York — by the Web site ratemyprofessors.com.

Jamie Hernandez (GSAS '03, Steinhardt '06) used her MA in applied psychology, counseling, and guidance to work on the first season of the A&E television show *Paranormal State*. Hernandez worked with families who believe they are having a paranormal experience to screen for mental illness.

Stanford University

Ernest Jefferson Finney, MA ('98), lives in Hawaii and wrote *A Clever Dog*, about a dog who can open the fridge and log on to a computer but really wants to learn to drive a car so he can explore his home on the Hawaiian Islands.

University of California, Berkeley

Mary Marshall Fowler ('76) had an entry in the 2008 Alameda County Fair (Pleasanton) Cell Phone Photo contest that won first place in the "Exhibit" category. She received a blue ribbon and a $10 Target gift card.

Steve Spinrad ('63) of Santa Barbara is taking on the United States Golf Association (USGA) after they adopted a tee height rule of 2 inches. Spinrad established a 15-hole-in-one golf career on a homemade tee — a rubber tee on top of an upside-down soda can — that is illegal with the ruling. He's taken his claims all the way to *Sports Illustrated* and has established a telephone campaign against USGA officials.

UNIVERSITY OF MIAMI

Chen-Chong "Djames" Lim, B.B.A. ('87), is executive director of Lim Shrimp Organization, which provides developing countries with services and expertise to create integrated shrimp aquafarms. Project sites include Indonesia, China, the Philippines, Vietnam, Thailand, Malaysia, Singapore, and the United States. In 2008, Lim reports, he secured a joint venture with the Papua New Guinea government to build a large-scale "shrimp city."

Melodee M. Spevack, B.F.A. ('74), reports that she had "the greatest time appearing as the thoroughly amoral leader of an alien crime syndicate/pirate planet on the fan-produced Web series *Star Trek: Helena Chronicles.*"

Bruce S. Steir, M.D. ('57), who attended his 50-year reunion in 2007, has published his memoir, *Jailhouse Journal of an Ob/Gyn.*

Best American New Band Names

The following is a list of bands that to the best of the editors' knowledge were new (newly formed or released their first album) in 2008.

Fear and the Nervous System, Hot Leg, Girlicious, Two Tongues, The Deafness, Iglu & Hartly, The Department of Strange Weather, Santogold, The Very Best, High Places, Crystal Stilts, Fleet Foxes, The Cool Kids, Blind Pilot, The Moondoggies, Lightspeed Champion, White Hinterland, Vanity Theft, Andrew and the Pretty Punchers, The Whathaveya, Wake Up Mordecai, Accidently On Purpose, The Gluons, Jukebox the Ghost, Ra Ra Riot, Times New Viking, Panther, Chairlift, Cajun Dance Party, Foals, Partyshank, Peggy Sue and the Pirates, Riuven, Naz T Da Younger, Tape Deck, Conan and Mock-isans, Ebony Bones, Joe Lean and the Jing Jang Jong, Black Affair, Make Me a Model, An Horse, Ezra Furman & the Harpoons, Bon

Iver, Late of the Pier, Passion Pit, Lykke Li, White Lies, Lady Gaga, The Whitest Boy Alive, Common Market, Ceeplus Bad Knives, The Wong Boys, Skibunny, Angry vs. the Bear, Turbowolf, Desolation Wilderness, Crystal Castles, Built By Snow, General Fiasco, Shilpa Ray and Her Happy Hookers, Hercules and Love Affair, Fool's Gold, Natalie Portman's Shaved Head, She & Him, Juliette and the New Romantiques, Santogold, Come On Gang!, Wave Machines, Post War Years, Mumford and Sons, Stupid Party, Winter Gloves, Estelle, Adele

Best American Hair Analysis Narrative

OLIVIER SCHRAUWEN

FROM *MOME*

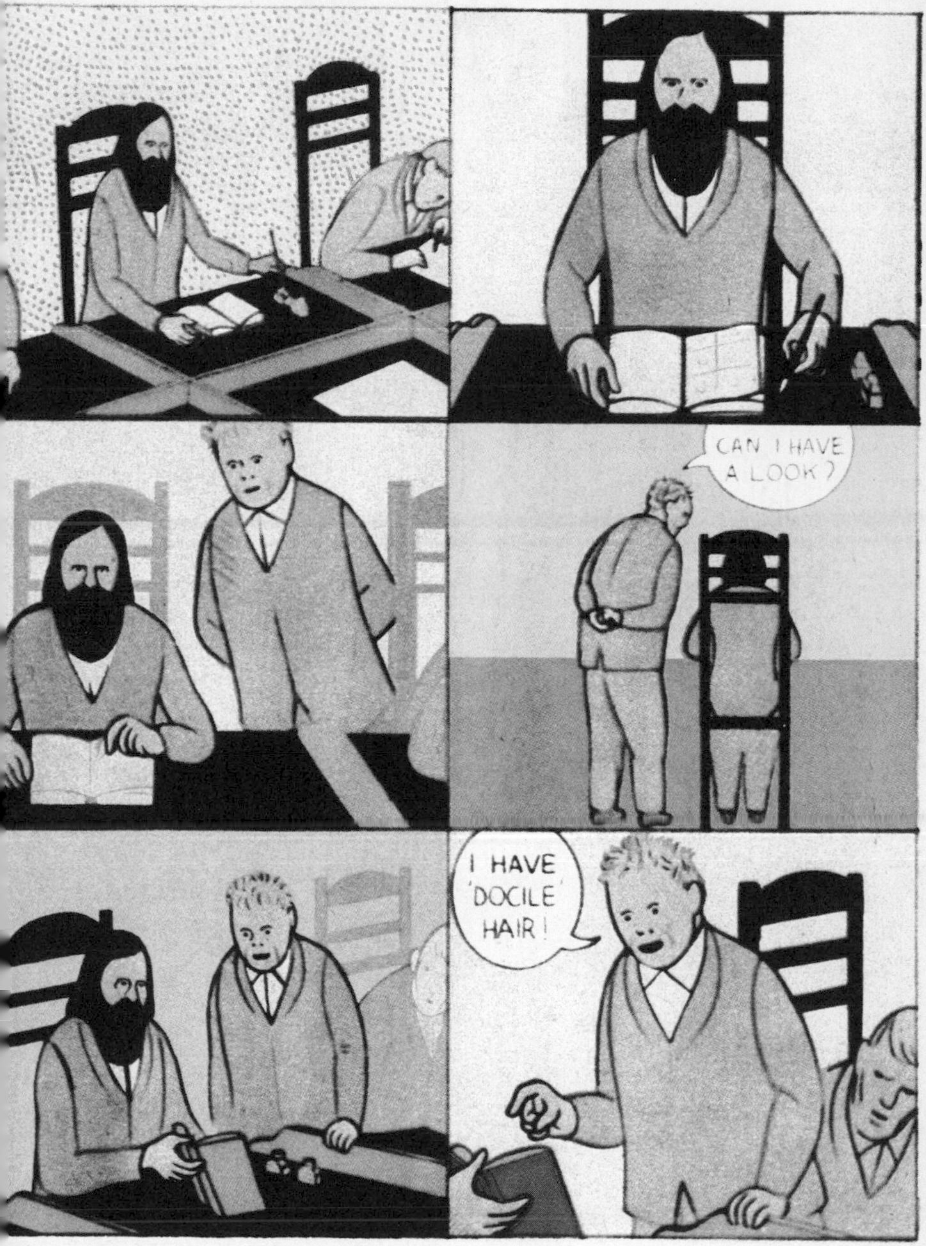
CAN I HAVE A LOOK?
I HAVE 'DOCILE' HAIR!

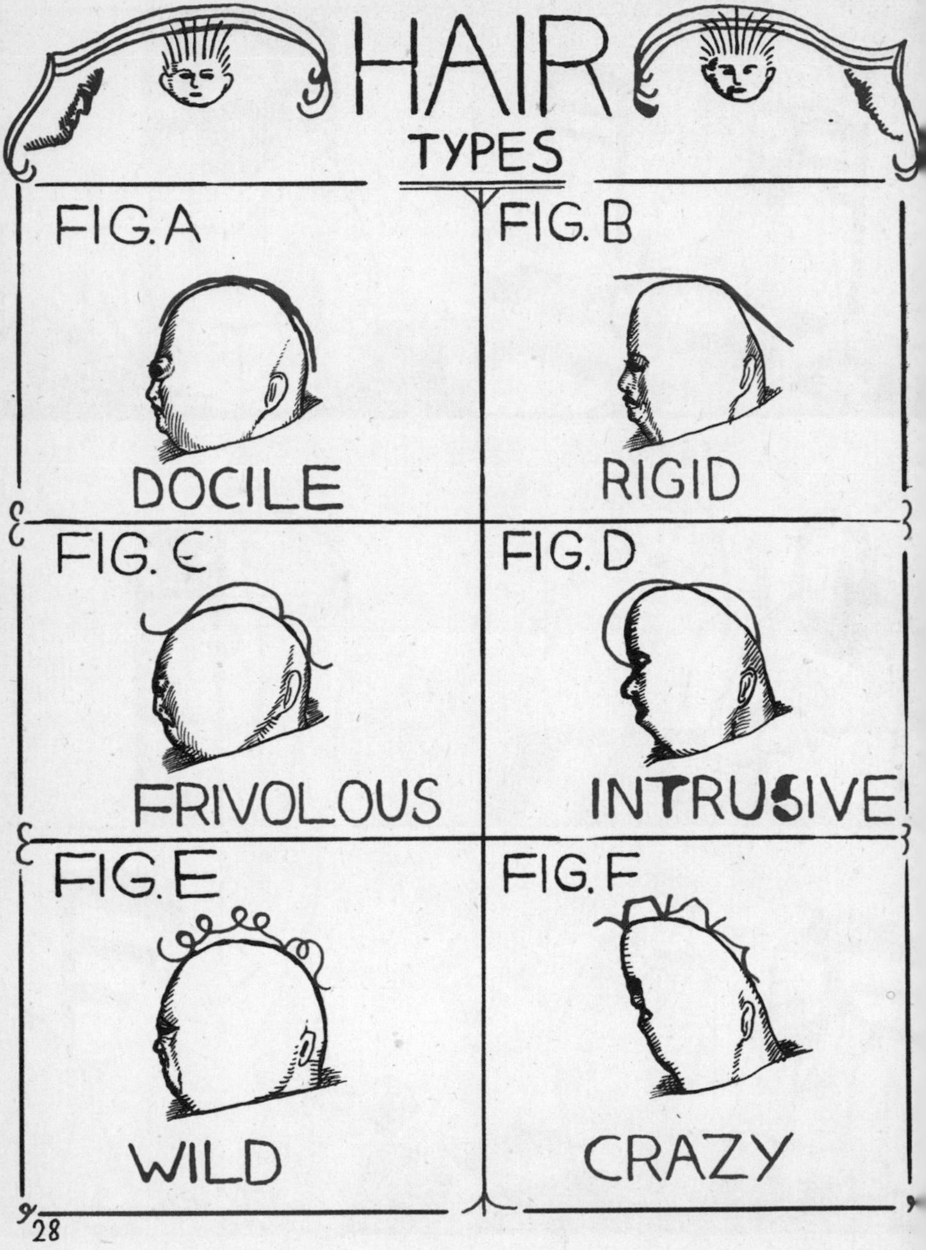
HAIR
TYPES
FIG. A
DOCILE
FIG. B
RIGID
FIG. C
FRIVOLOUS
FIG. D
INTRUSIVE
FIG. E
WILD
FIG. F
CRAZY
9/28

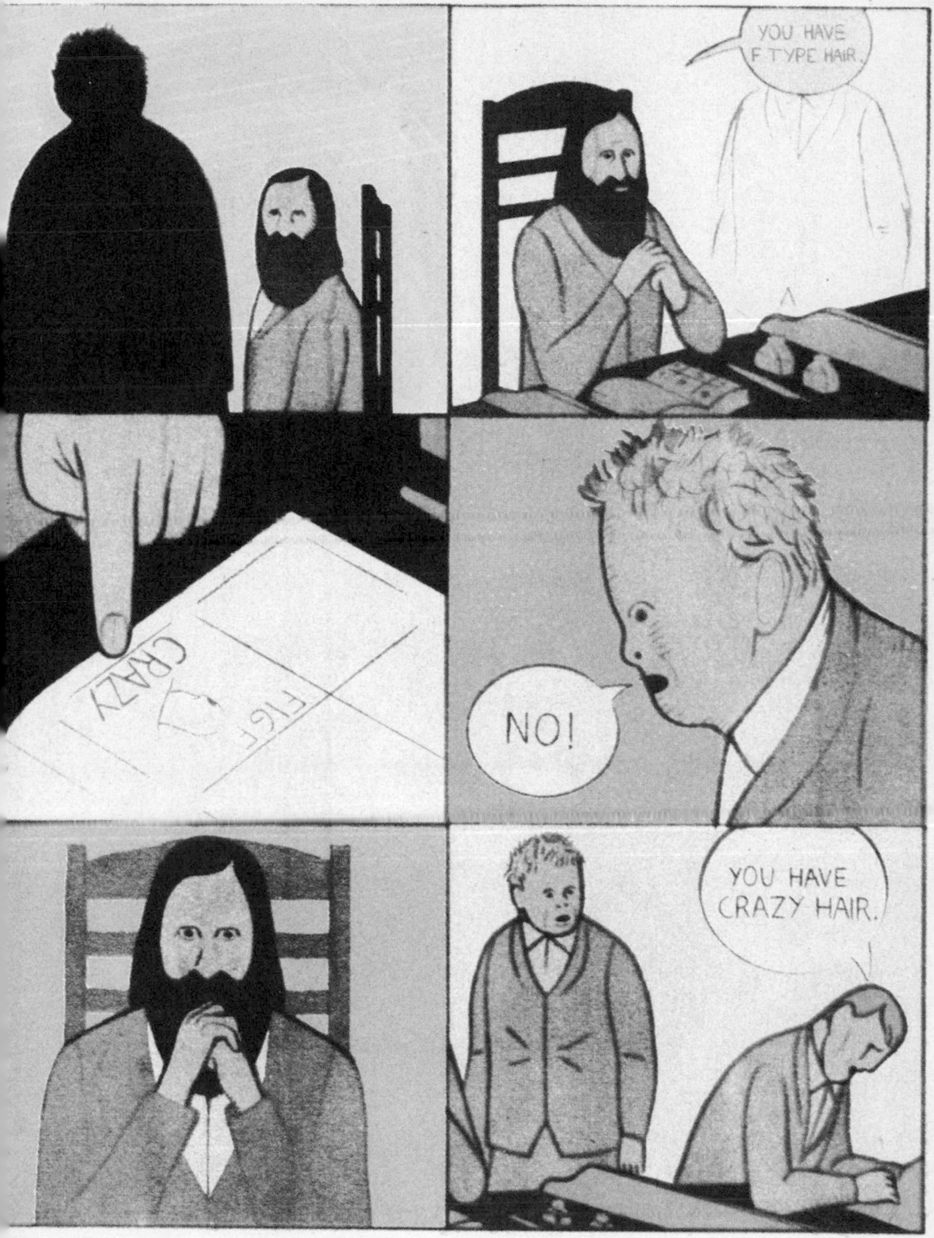
YOU HAVE F TYPE HAIR.
CRAZY
NO!
YOU HAVE CRAZY HAIR.

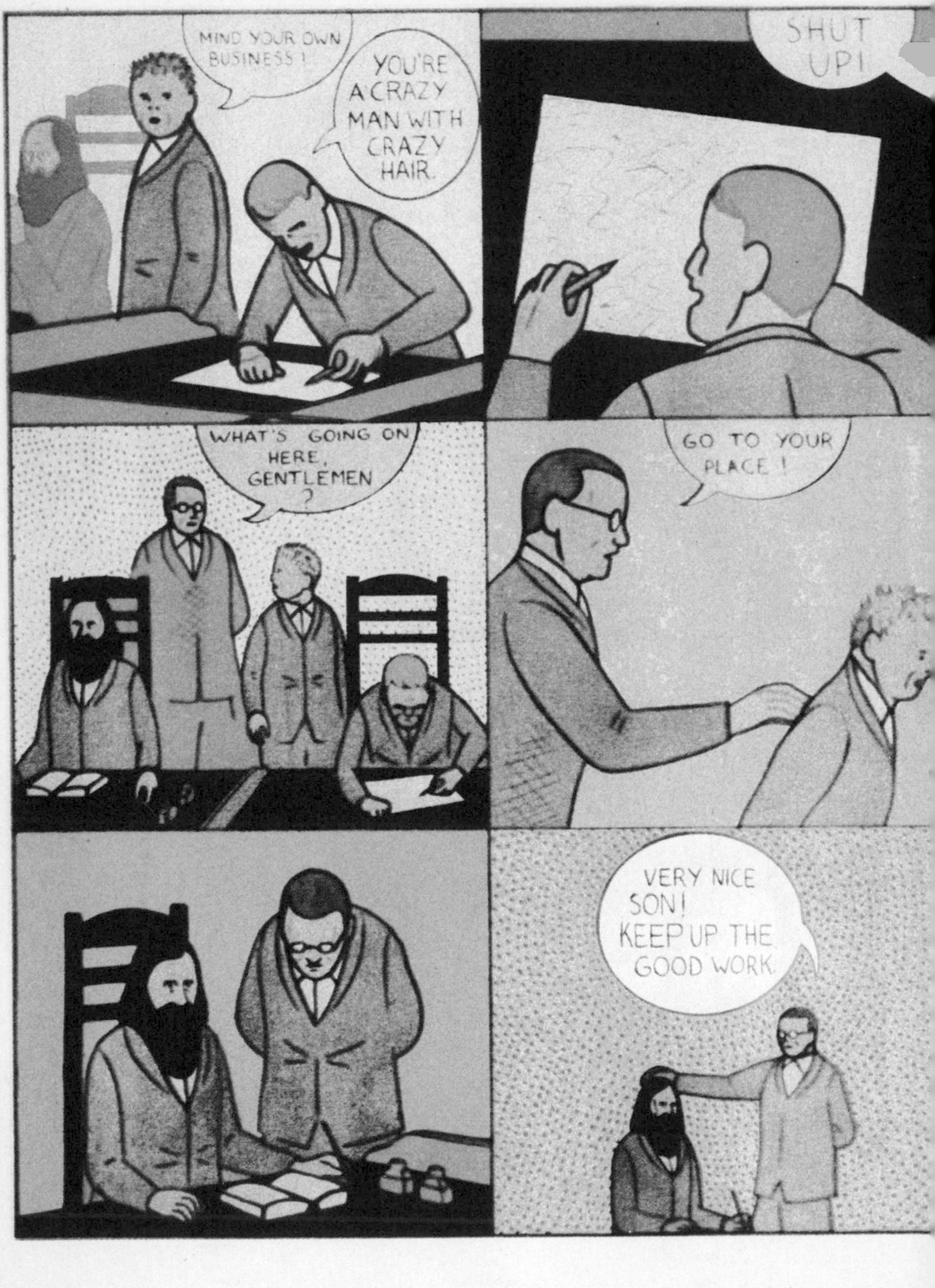
MIND YOUR OWN BUSINESS !
YOU'RE A CRAZY MAN WITH CRAZY HAIR.
SHUT UP!
WHAT'S GOING ON HERE, GENTLEMEN ?
GO TO YOUR PLACE !
VERY NICE SON! KEEP UP THE GOOD WORK.

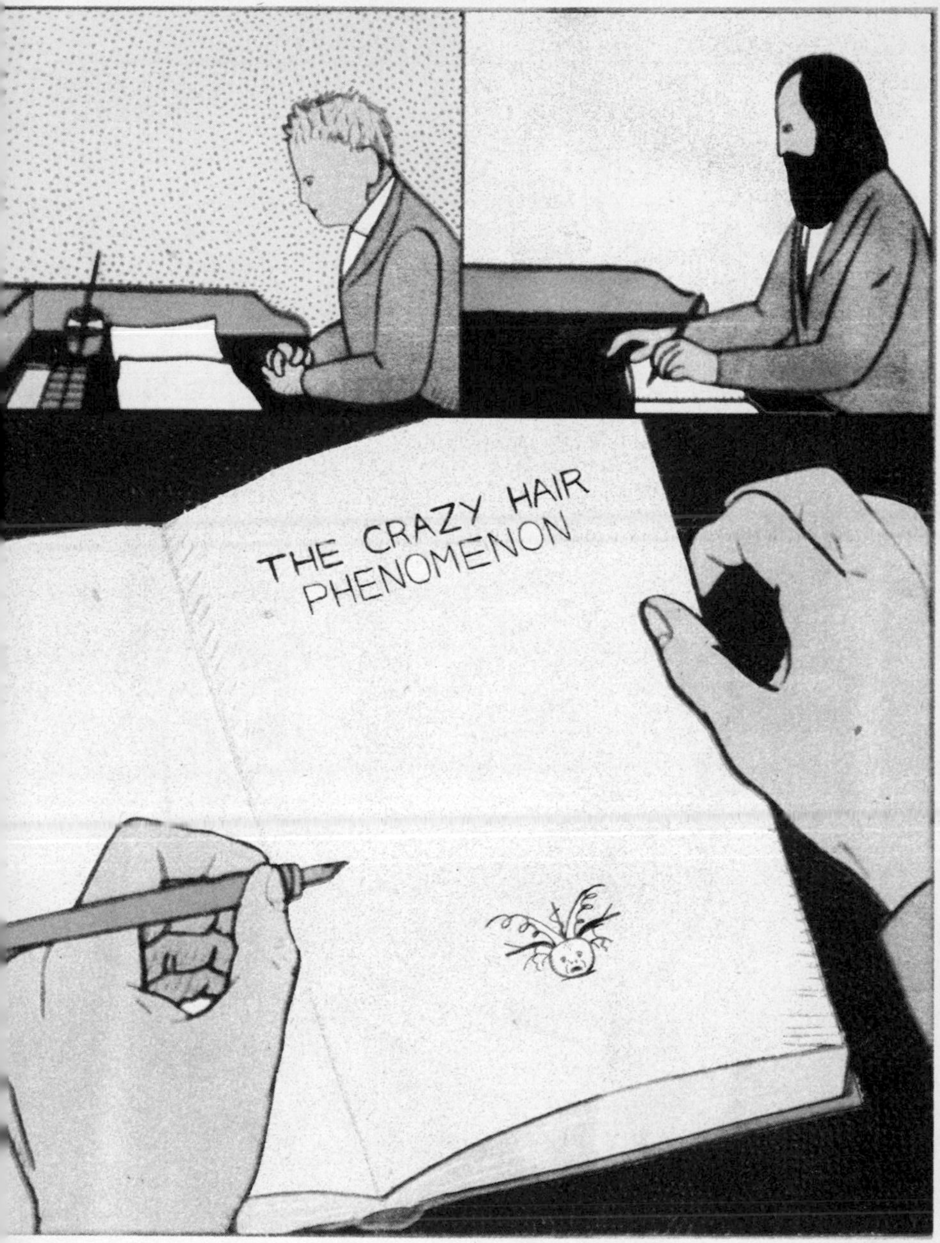
THE CRAZY HAIR
PHENOMENON

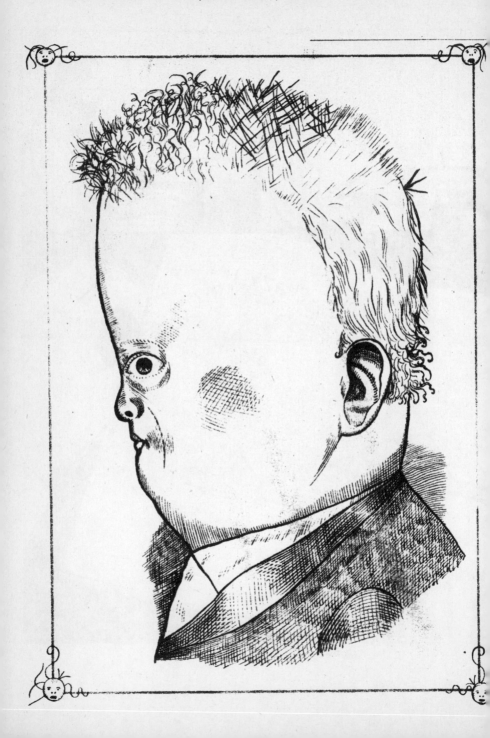

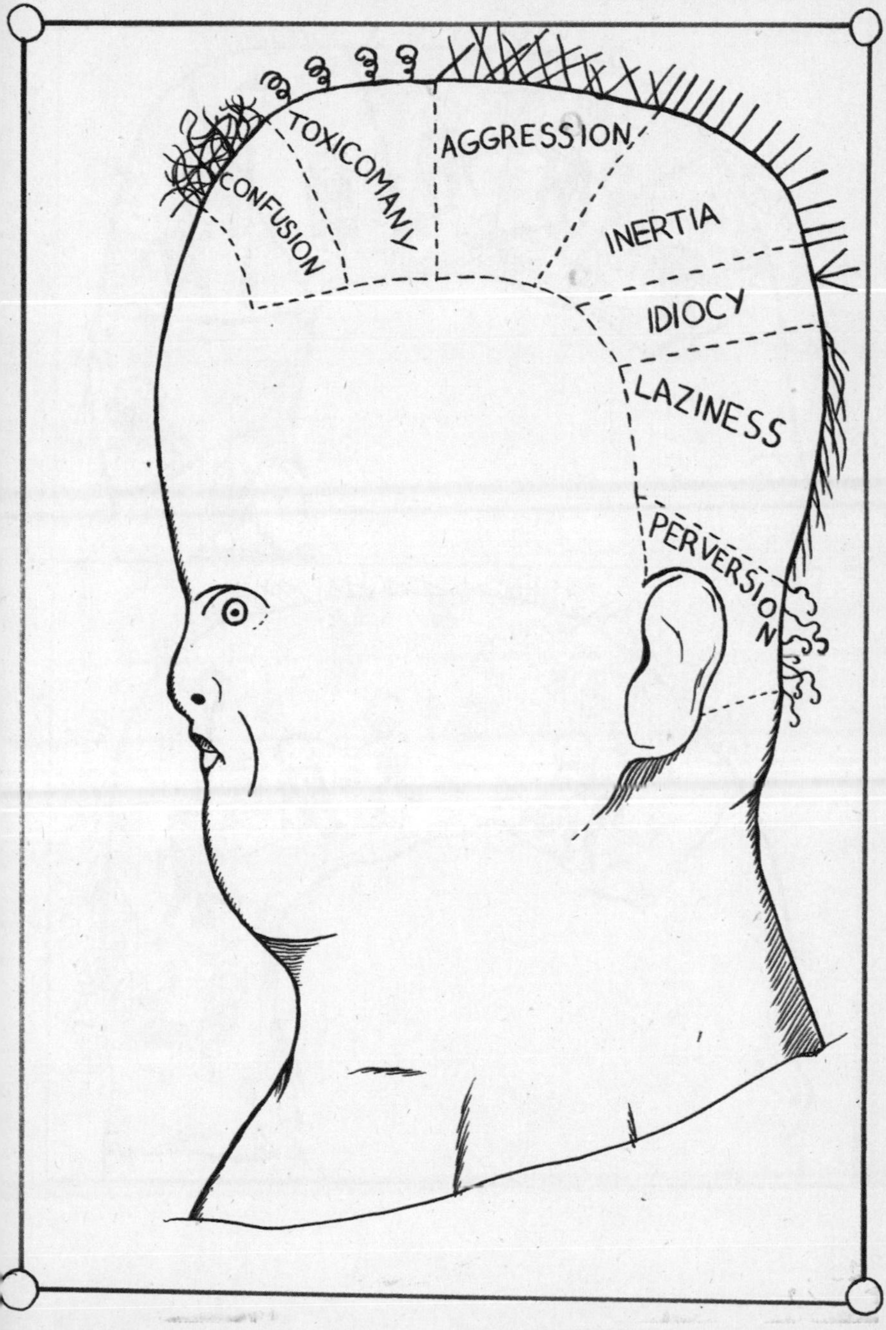
CONFUSION
TOXICOMANY
AGGRESSION
INERTIA
IDIOCY
LAZINESS
PERVERSION

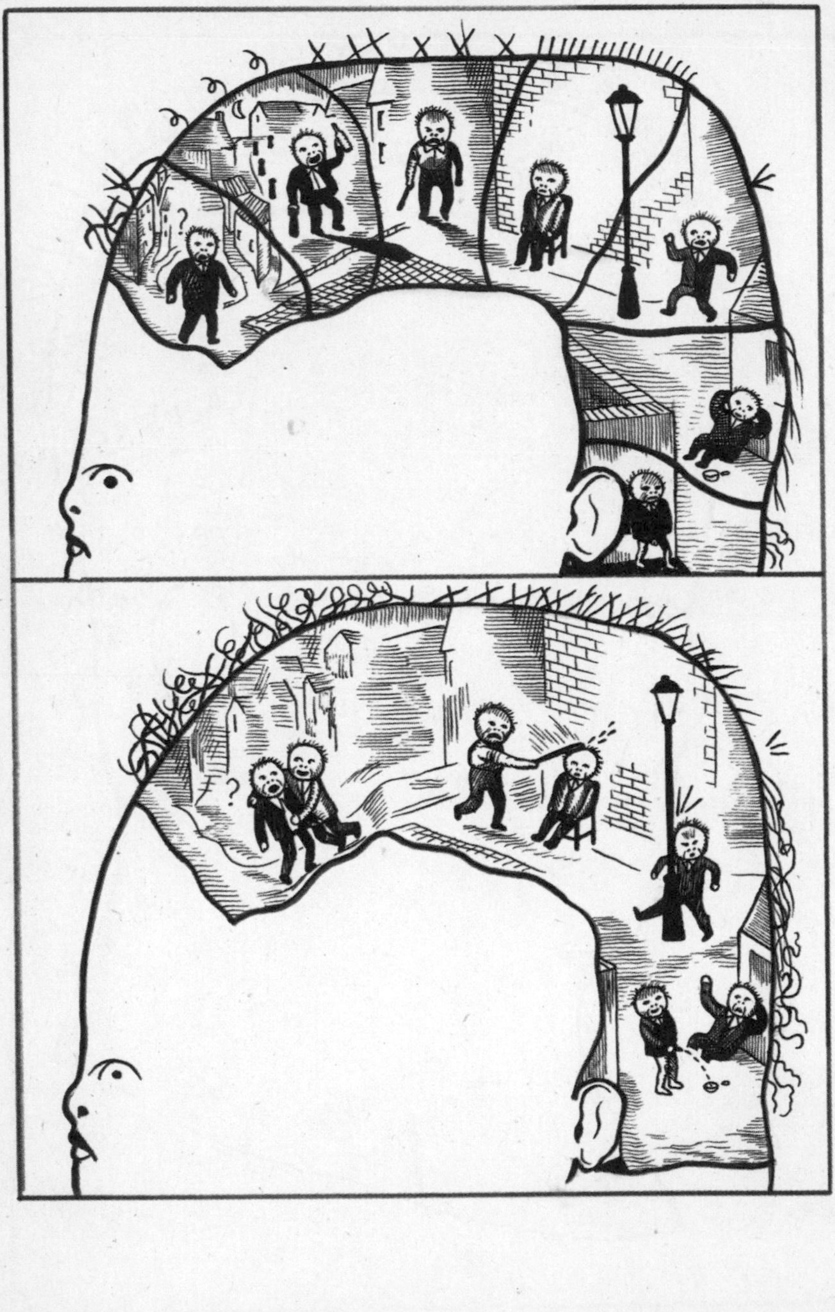

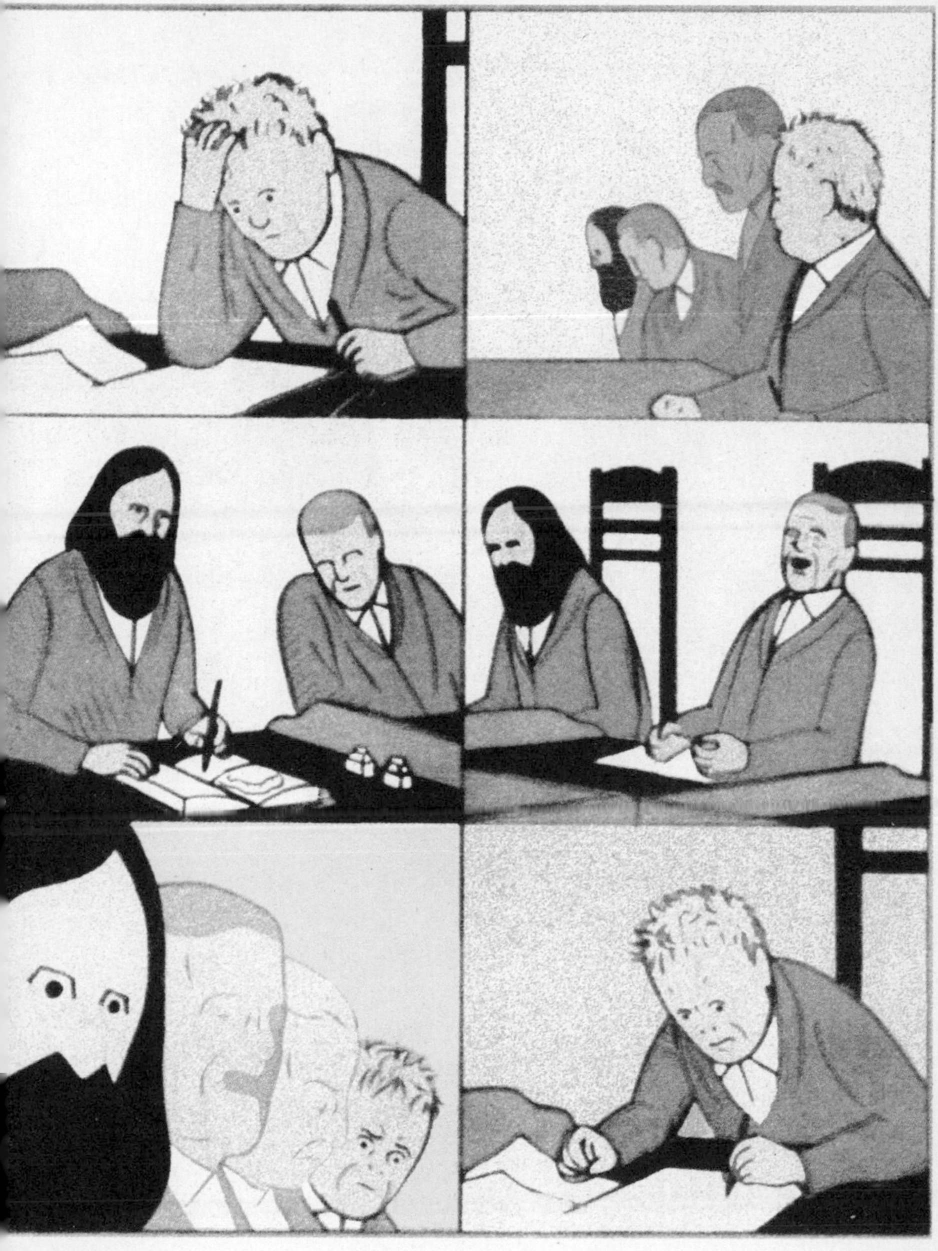

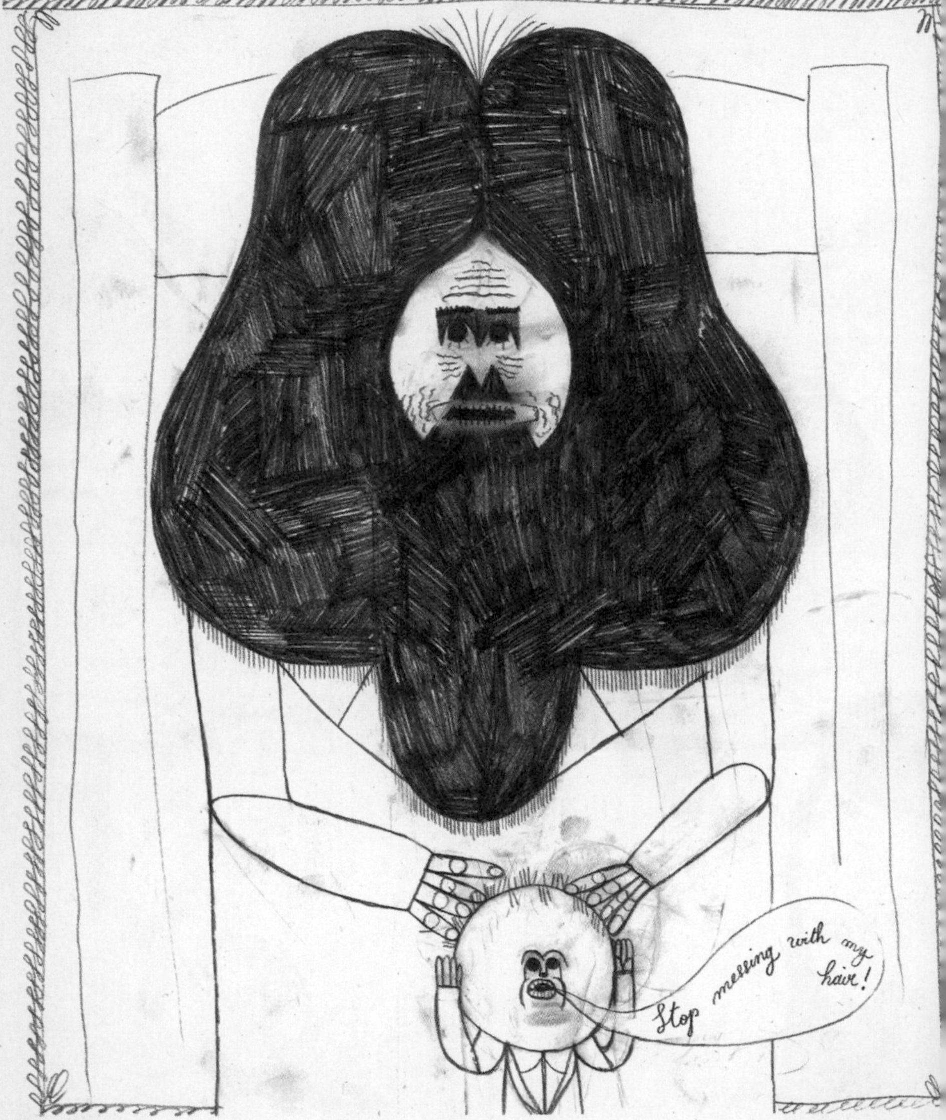
Stop messing with my hair!

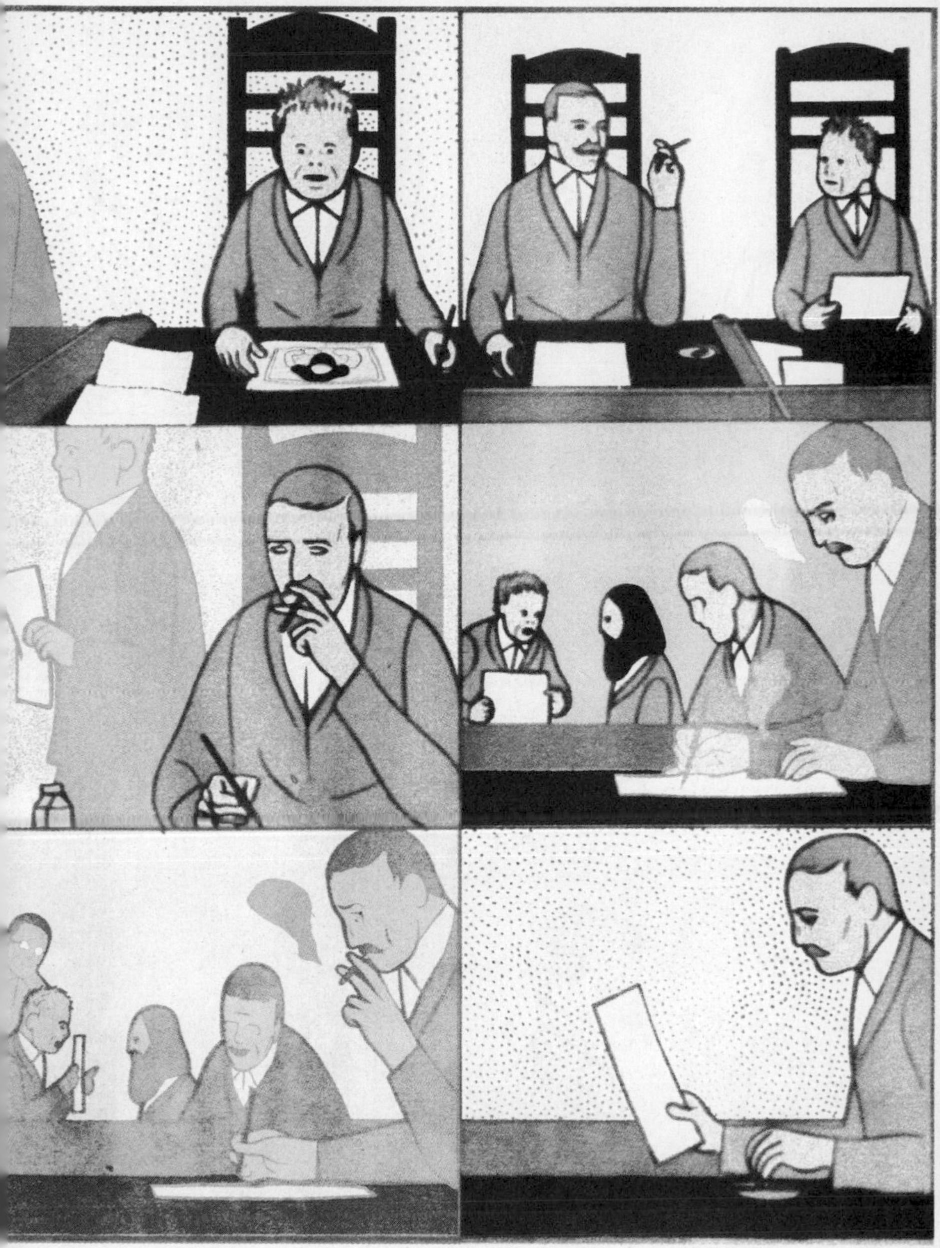

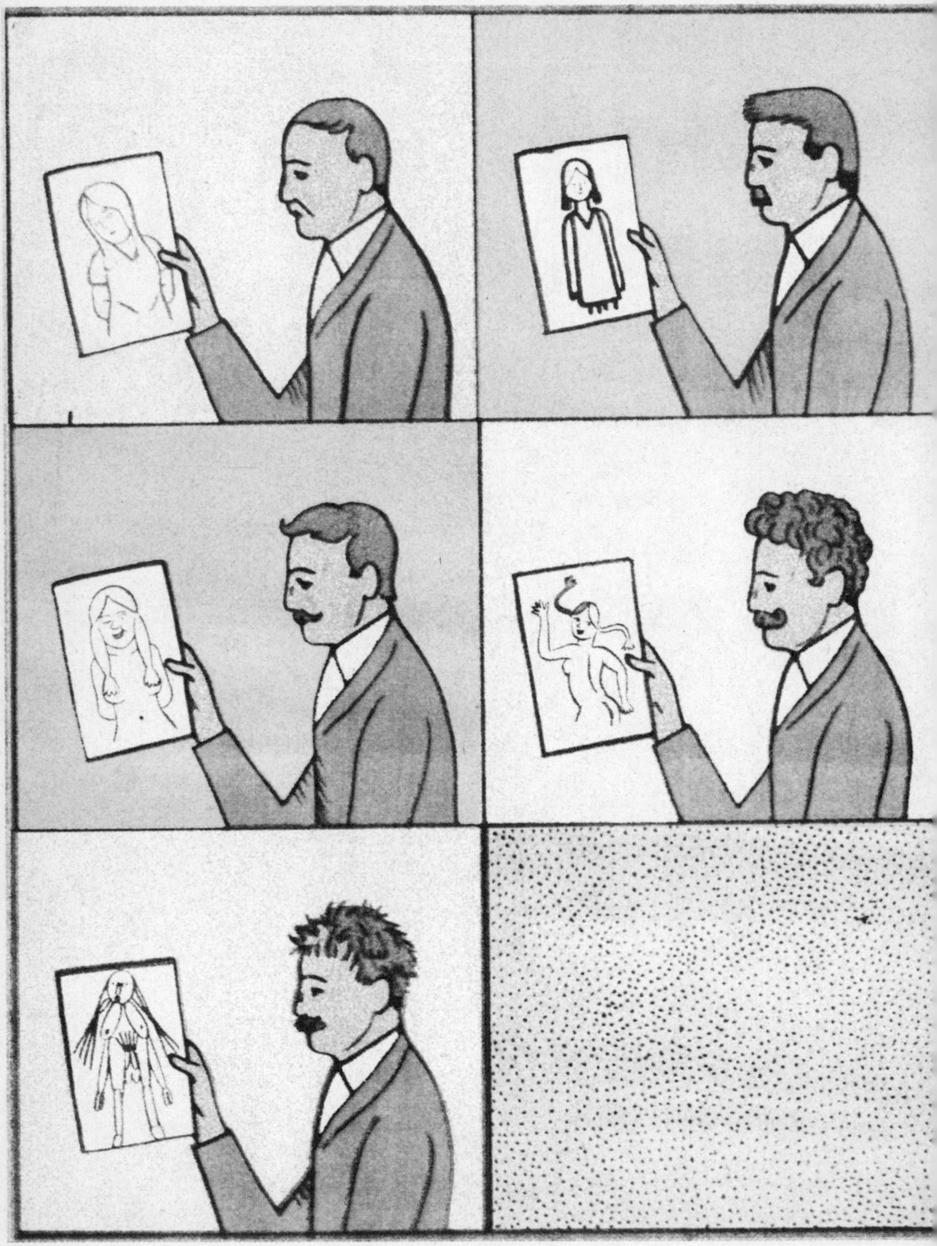

Best American Anonymous Postcards

FROM www.anonymouspostcard.org

Anonymous Postcard is the creation of artist Tucker Nichols. The website describes it as "a suggestion box for the world, designed to allow anyone to openly communicate to a third party without the complications of personal contact. Claims" — that is, suggestions and complaints — are "submitted by the public" and then "turned into vague and largely indecipherable postcards and mailed toward appropriate recipients" by Nichols.

CLAIM NUMBER: 009420081004
To: The person(s) living in our old house
CLAIM: Hi. We used to live here. We moved out in a hurry and didn't get a chance to paint all of the walls. Sorry that some walls look "splotchy" that's because we had a small amount of a lot of different shades of white. I never knew that white came in so many shades. I hope you enjoy the shed that I left behind in the side yard. That is, if the landlord didn't remove it for himself. If he didn't then I guess that kinda makes up for the "splotchy" walls.

Have an enjoyable day!

* * *

CLAIM NUMBER: 002820080822
To: Sonoma City Council
CLAIM: To support the trend towards healthier, locally grown food, lower transportation costs, and reduce the city's carbon footprint the Sonoma City Council proposed a measure to allow residents to keep 16 chickens (but no roosters — too noisy) and 8 rabbits (sex unspeci-

fied). Before the proposal goes to a final vote, I suggest they seek expert advice — maybe from a biology teacher at a local high school. Because even to the agriculturally unsophisticated that sounds a lot like a recipe for ending up with 1,000,000 rabbits and no chickens.

* * *

CLAIM NUMBER: 003820080905
To: Michigan
CLAIM: Michigan is my favorite state. It has had its share of troubles over the past couple of years and I am hoping this postcard will be a turning point for this wonderful state.

* * *

CLAIM NUMBER: 011920081017
To: The City of London
CLAIM: I counted 36 cranes on your skyline on October 17, 2008. That's too many.

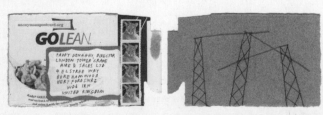

* * *

CLAIM NUMBER: 020420081204
TO: Hanukkah
CLAIM: With the tanking economy and poor sales of big ticket items, I think there's a real opportunity to gain a little ground on Christmas this year.

Hanukkah's always been smaller, and that's just what people will be looking for this time around. Strike while the iron's hot.

Best American Bank Heists

On December 30, 2008, five banks were robbed in New York City. It was an unofficial record. In a year of collapsing economies, bank robberies rose nationwide. In Jackson, Mississippi, for instance, there were more bank robberies in the first quarter of 2008 than there were in all of 2007. Here, from all over the country, are some of the strangest capers of the year.

The FBI had been looking for a serial bank robber who was suspected of robbing 10 banks in Oregon and Washington over a three-year period. They finally solved the case and arrested the "Waddling Bandit," a 63-year-old Portland man who pled guilty in federal district court. Dante Peter Dapolonia pled guilty to the 10 bank robberies and admitted robbing another 20 banks during the same period. Law enforcement's profile showed the suspect was likely a diabetic gambler well into his golden years, stocky, white and walked with a distinctive side-to-side gait. The robber had gotten away with more than $70,000 in the heists.

DRAWN FROM *The Portland Oregonian*

A would-be robber threatened to file an official complaint after he found that a Susquehanna Bank branch in Springettsbury Township, Pennsylvania, had no cash on hand when he came to hold it up on November 14. Local police say Joseph Goetz, 48, tried to rob the bank shortly after it opened. After finding out the bank had no cash on hand to give him, Goetz fled the scene and vowed to file a complaint with the bank's managers. Goetz was later arrested on suspicion of attempting to commit a robbery.

DRAWN FROM *The York Daily Record*

Beaumont, Texas, police arrived at a Wells Fargo branch early one morning to find an ATM missing and a forklift that was apparently used to remove the ATM still at the scene with its motor running. Police found the missing ATM in the back of a white truck that was pulled over later. The 42-year-old Houston resident driving the truck was charged with unauthorized use of a motor vehicle and felony theft of the ATM. Where he got the forklift is still a mystery.

DRAWN FROM www.kfdm.com/CBS News

A man pepper-sprayed an armored car driver who was parked and then wrestled a bag of money away from the reeling driver. This happened at a Bank of America in Monroe, Washington. Mitch Ruth, who was at work across the street from the bank, saw the incident. Ruth said he "first spotted the robber pacing along the bushes outside the bank while holding a garden sprayer and wearing a surgical mask, a wig and sunglasses." The robber took off with the money. Ruth pursued him on foot but lost him in the woods. The robber completed his escape via an inner tube on the Skykomish River.

DRAWN FROM www.komonews.com

Patrick Johnson, 33, handed a teller a note demanding cash written on the back of his own personal check. Johnson told a teller at the Ocala, Florida, branch of Bank of America that he had a .45-caliber pistol and wanted dough. The teller complied, handing over the cash. The robber also performed the same action at another Bank of America branch several hours later. The thief then fled from the second robbery scene in a taxi, which police later found, with the robber still in it. Both times, Johnson had handed the teller the holdup note, and both were written on the back of his personal checks.

DRAWN FROM www.wofl.com/Fox News

A man went through three tellers at a Wachovia branch in Dunedin, Florida, before getting cash. Gordon Ritchie, 55, hired a cab to drive him to the bank. Once there he gave a teller a demand note, but the teller explained she was assigned to the drive-through and had no access to cash. Richie hit up a second teller. She told him her window was, alas, closed. The robber gave his note to a third teller, and while she slowly complied with his demand, other employees called 911. The culprit fled in the same cab he'd arrived in, but was spotted in the cab 10 minutes later and pulled over.

DRAWN FROM www.tampabays10.com/CBS News

Best American Lawsuits

In 1995, Robert Lee Brock sued himself for $5 million. He claimed he'd violated his own civil rights and religious beliefs by allowing himself to get drunk and commit crimes that landed him in the Indian Creek Correctional Center in Virginia, serving a twenty-three-year sentence for grand larceny and breaking and entering. Because being in prison prevented him from having an income with which to pay himself, Brock demanded the state pay. The case was thrown out. Here are six cases from 2008 as mind-bending as Brock's.

A Maryland woman sued two state agencies, claiming they unfairly barred her from massaging horses. Mercedes Clemens of Damascus, Maryland, said she had to shut down her equine massage practice in the Washington, D.C., suburb after being told that only certified veterinarians were allowed to perform such services. Clemens is certified to massage humans. "This isn't just a career for me, it's my passion," Clemens said. "If I was independently wealthy and I didn't need an income, I would do this for nothing. That's how much I love it." Prior to the state's notice, Clemens had roughly thirty regular horse clients, including her own horse, Chanty. "If it was just me it wouldn't really be worth all this," she said. "But this is a much bigger constitutional issue."

DRAWN FROM *The Huffington Post*

Macrida Patterson, a 52-year-old Los Angeles traffic cop, filed suit against Victoria's Secret for an eye injury she claimed to have received as a result of a defective pair of thong underwear that had a rhinestone heart connected to the fabric by metal links. "I was putting on my underwear from Victoria's Secret, and the metal popped into my eye," Patterson said. "It happened really quickly. I was in excruciating pain. I screamed. That's what happened." Patterson is seeking more than $25,000 in damages. "This case is definitely about protecting the consumer from defective products," her lawyer said. "In terms of money, that's not what we really want here. We want to make Macrida fully redressed for her grievous injury. She's missed work. She's gone through a lot of suffering as well. We want to make Macrida Patterson whole again."

DRAWN FROM www.abcnews.go.com

The builders of the world's biggest particle collider were sued in federal court over fears that the experiment might create globe-gobbling black holes or never-before-seen strains of matter that would destroy the planet. Representatives at Fermilab in Illinois and at Europe's CERN laboratory, two of the defendants in the case, say there's no chance that the Large Hadron Collider would cause such cosmic catastrophes. The Large Hadron Collider, or LHC, was started up in 2008 at CERN's headquarters on the French-Swiss border. It's tackling some of the deepest questions in science: Is the foundation of modern physics right or wrong? What existed during the very first moment of the universe's existence? Why do some particles have mass while others don't? What is the nature of dark matter? Some folks outside the scientific mainstream have asked darker questions as well: Could the collider create mini–black holes that last long enough and get big enough to turn into a matter-sucking maelstrom? Could exotic particles known as magnetic monopoles throw atomic nuclei out of whack? Could quarks recombine into "strangelets" that would turn the whole Earth into one big lump of exotic matter? Former nuclear safety officer Walter Wagner has been raising such questions for years — first about an earlier-generation "big bang machine" known as the Relativistic Heavy-Ion Collider, and more recently about the LHC. Wagner and another critic of the LHC's safety measures, Luis Sancho, filed the lawsuit in Hawaii's U.S. District Court. The suit calls on the U.S. Department of Energy, Fermilab, the National Science Foundation and CERN to ease up on their LHC preparations for several months while the collider's safety was reassessed.

DRAWN FROM www.msnbc.com

Scott Anthony Gomez Jr. made his first break from the Pueblo County Jail two years ago. He pushed up a ceiling tile, hoisted himself into the ventilation system and climbed until he reached a roof. Then he shinnied down the wall on bedsheets fashioned into a rope. Caught two days later, he was back in his cell. The next time, Gomez again pried loose a ceiling tile and vanished into the guts of the building. But as he tried to rappel on bedsheets down the side of the 85-foot building, he fell. The would-be Houdini has sued the sheriff of Pueblo County, saying authorities caused his injuries by making it too easy to fly the coop. "Defendants . . . did next to nothing to ensure that the jail was secure and the plaintiff could not escape," said Gomez in his suit.

DRAWN FROM *The Los Angeles Times*

A construction worker named Brian Persaud, 38, sued New York Presbyterian Hospital for giving him an unwanted rectal examination. Persaud claimed that when he went to a hospital after being hit on the forehead by a falling wooden beam, emergency room staffers forcibly gave him a rectal exam. Persaud says in court papers that after he denied a request by emergency room employees to examine his rectum, he was "assaulted, battered and falsely imprisoned." His lawyer, Gerrard M. Marrone, said he and Persaud later learned the exam was one way of determining whether he had suffered spinal damage in the accident. Marrone said his client got eight stitches for a cut over his eyebrow. Then, Marrone said, emergency room staffers insisted on examining his rectum and held him down while he begged, "Please don't do that." He said Persaud hit a doctor while flailing around and staffers gave him an injection, which knocked him out, and performed the rectal exam. Persaud woke up handcuffed to a bed and with an oxygen tube down his throat, the lawyer said, and spent three days in a detention center.

DRAWN FROM Associated Press

Aaron and Christine Boring live in the country outside Pittsburgh. The couple is suing Google, the Mountain View, Calif., search giant, for invading its privacy by snapping a photo of the Boring house for Google Street View, a map feature that allows users to see pictures of streets. It caused the Borings "mental suffering and diminished value of their property," according to the suit filed in Pennsylvania state court. The Borings seek more than $25,000 in damages and ask that Google not take any more pictures of their property.

DRAWN FROM *The Recorder*

Best American Craigslist Items and Offers to Barter

FROM www.craigslist.com

Craigslist is an online conglomeration of classifieds founded in 1995 by Craig Newmark. It's the site of thousands of postings per day. In the last year or so, in addition to traditional want ads, a significant number of these have been offers to barter. Forthwith the best posts of 2008.

MY TEETH

I left my dentures in your Silverado last night. I gave you my number but did not get yours. Please call me asap. I need my teeth. We met in the parking lot of Margarita Jones. Get back to me asap please. Thank you.

* * *

STORAGE CART FOR VEGAN FOOD OR PAGAN STUFF

Will trade my rainbow storage cart; originally $50 at Costco.com. Would like vegan food or pagan stuff.

* * *

CATBUS

I have a 1995 MO' van that got transformed into this catbus. I brought it to a shop and I was like hey, can you turn this into a catbus? So they did. Then that day I drove it home. The catbus only has 50k, which are all highway miles as I drove it to work 2 days a week and that was it. It's in really good shape and all the fur is still all there. The steering wheel has a cat on it. I'm only asking 2900 for the catbus because it's really furry and sometimes people get sick on it.

* * *

BOAT WORK FOR YOUR WATER BOTTLES

Work on your boat (sail, kayak, etc.) for @ least 25 World Gym Water Bottles; the kind with the gorilla. I think these aren't available anymore, so I'm desperately looking.

* * *

THE LOUDEST VACUUM CLEANER ON THE FACE OF THE EARTH

Update: The vacuum cleaner has been picked up by the first person who had emailed me. I received a number of emails begging me not to delete the ad, so I'll leave it for a while.

Giving away absolutely free of charge, with no lien, mortgage, or other encumbrance of any sort, the undisputed world-record holder in the "loudest vacuum cleaner on the face of the Earth" category! Act now to take advantage of this truly unique opportunity! "Wow" your friends with this incredible Hoover!

To accurately describe this fine piece of machinery, I will need to be rather wordy, so please bear with me on this matter. Imagine you are on the runway at D/FW airport, right in front of one of the jet exhaust deflectors. A Boeing 747-400 has just taxied onto the runway about 8 feet in front of you, and holds there, awaiting clearance for takeoff.

After a few short moments, clearance is given. The pilot keeps the brakes firmly applied as the co-pilot gently places his hand on the throttles, then, in an instant, violently shoves all four of them forward to maximum thrust; right up against the stops. The ensuing cacophony resulting from the dissonance between the screaming whine of the turbines spinning at ten bazillion RPM and the 65,000 MPH blast of air and choking exhaust blasting you into the cold, sooty metal of the deflector is utterly deafening. That is not how loud this vacuum is. It's louder.

Just as the pilot of the 747 releases the wheel brakes, and the silvery, tubular behemoth commences its trip toward the other end of the runway and into the wild, blue yonder, air traffic control realizes they have made a deadly mistake; they had previously cleared an Airbus A380, the largest plane in the world, to land on the same runway, in the opposite direction!

Frantically, they radio the two planes in a vain attempt to prevent the impending disaster, but to no avail. The planes meet nose-to-nose in a gut-wrenching, mind-numbing collision. Add that noise to the already earsplitting din that was being emitted by the first plane. That is not how loud this vacuum is. It's louder.

While all of this is happening, the air traffic control supervisor has notified the airport's fire department and they have rolled to the scene just as this tragedy takes place. Their sirens are blaring as they pull up, only adding additional decibels to the already unbearable level of noise you are experiencing. Your eardrums feel like red hot razor blades fired from a 12-gauge shotgun are careening around inside your cranium. You honestly wish a 2-ton piece of the shrapnel flying from the ruins could just catapult your way and sever your head, putting you out of your misery once and for all. It never happens; you survive this, the most miserable moment of your entire life, surrounded by carnage, the noise level absolutely unbearable, with blood now flowing profusely from what used to be your ears. That is not how loud this vacuum is. It's louder.

Take the entire scene and insert it into the humungous wind tunnel at the Chrysler factory. Run the wind tunnel up to about 350 MPH. Take the noise you are now being subjected to, and triple it. Now, THAT'S how loud this damn vacuum is.

I've had people tell me I'm wrong, that this thing is much worse than I've described, and I'm being gentle just to be able to unload it on some poor, disadvantaged housewife in an act of masochism, thinly veiled as generous, selfless philanthropy.

I expect the competition for this beauty to be fierce, but if you want it, just email me and I'll set it out on the curb for you. If you need help finding the place after I give you the address, just let me know. I'll turn the lovely contraption on and you can follow the roar. Don't worry, it'll drown out the highway sounds from the semis, and the traffic choppers overhead and you'll have no problem getting here, even if you're just pulling out of your driveway in Guatemala.

Don't get me wrong, it does what it's supposed to do; it cleans the floor. I'm just tired of cleaning the blood from the walls that sprays out of my ears when I use this little gem.

Attachments Included
Allergen Filtration
Brushed Edge Cleaning
Won't Last
Act now to take this cream puff home with you today.

* * *

LIPSTICK FOR TIMERS, SOCKS, OR BRICKS
Bare Essentials lipstick; "Bread Pudding" is the name of the color. You can get an idea of what the color is on their website. New lip-

stick in sealed package, worth $15. Is sealed in tamper-proof plastic . . . could be given as a gift. I would like any of the following: Timers (electronic, kitchen, hourglass), clean cotton socks, clean wool hiking socks, two clean standard bricks.

* * *

NEMESIS REQUIRED. 6-MONTH PROJECT WITH POSSIBILITY TO EXTEND

I've been trying to think of ways to spice up my life. I'm 35 years old, happily married with two kids and I have a good job in insurance. But something's missing. I feel like I'm old before my time. I need to inject some excitement into my daily routine through my arm before it's too late. I need a challenge, something to get the adrenaline pumping again. An addiction would be nice, but, in short, I need a nemesis. I'm willing to pay $350 up front for your services as an arch-enemy over the next six months. Nothing crazy. Steal my parking space, knock my coffee over, trip me when I'm running to catch the BART and occasionally whisper in my ear, "Ahha, we meet again." That kind of thing. Just keep me on my toes. Complacency will be the death of me. You need to have an evil streak and be blessed with innate guile and cunning. You should also be adept at inconspicuous pursuit. Evil laugh preferred. Send me a photo and a brief explanation of why you would be a good nemesis. British accent preferred.

* * *

GET HER TO EAT THE VEGETABLES PLEASE

I'm desperate. My little girl won't eat vegetables of any kind. No matter what I do she won't. I am concerned about her health. I'm an architect and am willing to trade services if you can somehow get her to eat them on a permanent (not one-time) basis.

* * *

WHO PUT THE DEAD BIRD IN MY MAILBOX?
   a) how did you get into my mailbox in the first place, it is locked
   b) did you kill the bird
   c) it died horribly, that much was clear

d) you're psycho

e) do I know you

f) if I do know you I don't want to know you

g) if I don't know you, what did I do to inspire you to put a dead bird in my mailbox

h) I don't know how to disinfect a mailbox from a dead bird, I'm worried about diseases and have used five different kinds of cleaner but still feel like the bird's still in there still and like my bills and my catalogues and my coupons have dead bird on them

i) it was a hummingbird, I looked it up — they don't even live in New York — this is so f*ing psycho, I can't believe this

j) are you the mailman?

k) I'm always nice to the mailman

l) the super didn't care when I told him what happened

m) the neighbors didn't care either

n) do you have some kind of problem with birds

o) don't put anything else in my mailbox

p) unless it's an apology

q) no, I take that back, I don't even want an apology

r) what am I supposed to do with this bird — it's in bubblewrap in a bag in a shoebox in the freezer right now — am I supposed to bury it — where? how? in a construction site where they've jackhammered through the concrete — where is a person supposed to bury things in this city?

s) I could drop it in the Gowanus canal, but that seems undignified

t) I could drop it in the ocean, but the ocean is so big and it is such a small bird

u) I could drop it in the toilet but it would probably get stuck

v) I hear this whirring around my ears every time I go to the mailbox and I'm pretty sure it's ghost bird, and I'm all "it wasn't me that killed you, bird!" but still the whirring doesn't go away until I get to the stairwell

w) am I supposed to eat it — maybe you were trying to feed me — don't you know I'm a vegetarian

x) if this was Ricky, I'm gonna beat your ass, mama told you stop bothering the zoo

y) if this was Gina, I'm sorry, I'm sorry, how many times I gotta say I'm sorry

z) I could drop it off the roof, maybe it will reincarnate while falling and I can start reading my mail again

* * *

SUCCULENTS FOR PEACOCK FEATHERS

I have many succulent rooted plants I am willing to barter for your peacock feathers. I am NOT looking for the tail feathers, only the body feathers, male or female peacocks. Some of the succulents I have are: Felt plant (Kalanchoe beharensis), Jelly Bean Sedum (Sedum rubrotinctum 'Aurora'), Chocolate Soldier (Kalanchoe tomentosa), Mother of Thousands (Kalanchoe daigremontiana), and Finger jade (Crassula ovata), along with many, many others. Thanks!

* * *

AUTOGRAPHED COPY OF PLATO'S REPUBLIC

1st edition of the *Republic* signed by its author. There is of course a reasonable amount of wear and tear (light highlighting and underlining, dog-eared pages, back cover missing, etc.), but it is in overall good condition considering its age. First come first serve.

* * *

GOLF BALLS FOR CALCULATORS

About 100 used golf balls. Different brands and condition. Want calculators.

* * *

MARBLE SLABS FOR OLD CELL PHONES

I have marble slabs that I want to get rid of. I would like any old cell phones that could still be used with a new SIMS card.

* * *

LIGHTS FOR JACK DANIEL'S

Chandelier lights: selling both lights for half gallon of Jack Daniel's Old # 7 or $40 cash.

* * *

YOUR PETS WILL NOT BE FLAGGED FOR REMOVAL BY JESUS DURING THE RAPTURE

Over half the United States population has legitimate concerns about what will happen to their pets after the rapture occurs. Please respect their faith and allow this service to remain posted, just as the waste removal and grooming posts remain posted. Again, over half of the U.S. population feels that this is a concern to them. If there is a specific problem with the ad, please email me. Thank you.

Have you ever thought about what will happen to your pets after Jesus comes back to claim the souls of the saved during the Rapture and deliver them to heaven to  enjoy everlasting life? The bible clearly teaches that only those that have accepted Jesus as their savior will enter heaven (John 14:6, Romans 3:23) and we all know that pets do not have the cognitive ability to do this, so what will happen to your beloved pets? Surely without you there, they would be stuck inside your empty house, starving to death with no one to feed them, let them out to potty, or clean their litter box. This is probably not what you envision for your pets after you are gone. This is where I come in.

I am here to offer you pet care service for after the rapture. As an atheist, I will surely still be here on this earth post-Rapture and would love to look after your pets for a small fee and make sure they are still well taken care of after you and your family have been Raptured. You will be able to look down on them from heaven and see them being well cared for by me and living happy, healthy lives. Do not let my atheism scare you! I am a moral and loving pet owner and would never do harm to any animal.

For a small deposit of only $50, you can be assured that your pets will be well cared for from the time that you are Raptured until the end of their natural life. They will get adequate amounts of food, water, and shelter as well as plenty of exercise and socialization as I would imagine there will be a lot of pets that will be abandoned by Jesus The Pet Hater that will need to be cared for.

If interested, please email me for my PayPal address (you can also send me a check if you prefer) so you can assure that your pets will be taken care of after Jesus comes to take your soul to heaven. $50 is only a small price to pay to know that while you are enjoying everlasting bliss, your pets will be cared for until their end days.

Thanks and have a great day!

* * *

PANTIES FOR MONEY OR BRAS
Panties: These are new. Purchased for $50 (not including tax). They will fit a size Xs, small, or medium. Anywhere from 100 lbs–120 lbs. Very cute and playful. Leopard print on inside of crotch area, pink outsides, and lots of black lace. Willing to settle for $30 bucks or barter for some expensive bras. Willing to ship or meet up anywhere in SF. Thanks.

* * *

LEGAL SERVICES FOR MARTIAL ARTS LESSONS
Attorney is willing to trade legal services. Currently seeking martial arts lessons.

* * *

THE ABYSS FOR JACK HUGHMAN DVDS
Looking to trade *The Abyss* DVD for any DVDs with Jack Hughman in it. He's so hot. Will send through mail, but can also meet anywhere in Marin.

* * *

STUNT DOUBLE LOOK-ALIKE WANTED FOR FAMILY PHOTO
Hello, I am posting this ad to enjoy some times off from getting dressed, a hair cut and the whole 9 yards. I will pay someone 25 bucks to smile in a photo for me with my in-laws. Easy money!

Here's what I am looking for:

Asian male (26–29)
Short black hair
Handsome smiles
5'7
160 pounds
Handsome like myself
One messed up tooth
Please I don't feel like shaving etc.

* * *

TOY RAFT FOR FRESH FRUIT
Offering a blue transparent toy pool raft, about 7 feet 2 inches long
by 20 inches wide in exchange for fresh oranges or mangoes delivered every week by the pound. Preferably from a home-grown tree in
backyard; willing to negotiate.

Best American Police Blotter Items
for Johnson County, Kansas

FROM *The Kansas City Star*

*Johnson County is located in the northeast corner of Kansas, just out-
side Kansas City and bordering Missouri. It is 91 percent white, 4 percent
Latino, 2.8 percent Asian American, 2.6 percent African American,
.3 percent Native American, and .03 percent Pacific Islander. Johnson
County has a median income of $71,961 (the highest in Kansas and
the nineteenth-highest in the country), as well as an apparently under-
challenged police force. The following items are printed exactly as they
appeared in* The Kansas City Star.

North Parker Street, 100 block: Stolen beef jerky. 12:41 p.m.
North Parker Street, 100 block: Stolen personal care products,
slime potion and light stick. 4:23 p.m.
North Ridgeview Road and Santa Barbara Boulevard: Damaged
tunnel. 1:14 p.m.

West Fredrickson Drive, 1800 block: Stolen garage door opener and checks. 6:48 a.m.

West 133rd Street, 16100 block: Stolen boxes. 12:39 p.m.

West 135th Street, 16100 block: Stolen grilled cheese sandwich, french fries and soda. 11:03 p.m.

South Alden Street, 13600 block: Stolen allergy pills and cologne. 2:25 p.m.

West 107th Street, 21600 block: Stolen women's fleece jacket. 8:08 a.m.

East 151st Street, 1600 block: Stolen men's winter coat. 11:15 a.m.

East College Way, 1500 block: Damaged window and shoe. 7:50 p.m.

North Kansas Avenue, 100 block: Drugs. 8:41 a.m.

North Parker Street, 100 block: Stolen cosmetics. 7:07 p.m.

West 151st Street, 20100 block: Stolen athletic shoes. 3:45 p.m.

West 151st Street, 20300 block: Stolen framed photographs. 6:30 p.m.

North Iowa Street, 900 block: Stolen decorations. 10:30 p.m.

North Parker Street, 100 block: Stolen personal hygiene products, nose drops, cold medication and candy. 8:54 p.m.

North Parker Street, 100 block: Stolen beef steaks. 7:44 p.m.

West Santa Fe Street, 1000 block: Stolen piccolo. 1:10 p.m.

West 119th Street, 15300 block: Stolen gift cards. 3:24 p.m.

South Brougham Circle, 13900 block: Stolen landscape light. 9:13 a.m.

South Hagan Street, 12900 block: Damaged trees. 9:35 a.m.

South Strang Line Road, 11600 block: Stolen wedding dress, clothing, bedroom furniture, baby furniture, plasma television, household goods, sofa and chairs. 6:33 p.m.

Quivira Road, 9600 block: Unauthorized use of a financial card; stolen clothing and fast food. 6:26 p.m.

West 58th Street, 22300 block: Hole punched in wall. 6:42 p.m.

Antioch Road, 5800 block: Stolen plastic ice bucket. 3:46 p.m.

Frontage Road, 6600 block: Stolen intake snorkel, stereo, wheels, tires and headlights. 11:24 a.m.

Martway Street, 6600 block: Stolen toothbrush, shaving razor and DVD. 7:24 p.m.

Best American Karate Tribute

NICK TWEMLOW

FROM *jubilat*

I love karate. I love karate so much I sweat karate steak dinners. I love karate so much I eat karate cereal in the morning, karate sandwiches for lunch, and karate haiku for pleasure. But like a good karateka (that's the technical term for highly skilled karate person) I don't eat karate dessert. You know why? Because dessert takes the edge off. You might ask, Off what? but if you do, I'll perform a random karate move on you, as I did my mother when she tried to serve me non-karate cereal one morning. That was the morning when I realized that I was a true karateka. I refused the Empire's cereal. If you are a true karateka, you are a rogue. Rogues don't like the Empire. This means that rogues spend a lot of time building dojos in the woods. A dojo is the technical name for a rogue who spends a lot of time building cabins in the woods. There are some karate moves that I can't show you. Those are secret karate moves. Like all karate moves, they are designed to kill. But these secret strikes kill faster and harder. They are to regular karate moves what hardcore is to softcore pornography. I was sensitive once, but karate got rid of that. Now, I am tough on the inside as well as the outside. For example, if I was in the Oval Office partying with the President, smoking some grass (which I'd fake doing because karatekas don't smoke grass), I'd ask him to repeat what he said about kicking evil's ass and then I'd ask him to show me how he'd do it. Since I know the President isn't a karateka, I'd administer a very secret strike on him at the moment he showed me how he'd do it. That's pretty much how I'd do things. I want karate to be in the Olympics in Beijing because I want to be on the team and travel to Beijing and win a gold medal. Or at least that's what I'd trick everyone into thinking I was doing. Part of being a karateka means bolstering the Chinese economy. Sort of like ninjas except a karateka can beat a ninja fourteen out of ten times. So while people would think I wanted to go to Beijing to win a gold medal and hang out in the Olympic Village and have a really good time with all the other athletes and media and officials and tourists and stuff, I'd really have a secret agenda. Secret agendas are pretty common for most karatekas. Secret agendas ensure that no matter what you say, you really don't mean it. So when everyone else was having a good time at the Olympics in Beijing, seeing how Communism is really good on the citizens of China because the government rounded up, the year before, tens of thousands of homeless people and relocated them to work details in provincial labor camps, I'd slip out at night and administer random karate moves on officials of the Empire. This happened a lot in Atlanta, too, when we held the Olympics. The part about the homeless, I mean.

Best American Farmer's Calendar Column

CASTLE FREEMAN, JR.

FROM *The Old Farmer's Almanac*

The Old Farmer's Almanac has come out every September since 1792. It's chock-full of information useful to farmers and outdoorspeople, things like sunrise and tide schedules, long-term weather forecasts, and planting charts. Castle Freeman, Jr., has been writing a column called "The Farmer's Calendar" in the Almanac for twenty-five years — one missive for each month, twelve per edition. In them, he dispenses wisdom and tells stories. What follows is the March column from the 2008 Almanac.

Sugaring season. The sap gatherers are busy among the maples. Steam billows round the clock from the sugarhouses. For a couple weeks, people all over northern New England turn out to take their share of the woods' annual bounty of maple syrup and sugar. Some operate on a huge scale, drawing truckloads of sap from the sugarbushes. Others are amateurs who sugar for fun. Both are subject to what might be called maple sugaring's ruling ratio: You have to boil an awful lot of sap to get an awful little of syrup.

The backyard sugarer ignores this rule at his peril. I learned that some years ago when our family decided to make our own syrup. We had a big sugar maple in the yard, we had a bucket, and if we didn't have a proper evaporator, we had a kitchen range. We tapped the tree, collected the sap, and set to boiling.

We boiled and boiled. And boiled. The kitchen filled with steam. We boiled on. For hours we stumbled blindly through the fog, eventually to wind up with about a cup of syrup. What we had not counted on was the gummy film that covered the kitchen, deposited by the evaporation of gallons and gallons of sugar-rich sap. So sticky was our kitchen ceiling that the cats and dogs, and even the smaller children, could walk around up there easily, like houseflies.

Best American Kids' Letters to Obama

FROM *Thanks and Have Fun Running the Country*

Thanks and Have Fun Running the Country, edited by Jory John, is a collection of dozens of letters by kids to President Obama, written days after the election. These students, ages five and up, live in San Francisco, Ann Arbor, Ypsilanti, New York, Boston, Chicago, Los Angeles, and Seattle. Here are sixteen of the letters.

Dear President Obama,

I know you want to save the earth, but people don't want to clean. My life is to clean up all the world and help you to clean. I always dream of cleaning the world with you. I'll do anything for you because you are the president in this world.

Stephanie Gonzalez, age 7
Los Angeles

* * *

Dear Obama,

You are going to be a great president. My whole religion voted for you. I am happy you are going to be our present. Because you are going to do great stuff for the US. I wanted to tell you that I am Arabic and I heard that you were half way Arabic. I think that you deserve to be the president because you were going to do smart and good stuff, like give poor people homes and a life.

Bushra Habbas-Nimer, age 8
Ann Arbor

* * *

Dear President Obama,

If I want anybody to be president, it's me. I would clean the streets and give myself more money. I would also give everybody a piece of a Reese's candy. Every homeless guy or girl would get $50 for help and a place to sleep for the winter. My family and other families would get free gas for our cars; single people with no kids would have to pay.

The money would come from copying other bills. The $1, $2, $5, $10, $20, $50, and $100 bills would be copied one thousand times.

The paper would not come from trees, but hardened glue. The way to make it is by mixing water and glue together so that it looks like paper. You then put it in a fire, then let it cool in the freezer.

Weslie Jackson, age 12
Chicago

* * *

Dear President Obama,

Could you help my family to get housecleaning jobs? I hope you will be a great president. If I were president, I would help all nations, even Hawaii.

President Obama, I think you could help the world.

Chad Timsing, age 9
Los Angeles

* * *

Dear President Obama,

Why did you volunteer to be president? I like your good ideas. Don't let the USA down.

You come up with good ideas? Nothing? It's fine. It's all fine.

I did a screenplay. It was made into a movie by the Echo Park Film Center and people working with me.

I will do everything you say. You're nice and persuasive. You are one of the good presidents.

Alex Morones, age 10
Los Angeles

* * *

Dear President Obama,

You are just like a big me, because I am from Chicago and I am biracial and have curly hair. I live in Seattle now, but I'm still from Chicago.

How do you feel about being president?

I have an idea. Why don't you give everybody, even the homeless, ten dollars every day? Each person would need this money for food, clothes, toys, and many other needs. And don't forget to give the kids money, too.

My advice for you and your family is be yourself and you will change the world. If I were president, I would try to make the world a better place.

Sincerely,
Avante Price, age 7
Seattle

* * *

Dear President Obama,

I want to tell you hi. Do you work with Santa Claus? Can I meet you in your house? Can I say bye to you after I meet you? And then can I meet you again? And then again after that?

Sergio Magana, age 5
San Francisco

* * *

To President Obama,

If I were president, I would help the people. If we don't throw the trash away, we are going to get sick. I could walk around to check where there is trash.

Sincerely,
Kenia Zelaya, age 6
Los Angeles

* * *

Dear Barack Obama,

I have some comments about things going on in this place. You know, we really need to have some new cars to save our environment. We also need to persuade people to stop smoking — you can let people buy one more pack, but that would be their last pack. After that you have to stop selling cigarettes. You can have a little bit of beer, but not too much — don't go wild or anything.

You should also build cameras all around our city to find out who is breaking the law, and also in movie theaters so we can tell who is making illegal copies. We also need to save the forest. Another thing that you should do is that for all the people who are out there asking for money, you should help them get into college. That way those people can teach their kids, instead of being homeless.

Ray Crespo, age 12
Boston

* * *

Dear President Obama,

Are you going to be pictured on our money? How do you get in the White House? Do you like Abraham Lincoln? Do you have a big backyard? Martin Luther King Jr. had big fans. How many fans do you have? You could help us by giving us food. I am Luis Ramirez. I go to school at Mayberry. I like to play video games.

Luis Ramirez, age 8
Los Angeles

* * *

Dear Mr. Obama,

My name is Daniel and I am twelve. I live in Seattle, Washington and go to Asa Mercer Middle School. I am in sixth grade. My most favorite thing to do is to BMX. I hope you have BMXed before. If not, you should try it, because it is very fun. I go to Bike Works and learn to fix bikes. It's a really good place here in Seattle.

I really hope you can help with the crime problem and the violence that there is in my neighborhood. I live on Rainier Avenue and there are many crimes, like shooting and a lot of stealing. I had a beautiful Siberian Husky named Michael that was three years old and when I was working with my mom someone stole him. I was very sad. My brother David and I were crying.

I wish I was older than twelve so I could find a job and help my family since we are poor. My family is from Cuba, even though I was born in the United States. I have gone to Cuba three times. Cuba is very different than the USA because in Cuba you don't get to choose the religion you want to do. My family left because we are Jehovah's Witnesses and our lives were in danger. In Cuba, there are not any big cities and the people live on farms or close to the woods and there are animals that eat the crops and other animals and we must protect them. Most houses are made of mud and old wood. The best ones are made of old metal.

Also, the schools are waaaay different because only the best ones might have a roof.

I congratulate you and thank you.

Sincerely,
Daniel Gonzalez, age 12
Seattle

* * *

Dear President Obama,

Hi, my name is Brennon. I'm in fifth grade and I have good grades in school. Some advice I would give you and your family is don't stress out about being president and all the work you have to do, and spend a lot of time with your family. You should help your kids out a lot with their homework from school and spend time with your wife.

Some things I would like you to know about my family is that my dad lost his job but he was able to get one five weeks later, but it is in a different state. All of my friends live in Michigan, which is where I live right now. But we are going to have to move.

And if I could live in the White House the thing I would like the best about it is how big it is. And what I would like the least about the White House is that it might be hard to find my way through the house because of how big it is. And if I were president I would change the economy so that my mom, my dad, my brother, and my sister would have a better life.

Brennon Cole, age 10
Ypsilanti

* * *

Dear Obama,

My name is Kenia. Is it hard work to be president? I think it is hard because you have to help people not to die. If I were president I would have fun, because I could run fast.

From,
Kenia Zelaya, age 6
Los Angeles

* * *

Dear President Obama,

Congratulations on the election. My name is Moses Williams. I am twelve years old and I want to be a director. The job of president is kind of like being a director. Director of the country! I think if I were older, more experienced, and in this position I could help you with relationships with other countries because, well, most of the world doesn't really like us and a lot of my friends were people who didn't like me at first. Thank you for reading.

Sincerely,
Moses Williams, age 12
New York

Best American Comic by a French Artist

ÉMILE BRAVO

<small>FROM</small> *MOME*

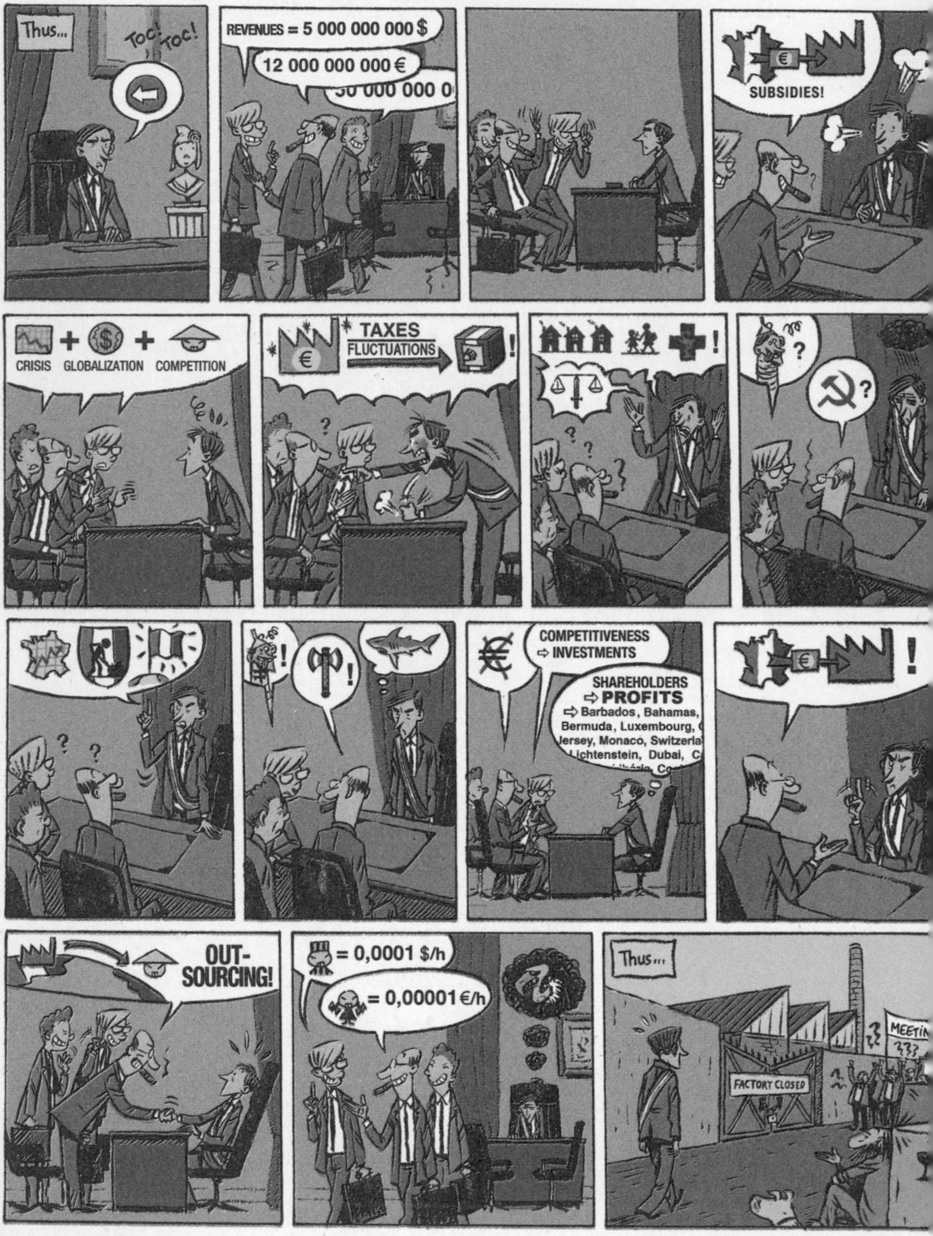
Thus...
TOC! TOC!
REVENUES = 5 000 000 000 $
12 000 000 000 €
SUBSIDIES!
CRISIS + GLOBALIZATION + COMPETITION
TAXES
FLUCTUATIONS
COMPETITIVENESS
⇨ INVESTMENTS
SHAREHOLDERS
⇨ PROFITS
⇨ Barbados, Bahamas,
Bermuda, Luxembourg,
Jersey, Monaco,
Dubai,
OUT-SOURCING!
= 0,0001 $/h
= 0,00001 €/h
Thus...
FACTORY CLOSED

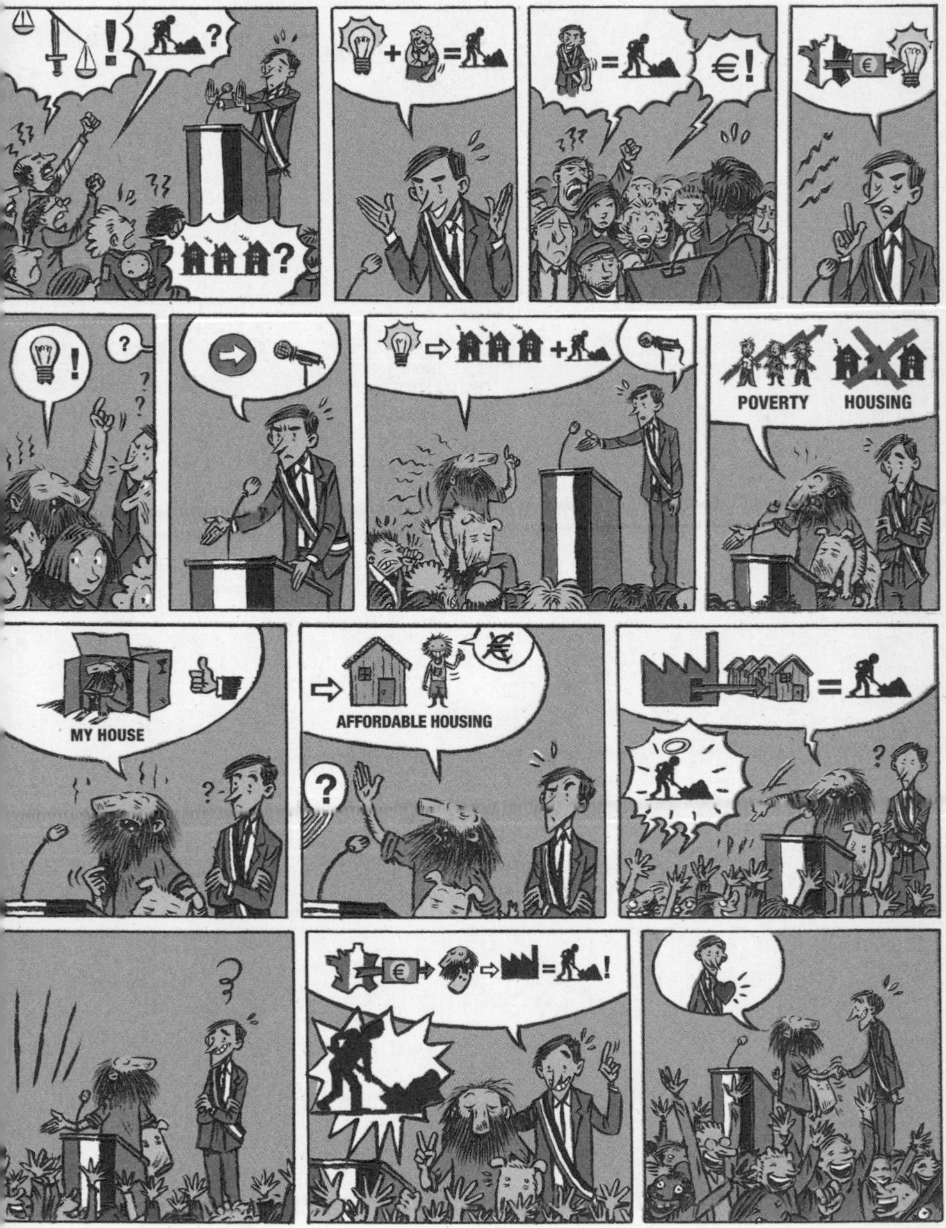
POVERTY
HOUSING
MY HOUSE
AFFORDABLE HOUSING

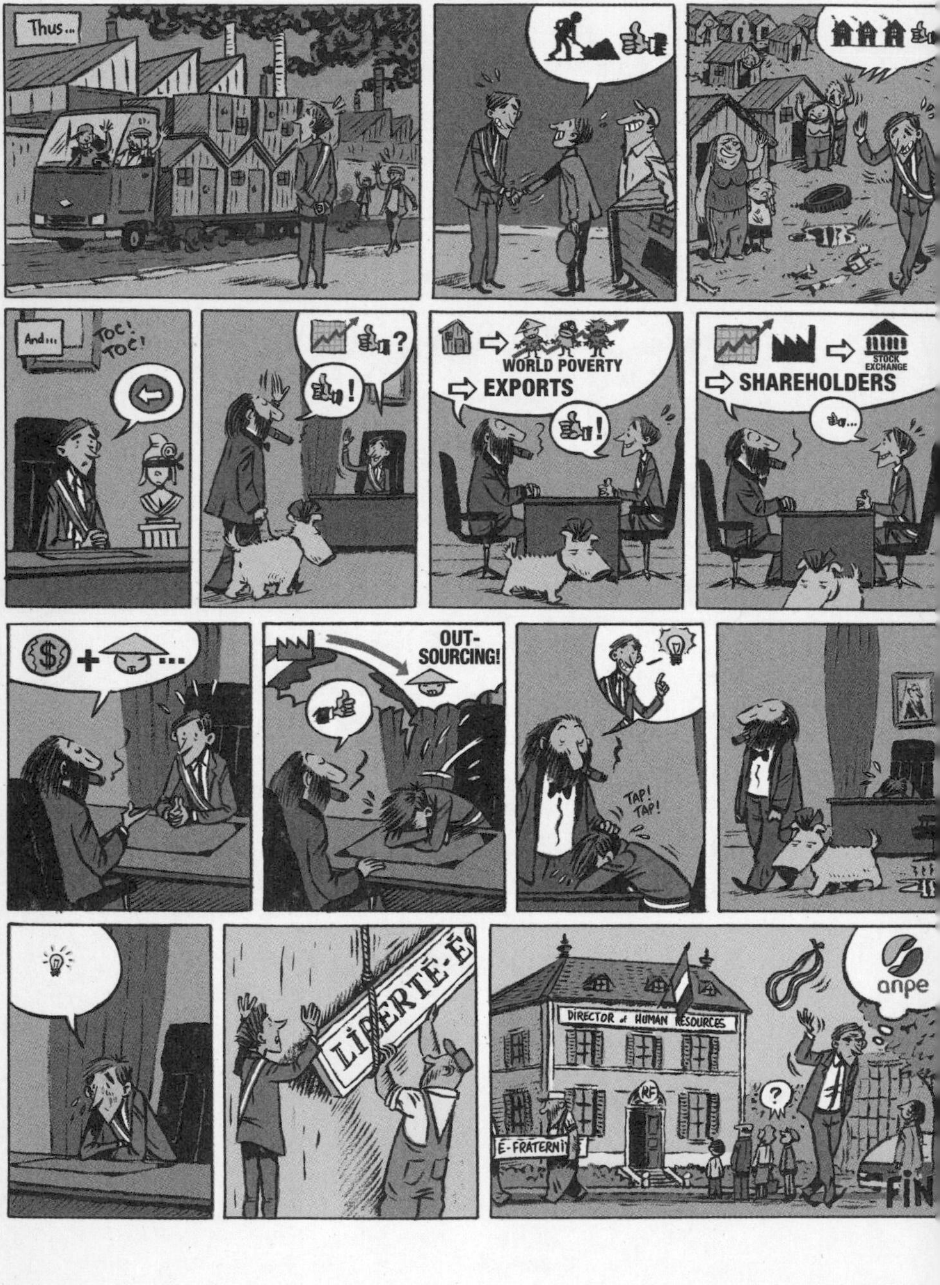
Thus...
And...
TOC! TOC!
?
!
WORLD POVERTY
EXPORTS
!
STOCK EXCHANGE
SHAREHOLDERS
...
OUT-SOURCING!
TAP! TAP!
LIBERTÉ-É
DIRECTOR of HUMAN RESOURCES
RF
E-FRATERNI
?
anpe
FIN

II

REBECCA BENGAL

∎

Captioning for the Blind

FROM a chapbook by Monofonus Press

CATS AND DOGS WERE DISAPPEARING in the Hill Country. Fliers
had been tacked to the bulletin board at the dock bar by the river, on
telephone poles that snaked along curving roads named for the trees
that had been cut down to build these houses: Chlöe last seen around
Whispering Woods, Cerberus on Spanish Oaks Drive, Vulcan on Juniper Trail, Sweetie Pie the tame deer on Vista Vu. There were color
copies, there were studded collars and markings and significant me-
ows, there were rewards. Guns were purchased. A seventy-eight-year-
old woman went walking with a baseball bat. There were rumors.
Parts of dogs and cats turned up in swimming pools. The cuts were
too clean. No, the job was too messy. Cat fur littered driveways, and
coyotes were seen zigzagging down the street. Theories abounded in
the papers. Unsupervised kids. The land was too developed. Predator
animals were growing bolder. It had happened in California. Drug
dealers. Satanists.

In Texas they remarked how strange it was that the dog-dying
seemed to have started when that girl showed up in town. Back in
Oregon her mother had claimed the change in Arlene began to show
when James was hired as a picker at the vineyard. In the note she
left for her parents, Arlene wrote that she was taking the rest of the
season off. She tore the page from a memo pad and left it on the
kitchen table. Then she took it back and slid it under the rubber
band stretched around the newspaper in the front yard and walked
around the corner to the waiting van and James. Her parents could do

what they wanted with her room while she was away, she'd written.

Away — she didn't say where.

James had promised Arlene that when they got to Austin they would live like pioneers, on the frontier of something new, but when the van pulled up the road, and the dirt cleared, and the canyon came into view, it became apparent that they had arrived years too late. The river that they would float down had become a silty, stagnant stream that plainly connected to a water treatment plant; the raft they'd planned to build from throwaway lumber would surely be shot at by security men paid to guard the docks and helicopter pads of the clay-colored mansions dotting the valley. Tawny, same-colored homes jutted from the cliffs and hills around and above. Trucks gleamed from their circular drives in the pre-dusk sun. Scale models of the mansions below, the smaller houses on the road James and Arlene traveled were moated by fresh piles of dirt, squares of sod just laid down, not yet grown together. Their van stalled, and James kissed Arlene and kissed the dash and turned the key and stepped several times on the gas with his worn-through boot to no avail.

"He called it a cabin," he said finally. The engine jerked, and they hurtled unexpectedly forward.

They were nineteen, Arlene and James. They had other things in common. For instance, they both got their GEDs so they could leave school early. That was three years ago, before they met. They made a point of liking things that were uncool, such as public television, such as wine coolers. They found an encyclopedia, Volume E, by a trash can near Grants Pass and read parts of it aloud as they drove down the coast at night toward someplace else. Éboli, *E. coli*, Edward the Confessor, egret. The reason Arlene fell for James, she told him, is because he was the only one of all of them who invited her along for the adventure of leaving.

He'd walked out of the orchard after his first day's work, with the other men and women. Arlene had watched him from the office where she pecked out orders on her father's typewriter. James was average height with brown hair that looked as though he cut himself, maybe while drunk or with extremely dull shears; he had tiny eyes that all Texans had, a genetic leftover, she'd always guessed, from years of squinting in the sun. His T-shirt and jeans were dirt-covered, sweat-stained; he was as normal as American rock 'n' roll. But he had an uncommon, celluloid look about him as though he were not really there, but somehow gliding over the moment, as though he had already lived it and knew what it contained.

He seemed older than he actually was, but younger, all at once. The same thing, people often remarked, was true of Arlene. Arlene had dropped out of college in Eugene a year ago. When James quit school, he had joined a traveling carnival, building and dismantling rides in a succession of county fairs; he left them somewhere in the Panhandle, in the middle of taking down the Heartstopper ride. He was a bastard, he told Arlene; his father was a blank on the birth certificate; his mother had never bothered to name any possible candidates. She lived in another state. The man she eventually married chose not to become James's stepfather, considered her past life an abomination and James its living representative.

James and Arlene had walked James's dog, a red-haired mutt with a black tongue, up and down the dirt road that led to the vineyard. Arlene was never allowed to have a dog as a child, was never a dog person, but James introduced them.

"Just don't make sudden moves," he said, taking Arlene's hand in his. He uncurled her fingers and held them out. Sonny sniffed them, expecting to see food in her palm. "Let her get to trust you. Let her smell your hand. Talk to her. She'll protect you and she won't forget you."

When it got dark, Arlene said she had to go home. She didn't know why she said this but once she had, she couldn't change her mind; it would look foolish. James didn't ask her to explain. He seemed to expect rejection. It fit into his exaggerated self-portrait of being from the wrong side of the tracks. Arlene thought she would probably not see him again. James was a Texas boy. She had known Texas people. They strayed from home but the way they told it, compared to Texas the rest of the world would always be small and insignificant. No other place could live up to its oversized myth.

Newlin was James's uncle. He had a face like a clear-cut forest, pocked and brown and stubbled and dry. He ran a landscaping company in Austin, sign slapped on a paint-chipped blue truck; he kept a wild garden grown from the spoils of his work; he had a garage out back fixed up for the two of them to live in, and they could stay as long as they liked. Why, he *insisted*. A glare shone from his gold tooth as he spoke.

"What have we here." He looked Arlene up and down without further comment. She was slight; dark bangs covered her face, splotchy from car sunburn. He reached inside his jean jacket as though grabbing a gun, but it was only a pocket, holding cans of beer, which he passed around. He and James attempted high-fives in the air, missed, tried again.

"Welcome to town, Arlene," he said, after his was mostly drunk. "Welcome back, James. You look a mile better than the last time I saw you."

"I've been working out, I been lifting weights," James drawled, his grin mocking and large, "in a tanning booth."

Newlin looked at him directly, a piercing, deep stare, as if to check for signs of bloodshot or lies. "I mean I'm fine," James said. "I feel good, I feel hopeful."

"Hopeful's another way of saying you're unsatisfied."

"Well, damn it." James drank down the rest of his beer and crushed the can in the dirt. "So I'm unsatisfied. Give me another, then."

Newlin motioned to the larger house, his, where a picnic cooler with more beers awaited them. They sat in striped lawn chairs repaired with tape on a concrete strip of patio as Newlin described the finer points of the property. He had spared the hackberry tree on the lot, for instance; its dead branches had been removed.

"That one's y'alls." Newlin pointed but didn't walk over to the garage, the only odd house out, ramshackle thing, brick, wood, scrap, tucked behind his own. "It's got two rooms and all you need. Pots and pans and light bulbs and a little chiming clock, even. Cute. But the plumbing's often tricky. No frills. No A.C."

"Guess we should take that up with the *landlord*," James said.

"Ah," Newlin answered drily, "but I hear he's a shiftless S.O.B."

Arlene and James's first home together was partially hidden from the street by the half-living tree. Rings of fire encircled the garage and licked at its little porch and windows. Arlene looked again and it was only bougainvillea, growing in the coils of an old bedspring leaned against the house. The porch was constructed from packing pallets and held, gingerly, a folding chair. More landscaping leftovers.

There was no move to go inside the house, so Arlene didn't. Sonny, who had been standing timidly between Arlene and James, ventured to sniff the perimeter of the garage and backyard with great, methodical interest.

"You said that dog was part Chow but she doesn't look like it one bit," Newlin said. "She resembles a fox, or a coyote!" There was barking, at some unseen thing, and Sonny burst out of the brush.

James whistled. "Sonny found me in Utah when I was headed west," he said. "She was begging by a gas pump. Just a homeless pup."

Sonny's bark changed to a low, disconsolate howl. Arlene went to her, pulled at the dry, ragged dreadlock on the back of her neck, a remnant of the dog's mysterious past life, before she walked into James's, suffering from mange in that particular spot, her leg fur thick with burs, a weird stripe of purple paint down her left side. Whoever she'd been with before them had *painted* her. All traces of it gone now but often she would bark and nothing would be there, some invisible presence passing down a hallway. Or like now, as she left Arlene and crept along the side of Newlin's truck.

"Sonny," Arlene said. And a second time, "Sonny," till the spell was snapped. A hawk flew across the mealy blue sky. Grackles snarled over something, an insect, a snake; it disappeared into a swath of silk tassel, and Sonny dove for it. Arlene stared after the dog, who was quickly becoming part of a landscape she knew only from books. Below, the limestone canyon was blunted with twisted leaf yucca and prickly pear. White mansions dotted the opposite side of the river, as if in agreement: this side, houses in colors of mud, that side, pure white.

James and Newlin popped the tops off new cans. They had moved past the point of pleasantry, and talked of things and people she didn't know. Arlene didn't know anyone outside of a two-state radius. It struck her that what she and James had done was totally senseless and wild, to run away from home, and after such a journey, to arrive here, to stay. She was overcome by the false but convincing physical sensation that she was still in motion.

Driving down the West Coast, they had eaten lunch stolen out of fruit trees, spooned out of tin cans, seasoned by packets of complimentary condiments; they had slept right by the shore and woke to the barking of seals gathered on the rocks. From San Diego to Arizona they hadn't stopped because Arlene was terrified of Yuma at night, the electrified borders, the guns. In her delirium she had seen things: mothers with children strapped to their backs, tearing across the border and collapsing in gunfire. How could James sleep? She had swerved into the median to avoid a man in a trenchcoat sprinting across the highway out of the desert. In the rear window there was no one. She sailed the van through storms, sheets of water, while James tried to wipe away the vapor fogging the windshield with a torn T-shirt. In El Paso the Rio was not so Grande, curled to a thin trickle. Sonny hung her head out the window, her huge mane whipping in the wind, perhaps looking enviously at another dog, who paddled freely between the United States and Mexico and then back again. Row after row of beef cattle faced the interstate, poked through head-sized holes in the fence to ingest feed. James was disgusted and tired, counting casino billboards. They passed through actual ghost towns. There was tumbleweed; there were longhorn cattle. A man rode a horse along the highway, the tallest man she'd ever seen, in extra-long, tight-creased blue jeans, a real cowboy, and she was sure she saw him because James did too.

"Hey, Arlene," James called now in a stage whisper. He was smiling in the way that people do around sleeping things. He nodded at Newlin.

"What time is it?" Arlene asked.

"Dark. Come on, I want to show you around." They left Newlin drowsing in his chair, the blue recycling box now full, James swiftly extricating the remains of a fifth of whiskey from Newlin's lap, and walked toward the lake through lawns that appeared blue and iridescent under streetlights. The cul-de-sacs were made of carefully choreographed sequences: porch and driveway light sensors flicked on in rapid succession. The dog trotted ahead, startled at the things she triggered. A lawn sprinkler suddenly erupted, sputtering in every direction, thwacking blasts of water, and then sobered again without warning like a sulking child.

"To hose down burglars," Arlene said.

"You mean horny teenagers," James said leerily and laughed and kissed her and pet the dog, who was standing at attention as if she expected them to leave again suddenly. They sat on a stranger's boat and no alarm sounded. Scattered lights, from houses, reflected in the water. Looking straight ahead, the land downriver appeared deceptively open and empty, resembling the part of the country Arlene thought they'd been trying to find. "Check out the aliens," James drawled, twisting her to face a range of mountainous hills in the opposite direction, where a row of radio towers stood, a half dozen of them. A series of flashing red lights appeared to climb vertically up the invisible towers, like otherworldly beings ascending into waiting spaceships. "That's us." He meant aliens, but that wasn't what Arlene thought, as the lights hovered in the air spookily and glowed for an instant, then descended back down the way they'd come and started the whole thing over again.

With her fur shorn only neck down to her tail, Sonny had resembled a cotton swab, or a rock star. By the time they reached Texas, her summer hairdo had filled in, her skinny body encased in a thick, even fuzz of reddish-blond fur. She lay at their feet all day long. James got a job delivering filtered water to offices and private homes; after he left each morning, Sonny followed Arlene in and out of the garage's two rooms, flopping on the floor tiles when she was ignored.

At night they drank wine coolers and watched television. Arlene opened the sliding garage door and nailed a sheet of window screen in its place, but the heat was incredible. Books had begun to tire her; it was impossible to concentrate; the sentences swam. James had found a huge old grandfather TV set on the street, and jerried together a set of rabbit ears, and on the sofa they lay, peach-breathed, watching a nature show.

Tiny sparrows scuttled through a woody thicket, accompanied by the faceless, yet sonorous voice of an announcer: "The song of the white-throated sparrow is a clear, crisp whistle succeeded by a sudden *chink*! and a slurry *tseet*. Generally, they continue on like this until nightfall, when some other nocturnal animal frights them into silence." His voice sounded like water being poured steadily into a very deep well, its echo reverberating within stone walls.

Out of nowhere another voice interrupted, forceful and bilious and breathless, swiftly overtaking the first: "In this image, the camera is eye level with the forest floor. In the left screen, sparrows with bold, alternating stripes on their heads and white throats gather pine needles. In the next image we see a setting sun through tall pine treetops against a graying sky."

The first man tried to stay firm, his cadence unchanged: "Like most passerine migrants, sparrows fly by night in small flocks as they leave for the southern states. During dusk prior to migration, they exhibit a marked restlessness which is termed *zugunruhe*."

But the second, like a lawyer aggressively blurting his objection, fired back: "At left, a nighttime sky. At center, a crescent moon. The sky is grainy, violet. Across the lower field of the screen, approximately a dozen sparrows fly toward the horizon." The first, mighty and strong, did not waver, no matter how minor his point. He had been entrusted with a script, with information, and he would, by God, deliver it in his deep rumble: "They may also sing at night during this period of pre-migration *zugunruhe*. Some fall prey to drift migration: birds blown off course by wind."

The second voice had retreated, was quieted at last. Sparrows flew across the screen in silence. The dog chased wine-cooler bottles that bumped and rolled on the tile. The little clock struck eleven; Newlin's house went dark. James wrapped his free arm around Arlene's waist and saw her alarmed look. "It's for *blind* people," he said, laughing, when Arlene reached for the set to turn it off.

"No, no, don't," he said to her. "I like it."

It was already hot, but only just light outside when James left with the water truck and a kiss goodbye, and a plea for her to join him somewhere after work, and Sonny pushed herself against the front door, waiting for Arlene. The streets were absolutely quiet except for the sound of Newlin's shovel, metal striking stone, down some other cul-de-sac.

This was the time of day she liked best. Arlene and Sonny walked down Juniper to the water's level, sticking their heads through the iron gates along the way to watch the people below leave their mansions for the day, a parade of child-size backpacks, and briefcases, and coffee mugs, and horns honking from expensive cars, and then economy ones and trucks pulling in as a few maids and nannies and house painters came to work. Arlene found the opening, through the trees, where they had gone on their first night here. There, on the ground next to the motorboat, was her own bra. Now it looked oddly exposed, like a piece of evidence, public. She chose to ignore it. She took off the jeans she was wearing and jumped in the water in just her long T-shirt, Sonny following, and they swam along the river's edge and she sat on a rocky outcropping in the shadow of a millionaire's home and tossed sticks in the water for Sonny to chase while her clothes dried.

They walked home. Sonny ran off the leash and reappeared with a crown of burrs. Tufted cactus spines stuck in her fur. Her ears lay flat against her head and she began to howl softly, sensing Arlene's drifting state. They crossed to avoid an oncoming jogger, who worked a pair of hand weights, bounced her head to a stereo wrapped like a tourniquet around her arm. The swishing of her shorts ceased as she stopped and lifted her large, tinted sunglasses to better see them.

"Is that a *fox?*" the woman exclaimed, and walked right over to inspect.

Arlene looked at her. The jogger wore red lipstick and dark foundation that had begun to sweat in orange streaks. Sonny barked.

"Yeah," Arlene said flatly. "You better watch your chickens."

Marriages were being tested over the losses of beloved family pets. A woman bemoaned the maiming of her dear departed Mister Samson, whose remains even taxidermy could not save. A study showed that, oddly, where there were more humans, there were more coyotes. The VFD was put on alert. Feral cats were trapped by a nonprofit group, neutered, vaccinated, and taken into town to be adopted into apartment buildings. A neighborhood association meeting boasted a record attendance. Anonymous tips had been received and leads were being chased by police: An initial investigation had turned up a BB gun that may or may not have been linked to the deaths, a stolen lawn mower, and an item of women's lingerie. It was recommended that small children remain indoors.

As they watched the news, Arlene rubbed Sonny's mane, pulling out the stuck burrs. "In a neighborhood where more than twenty cats and dogs have been mutilated," the announcer continued, "authorities now have reports of maimed deer . . ."

The blind captioner interrupted: "You can see the legs of the fawn cut off and scattered on a brick walkway leading to the engraved wooden door of a large estate. You can see various unidentified organs draped over the potted yellow hibiscus. You can see the gutted body of a young deer lying on a wooden doormat, partially covered by a plain white sheet. You cannot see any blood."

When Arlene saw her first dog body, she thought it was a discarded coat. It took her a minute to register the paws, the tail, the stomach, the blood. The absence of a head. It was, had been, a black Labrador retriever. It lay rigid in the spare early light. Sonny went to the dog, sniffing and then cocking her head strangely as she stared.

The cut was a clean slice. It was not the way they described it on the news. A headless animal lying in the bright-green imported grass. Arlene began to search about for the rest of the dog, but where was one to look? Car trunks, shrubbery, mantels. Lights showed in the windows of the houses in the hills about her, one by one by one, and she saw a face through a ruffle of curtains, and instinctively she ran.

She aimed for the garage, with Sonny fast and happy at her heels. Sonny seemed to have forgotten already what she had seen, or maybe it didn't matter, the sight of one of her species, fallen. Death, this unassailable thing, had come for a fellow dog, and well, that was that. She passed a telephone pole, a flier tacked there. *Mehitabel Is Lost!*, it read, above a photograph of a spaniel. Approaching on the sidewalk, a pair of walkers looked sharply at Arlene, then at one another, and she slowed to a sort of anxious jog.

In a little scraggly woods there was a bar. So this was the place James had been talking about. The pool table was propped up with a wadded section of newspaper. The roof was caving in. The bartender resembled her own grandfather, stern, not quite forgiving, nosehair needing a trim. He didn't question her age. "You look young," he said, "but no one's around."

"I just need some change." Arlene pushed a dollar across the counter. Inside the phone booth more *Mehitabel Is Lost!* posters had been taped to the walls. Apparently a private detective had been hired, and the reward had increased to a thousand dollars since the first round of fliering. *If you have any information, contact "Sherlock Bones" at this number.*

Arlene dialed long distance, collect. "It's your daughter," she told the operator, and waited while it beeped. Dad, she'd rehearsed, I'm fine. I'm in Texas. James is saving up money for us to move into our own place. If we stay around here, God, I don't know, we'll turn fifty in two seconds. I'm just learning my way around. I have some work, a job tomorrow, though. Mom's not there? Tell I miss her. I'll give you my address next time, I don't actually know it by heart. I hope things are okay. This morning I saw . . .

The line broke briefly, and the operator returned: "I'm sorry, your party did not answer. Please hang up and try again later."

She stood and let the dial tone sound for several seconds. How long had it been since she'd heard a dial tone? As she replaced the receiver in its cradle, a black Impala pulled up to the bar, and a policewoman got out and strode briskly toward Arlene.

"Ma'am," said the policewoman. Garbled talk sounded from the radio on her hip. "You live around here. You and your boyfriend bought dog food and feminine supplies and a dustpan from Wendell's Grocery the other night." Arlene nodded. This place had no secrets. "Know anything about this?" She thrust a Polaroid of the Labrador in Arlene's face.

Arlene studied it from one angle, then another. "I don't," she said carefully. "I don't know why this is."

"Well, we're treating it as an unsolved mystery," the policewoman said. "We're relying heavily on tips and calling on our residents to remain vigilant. If you see anything out there, give me a call." She handed Arlene a business card and looked down in surprise.

"Holy . . . ! That stopped me a second. I'd be damned if that dog of yours don't resemble a fox."

At six, they shoveled, Arlene and Newlin. It was not easy; the ground was limestone covered with shallow topsoil. They dug, and they struck rock, and they pulled the shovels out, and they struck again. "There are no basements in this town," Newlin said after about a half hour of this.

"No kidding," ten minutes later, came Arlene's response. They were working in the home of a woman who had requested stones to be arranged in neat slabs beside her goldfish pool. The river lay not twenty yards away.

"You can't begrudge someone for wanting a pool, Arlene," Newlin chided, and he was right. Fish did not thrive in that river. But other things did, less seemly life forms, algae and crawdads, which would certainly not be permitted to cohabit with the Gundersons' goldfish in the showpiece architectural garden. At seven-thirty, Mavis Gunderson's bronze Mercedes backed out of the drive and joined the fleet of other cars, disappearing down curving roads into the city.

As the morning grew late, the ground and air turned pink, orange, deepening. By noon, things were practically Martian. "I thought you were a farmer's daughter," Newlin said. Arlene lay sunglassed on the bed she'd made from piles of the sod they had purchased with the Gundersons' money and had yet to install. "This is no farm," she said. "My father's a supervisor, anyway."

"James said different."

"James says a lot different." She paused. Newlin smiled in the creepy, knowing way older people had; he was thirty, but an old, lived thirty. As if he thought he'd seen past hoping.

But love, what did he know? She sat up. "Look, you. I may not *know* James the way you do. But we're in love, right? You don't have to know someone to be in love with them."

"In my experience it's usually better if you don't," Newlin replied. "Knowing takes far longer."

He lit a second cigarette in one hand, finishing his sandwich with the other. "Just humor me for a while, Arlene. Couple hours after lunch, we knock off for the day."

"Lunch," Arlene moaned. "It's too hot for lunch." She poured her water thermos over her head and felt her skin dry almost instantly.

"Suit yourself, then."

They commenced to working. In a few hours, the cars would return to the driveways and the drivers would get out and curse at their overturned trash cans and plants, and call for their pets; the houses would refill with people trying to get to know each other, locking themselves in for another night against the unseen. Before they left, Arlene and Newlin unloaded some plants from the truck and set them in various spots among the rocks. They took panels of the sod and arranged them on the ground like a chessboard. "Now it looks like we've done something," Newlin said. He was pleased.

The captioner described a second tier of the world that was so blatant and crude, Arlene refused to listen anymore. She would talk James into donating their TV set to the dock bar. The bartender would have something to do; his bar would be visually-impaired-friendly. Occasionally they could still sit here with him, as they did now, with Newlin and the dog, watching the traffic flow home. Arlene was not interested in the city. She preferred to believe it was just as James said it was, rather than to see it for herself: "I delivered to a woman who yodels for a living. She wanted me to go to bed with her, but I told I only wanted to be with you." Newlin, hearing him, raised an eyebrow, but James continued: "She says she's been on *Hee Haw* and the *Grand Ole Opry*. I met a man who's bicycled across the country twelve times. His legs are ruined now but the maps on his wall are dark with Magic Marker lines showing the places he's been." As James talked, he seemed to join the mysterious world of which he spoke. He described a downtown building shaped like a drum; women with enormous sprayed hairdos like clouds; bats flying in and out of the state capitol at dusk; beautiful, garish Mexican churches sitting right next to shotgun houses with the paint stripped away.

James was glad to be back in Texas; he prospered. He was growing healthy and strong from all this work, Arlene noticed, tan especially on his left side, from the driving. He drank. They all did. There were three kinds of beer on display but only one of them in stock. There was a pool table, green as Mavis Gunderson's new grass, and a sliding-glass door that opened to the dock and a cluster of trees; past them, you could see the hills, see Newlin's house and their little garage. Arlene imagined fishermen here, shooting pool or throwing darts, in some other time. There was a filthy sink stained with a dozen paint colors, including the current one, gray, and a battered old jukebox filled with dusty, comforting songs of drinking and heartbreak and other lives she'd yet to know.

She followed Sonny to the back of the room. In the top half of the screen, the sun was going down. In the lower right corner, there was the river, bordered by a lean strip of land and the houses, which from here appeared as small as plastic toys. In the hills there was movement. Tiny and indistinct at first, like a black smudge on a screen, something approached, rapidly, coming into focus. Sonny made her strange, quiet howl, the sound she made for things she did not understand, for instance, squirrels that were beyond her reach. The coyote nudged its way forward, through the sage and the laurel, and stuck its head nosily into the missing door of one of Newlin's abandoned cars. It traveled down the road and came right up to the window, where Sonny stood, transfixed. They were the same size.

EULA BISS

■

Relations

FROM *Identity Theory*

IN NEW YORK CITY, in the spring of 1999, a story hit the newspapers of a Long Island woman who had given birth to twins — one white and one black. The woman and her husband were white and the black baby was not theirs, at least not biologically. The embryo that became that baby had been accidentally implanted in the woman's uterus with the embryo of her biological son, but it belonged to a black couple who were clients at the same fertility clinic, and they wanted their son back. After a DNA test, a custody battle, a state supreme court ruling, and an unsuccessful appeal, it was decided that the black baby was the child of the black couple, legally and entirely.

The story had its peculiarities, like the fact that the fertility clinic had notified the black couple that some of their embryos had been mistakenly implanted in another woman, but did not tell them anything more, so they eventually learned of the birth of their son through a private investigator. But even odd circumstances like this took on the sheen of metaphor, pointing, for those of us who were looking, to further evidence of a systematic failure of any number of services to reach black people intact, in the form in which they are typically enjoyed by white people. If both babies had been white, I doubt the story would have become the parable it became — playing out in the newspapers over the next few years as an epic tale of blood and belonging.

The fact that the story involved two babies and two mothers and, eventually, an agreement that gave both babies a family and both families a baby, would inspire some reporters to use the phrase "happy ending," but the story would resist that happy ending for quite some time, in part because the black baby was initially returned to his biological parents on the strict condition that he would continue to visit his twin brother, spending a week in summer and alternate holidays with the white family. On the question of whether a person can have a twin to whom he is not related, the New Jersey *Record* consulted an expert, who explained that the babies were not technically twins but that their situation was so unusual it was impossible to determine, without further research, how deep a bond they might share. Long after the black baby had been returned to his biological parents and given a new name, the question of what exactly his relationship was to the white baby persisted. The answer to this question would determine whether or not the courts would mandate visits between the black boy and the white family. "Are the baby boys brothers in the eyes of the law," asked the *New York Times*, "or two separate people who just happened to arrive in the world on the same subway car?"

When we were young, my sister and I had two baby dolls that were exactly alike in every way except that one was white and one was black. The precise sameness of these dolls, so obviously cast from one mold in two different colors of plastic, convinced me that they were, like us, sisters.

There is no biological basis for what we call race, meaning that most human variation occurs within individual "races" rather than between them. Race is a social fiction. But it is also, for now at least, a social fact. We may be remarkably genetically similar, but we are not all, culturally speaking, the same. And if that Long Island woman had raised the black boy to whom she gave birth, he might have been robbed of a certain amount of the cultural identity to which his skin would be assigned later in life, and might therefore find himself, as an adult, in an uncomfortable no-man's-land between two racial identities.

But this no-man's-land is already fairly heavily trafficked. Without denying that blacks and whites remain largely segregated and disturbingly polarized, and without denying that black culture is a distinct, if not uniform, culture, I think we ought to admit, as the writer Albert Murray once insisted, that American culture is "incontestably mulatto." A friend of mine used to tell a story about a segregated restaurant in the South where a sign on one side of the room advertised "Home Cooking" and a sign on the other advertised "Soul Food" and the customers on both sides were eating the same biscuits and gravy. "For all their traditional antagonisms and obvious differences," Murray wrote in *The Omni-Americans*, "the so-called black and so-called white people of the United States resemble nobody else in the world so much as they resemble each other."

Even so, we don't tend to make family out of each other. Marriages between whites and blacks amount to less than 1 percent of all our marriages. And even after the last state laws banning interracial marriage were declared unconstitutional in 1967, some states continued to ban interracial adoptions. The agencies that first began placing black children with white couples often viewed these placements as highly progressive. Not everyone agreed. The National Association of Black Social Workers, in particular, has continued to oppose the adoption of black children by white parents ever since the release of their somewhat notorious 1972 statement on the preservation of black families, which suggested that the likely outcome of such adoptions was "cultural genocide."

The bitterness of this statement, and its refusal to see white Americans as viable parents for black Americans, is probably best understood in the context of all the wrong that has been done to black children by white adults in this country. There was, during slavery, the use of black women for "breeding" purposes, the forced infidelities of that system, the denial of slave marriages as legitimate contracts, and the practice of selling members of the same family away from each other, so that sisters were separated from brothers, mothers were separated from fathers, and young children were separated from one or both parents. More than a century after emancipation, we still have the unmanning of black men by law enforcement, the incommensurate imprisonment of black fathers, and the troubling biases of the child-welfare system, in which a disproportionate number of black children are separated from their parents.

That doesn't mean white adults can't be good parents for black children, but the endeavor is fraught with history and complicated by all our current social failures. If the white woman on Long Island had given birth to two white babies, it might have been easier to ignore one of the uglier elements of her story: the fact that our claim on our children amounts to a kind of ownership. At one point, the biological parents of the black baby decided that they would rather pay the $200,000 fine mandated by their shared custody agreement than continue to allow the white couple visits with their son. The white couple balked at this, and their lawyer said, "They're not looking to, quote, 'sell' their son!"

If both babies had been white, I might have felt that the white woman was entitled to keep them both, no matter whom they were related to. I might have been wrong, and the courts would very probably not have agreed with me, but I would have believed in her right to keep any child she carried in her womb because that is what I would want for myself. As it was, because one of those babies was black, and because the black woman did not herself conceive — her treatments at the fertility clinic failed and she was childless — it did not seem right for the white woman to keep the black baby. It seemed like a kind of robbery, a robbery made worse by its echoes of history. But still — and perhaps this exposes exactly how wishful I really am — I wanted to believe in the white woman's desire to maintain a familial connection to the black child. I wanted the two boys to be brothers, and I wanted the original shared custody agreement to work out. And it might have, especially if the white woman had not made the mistake of saying "come to Mommy" to the black baby on one of those visits, and of calling him by the name she had given him, which was no longer his name.

The white doll was my sister's and the black doll was mine. My doll's proper name was Susannah, but her common name, the name I used more often, and the name my entire family used, was Black Doll. My mother finds this hilarious, but I don't enjoy revealing it. Even so, when I was young the fact that Black Doll was black became very ordinary to me very quickly, so that her name was nothing but her name.

The famous "doll studies" of Mamie and Kenneth Clark, which were conducted in a series of different schools in both the North and the South, used a set of identical black and white baby dolls bought at a Woolworth's in Harlem to reveal how racism affected children. In one experiment, sixteen black children were shown a white doll and a black doll and asked to pick which doll best represented certain words. Eleven of the children associated the black doll with the word "bad" and ten associated the white doll with the word "nice." This experiment later influenced the *Brown vs. Board of Education* decision to integrate the public schools.

In the years and decades following that decision, questions would be raised about what exactly, if anything, the doll studies proved. Black children in unsegregated schools had responded to the Clarks' dolls in much the same way as black children in segregated schools, which complicated the idea that the children were responding solely to segregation. But they were clearly responding to something. Perhaps the doll studies suggest that children are as sensitive to racial codes as adults. I do not know exactly how the word "nice" was used in 1939 when those studies began, but I do know what it means now to describe a neighborhood as "nice" or another part of town as "bad" and I know what "nice" hair is and I know what it means when my landlady tells me, as I'm applying for a lease, that she won't need my bank account number because I look like a "nice" person. And I suspect it is possible, especially in a racially aware environment, that the secondary meanings of these words are not lost even on six-year-olds.

"Maybe we love our dolls because we can't love ourselves," a friend of mine — an artist who made drawings of dolls missing legs or arms or eyes which all looked, somehow, eerily like her — once suggested. Perhaps this is the essential truth behind why we make effigies. And maybe this is why we tend to believe that children should have dolls that look like them, or at least that look like what they might eventually become. In 1959 Mattel introduced a doll that was not, like most other dolls marketed for children, a baby doll. This doll had breasts and wore makeup and was modeled after a doll sold in Germany as a gag gift for grown men. The man who designed the American version of the doll, a man who had formerly designed Sparrow and Hawk missiles for the Pentagon and was briefly married to Zsa Zsa

Gabor, was charged with making the new Barbie doll look less like a "German street walker," which he attempted in part by filing off her nipples.

In the past few decades quite a few people have suggested — citing most often the offense of impossible proportions — that Barbie dolls teach young girls to hate themselves. But the opposite may be true. British researchers recently found that girls between the ages of seven and eleven harbor surprisingly strong feelings of dislike for their Barbie dolls, with no other toy or brand name inspiring such a negative response from the children. The dolls "provoked rejection, hatred, and violence" and many girls preferred Barbie torture — by cutting, burning, decapitating, or microwaving — over other ways of playing with the doll. Reasons that the girls hated their Barbies included, somewhat poetically, the fact that they were "plastic." The researchers also noted that the girls never spoke of one single, special Barbie, but tended to talk about having a box full of anonymous Barbies. "On a deeper level Barbie has become inanimate," one of the researchers remarked. "She has lost any individual warmth that she might have possessed if she were perceived as a singular person. This may go some way towards explaining the violence and torture."

My own Black Doll, who is now kept by my mother as a memento of my childhood, was loved until the black of her hair and the pink of her lips rubbed off. Her skin is pocked with marks where I pricked her with needles, administering immunizations. She wears a dress that my grandmother sewed for her. And she has, stored in a closet somewhere, a set of furniture made for her by the German cabinet-maker who boarded with my family when I was young. There is something moving to me now about the idea of that man — who left Germany in the 1920s, just as the Nazi Party was gathering power — laboring at his lathe, perfecting the fancy legs of a maple dining table for a beloved toy known as Black Doll.

Although the two can be confused, our urge to love our own, or those we have come to understand as our own, is, it seems, much more powerful than our urge to segregate ourselves. And perhaps this is why that Long Island woman went to court to fight for shared custody of a child who was very clearly, very publicly, no blood relation to her or her husband. It was an act of thievery, but it was also an act of love.

In the agonized handwritten statement she released to the press just before she voluntarily surrendered to his biological parents the four-month-old child to whom she gave birth, long before the court decision that would decide she had no right to share custody of him, the white woman said, "We're giving him up because we love him." She had come to believe that it was in the best interest of the black baby to be with his biological parents. In a separate statement, her lawyer added, "She didn't look at them as a white baby and a black baby. She looked at them as her sons." This was already quite evident from the fact that she had insisted on a DNA test before she would consider giving the child back to the black couple whose embryos — as she had been informed by the fertility clinic — were implanted in her womb.

A group of white children and a group of black children were asked, in one of the Clarks' doll studies, to choose the baby doll that looked the most like them. The white children overwhelmingly chose the white doll. But seven of the sixteen black children also chose the white doll. Some of the others could not choose a doll, and a few broke into tears.

As a teenager I sometimes posed for my mother's sculptures. She worked in black porcelain, which is, when fired, as deep and rich a black as white porcelain is a cool and flawless white. At that time, my mother had just converted to a West African religion and was dating a black man. Her friends were black women and Puerto Rican women, and her imagination was full of African folklore. I posed for a mask she was making of the face of Oya — Yoruba goddess of the graveyard, of wind, and of change — standing in her attic studio with my lips pursed as though I were blowing. Why should I have been surprised, and somewhat hurt, when the mask was finished, to see that my face had become unmistakably African? My eyes were still almond-shaped, as they are, but my cheekbones were higher, my nose was flatter and wider, and my lips were fuller. Still, my face was in that face — I could see it there, especially in the mouth.

The topsy-turvy doll is a traditional doll peculiar to the United

States. These dolls have heads on both ends of their bodies and wear skirts that can be flipped up or down to reveal either one head or the other. In the antebellum South, many of these dolls had a white head on one end and a black head on the other. Some topsy-turvy dolls were sold with the slogan, "Turn me up and turn me back, first I'm white, and then I'm black."

The possibility of moving, through disguise, between one race and another is an idea so compelling that it keeps returning to us again and again. There was Nella Larsen's *Passing*, John Howard Griffin's *Black Like Me*, Eddie Murphy's *Saturday Night Live* skit in which he dressed as a white man and discovered that banks give money away to white people, and, most recently, there was *Black.White.*, a reality television show produced by R. J. Cutler and Ice Cube, an experiment that put two families, one white and one black, in a house together and used Hollywood makeup to switch their races.

I have a cousin whose race is sometimes perceived as black and other times as white. Her father is a black man from Jamaica, and her mother is my mother's sister. My cousin and I grew up on opposite sides of the country, she in Oakland, California, and I in upstate New York, but we both found ourselves in New York City in our twenties, and we shared an apartment in Brooklyn for a year. When I moved to New York I barely knew my cousin, but I was comforted by the idea that she was family. My cousin and I come from an extended family in which it is generally understood that even the most remote members cannot be strangers to each other.

And we were not. We looked alike, but in an oblique way that was probably most striking to us, because my cousin looked very much like my mother, and I looked very much like hers, but neither of us looked like our own mother. Beyond that, we recognized in each other the distinctively frugal and, we decided, hereditary habit of washing and saving bits of tinfoil and plastic sandwich bags. Neither of us seemed, by nature, capable of working full time, and we were always saving our money so that we could afford not to work. We both slept very poorly in the city, and we both considered ourselves in exile there. Both of us were inexplicably moved by the concrete cross outside our living room window. And we both had the same characteristic gesture of putting one of our hands to our neck protectively. We reveled in this sameness, in this twinning. We even called each other by the same name. "Cousin!" I would sing as I walked in the door. "Is that you, Cousin?" she would answer.

At some point during the year we lived together, I watched my cousin cut out pictures of black college beauty queens from *Ebony* magazine and glue them into a notebook. She didn't know what she wanted to do with them yet, she told me, she'd have to think about it. But she lined them up lovingly — Miss Norfolk State University, Miss Morris College, Miss Florida A&M University, Miss North Carolina Agricultural and Technical State University, Miss Southern University — like a paper-doll parade replete with heartbreaking plastic crowns and tiaras.

Years later, my cousin would send me a film called *A Girl Like Me*, in which a seventeen-year-old girl from New York recreates the Clarks' doll studies at a Harlem day-care center. In this 2005 re-creation, fifteen of twenty-one black children prefer the white doll over the black doll. "Can you show me the doll that looks bad?" a voice behind the camera asks a little black girl. The child immediately chooses the black doll, and when she is asked why, she reports flatly, "Because she's black." But when the voice asks her, "Can you give me the doll that looks like you?" she looks down, first reaching for the white doll but then, looking directly at the camera, reluctantly pushing the black doll forward.

As Barbie dolls became increasingly popular in the sixties, Barbie's family expanded to include her boyfriend Ken, her little sister Skipper, her twin siblings Tutti and Tod, and her cousin Francie. In 1967 Mattel released Colored Francie, a black version of cousin Francie. Notably, Colored Francie was intended to be understood as a friend for Barbie, not a cousin. One of the many objections to Colored Francie was that she was cast out of the same mold as the white Francie, and therefore had the same face and the same features. This oversight was seen by some as hostile, as another attempt to erase the Africanness of African Americans. Colored Francie did not sell well, and she was soon discontinued.

Despite this early failure, Mattel has maintained a long-standing tradition of releasing both a black version and a white version of many of their dolls. This was most problematic in 1997, when they teamed up with Nabisco to promote Oreo Fun Barbie. The cheerfulness of the black Oreo Fun Barbie, who was sold in packaging covered with pictures of Oreo cookies and whose dress was emblazoned with the word "Oreo," seemed to mock, chillingly, the predicament of the *Oreo* — the person who is seen as black on the outside but white on the inside. Oreo Fun Barbie was quickly recalled when Mattel realized that she evoked cultural abdication and self-loathing.

As a child, my cousin worried that her mother loved her brother more because he was not as brown as her. Even so, her skin is light enough to "pass." That was a household word for us in those days when we lived together. I remember, in particular, an evening when I invited a graduate student I'd met at a party over for dinner. We listened to Neil Young and talked about World War II, and sized each other up as material for love. When he left, just after I closed the door behind him, my cousin shot me a look. "What?" I said. "You were passing," she said, meaning that I had not been acting like myself. And she was right, although at the time I resented her accuracy.

Someone once accused my mother of adopting the cultural and racial identities of the men she was with. It does seem that my mother has been trying to escape her white, Protestant, middle-class background ever since she dropped out of high school and got on a Greyhound bus, but shouldn't she be allowed out if she wants out? Especially now that she has sacrificed, in various ways, just about all the privilege to which she could ever have laid claim. A multiracial society, Randall Kennedy recently wrote, "ought to allow its members free entry into and exit from racial categories."

If they are willing to make any sort of nod toward the existence of race as a legitimate category, most scientists agree that a person's race is self-identified, and the U.S. census now only categorizes people as they self-identify. But our racial categories are so closely policed by the culture at large that it would be much more accurate to say that we are collectively identified. Whenever we range outside the racial identity that has been collectively assigned to us, we are very quickly reminded where we belong.

Not long after I moved into my cousin's apartment in the historically black neighborhood of Fort Greene, I stopped at a small shop a few blocks away to buy her a birthday present of some hair oil I'd seen her admire. I was standing with my back to the register choosing between Nubian Woman and Jasmine, when I heard loud whispers and laughter from behind me. "White girl!" the sales women were saying, with every intention I would hear them.

In that part of Brooklyn, the people I passed on the street often greeted me with a summary description of what they noticed about me, as in, "You've got some short hair, girl." This was a phenomenon that my cousin and I found both arresting and amusing. For her part, my cousin discovered that the indicators of race she had learned in Oakland did not necessarily translate to Brooklyn. The way she walked, for example, the sharp switch of her gait, might have been read as black in Oakland, but it was not in Brooklyn. Here her identity became even more ambiguous. Walking home through the park after dark one night, my cousin passed a black man who nodded at her and said, "Mmm-hmmm, you're a bad-ass white girl."

I was mistaken for a white boy twice, and once I was mistaken for Asian. But I was never taken for black. And I could not have expected to be. As much as I believe racial categories to be fluid and ambiguous, I still know that there is nothing particularly ambiguous about my features, or my bearing, or my way of speaking. And although I was familiar, from my mother's religion, with the cowry shells and oiled wood carvings sold in the African shops of my neighborhood, I could not pass there.

At the beginning of the six-episode series of *Black.White.*, the white family needs coaching from the black family in order to learn to pass as black. But the black family, as they explain after an uncomfortable silence, already knows how to act white, of course, because that is the dominant culture within which they have to live their daily lives. Knowing how to act white is a survival skill for the black family. The white family, on the other hand, struggles with acting black, frequently committing tone-deaf errors, and ultimately not quite pulling it off.

Perhaps my inability to pass is part of why I feel so trapped within my identity as a white woman. That identity does not feel chosen by me as much as it feels grudgingly defaulted to. But I haven't worked to assimilate into any other racial group. And I have rarely turned down any of the privileges my skin has afforded me. When it became clear to me, for instance, that my landlady was looking for a "nice" tenant, I did not inform her that if she was under the impression I was white, she should at least know I was not nice.

In my mostly white high school, where the white boys who listened to rap and sagged their pants were called "whiggers," we were trained to feel disdain for anyone who ranged outside the cultural confines of whiteness. But later, in my mostly white college, among whiggers and punks and hippies and tattooed freaks, I began to understand the significance of the effort to advertise one's resistance to the mainstream and undo one's access to privilege through a modification of one's clothing or body or skin. Even so, my college was such a safe and nurturing place for misfits, especially rich misfits, that it was hard to believe dreadlocks and tattoos and piercings would really inhibit anyone's ability to get a job — they certainly weren't getting in the way of anyone's ability to get an education. And many of the punks and hippies whom I went to school with have now, after all that effort, found their way into positions of power and privilege.

But I still believe it is important for white folks to find ways to signal that we cannot necessarily be trusted to act like white folks — that we cannot be trusted to hold white values, that we cannot be trusted to be nice, that we cannot be trusted to maintain the status quo. Noel Ignatiev, editor of the journal *Race Traitor*, has suggested that the power of the entire white race can be undermined by just a few members who consistently refuse to act according to the rules, and who refuse to be who they seem to be. At the end of the *Saturday Night Live* skit in which he was made up as a white man, Eddie Murphy suggested exactly this possibility. "I got a lot of friends, and we've got a lot of makeup," he told the camera. "So the next time you're hugging up with some really super-groovy white guy, or you've met a really great super-keen white chick, don't be too sure. They might be black."

*

What exactly it means to be white seems to elude no one as fully as it eludes those of us who are white. In *Playing in the Dark: Whiteness and the Literary Imagination*, Toni Morrison observes that the literature of this country is full of images of impenetrable, inarticulate whiteness. And these images, she writes, are often set against the presence of black characters who are dead or powerless. She cites, as one example, Edgar Allan Poe's *The Narrative of Arthur Gordon Pym*, which ends with the death of a black man in a boat that is traveling on a milky white sea through a white shower toward a white veil behind which a giant white figure waits silently.

And so it is not surprising that what Marlow, the ferryboat captain in *Heart of Darkness*, finds deep in Africa, traveling on a boat manned by starving natives, is not darkness but a blinding white fog so thick it stops the boat, a white fog from behind which he hears chilling cries of grief. "Whiteness, alone, is mute, meaningless, unfathomable, pointless, frozen, veiled, curtained, dreaded, senseless, implacable. Or so our writers seem to say," writes Toni Morrison. We do not know ourselves, and worse, we seem only occasionally to know that we do not know ourselves. "It was the whiteness of the whale that above all things appalled me," Melville tells us in *Moby-Dick*, "but how can I hope to explain myself here; and yet, in some dim, random way, explain myself I must."

"It's hard for me," my cousin mused once as we waited for a train, "I have a lot of white family." At the time, I couldn't fully appreciate what she was saying because I was hurt by the implication that I was a burden to her. But I would remember that comment years later, when I was watching a public-television program in which Henry Louis Gates, Jr., was working with genealogists to trace the family trees of a series of African Americans including Oprah Winfrey, Quincy Jones, Whoopi Goldberg, and himself. Many of their ancestors were slaves, but the genealogists also revealed that some of their ancestors included free blacks and, of course, whites. In a particularly awkward moment, a genealogist informed Gates that one of his ancestors was a white man who fought in the Revolutionary War against Native Americans and left a will that freed his slaves. As I watched Gates struggle with that information, I saw how much the stories of our ancestors mark our identities.

It isn't easy to accept a slaveholder and an Indian killer as a grandfather, and it isn't easy to accept the legacy of whiteness as an identity. It is an identity that carries the burden of history without fostering a true understanding of the painfulness and the costs of complicity. That's why so many of us try to pretend that to be white is merely to be raceless. Perhaps it would be more productive for us to establish some collective understanding that we are all, white and black, damaged, reduced, and morally undermined by increasingly subtle systems of racial oppression and racial privilege. Or perhaps it would be better if we simply refused to be white. But I don't know what that means, really.

"I feel like an unknown quantity," my cousin remarked at some point during the year that we lived together. She was referring to the algebraic term, the unknown quantity x, which must be solved for, or defined, by the numbers in the equation around it. I remember, when I first encountered algebra, feeling the limits of my own comprehension break around the concept that one number in an equation could be unknown. And what baffled me most was that the answer, in algebra, was known, but the question was incomplete.

I could see two faces of the Brooklyn clock tower from my bedroom window in the apartment I shared with my cousin. The hands on those faces never told exactly the same time, and I often chose to believe the one I most wanted to believe. I was usually late, either way. The year we lived in that apartment was the year of the 2000 census. By chance, my cousin and I were chosen to complete the long form of the census, and we were visited in person by a census taker who was charged with ensuring that this form was completed accurately.

The census taker asked us to report the highest degree or level of school we had completed, how well we spoke English, and whether we did any work for pay. For every question he asked, my cousin asked one back. It became a kind of exchange, which is how we learned that our census taker was an artist when he wasn't taking the census. I laughed when my cousin asked him why he needed to know the address where she worked, and she cut her eyes at me. "It's not for him," I said, trying to help, "it's for the government." She pursed her lips. "I come from people," she informed me, "who have learned not to trust the government."

And then there was question six: *What is this person's race?* The census taker marked the box in front of "White" for me, with no discussion, but my cousin spent quite a bit of time on this question. "What are my options?" she asked first. The list was surprisingly long for a document conceived by the government of a country that does not readily embrace subtlety or accuracy in just about any form: *White; Black, African American,* or *Negro; American Indian* or *Alaska Native; Asian Indian; Chinese; Filipino; Japanese; Korean; Vietnamese; Other Asian; Native Hawaiian; Guamanian* or *Chamorro; Samoan; Other Pacific Islander;* or *Some Other Race.* Our census taker would list all of these options several times, stumbling over the words, until he eventually handed the form to my cousin in frustration. Part of the problem was that the list did not include her first choice — "Mixed Race." But it did, unlike the 1990 census, allow the census taker to mark more than one race. Eventually, he marked both "White" and "Black."

"He has two mothers," the Long Island woman said of the black baby to whom she gave birth, in a brazen refusal of the very terms in which her story was being told. She abandoned this idea only after it was suggested to her that this might be confusing for the child and perhaps even damaging. But she did not abandon her belief that the two boys who shared her womb should grow up knowing each other as brothers. "She wants him to know that she carried him and that she loved him and in the end made the ultimate sacrifice," her lawyer said shortly after she surrendered the black baby to his parents. "And secondly, she wants him to know he has a brother."

In the same statement, the white woman's lawyer also said, "The most important thing to her is that she wants this boy to know when he grows up that she didn't abandon him because of his race." If that was the most important thing to her and not simply her lawyer's bad idea of what needed to be said, then her story was even sadder than it first appeared. She already feared, when he was four months old, that the baby she birthed and held and fed would grow up to believe she was racist. She was giving him up because he was not hers, but the fact that he was not hers was all caught up, for her and for many others, in his race and her own.

It was not hard, in the end, to understand why the baby's biological parents in New Jersey were so adamantly opposed to sharing custody with this woman. And so it was all the more surprising, all the more touching, when, after the white woman had refused them contact with the baby for the first three months of his life, and after several years of custody disputes and court cases and appeals, the black couple told reporters that they still remained open to having some relationship with the white couple in the future. They suggested that when their son was "mature enough to understand his unique beginnings" they might be able to reach out to the white couple "in friendship and fellowship." They might be something less than family to each other, the black couple seemed to be suggesting, but they were more than strangers.

■

Triplet

FROM *Anderbo*

RAFAEL HAD BEEN IN TOWN for about a week. He was putting trim on the new house going up in the middle of Dooley's old apple orchard, that house being the most monumental thing to hit our town since my sisters and I were babies. It jutted up out of the flat, green landscape like something triumphant. It wasn't shaped like a regular house, but had odd turns and bends to it that made me think of knees and joints, that made me think it could get up and walk. Hell, it looked like it would chase me down Route 52, and I often looked in my rearview mirror, expecting to see that house jiggling with exertion, waving its eaves and shouting, "Watch out! Watch out!"

My mother thought it was outrageous that the house was so big. "Why does he need so much space?" she'd say, "What is he going to do in it?" But then the word came around town that the owner was building it because he was dying, that he wanted to secure a place for his daughter to live, and that he was drawn to the peacefulness of the area. Mother was dying herself, though so slowly that anyone else might have just said she was living out her life.

She liked me to park across from that house, so that she could absorb it. Sometimes I would lift her out of the car and set her down under one of the old apple trees. She would stare, curiously. "Look at that window, Alicia," she'd say. "Good luck trying to clean that." Look at that house, I wanted to say; some people do things even when they know they're going to die.

*

My sister Angela met Rafael at the Eagle's Nest Bar & Grill last Thursday night. She walked in, as she usually did, around 7 o'clock, around the same time the auto parts plant shift got out, which increased her odds. She noticed Rafael, which was easy enough, since he was the one man there she did not know. She told me later that he was staring at one of the pictures of us that hang on the walls. The whole bar is filled with pictures of us, the Dorsey Triplets, though all the pictures date from at least twenty years ago.

There we are, again and again, three bucktoothed girls in matching outfits. "The Dorsey Triplets" on the fire truck at the Memorial Day parade; "The Dorsey Triplets" at the Dutchess County Fair, standing in the booth which was right next to Dooley's cow, which was marked for butchering. Mr. Dooley was a soft touch and it was always the same cow that he showed, older and older. The cow actually outlasted us, because my mother got into a fight with the coordinators of the fair and they kicked us triplets out.

Back then, my mother sewed all of our clothes herself; in those golden days her fingers flew like fiddles over the fabric. She was healthy and happy. She'd whip up three dresses in an afternoon and then she'd sew a larger version of the dress for herself, always with a low-cut blouse. She felt that bearing triplets made her more of a woman than anyone around, and she liked to show off her equipment. She was particularly proud that she had breast-fed all of us. Once, years later, I asked her about that. Didn't that mean one of us was always waiting? But she just looked at me, irritated, as though there were something in my very demeanor that was an affront, and said, "Well, it doesn't look like it hurt *you* any, Alicia."

Rafael was looking at the picture of our kindergarten graduation when Angela first saw him. That happened to be my favorite picture. Amanda and Angela are standing in our regular triplet pose, arms around each other and heads thrown back, but I am standing a little apart, looking seriously at something that is in the distance. I look so wise, for a five-year-old. Angela said he was smiling at the picture and she went right up to him.

For a long time, people have called Angela a slut, but then people always were trying to label us. I think when you're a triplet people look for words to separate you; they pin any label they can on you. My sister Amanda is considered the *princess* because she's been married for three years but doesn't have children. I was considered the smart one, up until the day I dropped out of college, and then I was considered the good one, because I dropped out to take care of my mother. I don't know what they call me now.

Yes, Angela was called the slut, though I think really she just suffered from a want of imagination. For so many years people had been staring at our bodies and touching them, smelling them, that I think it didn't occur to her that she could use a different part of herself to interact with people — such as her mind.

Anyway, Angela saw Rafael smiling at her picture and she sat down and said to him, "Nice picture." She told me later that he looked like he was going to have a heart attack. He hugged her as though they were cousins, and said he had no idea, he had no idea. I wondered what that was like for him, to want something and have it walk right up to you and sit down.

Angela called me up late that night, after eleven. "Alicia," she said when I picked up the phone, which annoyed me right off the bat, because who else was going to pick up the phone? "How's Mom?" she asked.

"Fine. You want to talk to her?" Mom was sitting only about three feet away from me, staring at the phone with the sort of wobbly and hesitating look a turkey should have on the day before Thanksgiving. The TV bathed her in an unhealthy glow.

"No," Angela said, laughing. "But thanks." I could hear pinballs in the background and told her I knew she was at the Motel 8.

"How'd you know?" Everyone thought I was such a genius, just because I paid attention. I didn't even bother to answer her.

"You meet a guy?" I asked.

"He's kind of funky," she said.

"What do you mean?"

"Well, he has this thing about triplets. Like, he thinks we're really sexy."

"So?"

She started giggling and I knew that nothing I had said had tickled her. I found myself staring at the business cards on the wall of my mother's various doctors, and at the map of the gravesite where my father was buried and where she would be buried, in time.

"He'd like to meet you."

"Me?"

My mom was saying, "What? What?" and I knew she meant to be whispering, but she had a sinus infection and couldn't hear how loud her voice was. I shushed at her and looked at the phone. "What are you saying?"

"I know it sounds crazy. But remember that time with Jimmy D, how cool it was."

"I slept with him because I loved him. I didn't know you guys were going to trick him."

"Oh come on. You thought it was funny."

"I was fifteen then. I was a moron. I grew out of it."

Angela started clicking her tongue. "Oh, I forgot. You're better than we are."

"Because I'm discriminating."

"Discriminating," she said. "What's wrong with you? Look, Amanda's already been here and gone. I'll get her to call you."

Suddenly she breathed in really fast and a man's voice was on the phone. "You have a sexy voice, Alicia," he said.

"You're sick," I said back.

"Meet me at the Eagle's Nest," he said. "I'll wait for you." He hung up the phone then, and I sat and listened to the dial tone for about a minute.

"Do you have a date?" my mom asked me.

She was wearing a cute little scarf that looked like a dachshund around her neck and her black shoes gleamed. She always looked like she could go to a party, which I guess was a good way to live. I had on my Tweety Bird night shirt. "I don't want to talk about it," I said.

"I thought I heard a man's voice."

She looked so worried. She was so scared to die. That's what always got me. "I'm not leaving you, Mom. Don't worry."

"I'm ruining your life," she said, starting to cry.

"Yes you are," I said, sitting next to her. "But that's all right." And it was all right, I thought. You're supposed to ruin your life for the people you love. But the sound of Rafael's voice seemed to keep whispering in my ear.

Mom stayed up later than usual that night. She's like a dog that way, she picks up on my mood. I finally mashed up a little Valium and stuck it in her scotch. She fell asleep pretty quickly after that, and I got her in her nightgown and tucked her in. Funny how beautiful she still was. There is an aura around things that are beautiful, I think, and even when the beauty fades, the aura remains — that's why people go to see ruins, I suppose.

I sat in my room then, looking out the window at Route 52, which cuts like a zipper in front of our house. There wasn't much traffic on Route 52, even if it was a highway. The traffic came sporadically: a fruit truck, a moving van, a U-Haul. I used to wonder if that interrupted flow of traffic had stunted our lives. Did it make us spend too much time listening? Always expecting something from far away? If we had lived at the end of a dirt road, maybe we would all have been more content.

It's amazing how strongly a bad idea can grab hold of you. I didn't want to meet Rafael. I really did not want to set foot in the Eagle's Nest Bar & Grill, which I had successfully avoided doing for almost five years. But I felt a pull even so. Maybe it was knowing he wanted me. There's something very appealing about being wanted, which I suppose is why people join the army. Or maybe I was just tired of spending night after night with my mother.

The Eagle's Nest Bar & Grill sat at the south corner of the Cruikshank strip mall. There was a Dunkin' Donuts, a Laundromat and a vacant party store which closed down several years ago. The fire station was catty corner to the bar, and there was an auditorium there which was rented out for special occasions. That was where my sisters threw a party for me on the day before I left town to go to college. My mother was still healthy then, though she had a cough. The whole town thought I was some type of genius, because I'd gotten a scholarship. Some of them persist in calling me "Doctor."

There were still some of the party balloons hanging two months later when I dropped out. My mother had called me from the emergency room, right before my Calculus 101 midterm. She was doing fine and I shouldn't worry, but the doctors found a spot on her lung that was the size of an egg and she would probably be dead in a year. I dropped out the next day. I was happy to. I figured I could go back to college after she was dead. I didn't think it was going to ruin my life or anything. In those days I figured that destiny would find me wherever I was; it didn't even occur to me that I had to search it out.

I went into the bar. "It'll be easy," Amanda had said. "He's very sympathetic." She called me two minutes after Angela, after she'd got home from the same motel. "I know," she'd said. "I'm really surprised at myself." I could see her in my mind. She'd probably pulled her hair up and put on a lot of makeup. Painted her nails silver. "My life's gotten so *boring*, Alicia. I needed this for me. I think it will make our marriage healthier over the long term. Sometimes you have to do something for yourself."

Rafael was sitting at the biggest table in the bar. "Rafael?" I asked, in a voice that sounded funny to me.

"Alicia." There was something elastic about his face, as though it had been run over once and healed. Why did I find that arousing? "Your sisters were so sure you wouldn't come. They gave me no hope." He was actually rubbing his hands together.

"I'm not sure why I'm here. I'm not going to sleep with you."

I heard a sniggering sound behind me and turned to see Candy Link occupying the corner booth. When she met my eyes, her mouth dropped open as though she'd never seen me before, and I thought she might even have looked afraid. I supposed it was because it had been a long time since I'd been out. Probably since around the time my mother went on oxygen and it got just so damn hard to leave. I realized then that I still had on my Tweety Bird shirt and the tight green pants that made my legs look like drumsticks.

"What?" I said to Candy.

"Nothing," she answered, crossing her stiletto heels under the table.

"Good."

Rafael was standing, panting, wringing his hands. I had a feeling he was going to smile all night long, no matter what happened. I started to sit down, but he put out his hand like a policeman and said, "Stop." I didn't need to ask why. I was used to it. He wanted to look at me. I stood still then, figured there was no harm to letting him suck me up; everybody else had. My whole life had been one giant stage show. People would drive for hours just to get our autographs.

"You're beautiful," Rafael said. "You are the *most* beautiful."

"That's what you said to Amanda."

"You talked to her about me? What did she tell you?"

I considered telling him what Amanda had said on the phone; that he was the best thing that had happened to her in a long time, that he had taught her so much, so quickly. I decided against it. "She said you were nice," I said, doing my Amanda impression, which sounds as though she has a bell in her mouth, but I figured Rafael probably hadn't talked with her enough to get it.

Finally we sat down and I looked around the bar, which looked about the same as it always had. Some guy was singing country on the radio and he was singing something that sounded a lot like the thing some other guy had been singing last time I was there. There were still pictures of us all over the bar, though I noticed there were a few new ones of definite non-triplets. Jimmy D's eagle was still there in the window — he claimed that he'd found the eagle on the doorstep on the very day he intended to name the bar.

Rafael had discreetly put his hand between my legs, with the nonchalant manner of a man inserting paper into an envelope. I was disappointed by his height, but that was sort of comforting also — I knew I could knock him out if I had to. But he was so happy that I was there that it made him look innocent. Everything seemed topsy-turvy, as though *he* were the dewy bride and *I* the jaded groom. Rafael pulled me against his shoulder and I breathed in the smell of him, which was ripe with sawdust, and I found myself thinking of what the pharmacist had said about him, that he was working on the house single-handedly, lifting up doors by himself, carrying two banisters in at the same time. I laughed.

"What's so funny?"

"This is crazy. You're crazy," I said, a little more loudly than I meant to, because I noticed then that Jimmy D and Candy and even little Geneva Helms were all looking at me.

Rafael turned serious. "I grew up the oldest of fourteen," he said. "Do you know what that's like? In a poor town in Mexico?" He waved his hand to take in all of the Eagle's Nest Bar & Grill, which did not exactly seem to me like the cornucopia of plenty, though I got his point. "Here you have everything: cable TV, snacks, private bathrooms. We had nothing." His voice softened. "There was a mountain range there. Popactectel. Three mountains, broad at the waist with tiny little titties on top. I stared at those mountains day after day until it seemed to me that they spoke to me, until it seemed to me that they made love to me. My mother had fourteen children and then she died. Can you imagine? The only thing that kept me going was those mountains."

I understood him more than he realized, because I had spent a fair amount of time staring at distances myself. I remembered how I used to stare out at Orion every night, dainty Orion with his thin little wrists and heavy belt. I would watch him and be absolutely sure that he was staring in my direction, talking to me. I would turn out all the lights in my room and open the window, so that he could come into me and sometimes he did, or so it felt. I thought he was a knight and I was a lady, and that I would live an extraordinary life someday, maybe not with him exactly, but with someone like him.

Rafael was squeezing my hand like it was a pump and then I started to realize he was squeezing it with the same rhythm of his heartbeat, trying to make me his.

"You probably have a wife back in Mexico, right?"

He nodded.

"Guys with fantasies usually have someone at home. Women with fantasies usually don't."

He shrugged, took out a little comb and smoothed back his hair. I noticed his hands were shaking a little, which surprised me. "I can make you happy," he said.

I laughed and the sound came out of me like something biological, like something you should apologize for. "I don't think so," I said.

Rafael grabbed onto the table as though it were a ledge, and a pool of tears filled his eyes. I'd finished off my drink by then, not that I felt it. I'd found that no matter how much I drank I was sober, sober, sober and then I'd fall asleep. I knew I should probably go home; that's where I belonged, really. At least when I was with my mother I knew I was doing something important, even if it was driving me crazy. But I couldn't bring myself to go. I felt like if I went home, I'd never leave again and I wasn't sure if I was ready for that yet.

"You're so different from your sisters," he said.

"I know. My mother used to say I was adopted."

"What?"

"It was a joke."

"Oh."

"I actually am different," I said. "I have a scar on my nose from when I fell off a bicycle when I was ten. Once I had that scar everyone could figure out who I was. My mother figured it out. She'd say, 'Oh Alicia, you stay with me. You can help me.' You see, before then she wasn't always sure, and she would have been embarrassed to be wrong."

"You know your sister, the quiet one?"

"Her name is Amanda," I said.

"Amanda." He nodded. "She came right to my hotel. Just like that. She said she'd just had a fight with her husband; he'd told her she was getting old. Could I make her feel better? She was so warm. Even better than the other one, for all her tricks — Angela was *hot*. I was figuring you'd all be the same. *Triplets*."

A car went down Route 52 and its headlights swept through the bar. I noticed that the place had grown more crowded. There were a number of people from my high school class, also a number of my mother's friends. I hadn't seen them for years but they all looked the same. They were laughing, talking. They seemed so happy.

Just then Rafael put his hand back between my legs. I guess he had only a certain number of plans of attack, but I found myself pleased that he would try again, that he hadn't given up. I didn't move, didn't look at him. I didn't know what to do.

Jimmy D came over then with a drink on a tray. He looked good. He'd proposed to me once, a long time ago, in a car, up at the Ledge, on a night that smelled of wet grass and gasoline. I laughed at his proposal, something I still felt badly about. It was just that he was so different from what I was expecting. I told him I was hoping to marry someone who was more like Orion, which was, though a lame thing to say, honest. He married Carol Chanson a few months later, but the town never forgot that I thought I was too good for Jimmy D.

"How've you been?" he asked.

"OK."

"How's Mom?"

I shrugged. "You know."

"Good to see you."

"Thanks."

Rafael put his arm around my shoulder as soon as Jimmy D came over, and he was squeezing me to him as though we were teenagers on a date. He had a big ring on his finger, like the type you get when you join something or graduate, and the ring glistened against my shoulder as though I too might be something of value.

"You're in love with him," Rafael whispered, after Jimmy D left.

"No." I laughed at the thought.

"Well, he's in love with you."

"*You* see love *everywhere*," I said. He was still staring at Jimmy D and hanging on to me. He reminded me of my niece at Christmas, hanging on to her favorite toy for dear life. I was starting to feel the way I did when I was driving on Route 52 and hit a bank of ice and the only thing to do was ride it out; braking did no good, all you could do was skid and pray you didn't hit a tree. Rafael kissed me and I kissed him back and his breath smelled of meat and I remembered that Angela had said he told her he loved to eat meat patties. I heard Candy Link's chair scratch and heard her walk back to the bar. I found my body responding in spite of myself. I'd held myself apart for so long.

Rafael was running his hand over my hair; his touch felt so gentle. I closed my eyes because I knew everybody in the bar was staring at me. They would be talking about this for weeks. They would be laughing about it, because I knew that's what I had become. A joke.

"I don't want to be a number," I said to Rafael. "I don't want to think of you in the next town saying, *I did it with triplets*."

He kissed the scar on my nose. "Let's go," he said.

"I can't," I said. I started to cry a little, but I sagged against him and he supported me.

"Yes, you can. That's why you came here tonight."

He stood up and I stood up with him. We walked together to the door, he holding me up by the elbow, and I saw that Candy Link was smiling a little. *At* me? *For* me? The picture by the door was of my sisters and me on Halloween, three pretty girls dressed up as royalty. Jimmy D was wiping off the bar-top and he stared at me with concern, but I turned away.

We stepped outside and immediately the constellations sprung up in front of us, as though someone had turned on a switch. They were so beautiful, like millions of earrings thrown up into the sky by a careless hand. At the same time I was wary of looking at them. I turned back to look at Rafael, and I gasped, because there he was; there he stood on his small feet, with his heavy belt, bathed in yellow light from the bar — Orion made flesh.

PHILIP CONNORS

■

Diary of a Fire Lookout

FROM *The Paris Review*

FOR THE PAST SIX SUMMERS I've worked as a fire lookout in the Gila National Forest in New Mexico. Ten of every fourteen days I sit on a ten-thousand-foot peak and watch for smoke. From my tower I can see at least fifty miles in each direction — on clear days nearly a hundred. To the east stretches the Chihuahuan Desert: tan, austere, forbidding, dotted with a few lonely shrubs and home to a collection of horned and thorned species evolved to live without water. To the north and south, along the Black Range, a line of peaks rises and falls in timbered waves: piñon and juniper, ponderosa pine, spruce and fir, quaking aspen. To the west, the Mimbres River wanders by, its valley verdant with grasses, and beyond it rise more mesas and mountains — the Diablos, the Jerkies, the Mogollons. A peaceable kingdom, a wilderness in good working order, and my responsibiity if it burns.

The Gila covers more than three million acres; ten lookouts are employed to watch over it. Some of them live in their towers, four-teen-by-fourteen-foot boxes ringed with catwalks, but my tower is small and spare, just big enough to fit four people standing. A two-room cabin sits next to it, equipped with a bed, a propane refrigerator, and a stove. In the yard are a clothesline, a five-hundred-gallon cistern to catch rainwater, and an outhouse with a view of the sunrise if you prop the door open with a rock.

My tools are simple: a two-way radio for communication, and an Osborne Firefinder for locating fires. The Firefinder rests in the middle of the tower, mounted on a waist-high stand. It consists of a map inside a rotating metal ring. A sighting device sits on the ring, making it look a little like a miniature hula hoop with upright poles on either end. The lookout turns the ring and aims the crosshairs in the sighting device at the base of a smoke to get an azimuth reading. Having discerned the compass direction of the fire from his location, the lookout must then judge the fire's distance from his perch. The easiest way to do this is to alert another lookout able to spot the smoke, have her take an azimuth reading, and cross her line with yours on the map. The fire will be at the point of intersection. If that's not possible, topographic maps and guesswork have to suffice.

More than eight thousand lookouts used to keep watch over the forests of America. Now the number is in the hundreds. We remain on the Gila for three reasons: This is one of the most lightning-prone landscapes in North America — the two wilderness areas that comprise the heart of the forest get hit by lightning, on average, thirty thousand times per year — and thus one of the most fire-prone. It's also so rugged that communication with fire-fighting crews can be very difficult; it often falls to lookouts to relay messages between crews and dispatchers. Above all, lookouts remain on the Gila because we are less expensive than airplane surveillance: the Gila is so huge it would take multiple air observers to cover it all.

The summer of 2007 was atypical. Spring rains, unusual for southwest New Mexico, forestalled the beginning of the fires by several weeks, and there were none of the massive burns that have become common of late in the West, the kinds of fires that make the national news. Still, I know many people are glad we're there to keep watch, none more so than the residents of Kingston, a small town five miles to my southeast. It is the nearest town to my post, and the few dozen residents there can sleep a little easier at night knowing that if wind and fire were to conspire to work their ancient magic in the hills surrounding the village, someone high above them would be there to see it and sound the alarm.

April 16

I am a stranger to myself when I arrive on the mountain each year. I haven't carried a fifty-pound pack in months. My knees are crying,

I'm drenched in sweat, and the wind is blowing forty miles an hour. Before anything else I want to eat. I wonder: who is this alien winter-softened creature, this body barely able to walk five miles uphill with ten days' worth of food and books? Who is this man so hungry he could eat raw sugar with his bare hands?

April 17

First things first: the cabin must be cleaned, wood cut for the stove. Last night the temperature dropped into the teens. I fell asleep with a fire going and started another first thing this morning. I gathered wood and checked on the spring — running slow but steady — and slept half the afternoon. I could have stayed in bed all day. I want to sleep off the entirety of winter — the vampire hours of tending bar and baking bread, the worries over money — wipe the slate clean, begin again.

April 18

Morning was calm and early afternoon beautiful, with temps near sixty degrees. Then the wind rose out of the canyons and the trees on the mountaintop bowed to some unseen god in the east. The guy-wire cables that anchor the tower in bedrock swayed slightly, and the tower itself bobbed and dipped like a boat at sea. Now it is after dark, and a fire crackles in the stove. Even with the flue closed the fire burns hot and fast, the wind whistling down the stovepipe.

The greatest gift of life on the mountain is time. Time to think or not think, read or not read, scribble or not scribble — to sleep and cook and walk in the woods, to sit and stare at the shapes of the hills. I produce nothing but words; I consume nothing but food, a little propane, a little firewood. By being utterly useless in the calculations of the culture at large I become useful, at last, to myself.

April 25

Finally a calm day. I step gingerly into the meadow at dawn to piss, and the world is silent and still; for once I do not have to take care with my aim for fear of pissing all over myself. Over the course of the week the wind has insinuated itself in my cranium: whisper, whistle, moan and roar. It gave a sort of texture to the days, gaining power through the afternoon, barreling relentlessly through the night, easing briefly at dawn. The sudden quiet knocks me out of balance, forces me to recalibrate the truce I've made with solitude. The answer is to walk. On the east side of the peak, I hear the descending call of a Montezuma quail; down toward the spring I hear a turkey gobble and spot a hen lurching away through the trees. I even hear the first hummingbird of the season. Time to make some sugar water.

May 1

Lightning rattles the cabin windows. A cold rain falls. There are strikes within a half mile of the tower — a couple within a hundred and fifty yards, the flash and the crack simultaneous. A full moon rises over the trees on the southeast side of the peak. Long flotillas of clouds glide above the Mogollons. I climb the tower at dusk and the world is vast and cleansed by rain, all muted blues. Spidery jags flash in the twilight as the light drains into the west. The few remaining snowbanks on the north slope of the peak glow like molars under the moon.

May 7

Two hikers appeared on the trail midafternoon — Reno and Slouch. I always know the "thru-hikers" by their fancy walking sticks, their sunburned skin and general air of dinginess, and the scratches on their shins if they're wearing shorts, from bushwhacking through the thorny brush to the south. By the time they arrive here they've walked a hundred and twenty miles from the Mexican border on their way to Canada via the Continental Divide Trail. It shows, though not in their spirits: unfailingly gracious and cheerful, they shake hands, shed their packs, and climb the tower. They always smell strongly of underarm sweat.

Reno and Slouch said they'd been shadowed by a Border Patrol agent along part of their route; he came crawling out of the brush in the desert about the time they were met on the road by two guys in a Border Patrol vehicle, all of them armed with pistols and wearing shades. The agents took one look at their quarry and realized their error. Earlier, Reno had taken a few pictures of Palomas from the American side of the border, and they were both forced to show papers despite not having crossed. Reno worried about her passport smelling of weed, having kept it in the same little bag as her stash and not having expected to have to produce it. The border agent must not have noticed.

With many CDT hikers I sense a sort of mutual envy. I admire their courage and stamina and sheer physical gumption; they admire my solitude, my view, the sheer weirdness of my job. Their aim: three thousand miles in six months, Glacier National Park before the snow flies. Insane! Yet I envy that brand of insanity.

May 16

A real soaker yesterday: rain for nearly five hours, more than an inch in the end. Tremendous lightning all along the crest of the Black Range. In the evening, mist enveloped the mountain and the flashes of the lightning seemed to light the entire sky, strobing through the smoky-looking fog. Sometimes lightning stabs repeatedly, three or four times in the same spot, and you know the tree it hit has exploded in a blue ball of smoke. This morning more fog drifts up out of Kingston and Lake Valley. Deer lick for salt in the meadow.

When I look out on this stretch of country, I often think of Aldo Leopold, the man who wrote *A Sand County Almanac*, one of the handful of classic American ecotexts. He's associated with Wisconsin, where he lived much of his life. Yet it was here, in the Gila, as a young forest ranger fresh out of the Yale School of Forestry, that he formed his thinking about the natural world, and it was here that he made one of the most radical (and civilized) gestures of our American experiment. In 1922 he sat down with friends in the Forest Service and drew a line on a map of the Gila that barred incursion by anything motorized. The result was the first officially designated wilderness in the world, more than five hundred thousand

acres encompassing the Mogollon Mountains and the entire headwaters country of the Gila River, a land of slot canyons and strange
cliffs. No one in a position of comparable influence had ever argued
in favor of the restraint required to preserve so large a stretch of wild
country. (Although we should not forget it was one of the homes of
the Apache, who had to be driven out with violence to make it safe for
Anglos.)

Because of Leopold's bold and hopeful vision, most of that country
remains unmarred by industrial machines. It has been chipped away
at, certainly. A third of it was lopped off when a road was built in the
1940s, a road clamored for by hunters who complained about an explosion of the deer population. Deer had multiplied, Leopold would
come to see, because large predators — principally the Mexican gray
wolf — had been poisoned, trapped, and shot near extinction. His essay on shooting a wolf in *A Sand County Almanac* is the most powerful thing in the book, and probably the founding document of the
endangered species program now attempting to reintroduce the wolf
to the Gila, with mixed success. If country can be thought of as a text,
then the Gila Wilderness is the founding document of the wilderness
movement.

May 18

If you're a lookout long enough a day will come when the lightning
strikes so near, so frequently, and so fiercely that rather than brave
the seventy yards to the outhouse across the open meadow, you do
your business in an empty rice box, wipe your ass with a paper towel,
and burn the whole mess in the potbellied stove, a little embarrassed
but happy still to be alive in a high place.

I found a couple of trees struck by lightning not far from the top of
the peak, and although their trunks were corkscrewed and big splin-
ters lay fifty and a hundred feet away, there was not one black mark to
be seen, not an inch of charred wood. Still too wet for fire.

May 21

Being alone here I may not be my best self but I am perhaps my
truest self: lazy, contemplative, goofy, happiest when taking a nap or

staring dumbly at the shape of mountains. Whatever insights I have are fragmentary and fleeting. I am not so much seeking anything as I am allowing the world to come to me, allowing the days to unfold, the dramas of weather and wild creatures, the many different ways the world appears to the human eye — the colors and shapes constantly shifting.

May 22

Still not a fire within thirty miles of my perch. And I've been here nearly six weeks.

My dog Alice and I took a walk after dinner north of the peak above South Animas Creek. Everywhere the aspens have leafed out, big splashes of green on the north-facing slopes. It's still possible to follow the old trail to East Curtis Canyon, at least for a while, but cat-claw and gambel oak are crowding it, and every once in a while it disappears entirely and can only be picked up by the blazes on the trees. We made it nearly three miles down the trail, just above the point where we needed to turn around to make it back to the top by dark, when ahead I spotted something like a charred stump. The harder I looked, the more I realized the charred stump had a big tan-colored snout sniffing the air. I stopped and grabbed the dog's collar. Come on, Alice, I whispered, time to go home. By some miracle she neither saw nor smelled the bear; perhaps just as lucky the bear did not appear to see or smell her.

May 29

While I was away on days off, a real fire started — something bigger than a single snag — the Shelley Fire, about thirty miles west of here, just south of the Gila River. By today it had burned more than sixty acres. Two hotshot crews are at work on it. I can see the drift smoke from here, over a ridge top, but only barely.

Tonight I walked with Alice down to the pond, a mile below the top of the peak. Another six-tenths of an inch of rain fell while I was away, and the pond remains as full as I've ever seen it. The grass all around is lush and green, and the wild irises are beginning to bloom, their petals traced with thin purple veins. One of the fallen aspens, half submerged in the pond, has nevertheless leafed out, its root system still partially intact.

June 1

More than four inches of rain fell in May — very unusual. This season has felt more like a paid vacation than work. So far.

I was taking a nap in the tower this afternoon when a group of maybe three dozen ravens came overhead, calling to each other and circling. They wheeled and dipped and sang *cronk, cronk, cronk*. Two or three would fly seemingly straight up in the air, corkscrewing around each other, and then they would break apart and float away in big looping curlicues. Eventually they drifted off to the north.

As the sun moves overhead the dog likes to sit in the shadow cast by the tower. Like me she is mostly indolent, but also like me she serves as a first-alarm system, a lookout in canine form: at the first sight or sound of hikers she barks and howls to let me know our solitude is about to be sullied.

June 4

A thrill today: first fire of the year, for me anyway—the Loco Fire, just northwest of Loco Mountain. A little plume of gray-white smoke twenty two miles as the crow flies. It showed at five o'clock. I got a cross from Black Mountain, so we knew it to the quarter section. To be the first to spot a smoke is a sublime feeling. You know you're the only person in the world who sees it. A new smoke often looks beautiful: a wisp of white like a feather, a single snag puffing little fingers of smoke in the air. You see it before it even has a name. In fact, you are about to give it one, after you pinpoint where it is and call it in to dispatch. We try to name the fires after a nearby landmark — a canyon, peak, or spring — but there is often a touch of poetic license involved. I might have called the Jackass Fire, spotted by the Mogollon Baldy lookout this morning and named for Jackass Park, simply the Ass Fire, to see if I could get away with it. Worked when I named the Drum Fire after Drummond Canyon last year.

June 6

Simply being in the tower tests my resolve today. The wind gusts to near eighty miles an hour — my anemometer only goes to seventy, and the little ball marker shoots straight to the top, signaling a reading off the chart. The dog took one look out the door of the cabin this morning and went back to bed. Standing in place in the tower I feel like I'm dancing the jitterbug. There is a lip of metal overhang to the tower's roof, to shunt off the rainwater, and when the wind gusts the overhang sounds as if it's going to bend or snap upright and shear the roof off. Those CCC boys did a marvelous job erecting this old tower, still sturdy after seventy years in a high and windy place. Sturdy, but not impervious to an eighty-mile-an-hour wind. Luckily there are no big fires at present, and none along the Mogollon or Black Range crests, or they'd be hurling burning pinecones a quarter mile ahead and starting spot fires a dozen at a time. The Loco Fire is down in the low country, where the winds are much lighter. With all the rain we've had it hasn't burned very hot yet at all — maybe a few dozen acres.

I hung on in the tower all day except for lunch and another break midafternoon. The guy-wire cables twirled like jump ropes. I couldn't write or read. I lay on the cot with my eyes closed listening, rising now and then to make sure no fool had left a campfire unattended or thrown a cigarette from a car. The wind was a menacing symphony, discordant and brutal in the trees. An awesome performance — though not a show I'd pay to see again.

June 13

As a lookout in high country, I often tell people I get paid to look at trees. But I find myself lately thinking more and more of grass. For millennia fire and grass worked in tandem here. Grass burned quickly and fertilized the soil, from whence came more grass. Fires moved quickly through the forest understory, rarely torching in treetops. Fire kept the saplings in check. Trees lived in mature stands where most were hundreds of years old. An ancient juniper from the heart of the Gila shows that fire burned around it, on average, every seven years; fire helped it thrive. Ponderosa covered much of the forest in open parkland with trees forty to sixty feet apart, surrounded by grass.

Then, in the nineteenth century, the cow arrived.

The grass fires became fewer, brush began to encroach on grassland; piñon and juniper crept down the foothills. With the coming of the Forest Service at the beginning of the twentieth century, two values prevailed: respect for cattlemen and disdain for fire. The goal became to put out every fire by ten o'clock the morning after it was spotted. As late as 1826 a white explorer reported being "fatigued by the difficulty of getting through the high grass, which covered the heavily timbered bottom" of the Gila River drainage. The cattle that came soon after devoured the grass, trampled the stream beds, pushed the Gila trout to the edge of extinction, and subsisted many places with the aid of stock tanks rigged to capture running water. Low elevation canyons saw beaver slaughtered for the whims of Eastern fashion; dammed wetlands were drained and with them went the waterbirds. A century of fire suppression allowed the fir and pine and spruce to grow unchecked in the higher elevations, crowding out the aspen, which love big stand-replacement fires. Brushy ladder fuels took hold and created a link to old-growth crowns; the fires became harder to suppress, so the Forest Service responded with ever more military technology: airplanes, helicopters, chemical drops, a full-scale techno-industrial war on fire.

Now, for the first time, we see catastrophic fires that burn so hot they sterilize the soil on tens of thousands of acres. Prescribed fire is needed more than ever but has been used too capriciously, too often, diminishing the constituency of the reasonable. (Burn down someone's house with an intentionally lit fire and see if you win a friend.) "Wildland fire use" fires are the preferred tool here now: fires started naturally by lightning and allowed to burn within predetermined areas, mostly within the wilderness, far from human settlements. *Burn, baby, burn* — that is the mantra now in the Gila, and for that reason among others this place is healthier than most places like it in the West. But does it even remotely resemble its optimum post-Pleistocene state? Not by any means. Too many cows, too few fires.

Yet much of what makes the Gila special remains unchanged over the centuries. The shark-fin shapes of mountains, mist in the canyons, the smell of smoke like a whisper of campfire when the forest burns. Deep red cliffs along the river. Because it's been protected, it's been saved from irreversible destruction. We've done our best to sully it, of course, and global warming may yet do it in, but certain local restraints have thwarted us. Leopold came to believe in restraint, though not before succumbing to hubris. He helped exterminate Mexican gray wolves. He believed in total fire suppression. He later found his way out of the traps of conventional thinking and saw the world whole, as an almost infinite series of interlocking relationships, grass benefiting rivers, rivers benefiting beaver, beaver benefiting elk, elk chased by wolves, wolves thus ensuring more even browsing of grass, and grass at the center of a hundred or a thousand other relationships. Grass and fire.

June 15

Yesterday the clarity of the view was as good as it's been all season. Mountain range upon mountain range like a sea tide crashing on the horizon: the Caballos and Sacramentos, the Organs and Franklins and Floridas, the Tres Hermanas, the Cookes Range, the Peloncillos and Chiricahuas and Burros, the Silver City and Piños Altos ranges, the Jerkies and Diablos and Mogollons, the Black Range, the Wahoos, the San Mateos. A world of more mountains than a man could walk in a lifetime. I sit trancelike in the tower and feel myself begin to empty, to disappear almost, in the immensity of the country all around.

June 17

Two weeks on and the Loco Fire still burns, working its slow way through piñon and juniper country, burning coolly in the grass and brush, torching a few trees here and there but not many. It can't have burned more than a few hundred acres. If the weather cooperates it could burn for another month just the way a fire should — not catastrophically, leaving behind sterilized soil and torched old growth, but gently, burning up the understory and reinvigorating the grass.

After my lunch hour, the first thing I see when I reach the top landing of the tower is a little plume of white smoke about eleven miles north. Fire! I call Lookout Mountain on the radio.

I see it, she answers.

From my position it's at eight degrees; from hers, one hundred and sixty-six degrees. I run our lines on the map, cross them, and mark the spot. Township 14 South, Range 9 West, Section 3. I take a few deep breaths, try to even the flow of adrenaline coursing through my veins, and call dispatch with the news. The Lake Fire — right in the bottom of North Seco Creek, near some ancient lake beds.

June 18

I wake at six A.M. and make a pot of coffee, climb with it up the tower. I check in with the Lake Fire folks, and as I'm talking with them on the radio I see another smoke about seven miles south of theirs. A whitish smoke, its source obscured by Granite Peak, the drift blowing and dispersing to the east. I line it out and call it in: twenty-one degrees from me, Township 15 South, Range 9 West, Section 15. The Granite Fire.

It's going to be a busy day of radio chatter. I don't mind: I've done enough brooding for a while. Time to work a little. If you're going to be a lookout you've got to prepare yourself for the fact that everything can change in a moment. Two weeks of silence on the radio, quiet on the forest, immaculate weather, hikes in the evening after six o'clock — gone in a puff of smoke!

Obscured by Granite Peak indeed — turns out, after a helicopter recon, that I was off by six miles on the Granite Fire. Not a record, not even close — I've known lookouts to be off by double-digit mileage — but still. Six miles . . .

The Granite Fire has grown to two hundred acres. Much of the burn was in grass, where it moved quickly with minimal smoke. I'm accustomed to watching fires in timber so would have guessed it was much smaller. My boss has decided to let both fires burn, a sensible move. Steep terrain, deep canyons, far from any human settlement: no sense risking life and limb trying to suppress such fires. Rain is predicted by Wednesday. That will slow them some. They may yet burn for a month or more, a few acres here, a hundred acres there, several thousand all told. Depends on weather and fuels.

June 19

Up at five A.M. to make coffee. In the tower and on the radio at six. In the predawn light open flame is visible on the Granite Fire, little shifting dots of orange on the ridge tops. The wind has shifted and now blows out of the east, sure sign of impending storms. The forecast says dry lightning possible, winds of up to forty miles an hour.

By six P.M. the Granite Fire had burned more than nine hundred acres.

June 21

I will hike out today when Natalie, my replacement, arrives. I'm ready, this time, for a few days off. I've spent forty-four of the last seventy-two hours in the tower, and while I never feel claustrophobic, I do prefer a balance between sitting all day in a seven-by-seven room and all the other joys of the job — a morning and an evening walk, coffee on the porch in the sun, a game of Frisbee golf in the meadow. Exhaustion sets in after a few days of intense watching of the landscape, nonstop chatter on the radio, dawn till dark. Physical exhaustion is a piece of it — tired eyes, too few hours of sleep. But the exhaustion is more mental. The adrenal thrill of being a small part of a big fire wears off, but one's powers of concentration mustn't wane. More than anything, right now, I want to drink an ice-cold beer in a bar thick with smoke and conversation.

Yesterday the Lake Fire grew to one hundred and thirty-two acres, the Granite to eighteen hundred and twenty-six. The Lake more than quadrupled in size; the Granite doubled. All's well. Ops normal.

June 26

I return to a forest on fire: nine fires are being allowed to burn, mostly in the wilderness — a total of perhaps five thousand acres, still just a tiny fraction of the whole.

By listening to the radio and quizzing Mark at Lookout Mountain, I piece together the story of the fires. The Loco Fire has crossed Apache Creek and is now eight hundred acres. The Lake Fire is moving both east and west through North Seco Canyon and is two hundred acres. The Woodland Fire has reached the bluffs above the Middle Fork of the Gila River and is more than one thousand acres. The Ten Fire, at sixty acres, has run into the outline of two old burns, the Ten Cow and the Bull, where it has slowed and is burning only in downed heavies. There are others: the Aspen, the HL, the Pigeon, the Spring. All the visible world north of my post is murky with a haze of drift smoke.

June 29

The observer plane is up today. It will cost five hundred dollars an hour, and what will it find? Maybe, just maybe, a single snag burning on a ridge top in scree, zero to low potential for spread, somewhere deep in the wilderness.

Final score: observer plane 1, lookout 2.

The plane got the jump when my boss was driving toward the Wahoos and saw a smoke up Middle Seco Creek — another fire blocked from my view by Granite Peak. The observer happened to be flying farther north at the time, so my boss had it swing by and pinpoint the fire. It was only ten minutes later when I saw the smoke myself. Nonetheless — scooped.

About an hour and a half later I spotted a smoke about fifteen miles north, popping up in a little white column near Moccasin John Mountain. I called Lookout Mountain for a cross, and our triangulation put the fire on a ridge above Palomas Creek. Thus, the Palomas Fire.

Not more than half an hour later, just as the observer plane touched down at the airport, I saw another smoke, this one a mere mile and a half from the tower, on a west-facing slope to my east. A single tree struck by lightning, puffing little puffs of blue-gray smoke. It puffed off and on all day, got rained on for parts of an hour and a half, and then, just before dark, reappeared and began to burn a little hotter.

I could see open flame from the tower, as if someone were having a big campfire high on a ridge above Mineral Creek: the Mineral Fire.

Neither the Palomas nor the Mineral was suppressed today. Both will be handled by smoke jumpers in the morning. The Seco Fire — the one called in by the observer plane — was cold by seven o'clock in the evening, lined and patrolled by six firefighters whose arrival did nothing but confirm the fire was dead in its tracks. The plane ate two thousand dollars today — and all to spot one fire that put itself out. I spotted two fires and worked thirteen hours at thirteen dollars an hour plus overtime. Let's do the math:

Observer plane — two thousand dollars per fire spotted.

Lookout — one hundred dollars per fire spotted.

I'm a bargain!

June 30

There are days every summer when I'm reminded that even here, on the edge of the world's first wilderness, there is no escape from the world of machines. Today two helicopters and three airplanes — one of them a slurry tanker — circled and roared over the east side of the Black Range, the big-money forest circus at its most spectacular. At dawn the jumper plane was up and circling the Mineral Fire. No likely jump spots were apparent, so the plane began to circle my peak with the notion of dropping the jumpers in the meadow on top. After sending a couple of test streamers out they judged the wind a bit too brisk. So I was denied the spectacle of men and women descending by parachute into my front yard, combining, in the most romantic way imaginable, the elements of earth, wind, and fire.

The plane went north to the Palomas Fire, where it dropped five jumpers on a fire with a good head of steam. The jumpers immediately called for a slurry tanker. That brought out the observer plane to assess the situation; then a lead plane to guide the tanker on its drops; and finally the tanker itself, splashing its bright red chemical cocktail on the ridgelines. All the tools and tactics of warfare deployed on the enemy of fire. Why? Because that's the way it's been done for decades. No better reason than institutional habit. And fear — fear of the big fire.

Next up: the Mineral Fire. When the jump plane bailed, two heli-copters were called into service. The first managed to find a landing zone right near the fire, on a little open ridge, and began to shuttle in a crew. The second helicopter received some bad intelligence along the way, because it thought my peak was the LZ; it dropped two be-wildered firefighters on the landing pad below my tower. "We were told the fire was an eighth of a mile down the ridge," one of them shouted up to me.

Realizing what had happened, I invited them up in the tower. Their home base was Libby, Montana. They had no clue where they were on a map of the forest. Neither was much older than twenty. Both were still in college, making some serious summer cash — overtime and hazard pay — and having an adventure to boot. I pointed to the fire.

"It's a mile and a half from here, but there's not a good straight route. You'd first drop two thousand feet, then gain a thousand of it back. The easier way would be to hop from knoll to knoll and curve your way down to the fire, but that would run more like two and a half miles and it still wouldn't be fun."

They looked at each other and shook their heads. "We're fucked," one of them said. They looked forlornly at their gear below the tower, next to the helipad. Two hundred pounds of tools in three bags.

I took pity on them. It is, after all, part of my job to untangle a cluster, especially when it involves miscommunication. So I called the first helicopter on the radio and had it swoop down, pick the boys up, and fly them the rest of the way.

July 1

In the end, the Mineral Fire burned about a tenth of an acre. It was out within twenty-four hours of it starting. My boss requested total suppression, in part because of the fire's proximity to the lookout, but also because a stand of beetle-killed fir, with dead red needles still on, ran up a ridge adjacent to the fire. There could be no better fuel for a forest fire. It was a recipe for trees going up like Roman candles, which is not something the thirty-some residents of Kingston wish to see from their porches after dark.

A modest proposal for fire in the Gila: when it's in the wilderness, let it burn, and monitor it only with wilderness tools. No engines of any kind: plane, helicopter, truck, four-wheeler, chain saw. No suppression tactics at all. Use pack mules to supply the crews, who must walk in and out of wilderness-boundary trailheads. In fact, revolutionize the entire structure of fire fighting. Fewer *fighters* of fire and more *walkers* of fire. Make walking a fire the new prized skill. Walking with GPS in hand, tracing the perimeter as a fire does its ancient work. This would have to be done in teams on big fire-use fires — as it was on the Woodland Fire — so make a kind of fraternity of it, like the smoke jumpers are now and always will be. Call them smoke mappers, the new incarnation of John Muir and Bob Marshall, epic walkers of the woods.

July 2

Before they left, the folks on the Mineral Fire "improved" the helispot where they'd originally been dropped. A little terrace cut out with chain saws — from here it looks as neatly manicured as a putting green. All of this in the wilderness, where motorized machines of any kind are supposedly forbidden. Another day of mega-fuel usage on the forest. Eight hours of observer plane fuel. Four hours of slurry tanker fuel on the Hummingbird Fire. Four hours of lead-plane fuel. Eight hours of helicopter fuel. Helping to cook the planet, bit by infinitesimal bit, and hastening the eventual doom of the forest we are pledged to protect.

Despite my misgivings about the agency's bureaucratic blundering, its inability to entirely free itself from the habit of destructive practices, the Forest Service still offers the best job in the world: mine. To live in the wild for four or five months a year, to be paid for the privilege of watching mountains all day. To escape, for a while, the ugliness of the world we have made for ourselves, into the world we were given. To climb the tower after dark and watch a fire in the wilderness, torching trees and glowing red like lava running uphill. And all in the course of a job — that thing we find necessary and usually halfway loathe.

July 3

It's been exceedingly hot and dry — relative humidity was four percent at four in the afternoon today. In the mornings now inversion settles a gray-brown haze in the Gila River drainage, and the world smells sweetly of wood smoke and burning pine needles.

July 10

Lightning all along the Mimbres Valley, thunder overhead with a sound like massive sheets of roofing tin shaken by the hand of a giant.

One of the kicks of the job is to listen to the other lookouts pronounce Hispanic names such as Torres, Gallardo, Zapata, Martinez. All of us are gringos from elsewhere originally — Michigan, New Hampshire, Ohio, North Dakota, Texas, two from Minnesota. We couldn't roll an *r* if it was shaped like a wheel.

July 11

Yesterday's score: observer plane 4, lookouts 0. Whipped. Of course we were all socked in by rain, and three of the four fires got no bigger than a single snag doused by rain before anyone arrived on scene. If a tree smokes briefly in the forest but a lookout doesn't see it, is it really a *fire*?

July 18

Sweet and lazy days. Everything is green, flowers are everywhere, the hummingbirds arrive in abundance to feed. Eight, ten, twelve at a time buzzing around the feeder on the porch. Yesterday I called in a smoke just before six P.M. A single snag burning a few miles east of Signal Peak. It smoked till dark and was visible when I rose this morning at dawn; by the time I made coffee and looked again it was gone. I presume a little sunshine will revive it later, but there's little danger of it burning more than the original tree struck by lightning.

July 26

A profusion of wildflowers now paints the peak: yarrow, fleabane, bluebells, lupine, penstemon, Indian paintbrush, California fuchsia, coneflowers, wallflowers, skyrocket, sorrel, silene and sneezeweed. Yellow, red, pink, white, orange, lavender and blue. Hummingbirds chirp and buzz around the meadow all day long — broadtails, rufous, a couple of calliope, smallest bird in North America. An orgy of color and birdsong on the peak, and two days in a row of no rain.

July 30

Alice and I hit the trail for an evening hike. We were a half-mile below the tower when we came upon a tiny fawn alone by the side of the trail, in a little clearing. It didn't move — its legs were tucked beneath its quivering belly — but it appeared alert, and frightened by the dog's curiosity. It made a little mewling sound like a newborn kitten. I kept Alice at bay while I gingerly inspected the fawn for wounds. I found none. Figuring it had been abandoned — alone and helpless in an exposed place, right next to the trail — I cradled it in my arms to carry it back to the peak. It kicked its hind legs and bolted off. It ran perhaps thirty feet before its legs gave out and it collapsed, whining and crying. Alice of course gave chase and had to be restrained again. This time the fawn did not resist when I picked it up, and we marched up the hill, the dog circling us and jumping until I ordered her ahead of us on the trail. Shyly she obeyed, and we marched like some strange, half-comic parade through the woods. There must have been something about the fawn's coat that didn't jibe with me, because by the time I reached the cabin I was sneezing violently, on the verge of an asthma attack, and frightening the poor fawn even more than it was before.

I set it up in a bed of sweaters and jackets in the old tin bathtub. I heated some soy milk and a few drops of honey in a pan on the stove; I managed, by squeezing its jaw and tilting back its neck, to force it to swallow a little milk spooned onto its tongue. I was scared I might make it choke — its choices were choke, spit up, or drink — but with a little practice I became reasonably adept at making it take the milk.

I radioed the Kingston work station and asked the guy there to call Gila Wildlife Rescue, to see if I could get some guidance on how to feed and handle the fawn. I know the guy who runs GWR, and in fact I was just at his house a couple of weekends ago, where he showed me an owl, two kit fox, and a fawn he was nursing back to health. Unfortunately the listing for him in the phone book was out-of-date, so the guy in Kingston called and left a message with Game and Fish. We shall see what they say.

July 31

Yesterday Game and Fish called Kingston to say it would send an agent out of Las Cruces to pick up the fawn. I was surprised they didn't have someone closer, but relieved at least that help was on the way.

"Do they know it's a five-and-a-half-mile walk to get here?" I asked.

"I'm not sure," came the reply. "I'll check."

Ten minutes later he radioed back.

"Game and Fish says to return the fawn to the place where you found it and leave it there."

Translation: we don't hike. The final phrase of their message as relayed consisted of the words "let nature take its course." Nice.

I can understand the attitude, the kind of attitude it's easier to maintain in a fluorescent-lit office eighty miles from the scene. Animals die all the time in the wild. This one's life was accidentally prolonged on the basis of sheer chance — its abandonment near a trail Alice and I happened to be hiking. What I was really being told, between the lines, was that it was my fault for interfering in the first place — disrupting the natural order of things. I should undo my error, rewind the scene, return it to the place of its discovery, forget about it.

I began to entertain a host of questions: Had I doomed it merely by touching it? Would the scent of me, the scent of a human, ensure its rejection by its mother and the herd no matter what? Would its immune system have any defense for the microbes I carry? Was my own sentimentality the real cause of its doom? Had I (and the dog) frightened off its mother, a doe who would have returned when we passed?

At dawn the fawn was no longer in the old tin tub. I found it looking lifeless, curled under one of the bunks in the corner, an unmoving little coil. I felt its side: warm to the touch. I heated more soy milk and forced some down its gullet with a spoon.

In the afternoon I roused it and carried it outside, placed it on the ground. It wobbled and swayed but remained upright. I walked a little ways off. The fawn began to follow. Every moment afoot its legs appeared stronger, more sure of each step, until I jogged a few paces and it broke into an awkward lope, hind legs splayed and bent to maintain a precarious balance. I led it around the meadow for a hundred yards, the fawn following like the obedient pet I did not want it to become.

When we stopped the fawn moved between my legs, its muzzle in the air, searching for a nipple. What, I thought, do I have that resembles a nipple? A saline spray bottle, a nasal moistener. I emptied the bottle, rinsed it, and realized I'd run out of soy milk the day before. I remembered some powdered milk (years old) stowed in the back of the pantry. I heated water and added powder and suctioned the mixture into the spray bottle. I held the bottle between my legs like a nipple. To the fawn it did not feel like a nipple, of course — too cold and inflexible. But after several false starts and milk dripping down its chin it finally understood the mechanics and sucked for a few seconds on the nozzle, and I delivered perhaps half an ounce to its shriveled stomach.

Since it seemed strong, I thought now was the time to return it to the place I found it, if return it I must. When we reached the scene of our first meeting I sat on a log and waited to see if it would recognize the place. It came toward me, jaws in search of a nipple once more, its cries louder, and all of a sudden I began to cry. Streams of tears, a bowel-deep sobbing. The fawn wandered unsteadily along the slope below the trail, seemed to sniff at the earth in recognition, in a way I'd never seen it sniff. It walked a few feet and curled next to a log, and there I left it. It did not stir as I walked away up the hill.

In the night I came as close as I've ever come to prayer. More wish than prayer, in the end, but fervent in the way we think of the desperate and prayerful. I wished for the fawn to be wild, to run in high mountain meadows under moonlight, to feel the cold splash of crossing a creek in autumn. To know desire, pleasure, pain. To at least be given a chance. A life. Not merely birth and death.

This morning I ambled into the meadow to piss and heard its faint cries. By walking in ever larger concentric circles I discovered it lying next to a rock near a salt lick visited by its own kind, mature mule deer, whose droppings litter the ground there. It had walked up the hill god knows when. Surpassingly odd. I did not hear it in the night. What did it want? To lie in a place it knew through the power of its senses as a sort of social site for its species? Or did it know only enough to return to its source of milk? When it saw me — or maybe when it heard me, for its eyesight appeared poor — it came to me with its muzzle more insistent than ever for a nipple, its teeth gripping the inseam of my pants and gnawing, sucking. Again I filled the saline spray bottle with milk and got a little down its throat.

I called the dispatcher on the radio, in one last effort to enlist help. I told him to reach my friend at Gila Wildlife Rescue, to let him know I could either meet him at the pass or drive to town with the fawn — I would find a way to carry it the five miles down. The dispatcher tried two numbers and left messages at both. Then the district office got on the radio and said: Game and Fish instructed that you take it away from the tower, do not touch it, and let nature take its course.

I thought: Fine! While we're at it, let's let every fire burn as long as it wants. Stop fighting them at all. *Let nature take its course.*

Roger that, I said, furious and helpless.

Now the fawn lies curled beneath the sawhorse, ten feet from the cabin door, the place it seems to feel offers it a modicum of safety as its strength wanes.

Alice has been lovely with it, resisting her urge to sniff at it, paw at it, make it a plaything. The fawn even came to Alice and crouched beneath her in search of a teat, and Alice simply stood with her legs splayed and looked at me, uncomprehending and perhaps a little scared. She barks into the trees at the edges of the meadow, barks seemingly at nothing, at phantoms. As if to say: Do not come near the fawn. Do not prey on the defenseless.

The radio is quiet. I am socked in by clouds, humidity ninety percent. I am watching the fawn's torso rise and fall with each breath. I feel a tremendous sadness and something like love. As if I've entered a stupor of grief — here at my impromptu wildlife hospice on the hill.

August 1

In its last moments of strength the fawn lay on its side and galloped in place, all four legs going like pistons, like a dream of running. Its cries grew louder, higher pitched, more insistent. On what? Its sense of abandonment, its struggle for breath? For life? Its cries pierced me. Then it was still.

And so I built a pyre. I'd been saving dry wood for weeks under a tarp for late-season bonfires. I burned one batch down to a flaming bed of red-hot coals and then I placed the fawn on the bed and covered it with yet more wood. I piled it high as the stone circle would allow.

Before the fire burned completely down a deluge poured from the sky and reduced it to a core of molten coals and a drift of blue-gray smoke. It rained a quarter inch in half an hour. The meadow is perfumed with the smoke.

NATHAN ENGLANDER

∎

Everything I Know About My Family on My Mother's Side

FROM *Esquire*

1.

Watch the husband and wife walking down Broadway together. Even looking at their backs, even from a distance, you can see the wife is making big sweeping points, advising. There is wisdom being shared. But she is a kindly woman, the wife. You can see this, too. Because every few paces, the wife slows and reaches toward the husband, hangs an arm around his shoulder, and pulls him close. There is clearly love between them.

2.

If we weave through the crowd with a little gusto, we'll make progress. If we take advantage of the pause when the two stand by a table of trinkets — bracelets and lighters and watches, all of them, oddly, embossed with the faces of revolutionaries — we get close enough to become suspicious of their relationship, about the nature of its husband-and-wifeness.

3.

The two stop right in the middle of Canal Street. The wife faces the husband, and the point she argues is so large, it's as if the wife believes traffic will stop for it when the light changes, as if, should the cars roll on, it's worth being run down to see her point made.

It's then that we catch up, then that we're sure — as the woman smiles and hooks her arm through the man's, guiding him safely across — that the wife is not a wife and the husband not a husband.

4.

What they are, it seems clear now, is boyfriend and girlfriend. And that girlfriend, upon closer inspection, seems to be a cat-eyed and freckle-faced Bosnian. Standing next to her, looking ten years older and with a mess of curly hair, we see that the other one — the boy-friend one — is just a little Jew. And recognizing the face, taking it in, we see that the little Jew is me.

5.

It's because of how they walk and talk, in the way their shoulders bump and how her lower back is held and released by him at every corner, that we assume a different type of intimacy. There is an ease — a certain safety, you could call it — that just makes a person think husband and wife. From a distance, it just seemed another thing.

6.

The argument that they — that is, that she and I — settle in the mid-dle of Canal Street sounds, in a much truncated form, like this, with me earnest and at wit's end: "But what do you do if you're American and have no family history and all your most vivid childhood memo-ries are only the plots of sitcoms, if even your dreams, when pieced together, are the snippets of movies that played in your ear while you slept?"

"Then," the girl says, "those are the stories you tell."

7.

Her family tree is written into the endpapers of a Bible whose leather cover has worn soft as a glove. She was raised in the house in which her mother was raised, and her mother's mother, and in which, believe it or not, her great-grandmother was born. Think of this: The ancient photos around her had grown old on the walls.

When the Bosnian came to America with her parents, they took the Bible, but the pictures, along with the still-living relatives in them, were left behind.

8.

We're still in the street, arguing over my family history gone lost, and I say what I always say to this girl who was swaddled in a quilt sewn from her grandmother's dresses: "Oh, look at me, my uncle shot Franz Ferdinand and started World War I — then Count Balthus came to Sarajevo to paint a portrait of my mother playing badminton in white kneesocks." For this there's always a punch in the arm and a kiss to make up. This time I also want a real answer.

9.

"What you do is tell the stories you have as best you can."

"Even if they're about going to the mall? About eating bageldogs and kosher pizza?"

"Yes," she says.

"You don't mean that."

"I don't mean that," she says. "You find better stories than that." And looking at me, frustrated, "You can't, not really, know nothing! Tell me about your mother. Tell me an anecdote right now."

"Everything I know about my family on my mother's side wouldn't even make a whole story." And she knows enough of me, my girl does, to know that it's true.

10.

The Bosnian, my bean — and, admittedly, that's what I call her — she fills me with confidence. I go from saying it's hopeless to telling her about the Japanese beetles, about the body in the stairwell, about the soldier with the glass eye. "You see," she says. "There's story after story. Plenty of history to tell."

11.

My mother's father had two brothers, both of them long dead. My grandfather never told me about either brother. These are the stories he told me instead: "During Prohibition, we drank everything. Vanilla. Applejack. When I was down in Virginia, we used to go out to where the stills were hidden in the woods and buy moonshine. Always, you take a match to it first. If it burns blue, you're all right. If it burns clear, then it's methanol. If it burns clear and you drink it, you go blind."

12.

Applejack, it's just hard cider. My grandfather told me how to make it. You take fresh cider and you put it in a jar and throw in a bunch of raisins, for the sugar. You let it ferment, watching those raisins go fat over time. Then you put it in the freezer and you wait. Alcohol has a lower freezing point than water. When the ice forms, you take out the jar, you fish out the ice (or pour out the liquid), and what's not frozen, that's alcohol — easy as pie. I tried it one Thanksgiving, when suddenly, even in suburbia, cider abounds. I threw in the raisins. I waited and froze and skimmed and drank. I don't think I got drunk. I don't think anything happened. But neither did I go blind.

13.

If you were to climb into my childhood head and look out from my childhood eyes, you'd see a world of Jews around you: the parents, the children, the neighbors, the teachers — everyone a Jew, and everyone religious in exactly the same way. Now look across the street at the Catholic girl's house, and at the house next door to hers, where the Reform Jews live. Now what do you see? Is it a blur? An empty space? If you are seeing nothing, if your answer is nothing, then you are seeing as I saw.

14.

Now that I'm completely secular, my little niece looks at me — at her uncle — through those old eyes. She asks my older brother sweetly,

"Is Uncle Nathan Jewish?" Yes, is the answer. Uncle Nathan is Jewish. He's what we call an apostate. He means you no harm.

15.

My great-grandfather gave up on religion completely. And my grandfather told me why he did. This is true, by the by. Not true in the way fiction is truer than truth. True in both realms.

16.

What he told me is that his father and two other boys were up on the roof of a house in their village in Russia. One of the boys — not my great-grandfather — had to pee and peed off that roof. What he didn't see below him was a rabbi going by.

Like a story, every stream has an arc that has to come down somewhere. The boy pissed on the rabbi's hat. The three children were brought before the anointed party. They were, all three, soundly and brutally beaten. The punishment meted out was an injustice my grandfather couldn't abide. He thought, in Russia, in Yiddish, in his version, Fuck the whole lot, I'm done.

17.

Up until this story, all I knew was that our family was from Gubernia. That's where we hailed from. And when I tell my sweet Bosnian, who also speaks some Russian, she shakes her head — looking sad, as if maybe everything I know really isn't enough. "*Gubernia* just means 'state,'" she says, "like a county. To say you were born in gubernia would be like saying you were born in *state*. As in, New York State or Washington State. To be from there is to be from everywhere."

"Or nowhere," I say.

18.

It's when I'm asking my mother about the other side, about my grandmother's side, that she says, "Well, it's when Grandma's grandma, that is (*and here, the middle-distance stare, the ticking off on fingers*), when my mother's mother's mother came from Yugoslavia to Boston . . ." and that's when I stop her. Thirty-seven years old, and for the first time, in writing this, I find that my great-great-grandmother — my people — come from Yugoslavia. How does that not ever come up? I'm flabbergasted, and I want to call the Bosnian to say, "Hey, Neighbor, it's me, Nathan. Guess what?" But she is not the person to call with such news — not anymore. That's how quickly things change. Some truths, you can hide them forever, but when you finally face them, finally take a look . . . well, with me and the Bosnian, it's done.

19.

About Yugoslavia, about the news, my mother doesn't pity me over stories suppressed. She says, "You have nothing to complain about. I had it worse in my not-knowing." Her uncle, my grandfather's brother, died at age eight of a brain tumor. There was nothing to be done. A brain tumor killed the littlest brother of the three. My grandfather was twelve at the time, his middle brother ten, and his dead-of-a-brain-tumor brother, eight. And my mother worried about every headache I had in my life. She worried about every little twitch and high fever in my childhood. She waited for the malady to start, the disease that eats the brains of young boys.

20.

And then, in 2004 — "That spring," my mother says — she drives up to Boston because Cousin Jack needs a new hip, a new shoulder, a new valve; she drives up to Boston because Cousin Jack is getting fit for a replacement part. There she learns a different story from Jack, different from the one she's carried her whole life. My grandfather, all of twelve, was crossing Commonwealth Avenue with his littlest brother, with Abner, when a car came over the hill and clipped him. Knocked little Abner from my grandfather's grip. Abner got up. Abner looked fine, except for his right hand. A deep cut in the hand that might have been of concern to the driver had he taken a closer look. Instead, he got out of the car, stared at the little Jewboys looking fine enough, and drove off.

21.

My grandfather led his brother home. Great-grandma Lily (my grand-father's mother) screamed in shock. A car? An accident? Look at this cut. She cleaned the wound. She wrapped the wound. And she made her littlest son lie down. She cleaned and wrapped, but she did not call a doctor. My great-grandfather did not call a doctor. It would get better. It would get better even after the fever took, even when, run-ning up the arm, was a bright-red line, an angry vein. The boy would mend until he didn't, so that my grandfather's littlest brother died from nothing more than a cut to his hand. Lily would not recover. Her husband would not recover. My grandfather would not recover. But, in a sense, they did. Because on the outside they did. Because it turned into a brain tumor. It turned into what was so clearly God's will and so clearly unstoppable, a malady that begs no other response than a *tfu-tfu-tfu*.

22.

There were two brothers left. And then there was, a decade or so later, a world war. My grandfather, legally blind, could not be sent over. He was drafted, but worked an office job.

23.

His office mate was a soldier with a glass eye. At night, this soldier would drink and drink, and then when everyone was as drunk as he was, he'd pop out his regular glass eye and pop in one that, instead of an iris, contained one red swirl inside another — a bull's-eye. A little trick to get a laugh, to make the uninitiated think they'd had one too many, which they already had.

24.

My grandfather's brother was killed in the war. His brother died fighting. That is how it was, until right now.

25.

My favorite family story didn't come to me through blood. It's about Paul, my grandmother's father, and it came by way of Theo (who married Cousin Margot) and was, for the next thirty years, my grandfather's best friend. Inseparable. They were inseparable, those two.

26.

"Your great-grandfather Paul, he had a bull's neck. Eighteen, nineteen inches around. He was a tough motherfucker." Theo tells me this on the day we bury my grandfather. We're outside a restaurant near the graveyard, everyone else has already gone in. Theo and I stand in the parking lot. He stamps his feet against the cold. "One day, after work, me and your grandfather and Paul, we went to a bar for the train workers. We were sitting at the bar, the three of us, and the man right next to your great-grandfather, he turns to Paul and says, 'You know what the problem with this place is?' Your great-grandfather sizes him up. 'What's the problem?' he says. 'I'd like to know.' So the man tells him. 'Too many Jews,' he says. Your great-grandfather puts down his drink. He's still sitting, mind you. Still facing forward and seated on his barstool. Without even much of a look, he balls up a fist, and he just pops the guy — crosswise — just clocks that guy right in the jaw. Sitting down! And then your great-grandfather picks up his drink like it's nothing, and he throws it back. One quick punch, and he knocked him out cold." Theo shakes his head in remembering. "That mutt just fell off his stool like a sack of corn."

27.

And I can't even handle it, it's so good a story. "What'd you do?" I say. "What happened?" And Theo is laughing. "What do you think?" Theo says. "I said, 'Let's get the fuck out of here.' Then me and your grandfather, we grabbed Paul and got the hell out of that bar."

28.

And what can I contribute to my own family history, what stories have I witnessed firsthand? I can tell you about breakfast. My grandfather cooked like nobody's business. And, above all, it was breakfast he did best. Burnt coffee and burnt eggs and bacon burnt black. Bacon that we did not eat as a religious family — though our mouths watered at the smell. When we stayed at my grandparents' (my parents, my brother, and me), we'd wake to a cloud of burnt-bacon smoke filling the house. It would summon us, cartoonlike, lifting us with a curling finger of smoke, from bed.

29.

Right before the end of things, Bean and I walk to Greenpoint to buy chocolates at one of the Polish stores. We pass a Ukrainian grocery, which reminds Bean of her Ukie parts. She tells me of a great-uncle, a butcher, who slipped and fell into a vat of boiling hams. He was dead in an instant, leaving eight children behind. "Even your bad stories are good," I tell her. "A very bad story," she agrees. And I add, upon consideration, "That's possibly the least Jewish way to die." "Yes," she says. "Not the traditional recipe for Jews." And looking around at all the Polish stores, I agree. "Traditionally, yes, correct. Jews go in the oven. Pagans, burnt at the stake. And Ukrainian uncles . . ." "Boiled," she says. "Boiled alive."

30.

Theo tells me this: When he was three, he was left alone in his family's little bungalow in Denver. "Still standing," he says. "They've torn down practically all of them, but that one still stands." In his parents' bedroom, under his father's pillow, he found a loaded gun. Theo took the gun. He aimed at the window, at the clock, and then took aim at the family dog, a sweet, dumb old beagle asleep next to the bed. He pulled the trigger; Theo shot that dog through his floppy ear. The bullet lodged in the floor. "You killed him?" I ask. "No, no, the dog was fine as fine can be — fine but for a perfect circle through that ear." Sammy (the dog) just opened his sad, milky eyes, looked at Theo, and went back to sleep.

31.

Cousin Jack stands with me while Theo tells that story. Jack doesn't believe it. "What about kickback?" he says. "You were all of three.

Should have shot you across the room. You'd have a doorknob in your ass until this day."

"A .22," Theo says. "There doesn't have to be much kick. A .22-short wouldn't have to knock over a flea."

"Still," Jack says. "A little boy. Hard to believe it."

"I guess I handled it," Theo says, and looks off. And to me, there is nothing in that look but honesty. "I must have handled it," Theo says, "because I still remember the feel of that shot."

32.

It is "the feel of that shot" that does it. It is "the feel of that shot" that undoes another sixty years for Jack. Because out of nowhere, he is talking again, Jack who does not keep secrets — or keeps them for half a century until suddenly the truth appears. "Terrible," Jack says. "It was a terrible phone call to get, I can still remember. I was the one who picked up the phone."

33.

"What phone?" I say. "What call? What terrible?" I rush things out, desperate for any history to put things in place. I'm sure that I've already scared the story off with my eagerness, my panic. I'm sure it's about Abner, about the little boy dying.

"The call about your grandfather's brother."

"About Abner?" I say, because I can't keep my mouth shut, can't wait.

"No," he says. "About Bennie. The call from your grandfather to tell me Bennie had died."

34.

Margot is now standing there, her arm hooked through Theo's, her face full of concern. "You got the call about Bennie being killed in the war?"

"Yes," Jack says. Then, "No."

"You didn't get it?" she says.

"I did. I got the call. But it wasn't the war."

"He was killed in the war," Margot says. "In Holland."

"He was buried in Holland," Jack says. "Not killed there. And he wasn't killed in the war. It was after."

"After."

"After the fighting. After the end of the war. His gun went off on guard duty."

"You always said," Margot says, incredulously, "everyone always said: Killed in Holland during the war."

35.

Jack puts a hand on my shoulder, hearing Margot but talking to me. "'Guard duty' is what your grandfather told me that day. 'An accident.' Then, a few months later, we're out in my garage — I remember this perfect. I'm holding a carburetor, and he takes it, and he's looking at it like it's a kidney or something, weighing it in his hand. 'It was a truck,' he says. 'Bennie asleep in the back, coming off guard duty. Something joggled, something fired, and Bennie shot through the head.'"

It's Theo who speaks: "That's one in a million, that kind of accident. Spent my life around guns."

"It is," Jack says. "One in a million. Maybe more."

36.

What I'm thinking — and maybe it's the way my head works, maybe it's just the way my synapses fire — but in this Pat Tillman, quagmire-of-Iraq world, I'm thinking, I don't like the sound of it. And maybe I'm being truly paranoid. It is, as I said, sixty years later. The idea that it already sounds funny, and already is the cut hand turned brain tumor, is not for me to think. And then Jack says, "I never did like the sound of it. That story never sat right."

37.

Margot says, "I don't know why your grandfather never visited."

"There was talk," Jack says. "Right after. But then, like everything else in this family" — and no one has ever said such a thing before, no one ever acknowledged the not-acknowledging — "it just got put away and then it was gone."

38.

I'm in Holland on book tour. I'm at the Hotel Ambassade in Amsterdam, eating copious amounts of Dutch cheese and making the rounds. There is one day off. One day free if I want to see *The Night Watch* or the red lights or to go walk the canals and get high. My publisher, he offers me all these things. "No thank you," I say. "I'm going to Maastricht to visit a grave."

39.

When you tell the Americans you are coming, the caretaker goes out and does something special. He rubs sand into the marker of your dead. The markers are white marble, and the names, engraved, do not show — white on white, a striking field of nameless markers. But with the sand rubbed, the names and the dates, they stand out. So you walk the field of crosses looking for Jewish stars. When you find your star and see the toasted-sand warmness of the name, you feel, in the strangest way, as if you're being received as much as you're there to pay tribute. It's a very nice touch — a touch that will last until the first rain.

40.

Do you want to know what I felt? Do you want to know if I cried? We don't share such things in my family — we don't tell this much even. Already I've gone too far. And put being a man on top of it; compound the standard secretiveness and shut-down-ness of my family with manhood. It makes for another kind of close-to-the-vest, another type of emotional distance, so that my Bosnian never knew what was really going on inside.

41.

This happened at the bridge club, back in '84 or '85. My grandparents are playing against Cousin Theo and Joe Gorback. (Margot never plays cards.) Right when it's old Joe's turn to be the dummy, he keels over and dies. The whole club waits for the paramedics and the gurney, and then the players play on — all but for my grandparents' table, short one man.

They wait on the director. Wait for instruction.

And Theo looks at my grandparents, and looks at his partner's cards laid out, and over at the dead man's tuna sandwich, half eaten. Theo reaches across for the untouched half, he picks it up and eats it. "Jesus, Theo," is what my grandfather says. And Theo says, "It's not like it's going to do Joe any good."

"Still, Theo. A dead man's sandwich."

"No one's forcing you," he says. "You're welcome to sit quiet, or you can help yourself to a fry."

42.

My grandfather wasn't superstitious. But it's that half sandwich, he's convinced, that brings it on Theo — a curse. That's what he says when Theo parks his car at the top of the hill over by the Pie Plate and forgets to put his emergency brake on. He's heading on down to the restaurant when he looks back up to see his car lurch and start rolling. And he still claims it's the fastest he ever ran in his life. Theo gets run over by his own Volvo. He breaks his back, though you'd never tell to look at him today.

43.

My couch is ninety-two inches, it's a deep-green three-cushion. It seats hundreds. But that's not why I got it. I got it because, lying down the long way, in the spooning-in-front-of-a-movie way, in the head-to-toe lying with a pair of lamps burning and a pair of people reading, it fits me and it fits another — it fits her — really well.

44.

She is gone. She is gone, and she will be surprised that I'm alive to write this — because she, and everyone who knows me, didn't think I'd survive it. That I can't be alone for a minute. That I can't manage a second of silence. A second of peace. That to breathe, I need a second set of lungs by my side. And to have a feeling? An emotion? No one in my family will show one. Love, yes. Oh, we're Jews, after all. There's tons of loving and complimenting, tons of kissing and hugging. But I mean any of us, any of my blood, to sit and face reality, to sit alone on a couch without a partner and to think the truth and feel the truth, it cannot be done. I sure can't do it. And she knew I couldn't do it. And that's why it ended.

45.

It ended because another person wants you to need to be with them, with her, specific — not because you're afraid to be alone.

46.

My grandmother had one job in her life. She worked as a bookkeeper at a furniture store for a month before my grandfather proposed. The owner proposed first. She turned the owner down.

47.

She had another job. I thought it was her job, and I put it here because I put this scene into every story I write. I lay it into every setting, attribute it to every character. It's a moment that I add to every life I draw, and then cut — for it contains no meaning beyond its meaning to me. It comes from my grandmother and her Mr. Lincoln roses, my grandmother collecting Japanese beetles in the yard. She'd pick the beetles off the leaves and put them in a mason jar to die. And I'd help her. And I'd get a penny for every beetle, because, she told me, she got a penny for every beetle from my grandfather. I believed, until I was an adult, that this was her job. A penny a beetle during rose-growing season.

48.

About sacks of corn and the one time I felt like a man: My grandfather and I drive out to the farm stand. It's open but no one's in it. There's a coffee tin filled with money, under a sign that says SELF-SERVE. Folks are supposed to weigh things themselves and leave money themselves and, when needed, make change. This is how the owner runs it when she's short-staffed. We'd come out for corn, and the pickings are slim, and that's when the lady pulls up in her truck. She gets out, makes her greetings, and drops the gate on the back.

And in the way industrious folks function, she's hauling out burlap sacks before a full minute has passed. My grandfather says to me, "Get up there. Give a hand."

49.

I hop up into the bed of the truck and I toss those sacks of corn down. It's just the thing an able young man is supposed to do — and I'd never, ever have known. But I don't hesitate. I empty the whole thing with her, feeling quiet and strong.

50.

They are sacks of Silver Queen and Butter & Sugar, the sweetest corn in the world. She tells us to take what we want, but my grandfather will have no such thing. We fill a paper sack to overflowing and pay our money. At my grandparents', I shuck corn on the back steps, the empty beetle jar tucked in the bushes beside me and music from the transistor coming through the screen of the porch. And — suburban boy, Jewish boy — I've never felt like I had greater purpose, never so much felt like an American man.

51.

The woman I love, the Bosnian, she is not Jewish. All the years I am with her, to my family, it's as if she is not. My family so good at it now. My family so masterful. It's not only the past that can be altered and forgotten and lost to the world. It's real time now. It's streaming. The present can be undone, too.

52.

And I still love her. *I love you, Bean. (And even now, I don't say it straight. Let me try one more time: I love you, Bean. I say it.)* And I place this in the middle of a short story in the midst of our modern YouTube, iTunes, plugged-in lives. I might as well tell her right here. No one's looking; no one's listening. There can't be any place better to hide in plain sight.

53.

On Thanksgiving, this very one, I am looking for a gravy boat in the attic. I find the gravy boat and my karate uniform (green belt, brown stripe) and a shoe box marked DRESSER. Lifting the lid, I understand: It's the remains of my grandfather's towering chest of drawers — a life compacted, sifted down. Inside, folded up, is a child's drawing: a man on a chair, a hat, two arms, two legs — but one of those legs sticks straight out to the side, as if the man were trying to salute with it. The leg at a ridiculous and impossible angle. It's my mother's drawing. She hasn't seen it in years. She doesn't remember filling that box.

54.

The drawing is of Great-grandpa Paul. "Hit by a train," she says. And already — in a loving, not-at-all-angry, Jewish-son's way, I'm absolutely furious. She knows I'm writing this story, knows I want to know everything, and here, Great-grandpa Paul, a lifetime at the railroad and killed by a train. I can't believe it — cannot believe her.

"Oh, no, no," she says, "not killed, not at all. Eighteen when it happened. He survived it just fine. Only, the leg. He could never bend that leg again."

55.

The first time Bean brings me home, we walk to the river in Williamsburg. We stand next to a decrepit old factory on an industrial block and stare at Manhattan hanging low across the water, a moon of a city at its fullest and brightest.

56.

Bean takes out a key. Behind a metal door is a factory floor with no trace of the business that was. The cavernous space is now a warren of rooms, individual structures, like a shantytown sprouting up inside a box. "I've got a lot of roommates," she says. And then, "I only just finished building. The guys helped me put the ceiling on last night." Toward the back, behind a mountain of bicycle parts, is a grouping of tiny rooms with a ladder (which we climb) leading to a sort of cube on top. She's bracketed together scavenged frames of all shapes and sizes to make four window walls under a window ceiling through which one may stare at the rough beams above. It's a miracle of a room, a puzzle complete. "I guess I'll need curtains now," she says, as we sit on her bed. And I say, "You live in a house made of windows but," and I motion, "you can't see outside." She takes it well, and takes my hand.

57.

I mention him to my grandfather just once. Visiting from college, drinking whiskeys, playing gin. I mention his dead brother Bennie — the army brother — who I'd just found out existed. I say something awkward about the only guy at school called up for the first Iraq war — the good one. I say something about younger brothers, being a younger brother myself.

58.

My grandfather picks a card, arranges his hand — making sets. "For a while we owned a building. Two stories. We were landlords to a deli on the ground floor and a pair of tiny apartments upstairs. More than once," he says, "I found a body. I'd head over to check on things before work, and I'd find them. One time in the stairwell, and another, a stiff in the alley, still wearing his hat. These weren't crimes of passion, either. These were deals settled, people done in." He lays his cards facedown on the table. I look at their backs. "Gin," he says. And he goes out to the porch to smoke a cigar.

59.

I use the Freedom of Information Act to get at it. We don't have such a law in my family, but the government, the government will tell you things about a missing brother. The government will sometimes share secrets if you ask.

60.

Where is my Bean when I need her? Where is Bean when I'm having a feeling I can't face? It's not that I want to share it. It's the exact opposite; the old me in play. What I want is to turn pale for her, saying nothing. I want to go anxious and ask her — should anyone call — to come find me under the bed.

Where she is right then is out dancing on tables. That's what I see in my head. And that's our standard joke during the rare times we speak. Me saying, "I picture you out dancing on tables whenever I wonder what you're up to." "Oh, yeah," she says, "that's me. Out dancing every night."

61.

The letter is real — in both realms real. There is an envelope from the government, a pack of papers, forms typed uneven, faded reproductions, large spaces for the clipped explanation. In it is a letter written in my grandfather's hand. It's a beautiful, intelligent, confident (but not cocky) script. It's a polite letter to the government, a crisp-clean letter. He is writing on behalf of his mother, about her son — his brother, killed in (after) the war. They'd filled out the forms, and they'd still not received — he was wondering when they might get — his dead brother's things.

His effects.

Bennie's worldly effects.

62.

Here is me, fictionalized, sitting on the couch with a letter, written in my grandfather's hand. I am weeping. I don't know if I've ever seen his handwriting before. I think to call my mother, to tell her what I'm holding. I think to call my brother, or maybe Cousin Jack. But really, more than anyone, I think to call that missing love — that missing lover. Because it's her I wish was with me; it's her I want to share it with right now. And more so, to find myself weeping from a real sadness — not anxious, not disappointed, not frustrated or confused — just weeping from the truth of it, and the heartbreak of it, and recognizing it as the purest emotion I've ever had. It's this I want to tell her, that I'm feeling a pure feeling, maybe my first true feeling, and for this — I admit it — I'm proud.

63.

I am sad for my grandfather, ten years passed, and his mother dead forty, and his brother sixty years gone from this world. I'm on the couch alone, and I am weeping. It is the purity of the letter, the simplicity of it: Your last brother dead, and you're asking for his things.

NICK FLYNN

DRAWINGS BY DANIEL HEYMAN

∎

The Ticking Is the Bomb

FROM *Esquire*

Telegram Made of Shadows

THIS BLACK-AND-WHITE PHOTOGRAPH in my hand is an image of my unborn daughter. This is what I'm told. It is actually a series of photographs, folded one upon the other, like a tiny accordion. I was there when the doctor or the technician or whoever he was made it with his little wand of sound. I sat beside him, looked into the screen as he pointed into the shadows — *Can you see her nose, can you see her hand? Can you see her foot, right here, next to her ear?* I was there when each shot was taken, yet in some ways, still, it is all deeply unreal — it's as if I were holding a photograph of a dream, a dream sleeping inside the body of the woman I love, this woman now walking through the world with two hearts beating inside her.

At this same moment, or outside of this moment, outside of us, somewhere out there in the world, exists another set of photographs, photographs of prisoners and smiles and shadows. These photographs also have the texture of dreams — they seem so unlikely, yet I have held them in my hands.

Here's a secret: Everyone, if they live long enough, will lose their way at some point. You will lose your way, you will wake up one morning and find yourself lost. This is a hard, simple truth. If it hasn't happened to you yet, consider yourself lucky. When it does, when one day you look around and nothing is recognizable, when you find yourself alone in a dark wood having lost the way, you may find it easier to blame it on someone else — an errant lover, a missing father, a bad childhood — or it may be easier to blame the map you were given — folded too many times, out-of-date, tiny print — but mostly, if you are honest, you will only be able to blame yourself.

One day I'll tell my daughter a story about a dark time, the dark days before she was born, and how her coming was a ray of light. We got lost for a while, the story will begin, but then we found our way.

Who Died and Made You King?

If, one Saturday afternoon, watching cartoons when you really should be outside *(why not bike to the beach, or to a bridge, why not stand on the railing, watch the tidewater pass below, why not step off into the air, why not jump?)* — if, without taking your eyes from the television, you call out for a glass of water and your mother, stirring some onions in a pan, answers, *Who died and made you king?* — it might make you wonder if you were, in fact, a king — unknown, unrecognized, but still, a king.

Or if you call out for a glass of water and your mother, as she passes you on her way out, answers, *Who was your slave yesterday?* — it might mean something else. Or it might mean the same thing, for kings, after all, often have slaves, the two often go together, you know this.

Belly down on the floor, reading the funnies while your mother reads the obituaries, you look for *The Wizard of Id* — you like Spook, the troll-like guy chained up forever in the dungeon. You like how every time Spook appears, he tries to escape, and you want him both to make it and to be there the next time you visit.

In school you are studying the civil-rights movement, but you aren't interested in civil rights. You are interested in the Middle Ages, a time of kings and dungeons, which they don't teach in school — *medieval*, you like to say the word, it has the word *evil* in it. Today the teacher is talking about Martin Luther King — every year you learn the same four things about Martin Luther King — but you are thinking about Nebuchadnezzar, the king of ancient Babylon. God took away his kingdom in order to punish him for his pride, and then God condemned him to live in the woods like an animal. God, apparently, doesn't like one to have pride. For seven years Nebuchadnezzar lived without society or the ability to think — hair grew all over his body, his nails became claws. You look at your own hand, stretch your fingers out.

Martin Luther King sat in a Birmingham jail, locked up for supporting the right of a man to order a sandwich whenever and wherever he damn well pleased. Your father is in prison, your mother told you so, the prison is in Missouri, but that's all you've heard. From the big map on the wall, the one you stare at when you're supposed to be listening, you know Missouri is in the middle of nowhere. The teacher says that while in prison Martin Luther King wrote a letter — you were supposed to read the letter for homework. *Can anyone tell us one thing he wrote in his letter?* She looks straight at you as she says this — you blur your eyes and she dissolves.

When you were younger, for a year or so, your brother believed he was a termite. At a restaurant, when the waitress asked what he wanted, he'd answer, "Wood." You decide right then and there that you have to be something else as well, so you decide to be a monkey. For some months afterwards you run around the house dragging your knuckles, answering only in monkey — monkey sounds, monkey yells, grunts taken from Saturday-afternoon Tarzan movies. How else would you know what a monkey sounds like? Maybe from cartoons — *Magilla Gorilla*, maybe, though didn't he speak in full sentences? A distant relative has a spider monkey as a pet, you are alone in the same room with it once, you can't remember how you got there or why. What you remember is that it jumped on you and held on to your head with its little hands, and you stopped being a monkey after that.

Your mother passes on a letter your father has sent you from prison. Along with the one-page letter, you find he has included a clipping from the newspaper of *The Wizard of Id*. Spook is chained to a wall; a hooded man holding a whip stands behind him.

If you asked your mother why your father is in prison, she might say, *Your father is a reprobate,* and since you don't know what a reprobate is, you might think it's a type of king.

But it's more likely that you'll think it's a type of spook.

One day you will learn that Babylon is now called Iraq, and years later, after your country invades, its king, its president, will be found, some months later, hiding in what will be called a "spider hole" — his beard gone wild, his nails grown long. And some time after this, after he is sentenced to death, he will be hung by the neck by jeer-

ing hooded men. You will watch his execution the same day you see photographs of a lost pop star showing her pussy to the world.

But now it is still that beautiful summer day, and you are still inside, staring into your box of shadows. Now it's *The Three Stooges* — Curly's head is in a vise again, Moe is cutting into it with a hacksaw. Moe, it seems, is forever trying to carve his way into someone else's body.

Welcome to the Year of the Monkey

(2004) I hear word of the photographs before I see the photographs, I hear about them on the car radio. The man on the radio has seen them, he talks as if they are there in front of him, as if he is thumbing through them as he speaks — *The photographs are from our war*, he says, *and they are very, very disturbing.*

I'm driving north from Texas to New York in a 1993 Ford Escort wagon — good, reliable, unsexy, cheap — a basic a-to-b device, bought in Texas with the idea of taking it north because, unlike the Northeast, a used car from Texas will be unlikely to have rust. I hear about the photographs again and again even before I make it to the city limits. What connects the photographs, the man on the radio says, is that each depicts what appears to be torture, and that the people doing the torturing are wearing uniforms, or parts of uniforms, and that the uniforms appear to be ours.

The man on the radio says the words *abu ghraib*, words I've never heard before — at this point I don't know if "abu ghraib" is one word or two, a building or a city, a place or an idea. The man on the radio describes the photographs — there are prisoners, there are guards, there are dogs. Hallways and cinder blocks and cages. Leashes and smiles. Many of the prisoners are not wearing clothes, he says, and the reason for this is that there appears to be a sexual element to what is happening, as I float past a church the size of a shopping mall.

The man on the radio is a reporter. The first time I heard his name was nearly forty years ago, when he broke the story of a massacre in Vietnam — My Lai — the name of a hamlet that came to symbolize all that was wrong with that war — nearly four hundred unarmed civilians, mostly women and children, rounded up, herded into ditches

(ditches? isn't that how the Nazis did it?), and shot (did the U.S. soldiers see those earlier photographs as children and later imitate them?). Photographs document that day as well, and the photographs eventually made their way to the pages of *The New York Times*. WEL-COME TO THE YEAR OF THE MONKEY, banners over the streets of Saigon read that spring of 1968.

I finally break out of the vortex that is Houston, and now I'm driving east on I-10, approaching the exit for New Orleans, where I'd planned to stop, as I haven't been there for years, but I decide to push on, to make it to Tuscaloosa before nightfall, where friends have offered me shelter. And I never get to see New Orleans again.

As We Drive Slowly Past the Burning House

When a siren — police car or fire truck or ambulance — would puncture my Saturday-morning cartoons, twisting the blue from the sky, my mother would tell me to go start the car, *Let's see what's happening*, and we'd drive to the place the sirens called us to.

What was she hoping to find, what was she hoping I'd see?

It could be argued that she was teaching me to pay close attention to the world. Or it could be argued that she was teaching me to pay close attention to the afterworld. Or, as we drove slowly past the burning house, it could be argued that at least it wasn't our tragedy, that we were at least able to step outside our house for an hour, into the fresh air, witness something outside ourselves. To empathize, or to practice empathy, even though we never knew the people who'd lived in the burning house, nor did it seem we cared to, even after their house was gone.

Or maybe she simply wanted me to practice, like other families practiced fire drills, so that when the sirens came for her, I'd know what to do. I'd get in my car and drive, toward the sound, whatever it was — fire or heart attack, car crash or suicide — get out and stand on the sidewalk or on someone's lawn, or not even stop, make it a slow drive-by while the stranger is carried away on a stretcher.

In mythology, Scylla and the sirens called the sailors to strand their ships on the shoals — it could be argued that our sirens were merely calling out to strand us as well, to crash our ship, only it would take years to know that was what we were doing. Where do you drive to when the siren is outside your own house, when the strangers on the sidewalk are looking at you?

You Don't Take Pictures

(2004) On the day the photographs appear, a veteran of the Korean War is interviewed on the radio in a coffee shop in Tennessee, and it seems as if he is thumbing through the photographs as he speaks. By now the photographs are in every newspaper in the world. *You know,* he begins, slowly, searching for his words, *stuff like this happens in every war.* It's hard to tell if he's disgusted or merely baffled. He pauses, and his voice gets slightly more indignant — *but you don't take pictures.*

The next day a radio commentator weighs in — *This is no different than what happens at the Skull and Bones initiation. And we're going to ruin people's lives over it and we're going to hamper our military effort, and then we're going to really hammer them because they had a good time. You know, these people are being fired at every day. I'm talking about people having a good time. These people, you ever heard of emotional release? You heard of the need to blow some steam off?* This is the moment before the soldiers dragging prisoners on leashes and giving the thumbs-up behind naked pyramids of bodies will be referred to as "a few bad apples," this is the moment when the soldiers are just like us, which, strangely, is perhaps closer to the truth.

The Magic Monkey

The first book I could call mine, my first book, was a picture book, *The Magic Monkey* — it was adapted from an old Chinese legend by a thirteen-year-old prodigy named Plato Chan with the help of his sister. The monkey in the story, as I remember it, was a misfit — lost, wandering, aimless, trying to find his way home. He manages to finagle his way into a walled school and there finds that he has magical powers, powers of transformation — he can change into a tree, a bird, a waterfall — but each thing he transforms into has a price, a complication. The tree becomes rooted, the waterfall slips away, the bird must constantly fly. I'm making this all up now from memory. I have the book on my bookshelf but I'm afraid to open it, in case I find out that the power it held over me proves to be thin, silly, superficial.

Istanbul

(2007) In August I fly from L. A. to New York, to connect to another airline that will carry me to Paris, then on to Istanbul. Istanbul, I know, is far away — half in Europe, half in Asia — but still, I didn't expect it to take three days to get there, and it wouldn't have, if the jet from L. A. hadn't run out of gas on the way to New York. I'd never been on a jet that ran out of gas, it felt like when I was sixteen and would put fifty cents in my tank to make a run to the package store. We had to touch down in Rochester to refuel — "touch down," the pilot said, but seven hours later we were still stranded, and I had missed my connecting flight.

By the time I make it to Istanbul I'm so jet-lagged, so bone tired, that in the taxi to the hotel I'm almost hallucinating. We pass men in their underwear swimming in the Bosporus, we pass fields of weekend picnickers sprawled out on ornate fabrics in the sun. Traffic sounds, a muezzin, the pop song on the radio — everything is calling us to prayer.

Not only am I jet-lagged, but, if I am to admit it, I'm a little freaked out, though at this point I haven't acknowledged the depths of my freak-out, not to anyone, not even to myself. Part of the unease comes from the fact that the lawyer I'm meeting has been joking that now that we are in contact, my phone is likely tapped, my e-mails being read. By coming here, she makes clear, I am now on a list — a blacklist.

In my exhaustion I can almost convince myself that a jet running out of gas is part of a conspiracy to keep me from Istanbul, a bit of paranoia that will thankfully dissolve (nearly) in the morning light. I will wake up with a line from Billy Bragg in my head — *If you have a blacklist, I want to be on it.* I can't say exactly what it is I'm doing here, beyond that it seems important.

The Allegory of the Cave

My mother, the story goes, set our house on fire one summer night. The house was a ruin, she did it to collect the insurance money, so she could then have it fixed up. My brother and I were sleeping upstairs at the time. I was five, I remember being carried outside in my ghoulish pajamas, left to stand across the street on the lawn of the

neighbor we never met, watching it burn, then watching the shadows of it burning, like one of those prisoners in Plato's cave. It was only years later that I learned she'd set it, or I was told she'd set it, by the boyfriend she was with at the time. It made sense, when I heard it, though it doesn't mean it's true — not that our house caught fire, but that she had set it. If it is true, then maybe it explains why we were fated to go toward sirens, maybe it answers the question of why every burning house pulled us toward it — maybe she believed that she could tell by looking everyone in the eye as they came out of the house if it was a scam or not, or maybe she just wanted to make sure all the children made it out okay.

In Plato's Allegory of the Cave, prisoners are locked up in such a way that they cannot look away from the wall they are facing. Even their heads are fixed, somehow, in that one direction. Behind the prisoners, some still children, there's a walkway, slightly elevated, and along this walkway the jailers, or their assistants, carry various objects back and forth. And beyond the walkway there is a fire burning continuously, a large fire, and this fire casts light onto the objects, which then cast shadows on the wall for the prisoners to contemplate. The object may be something benign — a bunch of carrots, say, but as a shadow the carrots become something frightful, because each could be a knife. Or an apple could be a rock that could crush a man's hands, or his son's testicles. Or a jar of milk could be a jar of acid, if all one sees, all one is allowed to see, are shadows. And the jailers make sounds, grunts and snorts and such, which echo off the walls, and so appear, to the prisoners, to come from the shadows themselves. And don't forget the fire, which makes another sound, and which heats their backs, perhaps too much, and fills the cave with smoke, making it hard to breathe. It must seem a little like hell, with its silent goons carrying menacing shapes, with your head strapped into place, though this allegory came well before we invented the concept of hell.

A few days after the towers fall, our vice president, the second in command, who some claim is the first in command, goes on television to make a pronouncement — *It's going to be vital for us to use any means at our disposal. We're going to have to work toward the dark side, in the shadows, if you will.*

A few weeks after the vice president invites us over to the dark side, a man named Ibn Shaykh al-Libi is sent, via a secret program called "extraordinary rendition," to a dungeon in Egypt, where he utters a lie about chemical weapons and Saddam and Osama, a lie that will be used to justify a war, a lie extracted under torture. A year later Colin Powell, who is believed by most to embody a preternatural form of integrity, will repeat this lie, he will repeat it on a world stage, and most will believe him. I will believe him, for a moment, until a document, folded into the same lie, referring to the purchase of something called "yellowcake," reveals itself to be a clumsy forgery.

The Allegory of the Cave is often read as an allegory of perception, how we come to believe that the shadows on the wall, which terrify or entertain us, are real. But how did we end up in a cave, how did we end up, hour after hour, day after day, staring at shadows on the wall? Why don't we simply look away? And why are we so afraid?

If Plato had seen me standing outside my burning house in my ghoulish pajamas that summer night, what would he have said? What would he have written if he had seen me spending day after day watching the Three Stooges pummel one another in my box of shadows? What insight would he have if he saw me standing in a Best Buy on Broadway before a bank of televisions, watching the first tower fall, when I could have simply looked south and seen the real thing? Would he say I was caught up in the world as it appeared, unable to enter into its essence? Would he say my eyes were having trouble adjusting to the light?

My Teufelberg (Bewilderment)

My mother told me a story, just once, of how as a girl she'd been tied to a chair, the chair balanced at the top of the attic stairs, teetering, her captors threatening to send her end over end, tumbling down. I don't know if they did this more than once, and I don't know what they wanted — a question answered, a promise made — beyond the usual childhood cruelties, or if they ever got it.

And then there's my father, and the stories he tells. The two are nearly inseparable by now, my father and his stories — the same handful over and over again, his repertoire, always told the same way. A liar always tells his story the same way, I've heard said, except that some — most — of my father's stories have, improbably, turned out to be true. The story of his father inventing the life raft. The story of the novel he spent his whole life writing. The story of robbing a few banks.

One of his stories, one I found too bizarre to engage with at all, is of being locked up in federal prisons for two years, which is true, but while there, he claims to have been tortured — experimented on, sleep deprived, drugged, sexually humiliated — and I don't know if this is true or not. Understand, it is hard and getting harder to get a straight answer from my father, as his alcoholism slips into its twilight stage. When I ask him about his prison time now, he looks wildly around the room or park or coffee shop and whispers, *I can't talk about that here.*

This morning I find in my in-box this note from Julia, my friend in Berlin — "I was standing on the Teufelberg (The Devil's Mountain) with a friend last night, listening to Patti Smith playing in the stadium below, and I thought of you. The Teufelberg is made from all the junk of the war, the broken houses and so on. It is a big mountain, and we stood there looking out over my strange and terrible and beautiful city. Where are you?"

My Teufelberg. The Devil's Mountain. All the junk of the war.

Here I am, I think, writing about my mother (again), and here I am, writing about my father (again), writing about my shadow, writing about my unborn daughter, building my own Devil's Mountain, piling up all the junk of the war. When asked, I'll sometimes say I'm writing about torture, but I've found that when I say the word *torture*, many go glassy-eyed, as if I had just dropped a stone into a deep, deep well. When asked, I'll sometimes say I'm writing about the way photographs are a type of dream, or I'll say that I'm writing a memoir of bewilderment, and leave it at that, but what I mean is the bewilderment of what it is to wake up in an America that has legalized torture.

What I don't say, what I should say, is that what I'm really writing about is Proteus, the mythological creature who changes shape as you hold on to him, who changes into the shape of that which most terrifies you, as you ask him your question, your one simple question — the question is often simply a variation of *How do I get home?*

Istanbul

(2007) I had a dream about this room before I found myself here. In the dream the room was the size of a barn, with six spaces divided by hastily built half-walls. In each room there was a shackle screwed into the floor, nothing more than a large eyebolt, really, and I worried that this eyebolt wasn't strong enough — it needed to be strong enough to hold a man. It needed to be like the shackles I had seen in the photographs, cemented into the floors. The rooms were dark, empty, the prisoners hadn't been brought in yet. I thought to leave a candle, and a lighter, but then I thought the man would use the lighter to set fire to his shackles, or to himself, or to the whole barn. I ended up leaving the candle and lighter in a corner, and if the man could reach it, if he knew to look, then come what may.

By the time I finally land in Istanbul I'm a day late — everything has already started. The taxi drops me off at the Armada Hotel. I check in and ask where the lawyers are, and within a few minutes I knock on the door to room 223. After brief introductions I find myself sitting next to a man — call him Achmad — telling the story of how he ended up in a photograph, a photograph I have seen many times by now, a photograph the whole world has seen. A photograph is like a house — once it is made, we then start counting the days and then the years from when it was made. My eyes take a moment to adjust to the light. *Tell me what happened next,* the lawyer whispers.

The room turns out to be utterly mundane — well lit, carpeted, a hotel room that one could find in any major city. The bed has been removed, and in its place is a table. The lawyer sits at the table, across from the ex-detainee. She is here to gather his statement as part of a lawsuit against an American company that has allegedly profited from torture. Another lawyer sits next to her, typing out the tran-

script of the conversation on a laptop. The translator sits at the head of the table, between the lawyer asking the questions and the ex-detainee. There is also an artist present, seated away from the table, near the window, painting a watercolor portrait in a large book, its pages folded like an accordion. When he isn't painting the portrait, he fills in the white space around the painted head with bits of what is being said. The seat next to the ex-detainee is empty, and this is where I sit, my notebook open.

Transmogrification

When I was younger, I worked for gangsters for a few years, mostly they just smuggled drugs. In my mind I was being groomed to make a run, to take a boat down to Colombia, sail it back full of marijuana, and it is very likely this was true. It was simple — I'd grown up broke, my mother was still broke, and this was a way to get some money. Fast money, real money. Years later, when I first moved to New York, I lived in Brooklyn with an artist who would become one of my closest friends. He'd grown up with money, and after a few years, when I told him about my misspent youth, about my plan of making a run, he had a hard time processing it, especially the part where I knew I was putting myself in a position where I might have needed to carry a gun, which meant I might have needed to use it. No way, he said, you'd never do that, and I tried to explain that it wasn't something I was proud of, it wasn't something I would have wanted to have done, but at that time, when I was eighteen, nineteen, I was willing to put myself in the position where it might happen.

What I was trying to say, maybe, is that I don't know what it is I'm capable of transforming into. When I was nineteen, I knew the consequences of getting onto a boat laden with drugs, I knew the consequences of carrying a gun, and part of me was willing to do it anyway, or at least to consider doing it. But maybe it's more accurate to say what John Lennon said, in a fictionalized version of his life — the film *Backbeat* — when asked why he was so angry. *I'm not angry*, he answered — *Just fucken desperate.*

Istanbul

(2007) It is likely you have seen Achmad before — he is the naked man being dragged by a leash out of a cell by a girl named England. This is the third time the lawyers have met with Achmad. The first time was in Amman, Jordan, where he told about his years in Abu

Ghraib. The second time was in Istanbul, when a doctor examined him, to corroborate his scars. This time is for him to look through the binders of the now-famous photographs, to identify who and what he can.

Achmad was a businessman awaiting a shipment of air conditioners from Iran when the CIA broke into his hotel room and arrested him. He was in his late twenties then. When we get to the photograph of him being dragged by the leash, we stop. *I remember that night,* he says, *I remember everything.* And then he tells us the story. The lawyer never takes her eyes off his face as he speaks, softly repeating, *And then what happened, and then what,* as he tells of his body being dragged from room to room, cell to cell.

It is only a year since Achmad was released from prison. The soldiers called the day of his release "the happy bus day." *Tomorrow you will get to ride on the happy bus,* they told him. Today, a year later, Achmad shakes his head as he looks at the photographs of himself from that time — *I cannot recognize myself as that man,* he says. *Can you?*

Two Dogs

Two dogs live inside me, a woman in Texas tells me, *and the one I feed is the one that will grow.* She tells me this as a way to explain why she won't have coffee with me, ever — married, kids, happy, but sometimes her mind wanders, sometimes she thinks that another man, one that looks at her with kindness, one that seems to listen, is the answer, though she is unsure of the question. The thing is, her husband does all these things for her — he listens, he's kind, there is desire, they make love often, everything's fine. But still, still, she's got these two hungry dogs inside her.

But wait — this woman didn't say her dogs were hungry, but aren't all dogs hungry? *Here Shadow, here Thanatos. Here Eros, here Light.* The one she feeds is the one that will grow, but does that mean that the other one will grow smaller? Will it grow so small as to vanish? Do the dogs that live inside her come from some Alice-in-Wonderland world? Are they fighting inside her, does she love them both, does she sometimes think if one died it would be easier? But then she will have one dog inside her and the corpse of another dog —

what good would that do, in the long run, what with all the other corpses we eventually end up dragging around inside us?

Istanbul

(2007) There is a moment in Achmad's story when words are not enough, as there will be in every story, a moment when the only way to tell us what happened is to show us what they did to his body, and at this moment he pushes back from the table and stands — *They hang me this way*, he says, and raises his arms out to his sides as if crucified in the air. There is something about him standing, about his body suddenly rising up, that completely unhinges me, something about it that makes his words real in a way they hadn't been before. The word made flesh. At this moment I get it: These words are about his body, it was his body this story happened to, the body that is right here beside me, in this room I could barely even imagine just yesterday, his body that is now filling the air above our heads, our eyes upturned to see him. Achmad stands there like that, arms outstretched — the scribe has nothing to write, the painter has nothing to paint, the interpreter has nothing to interpret, the lawyer's eyes are fixed on his eyes, all his words have led to this moment, when his body is finally allowed to speak. The lawyer shakes her head slightly. *And what happened next?* she says softly, and he lowers his arms and sits.

Mexico

I have a packet of photographs from when my grandparents were first married, before they had children, or maybe they simply left the kids at home. The photographs are of a road trip to Mexico, clearly from a time before everything fell apart. In each of the photographs, they are smiling — maybe it was after my grandfather got back from the war, or else it was just before. It could have been in the thirties, they had money in the Depression, they could have afforded a road trip. These few photographs reveal more about their early life together than anything either one of them ever told me. In one blurry photograph my grandfather is flat on his back on a hotel bed, a bottle of what I imagine to be tequila rising straight up from his mouth to the ceiling, as if a flower is growing from his mouth, as if he is going to finally fill himself completely. I imagine my grandmother took this shot, and I imagine her laughing gleefully as she did, having just taken a pull herself.

Lexington, Kentucky

Here's a story my father tells about his time in federal prison: "They left me alone in a dark room for days on end, shackled to the floor, and when they moved me, which they did constantly and for no reason, they shackled me even more — penis included." What? Did he say *penis included*? This is one of his stories that I'd turn away from, it seemed too far-fetched, but as I learn more, I am not so sure.

One day I hear the historian Alfred McCoy on the radio, talking about the CIA's fifty-year involvement in developing the torture techniques we saw enacted in the Abu Ghraib photographs. The most effective technique, they found, was to combine sensory deprivation with self-inflicted pain — think of the iconic photograph of the man on the box, hooded, his arms outstretched. This position is not new. It's called the "Vietnam." At one point he mentions the medical wing of a federal prison as the site of early experimentation. Federal prisoners were used to test the limits of what the body, the psyche, could withstand. Two of the main sites of these clandestine and illegal experiments were the prisons in Lexington, Kentucky, and Marion, Illinois, both of which my father passed through during his stint behind bars.

Istanbul

(2007) At times, in the silence between when a question is asked and when the translator translates it and when the answer is given, the only sound is the *clink clink clink* of the artist cleaning his brush in a glass of water. After four hours, we finish going over the photographs with Achmad, and we are all completely drained. As we stand to thank him, he reaches into his bag and takes out a camera. It looks so odd in his hands. He asks the translator to ask us to stand against

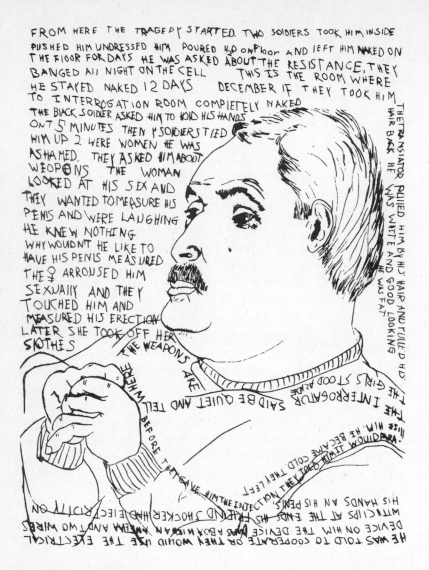

one wall — he gestures toward it. We all awkwardly move to one corner of the room, gather together in front of a painting of a hammam. Achmad raises the camera to his eye and smiles — *It's not only the Americans who like to take photographs*, he says, and we all break down laughing.

All Living Things Have Shoulders

I worked in New York City public schools for a few years as an itinerant poet — Crown Heights, Harlem — lugging a satchel heavy with books on the train every morning. These were the years of unprecedented wealth in the United States, and if you wanted to find the worst public school in any city, you just had to look up the one named after Martin Luther King. Much of what I taught was directed toward finding out what the students saw every day — it was a way to honor their lives, which isn't generally taught in public schools. The beginning exercises were very simple: Tell me one thing you saw on the way to school this morning, tell me one thing you saw last night when you got home. Describe something you see every day, describe something you only saw once and wondered about from then on. Tell me a dream, tell me a story someone told you, tell me something you've never told anyone else before. No one, in school at least, had ever asked them what their lives were like, no one had asked them to tell about their days. In this sense it felt like a radical act — I tried to imagine what might happen if each of them knew how important their lives were.

In the schools I'd visit, I'd sometimes pick up a discarded sheet of paper from the hallway floor, something a student had written in his notebook and then torn out. Sometimes I could tell that he had been given an assignment, and that he had tried to fulfill it, and by tearing it out it was clear that he felt he had somehow failed. Out of all the ephemera I've bent down to collect from black-and-green elementary-school linoleum floors over the years, one has stayed with me. Likely it was part of a research paper, likely for biology. It started with a general statement, which was, I imagine, to be followed by supporting facts. The sentence, neatly printed on the first line, was this: *All living things have shoulders* — after this there was nothing, not even a period, as if even as he was writing it, he realized something was wrong, that he would never be able to support what he was only beginning to say, that no facts would ever justify it. All living things have shoulders — the first word is pure energy, the sweeping *All*, followed by the heartbeat of *living* — who wouldn't be filled with hope having found this beginning? Then the drift begins, into uncertainty

— *things* — a small misstep, not so grave that it couldn't be righted, but it won't be easy. Now something has to be said, some conclusion. I can almost hear the teacher, I can almost see what she has written on the blackboard — "Go from the general to the specific" — and what could be more general than "All living things," and what could be more specific than "shoulders"? He reads it over once and knows it can never be reconciled, and so it is banished from his notebook. *All living things have shoulders* — this one line, I have carried it with me since, I have tried to write a poem from it over and over, and failed over and over. I have now come to believe that it already is a poem. All living things have shoulders. Period. The end. A poem.

Istanbul

(2007) As we meet with these men in the following hours and days, each will have the wrist tag they were issued and required to wear while in prison. The wrist tag has their name, birth date, date they were arrested, and who arrested them. It also lists where they were held — Abu Ghraib, Camp Cropper, Camp Bucca. Surprisingly, each wrist tag also has a tiny head shot of the man, which makes it easy for us now to verify their identity.

First it was the businessman, then it was a taxi driver, then a cleric (the translator calls him a "preacher"), then an ex-soldier, then a dentist, the week goes on and on — the butcher, the baker, the candlestick maker — could they be any more ordinary?

Now it is a thirty-year-old student, telling of being picked up in a sweep — beaten and shackled and hooded and thrown from Humvee to helicopter, to eventually arrive at a building he now believes is near the airport, either in Mosul or Baghdad. Once inside he finds himself in a large room, maybe the size of a gymnasium, filled with black boxes lined up in rows. Maybe a hundred boxes, maybe two hundred, hard for him to say — he was hooded constantly and quickly lost track of night and day. The boxes are about two and a half feet wide, six feet long. He is thrown into one of these boxes, for days that turn into weeks, unable to straighten his body, barely able to breathe. Every twenty or thirty minutes a soldier kicks the box, or hits it hard with a club, and it makes his shackled body jump. Around him he can hear the screams and pleadings of his fellow prisoners — those with stomach pains, those with infections, those slowly going mad. Among themselves the Iraqis call these boxes *tawabeet aswada*, or *nash aswada* — "black coffins."

Nash aswada, black coffins — I can't help thinking of them as the shadows of the flag-draped coffins we aren't allowed to see.

During a break in the interview, the artist tells the student how handsome he is. The student listens as this word, "handsome," is translated, smiles slightly, and murmurs, *Shukran*. One sometimes needs to be told that one is still beautiful.

The Falling Is the Rain

The week after I get back from Istanbul I go on a meditation retreat with Thich Nhat Hanh, the Vietnamese Zen master. I've been studying with him off and on (mostly off) for eighteen years now. I will sit for a week in silence, listen as he speaks, but I end up talking more than planned. My dharma discussion group's focus is addiction, and a handful of us addicts climb a great maple tree each afternoon to talk among the branches until sunset.

Thich Nhat Hahn says it is a mistake to say, "The rain is falling," to say, "The wind is blowing." *What is rain if it is not falling?* he asks. *What is wind if it is not blowing?* The falling is the rain, the blowing is the wind. The next day, in the tree, I bring it up. *He's talking about Impermanence*, someone says. *It's the same reason we climb trees*, someone else offers — *it's that we were once monkeys*.

Let's say you're a soldier in Iraq, assigned to a military prison. You've been told to soften the prisoners up, to get them ready to be interrogated the next day. Give them a bad night, you've been told, so you give them a bad night — you strip them naked, you throw cold water on them, you do not let them sleep. The rules have changed, you've been told, the gloves have come off. One guy, whenever you knee him, he cries, "Allah" — it becomes a game to see how many times you can make him cry Allah.

Let's say you've been trained as an interrogator, you've been told that one of the thousands before you has the answer that will save an

American city from an attack. It might be the city your wife and child live in, you don't know. You walk into a room, a man is hanging from the ceiling by his wrists, a sack over his head. You've been told that a bomb is ticking, and in this room you swear you can almost hear it. You remove the sack, you take hold of the man's shoulders, you look into his eyes.

In order to continue you need to be certain of the outcome, you must push aside any bewilderment you have, ignore any questions besides the one question. The falling is the rain, the blowing is the wind. If the Zen master were in that room with you, would he say that the ticking is the bomb? Telltale heart, would he ask if you were willing to set your house on fire to stop the sounds in your head? As our president said before the bombing of Baghdad, "The outcome of the current crisis is already determined" — this is the kind of certainty you need to continue.

So here I am, the man before me is Proteus. As I hold on to him, as I ask him my question, as I listen for his answer, he transforms, into a dog on a leash, into a man dancing with panties on his head, into a bruise, into a madman, into a waterfall, into a cockroach in a bowl of rice. Into a man strapped in a chair, into thirty men strapped into chairs, refusing to eat, thirty tubes forced down their noses.

So here I am, my fingers tight around Proteus's neck, asking that same question, over and over, as if the answer exists, inside the prisoner, inside the beloved, inside my mother, inside my father, inside me, as if the answer is there and just needs to be released.

And so here I am, holding my own head, dunking it into a bathtub full of water, repeating a meaningless question over and over, knowing that I will never get the question right.

And here I am, holding my breath, and then letting it go.

Immersion

Swim until the world becomes water, swim to the center of the pool, practice hanging, practice drowning, raise your arms above your head, let your body sink. Think of it as practice for when they come — there is only so much they can do with your body. Swim to the lad-

der, hang from it as you catch your breath, let your arms hang behind you like wings, then sink slowly into the water — your arms
will raise to shoulder height behind you, to your ears, any farther and
they will dislocate. No one is forcing you to do this, you do it because
you have heard that it is done to others. Sink farther and you will
sign the confession, you will give names, you will say whatever they
tell you to say. But when they check your story, it will be water, it will

OUR EYES WERE COVERED WITH PLASTIC WRAPS AND
GOGGLES AND MOVED TO 5C. WE WERE ASKED TO UNDRESS,
AND STAYED UNDER THE HOT SUN FOR HOURS HAND-
CUFFED.
WE WERE NOT GUILTY OF ANYTHING. IF I HAD DONE
SOMETHING, I WOULD
HAVE BEEN PROUD
BUT WE HAD NOT
DONE ANYTHING.

BORN 12 JANUARY 1973
ARRESTED 21 MAY

slip through their hands. On the confession you will have signed the name "bird," because that's what you think of, hanging there with your arms behind you. All living things have shoulders, you think, hanging there.

Slow-Moving Lava

A friend tells this story: While living in Hawaii, a volcano erupted near his village, and after the initial blast, which destroyed the top of the mountain and those villages in the vicinity, the lava continued to slowly ooze out over the next several months, so slowly that you could walk up to the wall of it, reach your hand out, press against it, feel its warmth. How high was this wall? I imagine twenty feet, more or less — so high that you'd have to tilt your head back to see the sky. The village my friend was staying in was downhill, spared the initial blast, but the lava kept oozing out, and the scientists came, to calculate its movement, how long it would take to reach the village, which house would be the first to be swallowed, to ignite, beneath the slow-motion wave. Is this better than a flood, better than a fire? It gives you time to move everything, if you are able, but it also gives you time to wonder if it's a waste of time to move, to wake up day after day and hope that the disaster won't reach you, in spite of what the scientists say. If you were able, if you had the resources, you could move the entire house, put it on a barge and float it to the next island. But I got the idea that the houses were not much more than thatch and mud, I got the idea that most simply went each day to the wall of lava, put a hand to it, hoped it would slow down, hoped it would run out of juice, hoped it would simply stop.

My grandmother does have one story she tells about that trip to Mexico, though she never mentions my grandfather when she tells it. She was walking down a village street, the village in the shadow of a volcano, and a boy came running up to her with a ball of hot lava in his hands, and he shaped it into a monkey right there in front of her. On one of her shelves sits a small statue of a monkey, and she holds it in her hands as she tells the story, as if it were still warm, as if she could still transform it.

JONATHAN FRANZEN

■

David Foster Wallace

FROM *Sonora Review*

*The following are remarks from a memorial service for David Foster Wallace,
held in New York City on October 23rd 2008.*

LIKE A LOT OF WRITERS, but even more than most, Dave loved to
be in control of things. He was easily stressed by chaotic social situ-
ations. I only ever saw him twice go to a party without Karen. One of
them, hosted by Adam Begley, I almost physically had to drag him to,
and as soon as we were through the front door and I took my eye off
him for one second, he made a U-turn and went back to my apartment to chew tobacco and read a book. The second party he had no
choice but to stay for, because it was celebrating the publication of
Infinite Jest. He survived it by saying thank you, again and again, with
painfully exaggerated formality.

One thing that made Dave an extraordinary college teacher was
the formal structure of the job. Within those confines, he could
safely draw on his enormous native store of kindness and wisdom
and expertise. The structure of interviews was safe in a similar way.
When Dave was the subject, he could relax into taking care of his interviewer. When he was the journalist himself, he did his best work
when he was able to find a technician — a cameraman following
John McCain, a board operator on a radio show — who was thrilled
to meet somebody genuinely interested in the arcana of his job. Dave
loved details for their own sake, but details were also an outlet for the
love bottled up in his heart: a way of connecting, on relatively safe
middle ground, with another human being.

Which was, approximately, the description of literature that he and I came up with in our conversations and correspondence in the early 1990s. I'd loved Dave from the very first letter I ever got from him, but the first two times I tried to meet him in person, up in Cambridge, he flat-out stood me up. Even after we did start hanging out, our meetings were often stressful and rushed — much less intimate than exchanging letters. Having loved him at first sight, I was always straining to prove that I could be funny enough and smart enough, and he had a way of gazing off at a point a few miles distant which made me feel as if I were failing to make my case. Not many things in my life ever gave me a greater sense of achievement than getting a laugh out of Dave.

But that "neutral middle ground on which to make a deep connection with another human being": this, we decided, was what fiction was for. "A way out of loneliness" was the formulation we agreed to agree on. And nowhere was Dave more totally and gorgeously able to maintain control than in his written language. He had the most commanding and exciting and inventive rhetorical virtuosity of any writer alive. Way out at word number 70 or 100 or 140 in a sentence deep into a three-page paragraph of macabre humor or fabulously reticulated self-consciousness, you could smell the ozone from the crackling precision of his sentence structure, his effortless and pitch-perfect shifting among ten different levels of high, low, middle, technical, hipster, nerdy, philosophical, vernacular, vaudevillian, hortatory, tough-guy, broken-hearted, lyrical diction. Those sentences and those pages, when he was able to be producing them, were as true and safe and happy a home as any he had during most of the twenty years I knew him. So I could tell you stories about the bickering little road trip he and I once took, or I could tell you about the wintergreen scent that his chew gave to my little apartment whenever he stayed with me, or I could tell you about the awkward chess games we played and the even more awkward tennis rallying we sometimes did — the comforting structure of the games versus the weird deep fraternal rivalries boiling along underneath — but truly the main thing was the writing. For most of the time I knew Dave, the most intense interaction I had with him was sitting alone in my armchair, night after night, for ten days, and reading the manuscript of *Infinite Jest*.

That was the book in which, for the first time, he'd arranged himself and the world the way he wanted them arranged. At the most microscopic level: Dave Wallace was as passionate and precise a punctuator of prose as has ever walked this earth. At the most global level: he produced a thousand pages of world-class jest which, although the mode and quality of the humor never wavered, became less and less and less funny, section by section, until, by the end of the book, you felt the book's title might just as well have been *Infinite Sadness*. Dave nailed it like nobody else ever had.

And so now this handsome, brilliant, funny, kind midwestern man with an amazing spouse and a great local support network and a great career and a great job at a great school with great students has taken his own life, and the rest of us are left behind to ask (to quote from *Infinite Jest*), "So yo then, man, what's your story?"

One good, simple, modern story would go like this: "A lovely, talented personality fell victim to a severe chemical imbalance in his brain. There was the person of Dave, and then there was the disease, and the disease killed the man as surely as cancer might have." This story is at once sort of true and totally inadequate. If you're satisfied with this story, you don't need the stories that Dave wrote — particularly not those many, many stories in which the duality, the separateness, of person and disease is problematized or outright mocked. One obvious paradox, of course, is that Dave himself, at the end, did become, in a sense, satisfied with this simple story and stopped connecting with any of those more interesting stories he'd written in the past and might have written in the future. His suicidality got the upper hand and made everything in the world of the living irrelevant.

But this doesn't mean there are no more meaningful stories for us to tell. I could tell you ten different versions of how he arrived at the evening of September 12, some of them very dark, some of them very angering to me, and most of them taking into account Dave's many adjustments, as an adult, in response to his near-death of suicide as a late adolescent. But there is one particular not-so-dark story that I know to be true and that I want to tell now, because it's been such a great happiness and privilege and endlessly interesting challenge to be Dave's friend.

People who like to be in control of things can have a hard time with intimacy. Intimacy is anarchic and mutual and definitionally in-compatible with control. You seek to control things because you're afraid, and about five years ago, very noticeably, Dave stopped be-ing so afraid. Part of this came of having settled into a good, stable situation here at Pomona. Another really huge part of it was his fi-nally meeting a woman who was right for him and, for the first time, opened up the possibility of his having a fuller and less rigidly struc-tured life. I noticed, when we spoke on the phone, that he'd begun to tell me he loved me, and I suddenly felt, on my side, that I didn't have to work so hard to make him laugh or to prove that I was smart. Karen and I managed to get him to Italy for a week, and instead of spending his days in his hotel room, watching TV, as he might have done a few years earlier, he was having lunch on the terrace and eat-ing octopus and trudging along to dinner parties in the evening and actually enjoying hanging out with other writers casually. He sur-prised everyone, and maybe most of all himself. Here was a genu-inely fun thing he might well have done again.

About a year later, he decided to get himself off the medication that had lent stability to his life for more than twenty years. Again, there are a lot of different stories about why exactly he decided to this. But one thing he made very clear to me, when we talked about it, was that he wanted a chance at a more ordinary life, with less freakish control and more ordinary pleasure. It was a decision that grew out his love for Karen, out of his wish to produce a new and more mature kind of writing, and out of having glimpsed a different kind of future. It was an incredibly scary and brave thing for him to try, because Dave was full of love, but he was also full of fear — he had all too ready access to those depths of infinite sadness.

So the year was up and down, and he had a crisis in June, and a very hard summer. When I saw him in July he was skinny again, like the late adolescent he'd been during his first big crisis. One of the last times I talked to him after that, in August, on the phone, he asked me to tell him a story of how things would get better. I repeated back to him a lot of what he'd been saying to me in our conversations over the previous year. I said he was in a terrible and dangerous place because he was to trying to make real changes as a person and as a writer. I said that the last time he'd been through near-death experiences, he'd emerged and written, very quickly, a book that was light-years beyond what he'd been doing before his collapse. I said he was a stubborn control freak and know-it-all — "So are you!" he shot back at me — and I said that people like us are so afraid to relinquish control that sometimes the only way we can force ourselves to open up and change is to bring ourselves to an access of misery and the brink of self-destruction. I said he'd undertaken his change in medication because he wanted to grow up and have a better life. I said I thought his best writing was ahead of him. And he said: "I like that story. Could you do me a favor and call me up every four or five days and tell me another story like it?"

Unfortunately I only had one more chance to tell him the story, and by then he wasn't hearing it. He was in horrible, minute-by-minute anxiety and pain. The next times I tried to call him, after that, he wasn't picking up the phone or returning messages. He'd gone down into the well of infinite sadness, beyond the reach of story, and he didn't make it out. But he had a beautiful, yearning innocence, and he was trying.

■

Monster

FROM *Post Road*

MOST OF THE TIME, THE PANTHER SLEPT. Its breaths were resonant and shallow in the apartment. Perhaps it was sick; Danny couldn't tell. His mother and father never heard it. When he looked up from his breakfast and cocked his head one way, they told him to go back to eating. He awakened his father in the middle of the night to tell him about it. "There's an animal in our house," Danny said. His father rolled over onto his side and said, "Danny, honey, whoever's picking on you at school, you just tell him to stop." It was almost dawn. Danny was alarmed by his father's apathy. He couldn't believe such a tall, smart man would be willing to risk his family's lives just to get some sleep. "Who will be here to pour milk on my cereal tomorrow?" Danny asked. "There is nothing in our house but us," his father said.

When Danny came home from school, he gave himself the job of trying to find the panther. He started in the kitchen, the north star of his compass, and waited for the breathing. It was a raspy breathing, like a grandfather's. Sometimes it spoke. These days were particularly frightening, and Danny always thanked the afternoon sun for being out. When the panther spoke, it said, "Kill me for the fun of it."

Or it said, "I'm very tired."

Or it said, "I'm under your chair right now."

It said all these things in the raspy grandfather's voice. It sounded like it smoked the Havana cigars Danny's father used to favor. Danny listened to it and wondered what it wanted. He knew from the start that he wouldn't be heard if he spoke back. He sat at the kitchen table like a pilot in his cockpit. If the breathing got louder, his neck started to tingle and he knew the panther was right behind him. He could feel the wetness of the animal's nostrils, the heavy abandon of its paws. He thought he'd go deaf from listening so much.

One day at school, Mrs. Welles was smiling broadly as her class took their seats. She told them something that didn't matter to them, something about talking to the principal and the other second-grade teacher for a long time.

"We will do a pen pal project," she said, the first thing they listened to.

Marcus, whom everybody hated, raised his hand. "Do we have to write to them first?"

"Let me explain," Mrs. Welles said. "Our pen pals live in Tangier, which is a city in Morocco. They go to the Darul Arqam School. We have been chosen to write to them because we are a magnet school, and all of you are excellent writers. They have sent us the first batch of letters. We will write letters back and forth for the next nine months. In May we'll get to meet our pen pals. They will fly to America and then spend three weeks here as part of an exchange program. We have been given the job of introducing them to our country before they come."

Emma, the girl who sat next to Danny, jabbed him in the ribs. "They can't speak English," she whispered.

At the end of the day, Mrs. Welles gave them the first batch of letters. Danny opened his. The letter was written in blue pen, in cursive, and had a picture of a dove drawn at the top.

Dear Pen Pal,

I am named Djamel Abd al-Hakiim. My last name is "servant of the wise." We are learning to speak the American langage.

Danny turned the letter over. There was nothing else. The bell rang and he stayed in his seat. Emma sat down next to him and looked at him, her eyes wide. She kissed him on the cheek.

"Stop it," he said.

"Mine's named Aisha," she whispered, ignoring him. "She has a pet monkey."

"No, she doesn't."

Emma produced a letter. Aisha had written two paragraphs. At the bottom, she'd pasted a picture of a scrawny, hairy thing.

"It's her pet," Emma said.

At home, Danny put the letter from Djamel up on the refrigerator. Then he opened the door and got out a carton of milk. There was a sudden loudness, the noise of glasses rattling. The kitchen became a threatening mauve. Danny held his breath and looked into the living room. His father was reading the paper; he had set a tray out in front of him with a variety of glass bottles, some orange and some red.

"What're you drinking?" his father asked.

A sudden warmth flooded Danny's body. "I'm having cookies," he said. He realized he hadn't really answered the question. "I just poured milk."

"I'm having a mixture of things," his father said. "Your mother won't be home for a while."

Danny almost corrected him, but he knew better. His father was not to be corrected. If Danny's mother wouldn't be home for a while, then Danny's mother would be staying out until midnight. As if by fault of a weak foundation, a smile cracked across his father's face.

"Danny, sit down here. Come sit down next to me."

Danny did.

"How was your day at school?"

"It was allright."

They sat in silence. Danny's father reached down and planted his hand on Danny's head. He began to pet Danny with heavy strokes. This lasted until Danny's hair became a disorganized nest, and his father looked down at him and grinned.

"You'll come back tomorrow and tell me how school went?"

Danny nodded. He stood up and went back into the kitchen. His father had begun humming a melody that would have been operatic had he opened his mouth to sing. Outside, a truck coming from the South Loop buckled loudly beneath its cargo. Danny became aware of the dull throb of radio voices in the living room, a noise that had been going on since he got home. He positioned three cookies on a plate and looked out the window at the sky. The sun was painfully bright, probably afraid to give up summer. He wanted to tell his father about this, or at least see if he had noticed it, and he leaned into the living room to announce his discovery apropos the sun. His father was not sitting in the chair. The panther had taken his place. It wore his father's robe and socks and held his father's glass of colors.

"You're here." It was all Danny could think to say.

The panther smiled, showing two rows of fragile, conical teeth. "I'm usually here." This was the first time it had responded to anything Danny said.

"You took my father's spot."

"I did."

"Did you eat him?"

It laughed at this.

"Did you eat him?"

"Of course not. How inelegant would that be? I've merely thrown him out the window."

Danny felt something catch in his throat. The panther set the glass of colors down and gestured to the window. Danny walked forward and pulled up the blinds. There was something on the pavement that looked like the remains of a baby bird. It had the wings and beak of a pigeon and the eyes and thin-lipped mouth of Danny's father.

Danny looked at the panther. "Is he dead?"

"Yes," it said.

He looked back out the window. A small pool of blood had formed around the bird. The blood was the deepest sort of crimson Danny had ever seen.

"I'll tell the police about you," he said.

The panther laughed again. It crossed its legs and the floor shifted with the terrifying weight of a real man.

Danny knew he had to tell his mother, but she wasn't home anymore to be told. She was usually teaching at the university. When she was home, she wanted to go straight to the kitchen to work on Danny's tux. She had decided a month ago that Danny needed a fancy outfit and had gone out and bought him a "crisp white shirt and a roll of the finest black silk," the latter of which she intended to make into a jacket. She had not given any thought to the pants. There was no reason for Danny to want or need formalwear, but he liked standing on the table while his mother pulled at the hem of his jacket, which sat on him Tarzan-like without a row of buttons.

While Danny's mother worked, Danny's father stood in the doorway or sat in a chair with his hands on his knees. The wife and son were two free agents independent of his influence. He could comment on the jacket, on how nice the fabric was, he could ask if anyone wanted dinner, but he never got a response. Ignored, he left the room and started making noise elsewhere in the apartment. He was always back in the kitchen doorway ten or fifteen minutes later. He was a failure. The place had a magnetic pull on him.

Danny's mother told Danny to smile and said he looked like a Nobel Laureate. She wrapped her hands around his waist to take a measurement of his hips. From above she looked older than she was. Danny could see pieces of silver in her hair. She was beautiful, but in a hidden way. She wore a strong prescription for farsightedness. She was always having to adjust her eyes to see Danny. When he was far away, she put her glasses on her head to see him. When he was close, she had to wear the glasses and squint at him through them. Her eyes were huge and white halos of light ringed her eyebrows when she looked up at him from below. The glasses ruined her face. Danny would gladly have guided her by the hand if she ever chose to give them up.

It was because his mother had such difficulty seeing that he didn't want to tell her about the panther. But it was necessary, it was important; if he didn't tell her, she'd die. While she worked on his tux jacket, while his father leaned in the doorway, Danny decided he couldn't postpone it any longer.

"There's no such thing as a creature living in our house," his mother said. "I'd know, honey."

"I'd be the first to know," his father said.

Danny looked over at his father. He was forlorn, bearlike.

"But it's hard to recognize because it acts like a person," Danny said.

"Are you having these dreams again?" His mother smiled a little.

"When I was little, I used to dream that I lived in a house of water. Everything in the house was liquid, and all of my toys were this really bright aquamarine. I couldn't touch anything without my hand going right through, but everyone else could."

"Could what?" his father asked.

"Could touch things," she said without looking at him. "I was completely powerless. I felt like a ghost."

Danny could feel the cold pressure of a pin against his side. There was a sharpness, and he winced. He placed two fingers under the jacket and then put them in his mouth. His mother had accidentally drawn his blood.

"I'm so sorry," she said.

He shook his head. He could feel tears forming in his eyes. His father turned around and went into the living room. The dusk made a specter of his huge frame.

"Danny, you have to put pressure on it," his mother said. She pressed her hand deep into his side. Danny thought he could feel his bones shifting.

"Don't prick me again," he said. She nodded.

Dear Djamel,

I go to a school called the Lab School Lower School. It is in Chicago wich is a city in Illinois. I am in the second grade. I like to play chess with my dad and meet new frends. My teacher says you are from Morocco, and that you are very smart. Plese tell me about what you have to eat there.

Yours,

Daniel J. Fein II

On a very rainy morning Mrs. Welles announced to the class that she was pregnant. She said jokingly that many of the preschool students had been asking her why she was looking fatter lately.

"I didn't think you could tell yet, but I guess you all could. I'm carrying a baby."

She smiled a haphazard smile that made Danny nervous.

"Can we feel it kicking yet?" a girl asked.

Mrs. Welles frowned. "It's just a shrimp now. We don't know if it's a boy or a girl."

"It looks like a shrimp?" Emma asked.

"Sort of, Emma. Do you all know that you start from a single cell that divides over and over again into many cells? A zygote?"

Marcus wanted to know how big a single cell was. A skinny girl in the front row reached across her desk to touch Mrs. Welles's stomach. The girl reeled back in delight.

"It's hard!" she said. "Hard like a rock!"

Danny walked home by himself in the rain. When he opened the door, the panther was standing on its haunches in the kitchen, reading Djamel's letter. Danny held his breath. Maybe catching the panther while it was distracted would make it go away.

"Were you busy at school?" it asked.

"I only answer questions like that when my dad asks them," Danny said.

The panther nodded and opened the freezer, staring at something pink.

"What are you doing?"

"Nothing," it said. It still hadn't turned around. "The refrigerator is pregnant, too."

Danny set his backpack down. The panther turned, making obvious the gruesome curvature of its spine. It was a hunchback today with a C-shaped neck.

"Pregnant with what?"

The panther said nothing. Danny stood on a chair and looked into the freezer. An infant was frozen in a block of ice, its spine bony like a crustacean's. It was breathing somehow, and it blinked every so often. A blue cord connected it at the belly to the ice machine.

"This refrigerator is pregnant," the panther said again. Danny didn't know why, but this made him cry. Tears froze on his cheeks and stung his skin. The panther reached a paw into the freezer to touch the frozen child.

Breathless, Danny stood at his mother's bedside.

"You can't keep ignoring it!" he said. "The panther put a baby in the fridge."

"What?" his mother asked. She kept her eyes closed when she spoke to him. "It's nighttime, Danny."

"There's a baby in the fridge. I saw it just now."

"You were dreaming," Danny's mother said.

"The panther was reading my pen pal letter."

Danny's mother opened her eyes. She put her glasses on and stood up. She walked without bending her knee joints, half her body still asleep. She was pushing Danny into his room. He lay in bed and she sat next to him.

"Will you go look in the kitchen?" he asked.

"Yes. As soon as you fall asleep, I'll check to see if it put a baby in the fridge."

Danny closed his eyes. He didn't want her to go, and he fidgeted every time the mattress threatened to leaven with her departure. He knew that she'd leave eventually, though, no matter how much he fidgeted. He knew he'd have to think of Mrs. Welles, and he'd have to imagine her stomach soft and sagging without a child in it. He would get in trouble for stealing her baby.

Danny was falling asleep. This was hard to postpone. Sleep was a demanding audience that insisted he stage dreams every night. His mother left the mattress slowly. He could feel himself rise. He grabbed the back of her shirt. She had to know by now that he was awake. She didn't. She stood up and went from the room without looking back. He saw a crescent of light blink on in the kitchen, and he watched her shadow. She was getting something from the cabinet. The light blinked off, and she hadn't checked the freezer. Danny pulled the covers up around his neck. She was too scared. She knew the truth.

Danny counted four weeks before Djamel sent him anything back. When he did send something, it wasn't a letter. The only thing in the envelope was a picture of two children with skin the color of bark, a boy and a girl. The boy looked to be about Danny's age with large eyes and a tall column of black hair. The girl was small, maybe four or five. They were both bare-chested and wet as if from a recent bath. The girl pointed to a hole in her mouth where she'd lost a tooth. Blood covered her lower lip. The boy looked at her as though she was a stranger, but he held her by the shoulders. There was a nervous excitement in the girl's face. Her cheeks were blotched from crying.

Danny put the picture in his backpack. He spent recess inside while the other children ran beneath the sky, which was a swollen dome of gray. He wrote three drafts of a letter and finally decided on one he liked:

Djamel,
There is a monster that lives in my house. It is a panther. My parent's don't think it is real. It has gigantic paws and oringe eyes. I'm very friht-ened of it, since it wants to kill everything. I dream about it a lot.
Yours,
Daniel J. Fein II

When he was done, he watched Mrs. Welles through the window. She had begun to wear long dresses with pleats just below the bust. Her stomach was a small hill upon which she rested both hands. Danny wondered if she had to stuff the bulge with cotton to keep it so large. He wondered how the baby had gotten in there in the first place, and imagined Mrs. Welles and a faceless man who was Mrs. Welles's husband standing naked in a room with a lot of sunshine, holding a wet infant between them. They rocked it to sleep and they rocked it awake and they never left the spot where they stood.

Danny's mother stopped being home enough to work on the tuxedo jacket, and Danny began to worry. He worried while watching cartoons, and his father mixed drinks of colors and said nothing. They never spoke. They let the TV speak. Every sound effect, joke, and indignant whistle contributed to their afternoon lingua franca. Sometimes, Danny's father would attempt eloquence by trying to speak with his eyes and mouth. He would look at Danny as if to say, *We are damned, and there is nothing we can do about it.* When Danny's mother finally came home at eight or nine or ten, the silence was broken. A new and frightening foreign tongue was introduced. She spoke loudly about overeager students keeping her until all hours talking about semiotics. She smelled like earth and dry flesh. When she was done taking off her coat and boots, she went down the hall to the master bedroom and called Danny's father, who rose from the couch majestically. They spoke together for a while, and the speaking became sharp; eventually they were yelling. This happened for several nights. Danny thought of Mrs. Welles's infant on these nights. He thought of what the noise in his house might sound like from inside the womb. He could only imagine the *thrum thrum thrum* of a woman's heartbeat. He held his chest and felt the pulse beneath his hands, drumlike, explosive.

"When will the baby be born?" he asked Mrs. Welles during class.

She had never heard him ask about the baby before. His question came as a surprise. "In four months. In the summertime, when you don't have school anymore."

Danny watched her touch the mound. She invited him to feel the child move. He didn't want to.

"I only want to see it when it's out of you," he said. "When it's alive."

"What do you mean, Danny?"

Some giggles could be heard from the back. One boy was practicing his whistling.

"I want to make sure it isn't dead inside of you. You know, from all the noise."

Nothing happened for a long time, and then Danny felt himself being pulled by the collar somewhere. Mrs. Welles was taking him to the principal. This sudden rift in their intimacy stunned him, and he felt betrayed.

"You are never to speak like that to me again," she said. Her face was dark. Her words sounded like barking. "Do you hear me, Mr. Fein?"

"I was just thinking about all the noise."

She left him at the office door. He thought he could see her crying.

When he came home from school that day, the baby was back in the freezer. It had grown since he'd last seen it. It had human features now: a smooth spine, toes, and fingers.

Djamel's second letter was shorter than his first:

Dear Daniel,

There was a lot of rain this week so that we never had playtime. During prayer today, I wished for your health.

Djamel Abd al-Hakiim

Djamel had drawn a picture of the boy he thought Danny was. The boy had blond hair and a large pair of glasses. His smile was an orange gash halfway across his face. A catlike black mass lurked behind him. Danny looked at the picture for a long time. Then he took a piece of paper from inside his desk and wrote "Dear Djamel" at the top. He erased it. He wrote the rest of the letter without thinking.

I bet there is a monster that follows you too.
Yours,
Daniel J. Fein II

Emma was looking at him. She smiled. It was easy to tell from her smile how she'd looked as a toddler.

"You're pale," she said.

"I know."

"You sad, Danny?"

Danny didn't say anything.

"You'll be all right," she said. He could smell something like lilacs on her breath. "It'll be all right."

Ren knocked on Danny's door one afternoon when neither of Danny's parents was home. He had the loose joints and lazy, haggard face of a teenager. He had white hair, which he wore long under a ski cap, and a white goatee. He smiled when Danny answered, and Danny saw that he was missing one of his front teeth.

"Does Professor Fein live here?" he asked. His eyes were glassy. "She gave me this address."

Danny watched him.

"Hey, little big man?"

"Professor Fein isn't home for another hour."

The teenager stood for a while, processing what he'd heard. When he was done, he offered his hand to shake.

"I'm Ren Wrolstad," he said.

Danny shook. He didn't introduce himself.

"Can I come in, Lieutenant?"

"Yes."

Ren stood in the kitchen and then looked in the living room. He wasn't satisfied with appreciating a room when he was actually in it; he always had to eavesdrop on the creaks and rattles of another room from afar. He did this in the living room, then the hallway, then in Danny's room. When he got to the master bedroom, however, he stopped pining for different rooms. He went to Professor Fein's vanity and began playing with her jewelry boxes. He tried several different perfumes on his neck until he sniffed with satisfaction — *That's the one* — and set the bottle down.

"Eau de lilac," Ren said. "So your mother smells good, right?"

Danny nodded. All he could see of Ren were his eyes, which glimmered a little when they caught the light from the window. Trucks drove by, casting obtuse, moving shadows on the opposite wall. One of these became the panther's uneven silhouette. It was sitting in a corner at the back of the room. It batted a paw against the wall and moved its mouth without speaking. It had metal teeth tonight, the top row golden and the bottom row bronze.

Danny almost screamed, but not because he was scared. He was angry now. The creature had appeared with a stranger in the house, the perfect time to make Danny look crazy "There's a monster behind you," he whispered.

"Oh yeah? What kind?"

"A panther. A panther that lives in my house." It was an embarrassed confession.

Ren sat down carefully. He was so close that Danny could feel their foreheads touching.

"Don't turn around," Danny said.

"Is it real?"

"Yes."

"You want me to fight it?"

"Yes."

The air became thick, unbreathable, and time slowed as Ren turned around to fight the panther. This would be the end. Danny knew it would be the end, because he was good at judging the beginning and end of things. He felt the finality, he felt Ren's strength, he felt the fibers of his own muscles stretch and ache with nervousness. There was a crashing noise, and a geometric beam of light was cast across the room. Danny's father was in the doorway, arms folded. He was home early from work. He looked at Danny and then Ren.

"Are you him?" Danny's father asked Ren.

Ren said, "*Jesus.*"

Danny's father grabbed Ren's collar and pulled him from the floor so fast his neck almost snapped. Then he took him to the kitchen. When Danny came out of the bedroom, Ren's face was a mosaic of purple and red, and his breaths were short and tortured.

Dear Daniel,
You are afrayed, afrayed. I know it because you write to me like that.
Remember: Only the bravest and wisest amonge us gets rewarded.
Djamel Abd al-Hakiim

Danny's mother started to be home every day, right when Danny got home. Danny stopped making snacks for himself and let his mother toast the bread, wash the apples, put the dishes in the dishwasher. He stood on the kitchen table and ate a peanut butter sandwich while his mother made adjustments to his tuxedo jacket. She pinned a felt rose to his lapel. Danny watched birds out the kitchen window. He counted four, ten, twelve pigeons, all of them flying straight up. He wondered how free they'd be, whether they'd meet the edge of the sky and burst into heaven, or singe their feathers and fall while trying to pass through the clouds.

He didn't write to Djamel for months. Djamel didn't write back. Mrs. Welles made the class sit in a circle and discuss what they had learned about Morocco: The flag is red with a green star. The motto is "God, Country, King." They eat mint, olives, and couscous for dinner. When you are a Muslim, you must follow the Five Pillars of Islam. You have to go to a mosque. The parents in the poor towns kill baby lambs right in front of the children. If they have to learn English, we should learn Arabic. Casablanca is a big city.

Mrs. Welles nodded. "Someone share something else they've learned. Someone who hasn't spoken."

Danny looked up at Mrs. Welles. He could barely see her face over her stomach.

"Mr. Fein?"

"My pen pal has nothing to tell me."

The whole class looked at him. Emma broke her posture to crawl to him, but Mrs. Welles wouldn't let her go.

"Why is that?"

Danny was silent.

Mrs. Welles scrutinized him and then leaned back in her chair. She rubbed her stomach. There was an oppressive silence that the class seemed unable to bear. She called on another student who hadn't spoken.

That night Danny felt something warm and heavy on his shoulder.

"Are you asleep yet?" it asked.

"What?"

There was a claw at his back, then one at his side.

"Don't prick me," he said.

"Wake up!" The panther's scream was furious. "Wake up!"

Danny turned over. The creature was lying in his bed, stretched long from post to post. He tried to get out, but it grabbed his shoulders.

"Don't leave or I'll get lonely."

"You're going to kill me," Danny said. "You've gotten sick of me."

The panther said nothing. It didn't even smile.

"I thought you were gone last time. What did you do?"

A cacophony of grinding metal ensued as it opened its mouth, which was mechanized tonight. Danny could see a steel tongue and jaws.

"What am I going to do?" it asked. Sparks flew in its mouth.

"No. What did you do?"

It pointed a claw at Danny's eye. He would be losing his sight. The panther was going to blind him. The claw stabbed his left eye, then his right. He blinked. He could see only the explosion of his vision, a webbed haze of red, then white, finally black. His head felt swollen. He kicked his feet against the covers. He could hear the creature breathing; he felt its tongue against his cheek, licking what tears or blood he could still muster from his damaged eyes. He tried to punch the creature, but his hands passed through it as through water.

Then there was someone's hand on his forehead, the heavy meter of adult breathing.

"Danny, honey," his father said. "Danny, you were yelling."

Danny pressed his fists against his eyes. His father would not like to see this. "I'm blind," he said.

"You're what?"

"I'm blind. The panther blinded me. It came when I was sleeping and stuck its claws in my eyes."

Danny started to cry the sort of climactic cry that invokes colors and shapes and skinny lines of neon. Danny's father pulled his son's hands from his face and pried his eyes open. He turned on a light. He waited for the pupils to get smaller. They did.

"You're not blind," he said. "Don't cry." He kissed Danny on the forehead and lay his head in the space between his son's chin and bent elbow. He waited until the wails became hiccups. Expressionless, Danny watched his father's face move as he spoke.

"Danny?" he said. His mouth was out of sync with his words. "You can see. You can see me."

Mrs. Welles's stomach had become so large and hard that it threatened to rip her skin apart. She never stood up from her chair to help the class with fractions or diagramming sentences. One afternoon, she left for a doctor's appointment. She didn't come back for two weeks. The substitute was a short, thin man named Mr. Song. He wrote his name on the chalkboard and then told the class that Mrs. Welles was having problems with her baby. Someone asked him what kind of problems and he said big ones. Bad ones. He'd have to accompany the class to the airport to meet the children from the Darul Arqam School.

Danny saw it when he opened the freezer to take out a Popsicle. The oppressive cold, the metal railings of the fridge like the edges of an examination table, the child's stomach girded with its umbilical cord. No breathing, no crying. A faceless, senseless blob of infant.

A smear of jaundice covering its eyes. The block of ice latticed with white cracks.

On the day he would meet Djamel, Danny's mother sent him to school in the tuxedo jacket. Mr. Song gave each student a piece of construction paper on which to write the name of his or her pen pal. Danny wrote "Djamel" in black marker. They took their papers with them to the bus, everyone laughing and throwing things at each other. Emma came up behind Danny and held his hand.

"Aren't you excited?"

"Yeah."

She giggled. She made him sit in a seat with her and grabbed his chin so he wouldn't look out the window. She had stretch pants and ribboned hair and a runny nose. She licked her upper lip. She had lost a tooth, most likely in the middle of the night, when she wouldn't feel pain.

"Aisha says she's going to bring me a flower necklace. She wrote me a letter about how I'm her sister."

The bus lurched, and they drove.

"She wants to meet you, too. I told her about you."

Danny nodded.

"She thinks you're like a brother."

Emma laid her head on his shoulder and he looked out the window. He could feel her breathing, and for a moment he believed he could synchronize their breaths.

They waited at the end of the airport for international flights, in front of a door labeled RABAT. There was a vulcanized hiss and a henlike matron appeared from inside the terminal, dressed in a pantsuit and scarf. A line of children followed her. It looked as if she had taken pains to Americanize them: they wore shorts and Velcro sandals, with shirts that advertised movie stars and beverages. They all looked tired and confused. Danny's class began to scream the names of their pen pals, holding the signs over their heads. Emma found Aisha and hugged her, whispered into her ear over her shoulder. The boys matched up with other boys, high-fived, offered each other metal cars and bottle caps. The girls stood across from each other at arm's length and compared bracelets and told each other secrets. Mr. Song shook hands with the matron and apologized that Mrs. Welles had to miss the occasion. Danny searched among the faces, all of them older-looking than his, all of them thin-lipped, and tried to see Djamel. He kept his sign behind his back.

The matron was dragging a stunned boy by the hand. His movements were mechanical, puppetlike, and he appeared to be dancing next to her as she moved with him. She stood him in front of Danny and announced that he was Djamel Abd al-Hakiim. Danny looked at him. He had a sunken face and very thick skin. He wore dark glasses. He was a withered version of the boy in the picture. The matron told them they'd get along fine. She said Djamel was very tired because he had been fasting for three days. She didn't say why.

"I'll leave you two boys alone." She smiled and left.

Djamel took off his glasses and looked directly into the sun.

"It's setting," Danny said. "It's almost nighttime here."

Djamel blinked and looked at Danny. "A monster chases you, Daniel?"

Danny said nothing.

"A monster is chasing you. I thought about it on the plane. A monster is chasing you, and it is trying to kill you."

Danny sighed. "Yes."

Djamel put his hand on Danny's shoulder. He hung his head and arched his back.

"You are afraid," he said.

Danny nodded.

"Your heart beats fast? When you are dreaming?"

"Yes."

Somewhere far off, the other children had begun to sing a song in Arabic. Their voices were a symphony of colors: reds, purples, oranges, greens.

"Do you dream of Heaven?"

"Once, maybe."

"You will look into my eyes?"

The boy raised his head and stared at Danny. His eyes were clouded, his pupils drowned. He looked to be asleep.

"You see it?"

Danny searched. He didn't know what he was looking for. He could feel Djamel's hand trembling as it gripped his shoulder. "See it?"

And Danny saw it at last, swathed in steam and smoke and dust. He imagined windows, staircases, the sounds of parents' voices. He could hear himself crying as a newborn. He imagined sky — cold, gray expanses of it — clouds weighty but soft. Then Djamel coughed and fell, and Danny caught him. He barely weighed anything at all.

"You've seen it?"

Danny nodded. Noises began to come back: the sounds of feet moving, whispers and screams, engines throttling. In the distance a plane took off from the runway, its nose pointed triumphantly toward the sky.

RIVKA GALCHEN

■

Wild Berry Blue

FROM *Open City*

THIS IS A STORY ABOUT MY LOVE FOR ROY, though first I have to say a few words about my dad, who was there with me at the McDonald's every Saturday letting his little girl — I was maybe eight — swig his extra half-and-halfs, stack the shells into messy towers. My dad drank from his bottomless cup of coffee and read the paper while I dipped my McDonaldland cookies in milk and pretended to read the paper. He wore gauzy plaid button-ups with pearline snaps. He had girlish wrists, a broad forehead like a Roman, an absolutely terrifying sneeze.

"How's the coffee?" I'd ask.

"Not good, not bad. How's the milk?"

"Terrific," I'd say. Or maybe, "Exquisite."

My mom was at home cleaning the house; our job there at the McDonald's was to be out of her way.

And that's how it always was on Saturdays. We were Jews, we had our rituals. That's how I think about it. Despite the occasional guiltless cheeseburger, despite being secular Israelis living in the wilds of Oklahoma, the ineluctable Jew part in us still snuck out, like an inherited tic, indulging in habits of repetition. Our form of *davenning*. Our little Shabbat.

Many of the people who worked at the McDonald's were former patients of my dad's: mostly drug addicts and alcoholics in rehab programs. McDonald's hired people no one else would hire; I think it was a policy. And my dad, in effect, was the McDonald's–Psychiatric

Institute liaison. The McDonald's manager, a deeply Christian man, would regularly come over and say hello to us, and thank my dad for many things. Once he thanked him for, as a Jew, having kept safe the word of God during all the dark years.

"I'm not sure I've done *so* much," my dad had answered, not seriously.

"But it's been living there in you," the manager said earnestly. He was basically a nice man, admirably tolerant of the accompanying dramas of his work force, dramas I picked up on peripherally. Absenteeism, petty theft, a worker OD-ing in the bathroom. I had no idea what that meant, to OD, but it sounded spooky. "They slip out from under their own control," I heard the manager say one time, and the phrase stuck with me. I pictured one half of a person lifting up a velvet rope and fleeing the other half.

Sometimes, dipping my McDonaldland cookies — Fryguy, Grimace — I'd hold a cookie in the milk too long and it would saturate and crumble to the bottom of the carton. There, it was something mealy, vulgar. Horrible. I'd lose my appetite. Though the surface of the milk often remained pristine I could feel the cookie's presence down below, lurking. Like some ancient bottom-dwelling fish with both eyes on one side of his head.

I'd tip the carton back in order to see what I dreaded seeing, just to feel that queasiness, and also the pre-queasiness of knowing the main queasiness was coming, the anticipatory ill.

Beautiful/Horrible — I had a running mental list. Cleaning lint from the screen of the dryer — beautiful. Bright glare on glass — horrible. Mealworms — also horrible. The stubbles of shaved hair in a woman's armpit — beautiful.

The Saturday I was to meet Roy, after dropping a cookie in the milk, I looked up at my dad. "Cookie," I squeaked, turning a sour face at the carton.

He pulled out his worn leather wallet, with its inexplicable rust stain ring on the front. He gave me a dollar. My mom never gave me money and my dad always gave me more than I needed. (He also called me the Queen of Sheba sometimes, like when I'd stand up on a dining room chair to see how things looked from there.) The torn corner of the bill he gave me was held on with yellowed Scotch tape. Someone had written over the treasury seal in blue pen, "I love Becky!!!"

I go up to the counter with the Becky dollar to buy my replacement milk, and what I see is a tattoo, most of which I can't see. A starched white long-sleeve shirt covers most of it. But a little blue-black lattice of it I can see — a fragment like ancient elaborate metalwork, that creeps down all the way, past the wrist, to the back of the hand, kinking up and over a very plump vein. The vein is so distended I imagine laying my cheek on it in order to feel the blood pulse and flow, to maybe even hear it. Beautiful. So beautiful. I don't know why but I'm certain this tattoo reaches all the way up to his shoulder. His skin is deeply tanned but the webbing between his fingers sooty pale.

This beautiful feeling. I haven't had it about a person before. Not in this way.

In a trembling moment I shift my gaze up to the engraved name-tag. There's a yellow M emblem, then *Roy*.

I place my dollar down on the counter. I put it down like it's a password I'm unsure of, one told to me by an unreliable source. "Milk," I say, quietly.

Roy, whose face I finally look at, is staring off, up, over past my head, like a bored lifeguard. He hasn't heard or noticed me, little me, the only person in line. Roy is biting his lower lip and one of his teeth, one of the canines, is much whiter than the others. Along his cheekbones his skin looks dry and chalky. His eyes are blue, with beautiful bruisy eyelids.

I try again, a little bit louder. "Milk."

Still he doesn't hear me; I begin to feel as if maybe I am going to cry because of these accumulated moments of being nothing. That's what it feels like standing so close to this type of beauty — like being nothing.

Resolving to give up if I'm not noticed soon I make one last effort and, leaning over on my tiptoes, I push the dollar further along the counter, far enough that it tickles Roy's thigh, which is leaned up against the counter's edge.

He looks down at me, startled, then laughs abruptly. "Hi little sexy," he says. Then he laughs again, too loud, and the other cashier, who has one arm shrunken and paralyzed, turns and looks and then looks away again.

Suddenly these few seconds are everything that has ever happened to me.

My milk somehow purchased I go back to the table wondering if I am green, or emitting a high-pitched whistling sound, or dead.

I realize back at the table that it's not actually the first time I've seen Roy. With great concentration, I dip my Hamburglar cookie into the cool milk. I think that maybe I've seen Roy — that coarse blond hair — every Saturday, for all my Saturdays. I take a bite from my cookie. I have definitely seen him before. Just somehow not in this way.

My dad appears to be safely immersed in whatever is on the other side of the crossword puzzle and bridge commentary page. I feel — a whole birch tree pressing against my inner walls, its leaves reaching to the top of my throat — the awful sense of wanting some other life. I have thought certain boys in my classes have pretty faces, but I have never before felt like laying my head down on the vein of a man's wrist. (I still think about that vein sometimes.) Almost frantically I wonder if Roy can see me there at my table, there with my dad, where I've been seemingly all my Saturdays.

Attempting to rein in my anxiety I try and think: What makes me feel this way? Possessed like this? Is it a smell in the air? It just smells like beefy grease. Which is pleasant enough but nothing new. A little mustard. A small vapor of disinfectant. I wonder obscurely if Roy is Jewish, as if that might make normal this spiraling fated feeling I have. As if really what's struck me is just an unobvious family resemblance. But I know that we're the only Jews in town.

Esther married the gentile king, I think, in a desperate absurd flash.

Since a part of me wants to stay forever I finish my cookies quickly.

"Let's go," I say.

"Already?"

"Can't we just leave? Let's leave."

There's the Medieval Fair, I think to myself in consolation all Sunday. It's two weekends away, a Saturday. You're always happy at the

Medieval Fair, I say to myself, as I fail to enjoy sorting my stamps, fail to stand expectantly, joyfully, on the dining room chair. Instead I fantasize about running the French fry fryer in the back of McDonald's. I imagine myself learning to construct Happy Meal boxes in a breath, to fold the papers around the hamburgers *just so*. I envision a stool set out for me to climb atop so that I can reach the apple fritter dispenser; Roy spots me, making sure I don't fall. And I get a tattoo. Of a bird, or a fish, or a ring of birds and fish, around my ankle.

But there is no happiness in these daydreams. Just an overcrowded and feverish empty.

At school on Monday I sit dejectedly in the third row of Mrs. Brown's class, because that is where we are on the weekly seating chart rotation. I suffer through exercises in long division, through bits about Magellan. Since I'm not in the front I'm able to mark most of my time drawing a tremendous maze, one that stretches to the outer edges of the notebook paper. This while the teacher reads to us from something about a girl and her horse. Something. A horse. Who cares! Who cares about a horse! I think, filled, suddenly, with unexpected rage. That extra white tooth. The creeping chain of the tattoo. I try so hard to be dedicated to my maze, pressing my pencil sharply into the paper as if to hold down my focus better.

All superfluous, even my sprawling maze, superfluous. A flurry of pencil shavings from the sharpener — they come out as if in a breath — distracts me. A sudden phantom pain near my elbow consumes my attention.

I crumple up my maze dramatically; do a basketball throw to the wastebasket like the boys do. I miss of course but no one seems to notice, which is the nature of my life at school, where I am only noticed in bland embarrassing ways, like when a substitute teacher can't pronounce my last name. The joylessness of my basketball toss — it makes me look over at my once-crush Josh Deere and feel sad for him, for the smallness of his life.

One day, I think, it will be Saturday again.

But time seemed to move so slowly. I'd lost my appetite for certain details of life.

*

"Do you know about that guy at McDonald's with the one really white tooth?" I brave this question to my dad. This during a commercial break from *Kojak*.

"Roy's a recovering heroin addict," my dad says, turning to stare at me. He always said things to me other people wouldn't have said to kids. He'd already told me about the Oedipus complex and I had stared dully back at him. He would defend General Rommel to me, though I had no idea who General Rommel was. He'd make complex points about the straits of Bosporus. It was as if he couldn't distinguish ages.

So he said that to me, about Roy, which obviously he shouldn't have said. (Here, years later, I still think about the mystery of that plump vein, which seems a contradiction. Which occasionally makes me wonder if there were two Roys.)

"I don't know what the story with the tooth is," my dad adds. "Maybe it's false?" And then it's back to the mystery of *Kojak*.

I wander into the kitchen feeling unfulfilled and so start interrogating my mom about my Purim costume for the carnival that is still two Sundays, eons, away. The Purim carnival is in Tulsa, over an hour's driving distance; I don't know the kids there, and my costume never measures up. "And the crown," I remind her hollowly. I'm not quite bold enough to bring up that she could buy me one of the beautiful ribbon crowns sold at the Medieval Fair, which we'll be at the day before. "I don't want," I mumble mostly to myself, "one of those paper crowns that everyone has."

Thursday night I am at the Skaggs Alpha Beta grocery with my mom. I am lingering amid all the sugar cereals I know will never come home with me. It's only every minute or so that I am thinking about Roy's hand, about how he called me sexy.

Then I see Roy. He has no cart, no basket. He's holding a gallon of milk and a supersized bag of Twizzlers and he is reaching for, I can't quite see — a big oversized box that looks to be Honeycomb. A beautiful assemblage. Beautiful.

I turn away from Roy but stand still. I feel my whole body, even my ears, blushing. The backs of my hands feel itchy the way they always do in spring. Seeking release I touch the cool metal shelving, run my fingers up and over the plastic slipcovers, over the price labels, hearing every nothing behind me. The price labels make a sandy sliding sound when I push them. He's a monster, Roy. Not looking at him, just feeling that power he has over me, a monster.

My mom in lace-up sandals cruises by the aisle with our shopping cart, unveiling to me my ridiculousness. Able now to turn around I see that Roy is gone. I run after my mom and when finally we're in the car again, back door closed on the groceries — I see celery stalks innocently sticking out of a brown paper bag when I turn around — I feel great relief.

I decide to wash my feet in the sink, this always makes me happy. On my dad's shaving mirror in the bathroom, old Scotch tape holding it in place, is a yellowed bit of paper, torn from a magazine. For years it's been there, inscrutable, and suddenly I feel certain that it carries a secret. About love maybe. About the possessed feeling I have because of Roy.

It says *And human speech is but a cracked kettle upon which we tap crude rhythms for bears to dance to, while we long to make music that —*

Next to the scrap is a sticker of mine, of a green apple.

I look again at the quote: the bears, the kettle.

Silly, I decide. It's all very silly. I start to dry my feet with a towel.

For the impending McDonald's Saturday I resolve to walk right past my tattooed crush. I'll have nothing to do with him, with his hi little sexys. This denouncement is actually extraordinarily painful since Roy alone is now my whole world. Everything that came before — my coin collection in the Tupperware, the corrugated cardboard trim on school bulletin boards, the terror of the fire pole — now revealed supremely childish and vain. Without even deciding to, I have left all that and now must leave Roy too. I commit to enduring the burden of the universe alone. The universe with its mysterious General Rommels, its heady straits of Bosporus. I resolve to suffer.

Saturday comes again. My mom has already taken the burner covers off the stove and set them in the sink. I'm anxious, like branches shaking in wind, and I'm trying the think-about-the-Medieval-Fair trick. I picture the ducks at the duck pond, the way they waddle right up and snatch the bread slice right out of my hand. I focus on the fair — knowing that time will move forward in that way, eventually waddle forward to the next weekend.

Buckling myself into the front seat of our yellow Pinto, I put an imitation Life Saver under my tongue, a blue one. When my dad walks in front of the car on the way to the driver's side, I notice that he has slouchy shoulders. Horrible. Not his shoulders, but my noticing them.

"I love you," I say to my dad. He laughs and says that's good. I sit there hating myself a little.

I concentrate on my candy, on letting it be there, letting it do its exquisitely slow melt under my tongue. Beautiful. I keep that same candy the whole car ride over, through stop signs, waiting for a kid on a Bigwheel to cross, past the Conoco, with patience during the long wait for the final left turn. In my pocket I have more candies. Most of a roll of wild berry. When I move my tongue just a tiny bit, the flavor, the sugary slur, assaults my sensations. I choke on a little bit of saliva.

When we enter I sense Roy at our left; I walk on the far side of my dad, hoping to hide in his shadow. In a hoarse whisper I tell my dad that I'll go save our table and that he should order me the milk and the cookies.

"Okay," he whispers back, winking, as if this is some spy game I am playing.

At the table I stare straight ahead at the molded plastic bench, summoning all my meager power to keep from looking feverishly around. I think I sense Roy's blond hair off in the distance to my left. I glimpse to the side, but see just a potted plant.

"How's the coffee?" I ask after my dad has settled in across from me.

He shrugs his ritual shrug but no words except the question of how is your milk. Is he mad at me? As I begin dipping my cookies with a kind of anguish, I answer that the milk is delicious.

Why do we say these little things? I wonder. Why do I always want the McDonaldland butter cookies and never the chocolate chip? It seems creepy to me suddenly, all the habits and ways of the heart I have that I didn't choose for myself.

I throw back three half-and-halfs.

"Will you get me some more half-and-halfs?" my dad asks.

He asks nicely. And he is really reading the paper while I am not. Of course I'm going to go get creamers. I'm a kid, I remember. He's my dad. All this comes quickly into focus, lines sharp, like feeling the edges of a sticker on paper.

"I don't feel well," I try.

"Really?"

"I mean I feel fine," I say getting out of the chair.

Roy. Taking a wild berry candy from my pocket I resolve again to focus on a candy under my tongue instead of on him. I head first toward the back wall, darting betwixt and between the tables with their attached swiveling chairs. This is the shiniest cleanest place in town, that's what McDonald's was like back then. Even the corners and crevices are clean. It's strange to me in that way. Our house — even after my mom cleans, it's all still in disarray. I'll unfold a blanket and there'll be a stray sock inside. Behind the toilet there's blue lint. That's what makes a home, I think, its special type of mess.

And then I'm at the front counter. I don't look up.

I stand off to the side since I'm not really ordering anything, just asking for a favor, not paying for milk but asking for creamers. Waiting to be noticed, I stare down at the brushed steel counter with its flattering hazy reflection and then it appears, he appears. I see first his palm, reflected in the steel. Then I see his knuckles, the hairs on the back of his hand, the lattice tattoo, the starched shirt cuff that is the beginning of hiding all the rest of the tattoo that I can't see.

Beautiful.

A part of me decides I am taking him back into my heart. Even if no room will be left for anything else.

Roy notices me. He leans way down, eyes level with my sweaty curls stuck against my forehead, at the place where I know I have my birthmark — a dark brown mole there above my left eyebrow — and he says, his teeth showing, his strange glowing white canine showing — "D'ya need something?" He taps my nose with his finger.

That candy — I had forgotten about it, and I move my tongue and the flavor — it all comes rushing out, overwhelming, and I drool a lit-

tle bit as I blurt out, "I'm going to the Medieval Fair next weekend."
I wipe my wet lips with the back of my hand and see the wild-berry
blue saliva staining there.

"Cool," he says, straightening up, and he interlaces his fingers and
pushes them outward and they crack deliciously, and I think about
macadamias. I think I see him noticing the blue smeared on my
right hand. He then says to me: "I love those puppets they sell there
— those real plain wood ones."

I just stare at Roy's blue eyes. I love blue eyes. Still to this day I am
always telling myself that I don't like them, that I find them lifeless
and dull and that I prefer brown eyes, like mine, like my parents',
but it's a lie. It's a whole other wilder type of love that I feel for these
blue-eyed people of the world. So I look up at him, at those blue eyes,
and I'm thinking about those plain wooden puppets — this is all half
a second — then the doors open behind me and that invasive heat
enters and the world sinks down, mud and mush and the paste left
behind by cookies.

"Oh," I say. "Half-and-half."

He reaches into a tray of much-melted ice and bobbing creamers
and he hands three to me. My palm burns where he touched me and
my vision is blurry; only the grooves on the half-and-half container
keep me from vanishing.

"Are you going to the fair?" I brave. Heat in my face again, the
feeling just before a terrible rash. I'm already leaving the counter so
as not to see those awful blue eyes and I hear, "Ah I'm workin'" and I
don't even turn around.

I read the back of my dad's newspaper. They have found more fossils at the Spiro mounds. There's no explanation for how I feel.

How can I describe the days of the next week? I'd hope to see Roy
when I ran out to check the mail. I'd go drink from the hose in our
front yard thinking he might walk or drive by, even though I had no
reason to believe he might ever come to our neighborhood. I got detention for not turning in my book report of *The Yellow Wallpaper*.
I found myself rummaging around in my father's briefcase, as if
Roy's files — I imagined the yellow Confidential envelope from Clue
— might somehow be there. Maybe I don't need to explain this be-

cause who hasn't been overtaken by this monstrous shade of love? I remember walking home from school very slowly, anxiously, as if through foreign, unpredictable terrain. I wanted to buy Roy a puppet at the Medieval Fair. One of the wooden ones like he'd mentioned. Only in that thought could I rest. All the clutter of my mind was waiting to come closer to that moment of purchasing a puppet.

So I did manage to wake up in the mornings. I did try to go to sleep at night. Though my heart seemed to be racing to its own obscure rhythm, private even from me.

Friday night before the fair, hopeless for sleep — my bedroom seemed alien and lurksome — I pulled my maze workbook from the shelf and went into the brightly lit bathroom. I turned on the overhead fan so that it would become noisy enough to overwhelm the sound in my mind of Roy cracking his knuckles, again and again. The whirring fan noise — it was like a quiet. I sat in the empty tub, set the maze book on the rounded ledge and purposely began on a difficult page. I worked cautiously, tracing ahead with my finger before setting pen to paper. This was pleasing, though out of the corner of my eye I saw the yellowed magazine fragment — *cracked kettle* — and it was like a ghost in the room with me, though its message, I felt sure — almost too sure considering that I didn't understand it — had nothing to do with me.

In the morning my mom found me there in the tub, like some passed-out drunk, my maze book open on my small chest. I felt like crying, didn't even know why. I must have fallen asleep there. I reached up to my face, wondering if something had gone wrong with it.

"Do you have a fever?" my mom asked.

It must have seemed like there had to be an explanation. When she left, assured, somewhat, I tried out those words — *Human speech is like a cracked kettle* — like they were the coded answer to a riddle.

I was always that kind of kid who crawled into bed with her parents, who felt safe only with them. If my mom came into my classroom because I had forgotten my lunch at home, I wasn't ashamed like other kids were, but proud. For a few years of my life, up until then, my desires hadn't chased away from me. I wanted to fall asleep on the sofa while my dad watched *The Twilight Zone* and so

I did. I wanted couscous with butter and so I had some. Yes, sometimes shopping with my mom I coveted a pair of overalls or a frosted cookie, but the want would be faint and fade as soon as we'd walked away.

I had always loved the Medieval Fair. A woman would dress up in an elaborate mermaid costume and sit under the bridge that spanned the artificial pond. I thought she was beautiful. People tossed quarters down at her. She'd flap her tail, wave coyly. It wasn't until years later that I realized that she was considered trashy.

Further on there was a stacked hay maze that had already become too easy by late elementary school but I liked looking at it from a distance, from up on the small knoll. I think every turn you might take was fine. Whichever way you went you still made it out. I remember it being upsetting, being spat out so soon.

We had left the house uncleaned when we went to the fair that Saturday. I was thinking about the wooden puppet but I felt obligated to hope for a crown; that's what I was supposed to be pining for. I imagined that my mom would think to buy me a crown for my Queen Esther costume. But maybe, I hoped, she would forget all about the crown. It wasn't unlikely. What seemed like the world to me often revealed itself, through her eyes, to be nothing.

We saw the dress-up beggar with the prosthetic nose and warts. We crossed the bridge, saw the mermaid. A pale teenage boy in stonewashed jeans and a tank top leaned against the bridge's railing, smoking, and looking down at her. Two corseted women farther along sang bawdy ballads in the shade of a willow and while we listened a slouchy man went by with a gigantic foam mallet. The whole world, it seemed, was laughing or fighting or crying or unfolding chairs or blending smoothies and this would go on until time immemorial. Vendors sold wooden flutes, Jacob's ladders. The smell of funnel cakes and sour mystery saturated the air. In an open field two ponies and three sheep were there for the petting and the overseer held a baby pig in his hands. We ate fresh ears of boiled corn, smothered with butter and cracked pepper. My mom didn't mention the price. That really did make it feel like a day in some other me's life.

But I felt so unsettled. Roy's tooth in my mind as I bit into the corn, Roy's fingers on my palm as I thrummed my hand along a low wooden fence. I had so little of Roy and yet he had all of me and the feeling ran deep, deep to the most ancient parts of me. So deep that in some way I felt that my love for Roy shamed my people, whoever my people were, whomever I was queen of, people I had never met, nervous people and sad people and dead people, all clambering for air and space inside of me. I didn't even know what I wanted from Roy. I still don't. All my life love has felt like a croquet mallet to the head. Something absurd, ready for violence. Love.

I remember once years later, in a love fit, stealing cherry Luden's cough drops from a convenience store. I had the money to pay for them but I stole them instead. I wanted a cheap childish cherry flavor on my tongue when I saw my love, who of course isn't my love anymore. That painful pathetic euphoria. Low-quality cough drops. That's how I felt looking around anxiously for the wooden puppet stand, how I felt looking twice at every blond man who passed, wondering if he might somehow be Roy, there for me, even though he'd said he wouldn't be there. Thinking about that puppet for Roy eclipsed all other thoughts, put a slithery veil over the whole day. How much would the puppet cost? I didn't have my own pocket money, an allowance or savings or anything like that. I wasn't in the habit of asking for things. I never asked for toys. I never asked for sugar cereals. I felt to do so was wrong. I had almost cried that one day just whispering to myself about the crown. But all I wanted was that puppet because that puppet was going to solve everything.

At the puppet stand I lingered. I was hoping that one of my parents would take notice of the puppets, pick one up. My dad, standing a few paces away, stood out from the crowd in his button-up shirt. He looked weak, sunbeaten. My mom was at my side, her arms crossed across an emergency orange tank top. It struck me, maybe for the first time, that they came to this fair just for me.

"I've never wanted anything this much in my whole life," I confessed in a rush, my hand on the unfinished wood of one of the puppets. "I want this more than a crown."

My mom laughed at me, or at the puppet. "But it's so ugly," she said, in Hebrew.

"That's not true," I whispered furiously, feeling as if everything had fallen silent, as if the ground beneath me was shifting. The vendor must surely have understood my mom, by her tone alone. I looked over at him: a fat bearded man talking to a long-haired bare-foot princess. He held an end of her dusty hair distractedly; his other hand he had inside the collar of his shirt. He was sweating.

"*Drek.*" My mom shrugged. Junk.

"Grouch," I broke out, like a tree root heaving through soil. "You don't like anything," I almost screamed, there in the bright sun. "You never like anything at all." My mother turned her back to me. I sensed the ugly vendor turn our way.

"I'll get it for you," my dad said, suddenly right with us. There followed an awkward argument between my parents, which seemed only to heighten my dad's pleasure in taking out his rust-stained wallet, in standing his ground, in being, irrevocably, on my side.

His alliance struck me as misguided, pathetic, even childish. I felt like a villain. We bought the puppet.

That dumb puppet — I carried it around in its wrinkly green plastic bag. For some reason I found myself haunted by the word *leprosy.* When we watched the minstrel show in the little outdoor amphitheater I tried to forget the green bag under the bench. We only made it a few steps before my mom noticed it was gone. She went back and fetched it.

At home I noticed that the wood of one of the hands of the puppet was cracked. That wasn't the only reason I couldn't give the puppet to Roy. Looking at that mute piece of wood I saw something. A part of me that I'd never chosen, that I would never control. I went to the bathroom, turned on the loud fan, and cried, feeling angry, useless, silly. An image of Roy came to my mind, particularly of that tooth. I felt my love falling off, dissolving.

He was my first love, my first love in the way that first loves are usually second or third or fourth loves. I still think about a stranger in a green jacket across from me at the waiting room at the DMV. About a blue-eyed man with a singed earlobe whom I saw at a Baskin-Robbins with his daughter. My first that kind of love. I never got over him. I never get over anyone.

J. MALCOLM GARCIA

■

A Product of This Town

Jena, Louisiana — January 2008

FROM *The Virginia Quarterly Review*

The Loop

OUTSIDERS, ALL OF YOU.

Your presence here a judgment on us. It was worst last September, when thousands of you descended with the indignation of embittered preachers. Businesses shut down. People stayed home behind locked doors. The silence of those days still lingers, still carries a warning of approaching tumult.

We pray for the people who come to Jena. God loves them no matter what their agenda, although we feel their agenda is misplaced. We pray for our community to be patient. We pray for everything to be back to normal.

Your judgment felt on this January night, by boys looping Oak Street, trolling endlessly up and down and through the center of town. Cruising, you would call it, but in Jena, it's called "looping."

The loop starts in the darkened parking lot of Chamlen's Furniture Store where teenagers sit in their idling pickups and lean out their windows, talking on weekend nights. Boys mostly. Some with their arms draped around their girlfriends. Then, as if by migratory compulsion, they slip their gears into drive and turn east through the unlit, empty streets.

The boys roll past the Dollar General Store, Ace Family Hardware, and McDonald's, where a teenager hands a sack of burgers out the drive-through window. A light illuminates the State Farm Insurance sign. A dog caught in its thin glow lopes past silent display windows. Brandon's Nails, Reid's Jewelry store, Honeycutt Drug.

Those white boys acted and we reacted. I'm just saying that's the way things happen in this little town.

Three minutes from Chamlen's the boys turn into the parking lot of Mitch's Restaurant (*today's special: the catfish plate*) and complete the loop. They pause, adjust their radios and then retrace their steps like panthers in a cage, back and forth, back and forth all night.

That used to be the whole, limited journey. But lately, it seems the loop has expanded. As if some of the youngsters kept going, looping the whole damn country, and then pulling it with them each time they turned back to Jena. More of you keep coming. And still the loop gets bigger.

Some of you all have returned this week for the Martin Luther King birthday march on Sunday, haven't you? You know about the protest by those fellas with the Nationalist Movement, right? A real party, yeah, buddy. Will there be fights? Will blood run? You'll tar and feather Jena for your own sport, won't you?

It's about where we're at. The South. This is being done to us because of geographics. We're the South, so outsiders say Jena's a racist town.

What is so different about Jena from your town?

What god made you judge and jury?

Just who are you anyway?

Crowd Control

In September 2006, nooses were hung from a tree in the high-school courtyard in Jena, Louisiana. The tree was on the side of campus that, by long-standing tradition, had always been claimed by white students, who make up more than 80 percent of the student body. But a few of the school's eighty-five black students had decided to challenge the status quo by pointing out their de facto exclusion: they asked the school administrators if they, too, could sit beneath the tree's cooling shade. The nooses were hung in retaliation, as a kind of threat.

Three white students were quickly identified as responsible, and the principal recommended that they be expelled. But Jena's school superintendent, Roy Breithaupt, who is white, intervened and ruled that the nooses were just an immature stunt. He suspended the students for three days, angering those who felt harsher punishments were necessary. Racial tensions flared throughout the month, and on November 30 a wing of the high school was destroyed by a fire; officials suspected arson. Tensions spilled out of the schoolyard and into the surrounding neighborhoods. One night at a predominantly white party, a young black student was assaulted by a group wielding beer bottles. In another incident, a white Jena graduate allegedly pulled a pump-action shotgun on three black students outside a local convenience store. The teens managed to wrestle the gun away from the twenty-one-year-old.

For the most part, local law enforcement stayed out of the way of these incidents, shrugging them off as testosterone-fueled teenage arguments. This approach shifted abruptly on December 4 — more than a month after the black students sat under the "white" tree — when a fight broke out in the lunchroom between a white student and a black student. The white student was knocked to the floor and allegedly attacked by other black students, one of whom was the same student assaulted earlier at the party. The white student sustained bruises and a black eye. He was treated at a hospital and released. According to court testimony, he attended a social event later that same evening.

The black students were not reprimanded with school suspensions or misdemeanor charges, as their white counterparts had been. Instead, five of the six black teens involved were charged as adults with attempted second-degree murder and were given bonds ranging from $70,000 to $138,000. Sixteen-year-old Mychal Bell was prosecuted as an adult and assigned a public defender, a black man, who never called a single witness. Under pressure by watchdog groups, the district attorney abruptly reduced the charges against Bell from second-degree murder to second-degree aggravated battery and conspiracy. The aggravated battery stems from the prosecutor's contention that the teen's gym shoes were used as weapons.

Donald Washington, a black U.S. attorney for the Western District of Louisiana, insisted race had nothing to do with the charges against Bell. He said that the hanging of nooses constituted a hate crime but that charges were not brought against those students because they were juveniles. Washington was unable to explain, however, why Bell was prosecuted as an adult by a white prosecutor. While teenagers can be tried as adults in Louisiana for some violent crimes, including attempted murder, aggravated battery is not one of those crimes. An appeals court tossed out the conviction that could have sent him to prison for fifteen years. But the four remaining students who could be tried as adults, because they were seventeen or older, were arraigned on battery and conspiracy charges.

In response to the treatment of the "Jena Six," more than five thousand protesters converged on Jena last September to express their outrage. The scene was reminiscent of a 1960s freedom march, and many of those old-school leaders, including Reverends Jesse Jackson and Al Sharpton, were in attendance. But there were also some new faces. Young faces. All excited to play a part in what some of them called "our Selma."

White supremacists did their part to resemble their 1960s counterparts as well. "The best crowd control for such a situation would be a squad of men armed with full automatics and preferably a machine gun as well," advocated an online blogger on the neo-Nazi Vanguard News Network. Another wrote, "I'm not really that angry at the nogs — they are just soldiers in an undeclared race war. But any white that's in that support rally I would like to . . . have them machine-gunned." Bill White, an especially virulent purveyor of race hate, posted the home addresses and phone numbers of some of the Jena Six under this headline: "Addresses of Jena 6 Niggers: In Case Anyone Wants to Deliver Justice."

The Road to Jena

My drive to Jena started Saturday, January 19, 2008 — three days after MLK's birthday — and took me through Little Rock, Arkansas, where I picked up a copy of the *Arkansas Democrat-Gazette*. On the editorial page, an article celebrated the birthday of Robert E. Lee ("It is January 19th again, Lee's birthday, now an official holiday in this state").

I was going to Jena in time to see the Martin Luther King birthday march, though I'd been warned that the Mississippi-based white supremacist National Movement was planning to disrupt the MLK march in Jena by demonstrating on the same day. The mostly black high-school marching band had already dropped out as parents became more and more concerned about safety. At the last minute, the march was moved to Sunday, January 20, a day before King's official celebration, to avoid conflict with the National Movement's Monday rally. Beth Rickey, the spokeswoman for Jena's mayor, told me that Jena had been turned into an armed camp of plainclothes cops anticipating a clash between the groups.

Before I left for Jena, I learned some history. The town was settled in 1802. The Bakers built a water mill for cornmeal and gin cotton, and the post office was named for the Hempill family. Between 1882 and 1965, more than 330 people, all black, were lynched in Louisiana — more than four a year. When Klan member David Duke ran for governor of Louisiana in 1991, spouting anti-black and anti-Jewish slurs, the vast majority of Jena voted for him.

Three Snapshots

I pull into Hughey Leggett's house just outside the Jena city limits. He is sipping a beer on the porch of his wood-frame house, which is a shrine to his dead brother, the country singer Johnny Leggett. A tiny bandstand is crowded with drums and cymbals, a small PA system, photos of Johnny. Dogs gambol in the yard beneath a Confederate flag. Leggett once had the Stars and Stripes but took it down. No particular reason. Louisiana is a Confederate state, Leggett tells me, as if that is explanation enough. He's been to Jena a bunch of times. Lots of whites and blacks. They all seem to get along. As long as they're involved in their own business and don't stir nothing up, everything's fine. No problems except last fall when Jesse Jackson and that Al Sharpton came here. They can't win the presidency so they go around the country and cause trouble. You have a scab on your finger, scratch it and it starts bleeding. Those two, they've been doing some serious scratching. Caused some bleeding they have. He sips his beer and says no more.

*

Down at a ramshackle club called the Yellow Cat, cigarette smoke froths the stale air above the heads of black men. The building is basically a barn — thick with cobwebs and faded beer signs. An old jukebox hums with 45s: Bobby Bland ("I Just Tripped on a Piece of Your Broken Heart"), Johnnie Taylor ("Good Love"), Billy Ray Charles ("What's Your Pleasure").

"Hear there's going to be another march."

"Ain't surprised."

"Nothing in Jena surprises me."

"Remember that black guy killed in '64?"

"The shoe shop guy?"

"He made too much money as far as white folks was concerned."

"Is it sleeting outside?"

"Raining. A bit."

"'Sixty-four, '04, makes no difference what year we in."

"It's 2008, fool."

"Like I said, makes no difference. Damn this weather."

Bernice Coleman Mack leans forward on her walker while a home-health nurse braids her hair. Her grandson, Robert Bailey, is one of the Jena Six. She suspects the devil's hand behind all this trouble. Old man Satan is busy going to and fro seeing who he can tempt. She doesn't know why it all happened. The noose-hangers heard they used to hang black folk. That's why they put up those ropes. A signal. If you do anything wrong, you'll hang. If they read Scripture they would know better. Something went wrong, but she doesn't know what. At eighty-four, her face a canyon of wrinkles etched with worry, she knows a thing or two. Satan, she says again.

Life Underground

My mother and father hail from Cuba and Puerto Rico, respectively, but through the mysteries of genetics, I look as white as most Caucasians. As a boy, I would hear my friends' parents discuss their dislike of minorities. I stopped introducing myself as Malcolm Garcia. I just said "Malcolm." Without my troublesome last name, I could "pass," but that never made me comfortable; I was always on the edge — both inside the white world and outside of it.

In 1997, I took a job in Philadelphia. I used to eat at a diner down the street from my apartment. One afternoon, I sat next to a man in a suit and tie, and we began exchanging pleasantries as we ate. I introduced myself and he paused, mouth open, full of partially eaten hamburger.

"Malcolm," he said repeating my name. "Your parents liberal?"

"What do you mean?"

"Why else would they name you after Malcolm X?"

I told him I wasn't named for Malcolm X, that my last name was Garcia.

"Garcia?" he asked. "You got a little color in you, don't you boy?"

I approach the people of Jena with caution.

Church

Pastors joke that eleven o'clock mass in Jena's thirteen churches is the most segregated hour of the week. Some black people have told white Pentecostal pastor Eddie Thompson they would attend his church, but they haven't. And there are no white people listening to the services of Rev. B. L. Moran at Antioch Baptist Church in Ward 10. Two white men ran over his sign after an NAACP meeting last year. Drove a big old mail truck over it twice. Said it was an accident; they were just turning around.

Rev. Thompson calls that sort of thing "stealth racism." You got some hotheads and knotheads, he says. Children of racism that have stained Jena and put the town up as a sacrifice on the racial altar of America. The country has not dealt with the spirit and hatred still lurking within. How, he asks, can we move forward if the heart has not been opened? America didn't transcend racism during some march in the 1960s, Thompson says; it's still floating down a river of racial divide. When the Jena Six came along, they poked everyone in the eye. A light was shined. He hopes Jena's critics shine as much light on their towns as they shine on his. God knows this little town didn't want the light. No town would. Will they see the way forward or is their shame too great?

Rev. Moran doubts most people are ready to see anything. Not yet. He tells his Sunday congregation, I have seen a lot of storms, but no storm lasts forever. There is something better in front of us all, amen. Change will come by the hand of our enemies — do I have a witness? They set off some things, those noose-hangers. Sure did. To say they didn't know — well — they know now, amen.

Snob Hill

Susan Ory Powers lives near First Street among Jena's better-off, including some middle-class black families, in a neighborhood known as Snob Hill. In fact, the modest two-story brick homes on the hill stand just one floor higher than the low ranch-style houses a few blocks away. I see nothing particularly ostentatious about them.

We sit at the dining-room table for a dinner of rice and black beans and steamed asparagus. Her refined peppermint drawl, rising and falling with each enunciated vowel and consonant, suits the manner in which she presents herself: slight and trim, sun-colored hair, wearing a yellow blouse. Her grandfather was a mayor here in the 1920s; her uncle, a school superintendent. Her father owned a chicken farm and her mother handled loan closings. When Susan Ory Powers was a child attending grammar school, she and her mother drove past an American Indian girl. *If you're anything but nice to that little girl,* her mother warned, *you'll be punished. You behave. No matter their color.*

"That is the Jena I know," Ms. Powers tells me.

She was raised by black women — hired nannies whose children are now nurses' aides or cashiers. They live in the unincorporated side of Jena, called Ward 10, once referred to by whites as "the quarters." It is much better now than it was then, she says. Nice homes coming up, not shacks. The people there have progressed. Not as much as she would expect of her own children, but considering where their families started out, enough.

After fourteen years in Los Angeles working as a set designer ("Every Southern woman knows how to set a table, so I went to USC and became a set decorator"), she returned to Jena and the white, box-shaped house she had grown up in. Just weeks later, the nooses appeared in the high school's tree.

"What's this about?" she had asked friends.

In Los Angeles, she sought out black people because they understood her Southern accent. A black man was a groomsman at her son's San Francisco wedding. He's family. If he wanted to marry her daughter, Powers would have no qualms other than her daughter's having to get divorced first. That won't happen, she trusts, and therefore is left with the comfort of her convictions. She would not wish divorce on anyone.

She recalls the 1960s when the term *colored* was replaced by *black*. In Jena, white people asked, What difference does it make? We've always called them "colored." It's part of our culture. What part of our culture are we allowed to keep without being accused of bigotry? "Hard to understand a word would make any difference then, isn't it?" She poses the questions rhetorically.

"More wine?"

Rabbit Hunting

A drizzly morning, first day of rabbit hunting season.

Haze Harrison hefts thirteen beagles, one after another, into cages on the back of his pickup. It's sunrise in Ward 10, and he's going hunting. Whatever rabbits he kills, he'll give to old folks. As the son of a sharecropper, he grew up eating wild meat because they could afford little else. Long ago, he lost his taste for it.

His one-story ranch-style house sits on a wooded street lined with warped trailer homes black-streaked from rainwater, their backyards wet as marshes. The asphalt street buckles into long stretches of dirt and gravel. Ward 10 might have improved from the days when people called it the quarters, but Harrison says it still ain't nothing to write home about.

Since 1970, Harrison has made Ward 10 his home. His front windows have looked out on burning crosses since then. For seventeen years he worked as the only black person among seventy-five white employees. He heard the word *nigger* at least three times a day, but Harrison won't work a job where most of the employees are black. No benefits. Just a lot of hard work and low pay. And most black people don't have money to hire anyone.

"Suzie, Sunshine," he calls to the remaining dogs dodging his out-stretched hands.

He disagreed with the attempted-murder charge for what he considers a schoolyard fight, but he won't excuse the Jena Six for beating up that white boy. Kids aren't raised now like he was. He doesn't understand the younger generation of black people. He counts his dogs. These days, kids kill dogs if they get out of their pens and run loose. When he was a child, if it wasn't yours you didn't touch it.

"Spot, Shorty! Hush up!"

At Dewey Wells Preserve, about a half-hour drive from his house, Harrison parks on a mud road made gooey from rain and lets the eager dogs out of their cages. He listens to them howl and take off after something, rabbit or deer he doesn't know, and follows eagerly, sinking into soggy ground.

As a black man, Harrison can go anywhere in Jena these days, eat anywhere, work anywhere — at least in theory. But blacks and whites still don't mingle. There are no white faces in Ward 10, except for a few spouses from mixed marriages. The town has grown subtler in its expression of its likes and dislikes. They don't just come out and say "nigger," but Harrison believes they think it. If a child grows up with that kind of talk, by the time he turns thirteen he's too far gone to think differently. Harrison doesn't know why that is. It's just what he has concluded about kids. Not all white teenagers. Some. That's enough.

"Hup! Hup!" Harrison calls to the dogs.

He heard about the tree long before it became national news. Black kids told him nooses were routinely left in a high-school tree like it was nothing. He understood what was going on. It's not like it's anything new.

Harrison does not hate. His mother was religious. Not him, although he considers himself God-fearing. His older sister was killed by her husband. Harrison's mother raised his sister's children like her own and taught them to love their father despite his crime. Harrison visited with him when he was released from prison. Just the way Harrison was taught. Forgive the sinner. His stride picks up, propelling him through the woods after his dogs. Hate destroys you, he says.

Her Town Now

When teacher's aide Bobbi Cornett tells strangers she lives in Jena, she sees in their faces the hard look of distaste. *You're one of those noose-hangers,* they're thinking, and she knows it.

The unspoken accusation burns. She's half Mexican. The charge of racism is way off, she tells me. She feels misunderstood, abused. On the day of the big September demonstration, Cornett woke up to the sound of helicopters, busloads of people, police everywhere. It was as if she had awakened in Iraq. Yes, that's it. She says that the demonstrators were misled about Jena, just like the country was misled about Iraq.

Cornett has lived in Jena with her husband and two children since 1980. Her father was an oilman, and as a child she roamed the world. Europe, the Middle East, Africa. Setting up house in Jena, she wondered, Where the hell did we move? At the supermarket she was unable to find fresh parsley and bottles of wine. Only beer. It took sixteen years before Jena no longer considered her an outsider. Now she stands up for her town.

The marchers were socially conscious, she'll give them that. But terribly naïve. Cornett knows the mother of one of the noose-hangers, a special-education teacher who ministers to the homeless and attends church. She had even helped some of the Jena Six boys. What Cornett has been told: The nooses were a prank. The boys didn't understand how a noose would be perceived. They weren't born in the time of Jim Crow. They had no notion. Who knows what kids are thinking? They aren't talking now. Can you blame them?

She had no problem with the attempted-murder charge. Knock a boy down, keep hitting him in the head, what would you call it? A schoolyard fight? She doesn't think so.

"Was there not violence implied in the noose?" I ask.

She waves the question away. She's not a lawyer and won't comment further on the attempted-murder charge. That's for attorneys to decide, not the public.

"The Jena Six should be punished according to our laws," she says.

Her husband wanted to leave town the day of the September demonstration, but Cornett refused. No one was pushing her out of her house. I'm planting my flower bed as I planned, she told him. If the demonstrations turned violent, she would shutter the house.

In fact, she says, the demonstrators were very considerate and stayed off everyone's lawn. But they left Jena divided. This mess has plunged race relations back fifty years. She shakes her head.

"I'm half Mexican," she tells me again. "Why is this happening to us?"

The Best Crops

When white people called Cleveland Riser "nigger," he mocked them. You don't have the education to pronounce *Negro*, he told them. Your parents didn't teach you that. Their words didn't hurt Riser. He knows that a lack of intelligence causes fools to say "nigger," and he can get along ignoring them.

Riser is a retired assistant superintendent of schools. His defense is an educated mind. He dismisses racists by joking: They may hate him, but they still have to pay the taxes that support his well-earned Social Security checks. He just loves those people to death. "The money is not black or white," he says and chuckles, covering his mouth to be polite.

He chose education over the plow and mule of his forebears, but his father and grandfather taught him the value of hard work and the self-esteem that comes with success. His grandfather grew the best crops, just outside Jena in Winnfield. Riser's father worked in the salt mines, but he emphasized education second only to religion. School buses didn't serve the black neighborhood they lived in, so every day he drove his son to the house of an elderly couple who lived along the bus route. He offered rides to fourteen other children, too. He asked the school district for help with gas money but was turned down. Instead, black families paid him half a ham, potatoes, a quarter a day, anything they could afford to get their kids to school. All but two of the fourteen children attended college. Now, Riser sees his education — the skills of the mind — as the best kind of empowerment, even against those who hate him for those skills.

Without skills, derogatory words cast a pall. Black people get tired

of getting hit in the head with *nigger*. The Jena Six, he believes, reacted in a physical way because they didn't have the words, the right
words, to fight back with their tongues and intellects.

"Some people have not accepted the fact of all these ethnic groups
in Jena," Riser tells me. "You find this in any town. It exists wherever
there are barriers." Riser pauses, collecting his thoughts, the right
words. You find this anywhere, he says. New York, Chicago, Los Angeles. Anywhere. Jena's not so different in that respect. Barriers can
be overcome, but conversation is better than battery. Words, used
correctly, help to dispel fear. And fear, he says, still overpowers the
residents of Jena. If your boss hates black people and you're dependent upon him, what words do you use? Do you use any? I work for
him, I attend his church. I keep my mouth shut when blacks are dis-
cussed. I say I don't like them either, to please him. I stop thinking
for myself.

Riser was pleased to see all those people descend on Jena for the
big fall protest. They brought an awakening to Jena. Good. Now some
white supremacists plan to protest on Martin Luther King's birthday. Good, Riser says. Let them come. Black folks should react by not
showing up. Think of it. No audience. Don't go, don't listen. Nothing
would happen except the hate would be ignored like so much wasted
breath, wasted words.

Another Civil War

The two little Dupre boys, not yet teenagers, dress like their daddy
and granddaddy — army fatigues and black lace-up boots. They know
how to handle a gun, though they don't carry one holstered on their
hips like the older men do. "It's going to come down to another Civil
War," their granddaddy David Dupre Sr. says and strokes his white
beard. "I might not live to see it, but these boys will."

The boys look at him and then away, feeling awkward to suddenly
be the center of attention. They play with a gray Chihuahua near a
wall of mounted guns: .22 Magnum, .243 Remington, Winchester
Model 94, Benjamin Air Rifle. Their mother works as a bank teller.
This Saturday, the boys are alone with the men. "We have plenty of
artillery. More in the attic," their daddy says.

"Ain't going to be between North and South, but between black and white," Granddaddy continues. "Blacks make it a race issue. I got kinfolk way back in history hung with a noose. It's a form of saying if you screw up, you get punished. It's got nothing to do with blacks."

He pauses, asks me if I'm all right. Am I sure I don't want to hang my jacket? Am I sure I don't want some coffee? Bathroom just down the hall if I need it. Something seductive in his hospitality. Gentle, so disconnected from his rage. You seem like a good fella, Granddaddy Dupre tells me. But if you're not, if you're some white liberal aligned with the Black Panthers . . . well, just because you got by me coming in, doesn't mean you'll get by me going out. Do you understand that?

The threat is expressed in such a quiet way that it doesn't quite register with me. I can't quite fully comprehend the fury beneath his soft tone of voice.

"Obama. Someone will kill him," Granddaddy says of the senator's presidential bid. "We'll have Obama Day. Ain't time for a black president. That nigger wins, I'll pack my shit and go to Mexico."

"I ain't that extreme, like they should go back to Africa, or anything like that," his son says. "I just don't like them."

He glances at his boys. Makes sure they're listening and understand.

Starting Over

Setting: *Two seventeen-year-old boys, one black and one white, lounge on steps leading into the Jena courthouse on an overcast afternoon, waiting for a mutual friend who is inside appealing a speeding ticket.*

White kid: There's nothing to do here but go out of town. Ride around, watch ESPN.

Black kid: I'm trying to go to college. When I get my income tax refund, I'm leaving.

White kid: No future here. This mess with the high school, it's so big it's become my only memory of Jena. I don't want to say I'm from Jena anymore.

Black kid: The nooses made black people further mad than they already are. What did that mean? They'd hang us for speaking the truth? I feel like whipping some ass.

White kid: I'm leaving. But you know those boys made some money. My momma's boss is a black man. He said he saw one of the Six walking out of the mall in Monroe, hands full of bags.

Black kid: My manager at McDonald's — he's white, he's nice. Most people aren't racist. When I'm not at work, I stay in the house. I remember as a little kid selling blackberries in the white community. I was eight years old. Someone broke into a house somewhere around us. The police picked us up.

White kid: The way this has been handled, more mistakes are going to be made. My momma says I should go to New Orleans.

Black kid: Yeah, start over in a place where everyone's starting over.

The Parade

There is no band. People silently carry placards. DR. KING SAID HATE CANNOT DRIVE OUT HATE. KEEP THE DREAM ALIVE. BLACK POWER IN JENA. IT'S A NEW DAY. Down Oak Street, cars follow the marchers. Their arms are linked; others throw candy to children on the sidewalk. Without music, the march assumes the funereal quiet of news footage from another era. Ignore the wrinkles and gray hair, and a moment of youthful 1960s activism seems to stand resurrected.

The opposition, carrying NO TO MLK signs, seems equally lost in time. Some of them stomp back and forth in army fatigues. *Do we want the values of Jena or the values of a Detroit crack house?* Handguns holstered on their hips, living caricatures of white rage. Some walk dogs with nooses instead of leashes, demand rights for the "white majority."

Half a dozen rotund members of the "New Black Panther Party," outfitted in black lace-up boots, black military uniforms, black berets, and Ray-Ban sunglasses, stand apart and refuse to speak with white people. They pick fights with police and shout triumphantly when one of them is handcuffed and dragged away, caricatures of a dated militancy that Jena's black youth are too young to recall.

And then I see Susan Ory Powers holding hands with a black

woman, and Bobbi Cornett in a van with black kids. I'm relieved by this, but their presence here isn't enough, any more than mine is. We seek absolution, but we are not absolved.

"I tell you what, Jena became the perfect storm of racial incidents," Rev. Thompson told me. "Yes sir, it became the perfect stage for America to play out its racial drama."

The Loop

On a wet Tuesday morning, I check out of my motel and join the small procession of cars on Oak Street. Our headlights sweep past the vacant parking lots of Chamlen's Furniture Store, Sonic, and McDonald's. The Martin Luther King birthday parade and the white rally that followed it left no trail of disruption. This new week brings a sense of relief that there will be no more commotion. For the time being at least, Jena will be quiet.

Dollar General, Auto Zone, Popeye's. My headlights sweep the side streets and dark houses, as if to pinpoint a sleeping unease, the discomfort of distorted dreams, of something amiss. If it can be found, whatever *it* is, perhaps it will dissipate, be absorbed without interruption, or at least forgotten, in the days, weeks, months, and years that compose a life grounded in routine and unhindered by doubt. Or perhaps the marches will keep coming, the people will continue to talk, to try to understand, to forgive.

Minutes outside Jena, I merge onto Louisiana State Highway 127 and then onto US 165; hours later I reach Interstate 530 and US 71, and on and on, each household between Jena and my Kansas City home entwined in a loop of my own making, pulled together by our uncertainty and our yearning, each one of us an outsider in a collective search for common ground.

ANNE GISLESON

■

Your Exhausted Heart

FROM *Oxford American*

A CONVOY OF TOUR BUSES ROLLED UP from St. Bernard Parish, up through the Lower Ninth Ward, and over the St. Claude Avenue Bridge. If it didn't visit the site outright, the convoy probably passed within blocks of the levee breach at the Industrial Canal, where during the storm, a barge came to rest on Jourdan Avenue near the concrete foundations of houses whose former lives were now mapped out in abject squares and rectangles, linoleum flooring still retaining the scuff and tread of their inhabitants. The nose of a yellow school bus was crushed beneath the barge, the tatters of everyday life embedded in the puzzle-patterned mud cracked around it: chairs, tables, toys, appliances, intact jars of baby food, air conditioning units, abandoned wheelchairs and walkers. The destruction went on for mile after numbing mile, all the way down to the Gulf of Mexico.

But the convoy had now crossed the Industrial Canal, going west toward downtown, and was edging along the Bywater, a Ninth Ward neighborhood a few blocks from the Mississippi River, which had little flooding but was rocked by looting and fires and months of abandonment. Then, from their plush-seated, window-tinted vantage point, the passengers — politicians or engineers or disaster tourists — looked down at a corner bar with a few dozen people on the sidewalk and seemingly hundreds more packed into the bar's midday murk. In the cool, late-January drizzle, the people gathered in loose groups on the corner seemed unclassifiable, nattily dressed retirees to tattoo-faced gutterpunks, and many of them cheered the buses as they passed, raised their beer bottles in defiant acknowledgment. The folks on the sidewalk knew what the buses had just witnessed on their tour, were aware of the incongruity of what they were seeing now at barely past noon: a party under the spent neon trimmings of an old corner bar amid hundreds of blocks of desolation, across the street from debris piles as tall as the partygoers.

It was January 28, 2006, and the city was wrecked. The gathering was a memorial celebration. O'Neil Broyard, who owned the Saturn Bar on the corner of Clouet Street and St. Claude Avenue for forty-five years had died at the age of sixty-seven on December 22. He was a victim of a subset of post-Katrina fatalities — older residents who succumbed to the heartbreak, hardship, and fatigue of life in the new New Orleans, where even the most youthful and energetic residents were overwhelmed and working at a near breaking point. When, and if, older evacuees made it back to town, many of them found their houses, neighborhoods, and friends gone. For many of them, "starting over," or even the possibility of another arduous evacuation, was more than daunting, it was the finishing blow. As one elderly gentleman said to a *Times-Picayune* reporter as he stood in his flood- and mold-ravaged living room seven months after the storm, "My future is behind me now."

O'Neil didn't evacuate before the storm, but stayed behind in the leaden August heat and fetid water with a shotgun, two toy poodles, a few cats, and the chickens he'd raised himself from hatchlings. He didn't want anyone messing with his business and the properties he'd accumulated along St. Claude. In the days following the levee breaches, bars all over the Ninth Ward were being looted. My husband, son, and I live four blocks down from the Saturn Bar toward the river. We evacuated at the last minute, but our next-door neighbor, Craig, who, like O'Neil, didn't leave at first either, said he knew it was time to go when he saw a man walking down Clouet carrying armloads of liquor bottles, dropping them in the street as he walked. Craig, a fastidious forensic pathologist who spent the day tidying up his garden as soon as the hurricane had passed, not realizing what was happening at the nearby Industrial Canal and what was happening all over town, kept an errant bottle of Dark Eyes Vodka as a souvenir. Another neighbor said the worst sound during the ordeal of the aftermath was the night howling of the dehydrated drunks in the water-deprived and electricity-dead Bywater. When my husband and I returned to our blasted and beaten neighborhood in early October, one of these drunks, a bedraggled and aging transvestite, staggered up to us as we unloaded the trunk of our car, a go-cup of beer in hand. "Welcome back." After exchanging a few inquiries, he got to what he really wanted to relay. "You know, I stayed. I never went any-where." He stumbled and slurred this badge of honor. "But welcome back." Over the next few months we'd piece together what happened during those first few days and weeks, before O'Neil was taken away at gunpoint by the National Guard, which locked down the neighbor-hood with its Humvees and razor wire.

Life in New Orleans in the months following the storm was heavy and complicated. Layers of bureaucracy collapsed like the floors of an imploded building, one slamming against another: government, in-surance, utilities, government, insurance, utilities, and you could feel the aftershocks reverberate throughout your being. On any given day, nearly every person you encountered, a cashier, waitress, co-worker, an old high-school buddy, had suffered catastrophic loss — homes or jobs or loved ones or all three. In the evenings, my husband and I would go over what we called the "Daily Calamity Report" — fresh news of disaster, who'd lost what, or was leaving town, what places we loved that had just burned down or were not salvageable, any re-cent political bungling or infuriating Army Corps of Engineers rev-elation. Though we lived in the lucky twenty percent of the city that hadn't flooded, the "sliver by the river," or if you lived farther uptown in the more affluent area, "the isle of denial," the mingled sense of urgency and despair was taking its toll, as was watching people you love evolve into strangers under the pressure.

All of this in a landscape of shredded, damaged, or destroyed signs. Literally. Upon returning to New Orleans, one of the more dis-concerting civic casualties was the lack of traffic signals and street signs, though liberating in an anarchical kind of way. Billboards, if still upright, became surrealist collages as years of advertising re-emerged in shredded layers. Almost all contemporary plastic signs were either gone or had had giant wind-fists busted through them. In some cases, the under-layer of old, suspended metal signs revealed their businesses' original monikers (TINA'S CAFÉ on St. Claude was once again PALACE PRIDE HAMBURGERS, the sign replete with turrets) or blown-off siding uncovered the stoic, homely elegance of hundred-year-old signs painted right on buildings, like the huge DRINK REGAL BEER command that emerged down on a Chartres Street restaurant facing the levee. Hurricane as both destroyer and cultural archeologist.

Miraculously, the Saturn Bar's iconic red and turquoise sign featuring the ringed, tilted planet with its swirling surface hung undamaged, one of the few things along St. Claude Avenue that was still intact when we returned. And beneath it we'd sometimes see O'Neil, sitting in front of the propped-open double doors taking a break from the clean-up, trying to catch a breeze and let in some light (as there was still no electricity on that side of the street), his two poodles skittering around the entrance. In the great mess that was everything, it was hard to tell if he was making any progress, but it was just a relief to see him there, back from his forced exile.

Most of the times I laid eyes on O'Neil, he was behind the counter, underneath the flickering black and white television. He and a skulking cat were the only animated elements in the dense landscape of bottles, ephemera, keepsakes, fetishes, and trash that had piled up in front of the bar's clouded, beveled mirror for decades. A former boxer, O'Neil's tough countenance and heavy features were somewhat blurred from a lifetime of bar-owning. He kept his dark hair short and greased and his brown eyes were still bright and wary. He often wore guayaberas wilted from his decades-long battle with the Saturn's air conditioning system, one of his many projects whose fallout accumulated in tangled piles of machinery on the pool table and in the leopard-print booths. Though he had a reputation for sometimes being a little ornery, over the years he was unequivocally nice to me because I was polite, blonde, knew what I liked to drink, and never ordered anything fancy. But if you grilled him about the variety of beers or cigarettes he carried, paid with a twenty-dollar bill on a slow night, or if you ordered a complicated shot ("the layers, they want the layers,") then there was a good chance he'd become surly or downright belligerent.

But he didn't speak much, at least to me. The bar seemed to do the talking for him, both effusive and mysterious in its volume and range of material, open to all species of interpretation. For a long time the Saturn was known for its eccentric décor (mummy suspended from the ceiling, neon-trimmed stuffed sea turtle, decades of Ninth Ward garage-sale finds) and for the wild, apocalyptic paintings of O'Neil's friend Mike Frolich. But as O'Neil's health suffered, even before the storm, the slag heaps and general mayhem of the place drove some patrons away and attracted others. Some, who only knew the place in its later incarnation, swore by the "authenticity" of its decrepit state. But to me that was akin to being intrigued by a barely comprehensible derelict at the end of a bar but never acknowledging whatever detour brought him to that place, what vibrant life he may have lived before, or what fragment of that life was still active in some bright corner of his mind, shining an indirect light on the dimness and chaos.

Before his death, O'Neil willed the Saturn to his nephew on his brother's side, Eric Broyard, who along with most of his extended family had lost everything down in St. Bernard Parish. At first, Eric just wanted to sell his uncle's crazy Ninth Ward bar. Back in the '70s, he and his family had fled that part of town for the burgeoning Parish, where folks were setting up to escape New Orleans' various and growing urban ills. After all, Eric had some good offers and he was trying to get his flooring business back off the ground and take advantage of the building boom that was about to occur. But as they began the clean-up in the requisite hazmat suits and respirators, the Broyard family unearthed signs that maybe the Saturn was more than just an old dive, a big mess they'd been bequeathed. Hidden throughout the bar were old letters requesting bar paraphernalia, testimonials from all over the world about the Saturn's significance to the letter-writer. At the moment, though, what they had was a bar filled with debris comparable to the ratio of the debris that filled the city, the whole parish.

When I first met Eric Broyard in January, he had the increasingly familiar look of a lot of people around town, the tired, uneasy attitude of a man who was faced with so much inconceivable loss, that if he stopped moving, stopped working, he might just fall apart. When you passed by the bar, he was usually shoveling out the soggy wreckage or laying down vinyl floor tiles, and if he paused to speak to you his large body would retain a tense, restless posture. As Eric and his wife, son, daughter, nieces, nephews, and sisters began cleaning out the place in earnest, the neutral ground across the street from the bar filled up with refuse that they carted over in abandoned shopping carts and wheelbarrows. The Army Corps of Engineers, charged with debris removal, would clear the wide, once-grassy neutral ground away and within hours, more would emerge. This cycle was still happening nine months after the storm, stores disgorging themselves of their rotted contents and ruined fixtures onto the neutral ground along St. Claude Avenue. When people saw that Broyard was fixing up the bar, hauling out load after load of junk, people told him to stop, warned that he would ruin the character of the place, the primary draw of the bar. People started sifting through the piles, like the French gleaners, hoping for some treasure or memento. This mess was too huge and it seemed a physical impossibility that a two-room bar with an upstairs gallery could hold that much stuff. But among the picked-over slag piles, my sister found a set of twenty-odd high ball glasses and a case of Saints football-helmet car-antenna ornaments. I myself scored a cut-glass fruit bowl, a promotional Sambuca ashtray, and a silk screen of an old AJ's Produce advertisement from the '60s, whose warehouse at the end of our street exploded and ignited a six-block-long wharf-fire that raged for days in the aftermath of the hurricane.

O'Neil's memorial was just a few weeks into the Carnival season, which begins every year on January 6, the Feast of Epiphany, and on the pool table, along with fried chicken and finger sandwiches were enormous king cakes from Randazzo's Camellia City Bakery. My sister Susan picked the piece of cake with the tiny plastic baby buried in it, which, of course, represents the discovery of the baby Jesus by the Three Wise Men, and promptly handed it over to me, who was six months pregnant at the time. A few months earlier, when we were all still in exile, she's the sister who had told me over a tenuous cell phone connection, "You know, I can totally believe that three-quarters of the city has been all but destroyed, but I still can't believe you're pregnant." I was thirty-seven and had taken my time with the family-making enterprise, marrying the year before, inheriting a seven-year-old stepson, and then getting pregnant during the Mexican honeymoon we returned from a few weeks before having to evacuate. Though I couldn't take part in the triumphant midday send-off for O'Neil as fully as I would have liked, with at least a few beers thrown back in the smoky clamor of the barroom, at least I had the symbolic contribution of my crowd-parting belly.

And the memorial did feel triumphant. Also raising their Budweisers to that passing convoy of buses were guys who used to box in the back room at the Saturn in the '60s, when it housed a ring O'Neil made himself, the upstairs gallery rigged to hold twenty or thirty spectators. These tight, compact men, Jimmy, Tony, and Charles, neighborhood toughs back in the day, had fled the Ninth Ward with their families thirty years before when crime and desegregation pushed too hard against their communities — mostly Italian, Spanish, Irish, and German. Crescents of tank tops visible beneath their ironed shirts, gold crucifixes around their necks, and, in one case, dangling from an ear, with cinched alligator belts and a subdued swagger, they were once again hanging out on the same corner they did as teenagers, beneath the same SATURN BAR sign, looking expectantly up and down a decimated St. Claude Avenue. One gentleman had a Tony Montana cell phone case hitched to his belt, a recent symbol of the thug life that developed from the culture that had driven these guys out to the suburbs of St. Bernard Parish in the '70s.

The gathering was palimpsest of the bar's history, revealing itself with every person I'd bump into, all of its decades represented. Among the hundreds, there was Kenny, the *Times-Picayune* illustrator who'd left his five-foot-tall Dixie beer can costume there one Mardi Gras in the early '80s because it became too cumbersome, and consequently was assumed into the bar's décor. And Jeff Treffinger, owner of the Truck Farm Recording Studios across the street, who twenty years ago was the delivery guy at the Uptown po-boy shop where I worked in high school. I had a big crush on him then, and now his high-school-aged daughter attends the school where I teach. That's the kind of thing that happens when you un-Americanly stay put where you grew up. Life starts to fold back on you. And there were clownish gutterpunks with tattoos and shredded clothes self-consciously pinned back together, who thought they'd found their level in the disturbing decay of the bar, though in reality O'Neil disliked their lack of manners and proclivity to sneak booze into the bar and hang out for hours on the purchase of a couple of Cokes. And aging hipsters, more Broyard family members and friends, more recording studio owners, artists, neighbors, all gathered for the shared purpose of honoring O'Neil and his unwitting life work: the Saturn Bar.

Though the bar's walls are crowded with snapshots of parties, parties, parties, including many for the wrap of a Nicolas Cage movie from the mid–'90s (celebrities like Sean Penn, John Goodman, and Tommy Lee Jones were also drawn to its wacked glamour and obscurity) and once you could spend evenings in the storied booths watching people come through the swinging doors and step into the transformative air of the Saturn, the place had never, ever seemed so alive. Though there were no movie stars, this gathering felt like a cinematic finale, filled with reunions and pronouncements and atmospheric import. No Uptown frat boys ordering shots of Jägermeister only to throw the glass against the wall, no tourists who'd read about it in *Esquire* or in an online travel magazine. It was the people who'd known and loved O'Neil and his bar and who, for whatever reason, were still in New Orleans five months after the storm when hundreds of thousands couldn't, or wouldn't, come back.

Above all, there was the Broyard family. They had invited everyone they knew and had done some modest advertising, but had had no idea what to expect. They were earnestly shocked by the large turnout and Eric later said it gave them the confidence to make a go out of reopening the place, even with O'Neil being gone, even with the local economy in shreds. They rushed around in black SATURN BAR T-shirts, bussing tables, taking pictures, and serving drinks, ebullient and proud, embodying the vanishing New Orleans tradition of the generational family business. O'Neil himself was even there, back behind his bar. His ashes had been interred in a brass urn and placed by the cash register, where he is forever remembered by thousands and forever at one with his clutter.

The event was a small but concentrated triumph for the city's past and maybe its future, so on that Saturday afternoon when the buses passed us by, loaded with these outsiders, come to check out our devastation, our progress and lack of it, our piles of debris and our pain, mile after mile of this complicated, colossal failure, we found ourselves speculating about the passengers' speculation. Did they think we should be out gutting and rebuilding and cleaning, not drinking, in the middle of the afternoon in what appeared to be the only functioning business for miles? But of course, it wasn't really functioning. It was merely open. Liquor licenses had lapsed after the storm and the Broyards were giving the beer away, as O'Neil would've wanted it. No commerce, just generosity and gratitude. And we weren't just partying; it was a respite from the overwhelming work of reconstruction. During those few months, immediately following the storm, when there was much concern about the city's diminished population, any critical mass of people felt strangely victorious, a desperate grab at a handful of social fabric. This memorial was a loaded moment of many loaded moments in the new New Orleans, a place and time when everything you did carried meaning, getting a piece of mail, buying a cup of coffee, walking your kid to school. The stakes were high, and everyone seemed to be making big decisions all the time. So this was what it was to live inside of history. Your exhausted heart was always on the verge of something, breaking in despair or bursting with gratitude, and your soul stretched in ways that weren't pleasant but that made you feel very alive.

The convoy of buses would continue along St. Claude Avenue, passing collapsed furniture stores, and burned-out businesses, stolen (then abandoned) city buses, and rescue boats grounded when the water finally receded. They would roll back to their hotels downtown, the ones that were open and not filled with relief workers and journalists and FEMA recipients. But first they would pass the storefronts along Canal Street from Claiborne Avenue to the river, some still closed and blank with plywood, others broken open and glittering with shattered shop windows.

DAVID GRANN

■

The Chameleon

FROM *The New Yorker*

ON MAY 3, 2005, IN FRANCE, a man called an emergency hot line
for missing and exploited children. He frantically explained that he
was a tourist passing through Orthez, near the western Pyrenees,
and that at the train station he had encountered a fifteen-year-old
boy who was alone, and terrified. Another hot line received a similar
call, and the boy eventually arrived, by himself, at a local government
child-welfare office. Slender and short, with pale skin and trembling
hands, he wore a muffler around much of his face and had a baseball
cap pulled over his eyes. He had no money and carried little more
than a cell phone and an ID, which said that his name was Francisco
Hernandez Fernandez and that he was born on December 13, 1989,
in Cáceres, Spain. Initially, he barely spoke, but after some prodding
he revealed that his parents and younger brother had been killed in
a car accident. The crash left him in a coma for several weeks and,
upon recovering, he was sent to live with an uncle, who abused him.
Finally, he fled to France, where his mother had grown up.

French authorities placed Francisco at the St. Vincent de Paul shelter in the nearby city of Pau. A state-run institution that housed about
thirty-five boys and girls, most of whom had been either removed
from dysfunctional families or abandoned, the shelter was in an old
stone building with peeling white wooden shutters; on the roof was a
statue of St. Vincent protecting a child in the folds of his gown. Francisco was given a single room, and he seemed relieved to be able to
wash and change in private: his head and body, he explained, were
covered in burns and scars from the car accident. He was enrolled at

the Collège Jean Monnet, a local secondary school that had four hundred or so students, mostly from tough neighborhoods, and that had a reputation for violence. Although students were forbidden to wear hats, the principal at the time, Claire Chadourne, made an exception for Francisco, who said that he feared being teased about his scars. Like many of the social workers and teachers who dealt with Francisco, Chadourne, who had been an educator for more than thirty years, felt protective toward him. With his baggy pants and his cell phone dangling from a cord around his neck, he looked like a typical teenager, but he seemed deeply traumatized. He never changed his clothes in front of the other students in gym class, and resisted being subjected to a medical exam. He spoke softly, with his head bowed, and recoiled if anyone tried to touch him.

Gradually, Francisco began hanging out with other kids at recess and participating in class. Since he had enrolled so late in the school year, his literature teacher asked another student, Rafael Pessoa De Almeida, to help him with his coursework. Before long, Francisco was helping Rafael. "This guy can learn like lightning," Rafael recalls thinking.

One day after school, Rafael asked Francisco if he wanted to go iceskating, and the two became friends, playing video games and sharing school gossip. Rafael sometimes picked on his younger brother, and Francisco, recalling that he used to mistreat his own sibling, advised, "Make sure you love your brother and stay close."

At one point, Rafael borrowed Francisco's cell phone; to his surprise, its address book and call log were protected by security codes. When Rafael returned the phone, Francisco displayed a photograph on its screen of a young boy who looked just like Francisco. "That's my brother," he said.

Francisco was soon one of the most popular kids in school, dazzling classmates with his knowledge of music and arcane slang — he even knew American idioms — and moving effortlessly between rival cliques. "The students loved him," a teacher recalls. "He had this aura about him, this charisma."

During tryouts for a talent show, the music teacher asked Francisco if he was interested in performing. He handed her a CD to play, then walked to the end of the room and tilted his hat flamboyantly, waiting for the music to start. As Michael Jackson's song "Unbreakable" filled the room, Francisco started to dance like the pop star, twisting his limbs and lip-synching the words. "He didn't just look like Michael Jackson," the music teacher subsequently recalled. "He *was* Michael Jackson."

Later, in computer class, Francisco showed Rafael an Internet image of a small reptile with a slithery tongue.

"What is it?" Rafael asked.

"A chameleon," Francisco replied.

On June 8th, an administrator rushed into the principal's office. She said that she had been watching a television program the other night about one of the world's most infamous impostors: Frédéric Bourdin, a thirty-year-old Frenchman who serially impersonated children. "I swear to God, Bourdin looks exactly like Francisco Hernandez Fernandez," the administrator said.

Chadourne was incredulous: thirty would make Francisco older than some of her teachers. She did a quick Internet search for "Frédéric Bourdin." Hundreds of news items came up about the "king of impostors" and the "master of new identities," who, like Peter Pan, "didn't want to grow up." A photograph of Bourdin closely resembled Francisco — there was the same formidable chin, the same gap between the front teeth. Chadourne called the police.

"Are you sure it's him?" an officer asked.

"No, but I have this strange feeling."

When the police arrived, Chadourne sent the assistant principal to summon Francisco from class. As Francisco entered Chadourne's office, the police seized him and thrust him against the wall, causing her to panic: what if he really was an abused orphan? Then, while handcuffing Bourdin, the police removed his baseball cap. There were no scars on his head; rather, he was going bald. "I want a lawyer," he said, his voice suddenly dropping to that of a man.

At police headquarters, he admitted that he was Frédéric Bourdin, and that in the past decade and a half he had invented scores of identities, in more than fifteen countries and five languages. His aliases included Benjamin Kent, Jimmy Morins, Alex Dole, Sladjan Raskovic, Arnaud Orions, Giovanni Petrullo, and Michelangelo Martini. News reports claimed that he had even impersonated a tiger tamer and a priest, but, in truth, he had nearly always played a similar character: an abused or abandoned child. He was unusually adept at transforming his appearance — his facial hair, his weight, his walk, his mannerisms. "I can become whatever I want," he liked to say. In 2004, when he pretended to be a fourteen-year-old French boy in the town of Grenoble, a doctor who examined him at the request of authorities concluded that he was, indeed, a teenager. A police captain in Pau noted, "When he talked in Spanish, he became a Spaniard. When he talked in English, he was an Englishman." Chadourne said of him, "Of course, he lied, but what an actor!"

Over the years, Bourdin had insinuated himself into youth shelters, orphanages, foster homes, junior high schools, and children's hospitals. His trail of cons extended to, among other places, Spain, Germany, Belgium, England, Ireland, Italy, Luxembourg, Switzerland, Bosnia, Portugal, Austria, Slovakia, France, Sweden, Denmark, and America. The U.S. State Department warned that he was an "exceedingly clever" man who posed as a desperate child in order to "win sympathy," and a French prosecutor called him "an incredible illusionist whose perversity is matched only by his intelligence." Bourdin himself has said, "I am a manipulator . . . My job is to manipulate."

In Pau, the authorities launched an investigation to determine why a thirty-year-old man would pose as a teenage orphan. They found no evidence of sexual deviance or pedophilia; they did not uncover any financial motive, either. "In my twenty-two years on the job, I've never seen a case like it," Eric Maurel, the prosecutor, told me. "Usually people con for money. His profit seems to have been purely emotional."

On his right forearm, police discovered a tattoo. It said "*caméléon nantais*" — "Chameleon from Nantes."

"Mr. Grann," Bourdin said, politely extending his hand to me. We were on a street in the center of Pau, where he had agreed to meet me one morning last fall. For once, he seemed unmistakably an adult, with a faint five-o'clock shadow. He was dressed theatrically, in white pants, a white shirt, a checkered vest, white shoes, a blue satin bow tie, and a foppish hat. Only the gap between his teeth evoked the memory of Francisco Hernandez Fernandez.

After his ruse in Pau had been exposed, Bourdin moved to a village in the Pyrenees, twenty-five miles away. "I wanted to escape from all the glare," he said. As had often been the case with Bourdin's deceptions, the authorities were not sure how to punish him. Psychiatrists determined that he was sane. ("Is he a psychopath?" one doctor testified. "Absolutely not.") No statute seemed to fit his crime. Ultimately, he was charged with obtaining and using a fake ID, and received a six-month suspended sentence.

A local reporter, Xavier Sota, told me that since then Bourdin had periodically appeared in Pau, always in a different guise. Sometimes he had a mustache or a beard. Sometimes his hair was tightly cropped; at other times, it was straggly. Sometimes he dressed like a rapper, and on other occasions like a businessman. "It was as if he were trying to find a new character to inhabit," Sota said.

Bourdin and I sat down on a bench near the train station, as a light rain began to fall. A car paused by the curb in front of us, with a couple inside. They rolled down the window, peered out, and said to each other, "Le Caméléon."

"I am quite famous in France these days," Bourdin said. "Too famous."

As we spoke, his large brown eyes flitted across me, seemingly taking me in. One of his police interrogators called him a "human recorder." To my surprise, Bourdin knew where I had worked, where I was born, the name of my wife, even what my sister and brother did for a living. "I like to know whom I'm meeting," he said.

Aware of how easy it is to deceive others, he was paranoid of being a mark. "I don't trust anybody," he said. For a person who described himself as a "professional liar," he seemed oddly fastidious about the facts of his own life. "I don't want you to make me into somebody I'm not," he said. "The story is good enough without embellishment."

I knew that Bourdin had grown up in and around Nantes, and I asked him about his tattoo. Why would someone who tried to erase his identity leave a trace of one? He rubbed his arm where the words were imprinted on his skin. Then he said, "I will tell you the truth behind all my lies."

Before he was Benjamin Kent or Michelangelo Martini — before he was the child of an English judge or an Italian diplomat — he was Frédéric Pierre Bourdin, the illegitimate son of Ghislaine Bourdin, who was eighteen and poor when she gave birth to him, in a suburb of Paris, on June 13, 1974. On government forms, Frédéric's father is often listed as "X," meaning that his identity was unknown. But Ghislaine, during an interview at her small house, in a rural area in western France, told me that "X" was a twenty-five-year-old Algerian immigrant named Kaci, whom she had met at a margarine factory where they both worked. (She says that she can no longer remember his last name.) After she became pregnant, she discovered that Kaci was already married, and so she left her job and did not tell him that she was carrying his child.

Ghislaine raised Frédéric until he was two and a half — "He was like any other child, totally normal," she says — at which time child services intervened at the behest of her parents. A relative says of Ghislaine, "She liked to drink and dance and stay out at night. She didn't want anything to do with that child." Ghislaine insists that she had obtained another factory job and was perfectly competent, but the judge placed Frédéric in her parents' custody. Years later, Ghislaine wrote Frédéric a letter, telling him, "You are my son and they stole you from me at the age of two. They did everything to separate us from each other and we have become two strangers."

Frédéric says that his mother had a dire need for attention and, on the rare occasions that he saw her, she would feign being deathly ill and make him run to get help. "To see me frightened gave her pleasure," he says. Though Ghislaine denies this, she acknowledges that she once attempted suicide and her son had to rush to find assistance.

When Frédéric was five, he moved with his grandparents to Mouchamps, a hamlet southeast of Nantes. Frédéric — part Algerian and fatherless, and dressed in secondhand clothes from Catholic charities — was a village outcast, and in school he began to tell fabulous stories about himself. He said that his father was never around because he was a "British secret agent." One of his elementary school teachers, Yvon Bourgueil, describes Bourdin as a precocious and captivating child, who had an extraordinary imagination and visual sense, drawing wild, beautiful comic strips. "He had this way of making you connect to him," Bourgueil recalls. He also noticed signs of mental distress. At one point, Frédéric told his grandparents that he had been molested by a neighbor, though nobody in the tightly knit village investigated the allegation. In one of his comic strips, Frédéric depicted himself drowning in a river. He increasingly misbehaved, acting out in class and stealing from neighbors. At twelve, he was sent to live at Les Grézillières, a private facility for juveniles, in Nantes.

There, his "little dramas," as one of his teachers called them, became more fanciful. Bourdin often pretended to be an amnesiac, intentionally getting lost in the streets. In 1990, after he turned sixteen, Frédéric was forced to move to another youth home, and he soon ran away. He hitchhiked to Paris, where, scared and hungry, he invented his first fake character: he approached a police officer and told him that he was a lost British teen named Jimmy Sale. "I dreamed they would send me to England, where I always imagined life was more beautiful," he recalls. When the police discovered that he spoke almost no English, he admitted his deceit and was returned to the youth home. But he had devised what he calls his "technique," and in this fashion he began to wander across Europe, moving in and out of orphanages and foster homes, searching for the "perfect shelter." In 1991, he was found in a train station in Langres, France, pretending to be sick, and was placed in a children's hospital in Saint-Dizier. According to his medical report, no one knew "who he was or where he came from." Answering questions only in writing, he indicated that his name was Frédéric Cassis — a play on his real father's first name, Kaci. Frédéric's doctor, Jean-Paul Milanese, wrote in a letter to a child-welfare judge, "We find ourselves confronted with a young runaway teen, mute, having broken with his former life."

On a piece of paper, Bourdin scribbled what he wanted most: "A home and a school. That's all."

When doctors started to unravel his past, a few months later, Bourdin confessed his real identity and moved on. "I would rather leave on my own than be taken away," he told me. During his career as an impostor, Bourdin often voluntarily disclosed the truth, as if the attention that came from exposure were as thrilling as the con itself.

On June 13, 1992, after he had posed as more than a dozen fictional children, Bourdin turned eighteen, becoming a legal adult. "I'd been in shelters and foster homes most of my life, and suddenly I was told, 'That's it. You're free to go,' " he recalls. "How could I become something I could not imagine?" In November, 1993, posing as a mute child, he lay down in the middle of a street in the French town of Auch and was taken by firemen to a hospital. *La Dépêche du Midi*, a local newspaper, ran a story about him, asking, "Where does this mute adolescent . . . come from?" The next day, the paper published another article, under the headline "THE MUTE ADOLESCENT WHO APPEARED OUT OF NOWHERE HAS STILL NOT REVEALED HIS SECRET." After fleeing, he was caught attempting a similar ruse nearby and admitted that he was Frédéric Bourdin. "THE MUTE OF AUCH SPEAKS FOUR LANGUAGES," *La Dépêche du Midi* proclaimed.

As Bourdin assumed more and more identities, he attempted to kill off his real one. One day, the mayor of Mouchamps received a call from the "German police" notifying him that Bourdin's body had been found in Munich. When Bourdin's mother was told the news, she recalls, "My heart stopped." Members of Bourdin's family waited for a coffin to arrive, but it never did. "It was Frédéric playing one of his cruel games," his mother says.

By the mid-nineties, Bourdin had accumulated a criminal record for lying to police and magistrates, and Interpol and other authorities were increasingly on the lookout for him. His activities were also garnering media attention. In 1995, the producers of a popular French television show called *Everything Is Possible* invited him on the program. As Bourdin appeared onstage, looking pale and prepubescent, the host teasingly asked the audience, "What's this boy's name? Michael, Jürgen, Kevin, or Pedro? What's his real age — thirteen, fourteen, fifteen?" Pressed about his motivations, Bourdin again insisted that all he wanted was love and a family. It was the same rationale he always gave, and, as a result, he was the rare impostor who elicited sympathy as well as anger from those he had duped. (His mother has a less charitable interpretation of her son's stated motive: "He wants to justify what he has become.")

The producers of *Everything Is Possible* were so affected by his story that they offered him a job in the station's newsroom, but he soon ran off to create more "interior fictions," as one of the producers later told a reporter. At times, Bourdin's deceptions were viewed in existential terms. One of his devotees in France created a website that celebrated his shape-shifting, hailing him as an "actor of life and an apostle of a new philosophy of human identity."

One day when I was visiting Bourdin, he described how he transformed himself into a child. Like the impostors he had seen in films such as *Catch Me If You Can*, he tried to elevate his criminality into an "art." First, he said, he conceived of a child whom he wanted to play. Then he gradually mapped out the character's biography, from his heritage to his family to his tics. "The key is actually not lying about everything," Bourdin said. "Otherwise, you'll just mix things up." He said that he adhered to maxims such as "Keep it simple" and "A good liar uses the truth." In choosing a name, he preferred one that carried a deep association in his memory, like Cassis. "The one thing you better not forget is your name," he said.

He compared what he did to being a spy: you changed superficial details while keeping your core intact. This approach not only made it easier to convince people; it allowed him to protect a part of his self, to hold on to some moral center. "I know I can be cruel, but I don't want to become a monster," he said.

Once he had imagined a character, he fashioned a commensurate appearance — meticulously shaving his face, plucking his eyebrows, using hair-removal creams. He often put on baggy pants and a shirt with long sleeves that swallowed his wrists, emphasizing his smallness. Peering in a mirror, he asked himself if others would see what he wanted them to see. "The worst thing you can do is deceive yourself," he said.

When he honed an identity, it was crucial to find some element of the character that he shared — a technique employed by many actors. "People always say to me, 'Why don't you become an actor?' " he told me. "I think I would be a very good actor, like Arnold Schwarzenegger or Sylvester Stallone. But I don't want to play somebody. I want to *be* somebody."

In order to help ease his character into the real world, he fostered the illusion among local authorities that his character actually existed. As he had done in Orthez, he would call a hot line and claim to have seen the character in a perilous situation. The authorities were less likely to grill a child who appeared to be in distress. If someone noticed that Bourdin looked oddly mature, however, he did not object. "A teenager wants to look older," he said. "I treat it like a compliment."

Though he emphasized his cunning, he acknowledged what any con man knows but rarely admits: it is not that hard to fool people. People have basic expectations of others' behavior and are rarely on guard for someone to subvert them. By playing on some primal need — vanity, greed, loneliness — men like Bourdin make their mark further suspend disbelief. As a result, most cons are filled with logical inconsistencies, even absurdities, which seem humiliatingly obvious after the fact. Bourdin, who generally tapped into a mark's sense of goodness rather than into some darker urge, says, "Nobody expects a seemingly vulnerable child to be lying."

In October 1997, Bourdin told me, he was at a youth home in Linares, Spain. A child-welfare judge who was handling his case had given him twenty-four hours to prove that he was a teenager; otherwise, she would take his fingerprints, which were on file with Interpol. Bourdin knew that, as an adult with a criminal record, he would likely face prison. He had already tried to run away once and was caught, and the staff was keeping an eye on his whereabouts. And so he did something that both stretched the bounds of credulity and threatened to transform him into the kind of "monster" that he had insisted he never wanted to become. Rather than invent an identity, he stole one. He assumed the persona of a missing sixteen-year-old boy from Texas. Bourdin, now twenty-three, not only had to convince the authorities that he was an American child; he had to convince the missing boy's family.

According to Bourdin, the plan came to him in the middle of the night: if he could fool the judge into thinking that he was an American, he might be let go. He asked permission to use the telephone in the shelter's office and called the National Center for Missing and Exploited Children, in Alexandria, Virginia, trolling for a real identity. Speaking in English, which he had picked up during his travels, he claimed that his name was Jonathan Durean and that he was a director of the Linares shelter. He said that a frightened child had turned up who would not disclose his identity but who spoke English with an American accent. Bourdin offered a description of the boy that matched himself — short, slight, prominent chin, brown hair, a gap between his teeth — and asked if the center had anyone similar in its database. After searching, Bourdin recalls, a woman at the center said that the boy might be Nicholas Barclay, who had been reported missing in San Antonio on June 13, 1994, at the age of thirteen. Barclay was last seen, according to his file, wearing "a white T-shirt, purple pants, black tennis shoes and carrying a pink backpack."

Adopting a skeptical tone, Bourdin says, he asked if the center could send any more information that it had regarding Barclay. The woman said that she would mail overnight Barclay's missing-person flyer and immediately fax a copy as well. After giving her the fax number in the office he was borrowing, Bourdin says, he hung up and waited. Peeking out the door, he looked to see if anyone was coming. The hallway was dark and quiet, but he could hear footsteps. At last, a copy of the flyer emerged from the fax machine. The printout was so faint that most of it was illegible. Still, the photograph's resemblance to him did not seem that far off. "I can do this," Bourdin recalls thinking. He quickly called back the center, he says, and told the woman, "I have some good news. Nicholas Barclay is standing right beside me."

Elated, she gave him the number of the officer in the San Antonio Police Department who was in charge of the investigation. This time pretending to be a Spanish policeman, Bourdin says, he phoned the officer and, mentioning details about Nicholas that he had learned from the woman at the center — such as the pink backpack — declared that the missing child had been found. The officer said that he would contact the FBI and the U.S. Embassy in Madrid. Bourdin had not fully contemplated what he was about to unleash.

The next day at the Linares shelter, Bourdin intercepted a package from the National Center for Missing and Exploited Children addressed to Jonathan Durean. He ripped open the envelope. Inside was a clean copy of Nicholas Barclay's missing-person flyer. It showed a color photograph of a small, fair-skinned boy with blue eyes and brown hair so light that it appeared almost blond. The flyer listed several identifying features, including a cross tattooed between Barclay's right index finger and thumb. Bourdin stared at the picture and said to himself, "I'm dead." Not only did Bourdin not have the same tattoo; his eyes and hair were dark brown. In haste, he burned the flyer in the shelter's courtyard, then went into the bathroom and bleached his hair. Finally, he had a friend, using a needle and ink from a pen, give him a makeshift tattoo resembling Barclay's.

Still, there was the matter of Bourdin's eyes. He tried to conceive of a story that would explain his appearance. What if he had been abducted by a child sex ring and flown to Europe, where he had been tortured and abused, even experimented on? Yes, that could explain the eyes. His kidnappers had injected his pupils with chemicals. He had lost his Texas accent because, for more than three years of captivity, he had been forbidden to speak English. He had escaped from a locked room in a house in Spain when a guard carelessly left the door open. It was a crazy tale, one that violated his maxim to "keep it simple," but it would have to do.

Soon after, the phone in the office rang. Bourdin took the call. It was Nicholas Barclay's thirty-one-year-old half sister, Carey Gibson. "My God, Nicky, is that you?" she asked.

Bourdin didn't know how to respond. He adopted a muffled voice, then said, "Yes, it's me."

Nicholas's mother, Beverly, got on the phone. A tough, heavyset woman with a broad face and dyed-brown hair, she worked the graveyard shift at a Dunkin' Donuts in San Antonio seven nights a week. She had never married Nicholas's father and had raised Nicholas with her two older children, Carey and Jason. (She was divorced from Carey and Jason's father, though she still used her married name, Dollarhide.) A heroin addict, she had struggled during Nicholas's youth to get off drugs. After he disappeared, she had begun to use heroin again and was now addicted to methadone. Despite these difficulties, Carey says, Beverly was not a bad mother: "She was maybe the most functioning drug addict. We had nice things, a nice place, never went without food." Perhaps compensating for the instability in her life, Beverly fanatically followed a routine: working at the doughnut shop from 10 P.M. to 5 A.M., then stopping at the Make My Day Lounge to shoot pool and have a few beers, before going home to sleep. She had a hardness about her, with a cigarette-roughened voice, but people who know her also spoke to me of her kindness. After her night shift, she delivered any leftover doughnuts to a homeless shelter.

Beverly pulled the phone close to her ear. After the childlike voice on the other end said that he wanted to come home, she told me, "I was dumbfounded and blown away."

Carey, who was married and had two children of her own, had often held the family together during Beverly's struggles with drug addiction. Since Nicholas's disappearance, her mother and brother had never seemed the same, and all Carey wanted was to make the family whole again. She volunteered to go to Spain to bring Nicholas home, and the packing-and-shipping company where she worked in sales support offered to pay her fare.

When she arrived at the shelter, a few days later, accompanied by an official from the U.S. Embassy, Bourdin had secluded himself in a room. What he had done, he concedes, was evil. But if he had any moral reservations they did not stop him, and after wrapping his face in a scarf and putting on a hat and sunglasses he came out of the room. He was sure that Carey would instantly realize that he wasn't her brother. Instead, she rushed toward him and hugged him.

Carey was, in many ways, an ideal mark. "My daughter has the best heart and is so easy to manipulate," Beverly says. Carey had never traveled outside the United States, except for partying in Tijuana, and was unfamiliar with European accents and with Spain. After Nicholas disappeared, she had often watched television news programs about lurid child abductions. In addition to feeling the pressure of having received money from her company to make the trip, she had the burden of deciding, as her family's representative, whether this was her long-lost brother.

Though Bourdin referred to her as "Carey" rather than "sis," as Nicholas always had, and though he had a trace of a French accent,

Carey says that she had little doubt that it was Nicholas. Not when he could attribute any inconsistencies to his unspeakable ordeal. Not when his nose now looked so much like her uncle Pat's. Not when he had the same tattoo as Nicholas and seemed to know so many details about her family, asking about relatives by name. "Your heart takes over and you want to believe," Carey says.

She showed Bourdin photographs of the family and he studied each one: this is my mother; this is my half brother; this is my grandfather.

Neither American nor Spanish officials raised any questions once Carey had vouched for him. Nicholas had been gone for only three years, and the FBI was not primed to be suspicious of someone claiming to be a missing child. (The agency told me that, to its knowledge, it had never worked on a case like Bourdin's before.) According to authorities in Madrid, Carey swore under oath that Bourdin was her brother and an American citizen. He was granted a U.S. passport and, the next day, he was on a flight to San Antonio.

For a moment, Bourdin fantasized that he was about to become part of a real family, but halfway to America he began to "freak out," as Carey puts it, trembling and sweating. As she tried to comfort him, he told her that he thought the plane was going to crash, which, he later said, is what he wanted: how else could he escape from what he had done?

When the plane landed, on October 18, 1997, members of Nicholas's family were waiting for him at the airport. Bourdin recognized them from Carey's photographs: Beverly, Nicholas's mother; Carey's then husband, Bryan Gibson; Bryan and Carey's fourteen-year-old son, Codey, and their ten-year-old daughter, Chantel. Only Nicholas's brother, Jason, who was a recovering drug addict and living in San Antonio, was absent. A friend of the family videotaped the reunion, and Bourdin can be seen bundled up, his hat pulled down, his brown eyes shielded by sunglasses, his already fading tattoo covered by gloves. Though Bourdin had thought that Nicholas's relatives were going to "hang" him, they rushed to embrace him, saying how much they had missed him. "We were all just emotionally crazy," Codey recalls. Nicholas's mother, however, hung back. "She just didn't seem excited" the way you'd expect from someone "seeing her son," Chantel told me.

Bourdin wondered if Beverly doubted that he was Nicholas, but eventually she, too, greeted him. They all got in Carey's Lincoln Town Car and stopped at McDonald's for cheeseburgers and fries. As Carey recalls it, "He was just sitting by my mom, talking to my son," saying how much "he missed school and asking when he'd see Jason."

Bourdin went to stay with Carey and Bryan rather than live with Beverly. "I work nights and didn't think it was good to leave him alone," Beverly said. Carey and Bryan owned a trailer home in a desolate wooded area in Spring Branch, thirty-five miles north of San Antonio, and Bourdin stared out the window as the car wound along a dirt road, past rusted trucks on cinder blocks and dogs barking at the sound of the engine. As Codey puts it, "We didn't have no Internet, or stuff like that. You can walk all the way to San Antonio before you get any kind of communication."

Their cramped trailer home was not exactly the vision of America that Bourdin had imagined from movies. He shared a room with Codey, and slept on a foam mattress on the floor. Bourdin knew that, if he were to become Nicholas and to continue to fool even his family, he had to learn everything about him, and he began to mine information, secretly rummaging through drawers and picture albums, and watching home videos. When Bourdin discovered a detail about Nicholas's past from one family member, he would repeat it to another. He pointed out, for example, that Bryan once got mad at Nicholas for knocking Codey out of a tree. "He knew that story," Codey recalls, still amazed by the amount of intelligence that Bourdin acquired about the family. Beverly noticed that Bourdin knelt in front of the television, just as Nicholas had. Various members of the family told me that when Bourdin seemed more standoffish than Nicholas or spoke with a strange accent they assumed that it was because of the terrible treatment that he said he had suffered.

As Bourdin came to inhabit the life of Nicholas, he was struck by what he considered to be uncanny similarities between them. Nicholas had been reported missing on Bourdin's birthday. Both came from poor, broken families; Nicholas had almost no relationship with his father, who for a long time didn't know that Nicholas was his son. Nicholas was a sweet, lonely, combustible kid who craved attention and was often in trouble at school. He had been caught stealing a pair of tennis shoes, and his mother had planned to put him in a youth home. ("I couldn't handle him," Beverly recalls. "I couldn't control him.") When Nicholas was young, he was a diehard Michael Jackson fan who had collected all the singer's records and even owned a red leather jacket like the one Jackson wears in his "Thriller" video.

According to Beverly, Bourdin quickly "blended in." He was enrolled in high school and did his homework each night, chastising Codey when he failed to study. He played Nintendo with Codey and watched movies with the family on satellite TV. When he saw Beverly, he hugged her and said, "Hi, Mom." Occasionally on Sundays, he attended church with other members of the family. "He was really nice," Chantel recalls. "Really friendly." Once, when Carey was shooting a home movie of Bourdin, she asked him what he was thinking. "It's really good to have my family and be home again," he replied.

On November 1st, not long after Bourdin had settled into his new home, Charlie Parker, a private investigator, was sitting in his office in San Antonio. The room was crammed with hidden cameras that he deployed in the field: one was attached to a pair of eyeglasses, another was lodged inside a fountain pen, and a third was concealed on the handlebars of a ten-speed bicycle. On a wall hung a photograph that Parker had taken during a stakeout: it showed a married woman with her lover, peeking out of an apartment window. Parker, who had been hired by the woman's husband, called it the "money shot."

Parker's phone rang. It was a television producer from the tabloid show *Hard Copy*, who had heard about the extraordinary return of sixteen-year-old Nicholas Barclay and wanted to hire Parker to help investigate the kidnapping. He agreed to take the job.

With silver hair and a raspy voice, Parker, who was then in his late fifties, appeared to have stepped out of a dime novel. When he bought himself a bright-red Toyota convertible, he said to friends, "How ya like that for an old man?" Though Parker had always dreamed about being a PI, he had only recently become one, having spent thirty years selling lumber and building materials. In 1994, Parker met a San

Antonio couple whose twenty-nine-year-old daughter had been raped and fatally stabbed. The case was unsolved, and he began investigating the crime each night after coming home from work. When he discovered that a recently paroled murderer had lived next door to the victim, Parker staked out the man's house, peering out from a white van through infrared goggles. The suspect was soon arrested and ultimately convicted of the murder. Captivated by the experience, Parker formed a "murders club," dedicated to solving cold cases. (Its members included a college psychology professor, a lawyer, and a fry cook.) Within months, the club had uncovered evidence that helped to convict a member of the Air Force who had strangled a fourteen-year-old girl. In 1995, Parker received his license as a private investigator, and he left his life in the lumber business behind.

After Parker spoke with the *Hard Copy* producer, he easily traced Nicholas Barclay to Carey and Bryan's trailer. On November 6th, Parker arrived there with a producer and a camera crew. The family didn't want Bourdin to speak to reporters. "I'm a very private person," Carey says. But Bourdin, who had been in the country for nearly three weeks, agreed to talk. "I wanted the attention at the time," he says. "It was a psychological need. Today, I wouldn't do it."

Parker stood off to one side, listening intently as the young man relayed his harrowing story. "He was calm as a cucumber," Parker told me. "No looking down, no body language. None." But Parker was puzzled by his curious accent.

Parker spied a photograph on a shelf of Nicholas Barclay as a young boy, and kept looking at it and at the person in front of him, thinking that something was amiss. Having once read that ears are distinct, like fingerprints, he went up to the cameraman and whispered, "Zoom in on his ears. Get 'em as close as you can."

Parker slipped the photograph of Nicholas Barclay into his pocket, and after the interview he hurried back to his office and used a scanner to transfer the photo to his computer; he then studied video from the *Hard Copy* interview. Parker zeroed in on the ears in both pictures. "The ears were close, but they didn't match," he says.

Parker called several ophthalmologists and asked if eyes could be changed from blue to brown by injecting chemicals. The doctors said no. Parker also phoned a dialect expert at Trinity University, in San

Antonio, who told him that, even if someone had been held in captivity for three years, he would quickly regain his native accent.

Parker passed on his suspicions to authorities, even though the San Antonio police had declared that "the boy who came back claiming to be Nicholas Barclay is Nicholas Barclay." Fearing that a dangerous stranger was living with Nicholas's family, Parker phoned Beverly and told her what he had discovered. As he recalls the conversation, he said, "It's not him, Ma'am. It's not him."

"What do you mean, it's not him?" she asked.

Parker explained about the ears and the eyes and the accent. In his files, Parker wrote, "Family is upset but maintains that they believe it is their son."

Parker says that a few days later he received an angry call from Bourdin. Although Bourdin denies that he made the call, Parker noted in his file at the time that Bourdin said, "Who do you think you are?" When Parker replied that he didn't believe he was Nicholas, Bourdin shot back, "Immigration thinks it's me. The family thinks it's me."

Parker wondered if he should let the matter go. He had tipped off authorities and was no longer under contract to investigate the matter. He had other cases piling up. And he figured that a mother would know her own son. Still, the boy's accent sounded French, maybe French Moroccan. If so, what was a foreigner doing infiltrating a trailer home in the backwoods of Texas? "I thought he was a terrorist, I swear to God," Parker says.

Beverly rented a small room in a run-down apartment complex in San Antonio, and Parker started to follow Bourdin when he visited her. "I'd set up on the apartment, and watch him come out," Parker says. "He would walk all the way to the bus stop, wearing his Walkman and doing his Michael Jackson moves."

Bourdin was struggling to stay in character. He found living with Carey and Beverly "claustrophobic," and was happiest when he was outside, wandering the streets. "I was not used to being in someone else's family, to live with them like I'm one of theirs," he says. "I wasn't ready for it." One day, Carey and the family presented him with a cardboard box. Inside were Nicholas's baseball cards, records, and various mementos. He picked up each item, gingerly. There was a letter from one of Nicholas's girlfriends. As he read it, he said to himself, "I'm not this boy."

After two months in the United States, Bourdin started to come apart. He was moody and aloof — "weirding out," as Codey put it. He stopped attending classes (one student tauntingly said that he sounded "like a Norwegian") and was consequently suspended. In December, he took off in Bryan and Carey's car and drove to Oklahoma, with the windows down, listening to Michael Jackson's song "Scream." The police pulled him over for speeding, and he was arrested. Beverly, Carey, and Bryan picked him up at the police station and brought him home.

According to his real mother, Ghislaine, Bourdin called her in Europe. For all his disagreements with his mother, Bourdin still seemed to long for her. (He once wrote her a letter, saying, "I don't want to lose you. . . . If you disappear then I disappear.") Ghislaine says Bourdin confided that he was living with a woman in Texas who believed that he was her son. She became so upset that she hung up.

Shortly before Christmas, Bourdin went into the bathroom and looked at himself in the mirror — at his brown eyes, his dyed hair. He grabbed a razor and began to mutilate his face. He was put in the psychiatric ward of a local hospital for several days of observation. Later, Bourdin wrote in a notebook, "When you fight monsters, be careful that in the process you do not become one." He also jotted down a poem: "My days are phantom days, each one the shadow of a hope; / My real life never was begun, / Nor any of my real deeds done."

Doctors judged Bourdin to be stable enough to return to Carey's trailer. But he remained disquieted, and increasingly wondered what had happened to the real Nicholas Barclay. So did Parker, who, while trying to identify Bourdin, had started to gather information and interview Nicholas's neighbors. At the time that Nicholas disappeared, he was living with Beverly in a small one-story house in San Antonio. Nicholas's half brother, Jason, who was then twenty-four, had recently moved in with them after living for a period with his cousin, in Utah. Jason was wiry and strong, with long brown curly hair and a comb often tucked in the back pocket of his jeans. He had burn marks on his body and face: at thirteen, he had lit a cigarette after filling a lawn mower with gasoline and accidentally set himself on fire. Because of his scars, Carey says, "Jason worried that he would never meet somebody and he would always be alone." He strummed Lynyrd Skynyrd songs on his guitar and was a capable artist who sketched portraits of friends. Though he had only completed high school, he was bright and articulate. He also had an addictive personality, like his mother, often drinking heavily and using cocaine. He had his "demons," as Carey put it.

On June 13, 1994, Beverly and Jason told police that Nicholas had been playing basketball three days earlier and called his house from a pay phone, wanting a ride home. Beverly was sleeping, so Jason answered the phone. He told Nicholas to walk home. Nicholas never made it. Because Nicholas had recently fought with his mother over the tennis shoes he had stolen, and over the possibility of being sent to a home for juveniles, the police initially thought that he had run away — even though he hadn't taken any money or possessions.

Parker was surprised by police reports showing that after Nicholas's disappearance there were several disturbances at Beverly's house. On July 12th, she called the police, though when an officer arrived she insisted that she was all right. Jason told the officer that his mother was "drinking and scream[ing] at him because her other son ran away." A few weeks later, Beverly called the police again, about what authorities described as "family violence." The officer on the scene reported that Beverly and Jason were "exchanging words"; Jason was asked to leave the house for the day, and he complied. On September 25th, police received another call, this time from Jason. He claimed that his younger brother had returned and tried to break into the garage, fleeing when Jason spotted him. In his report, the officer on duty said that he had "checked the area" for Nicholas but was "unable to locate him."

Jason's behavior grew even more erratic. He was arrested for "using force" against a police officer, and Beverly kicked him out of the house. Nicholas's disappearance, Codey told me, had "messed Jason up pretty bad. He went on a bad drug binge and was shooting cocaine for a long time." Because he had refused to help Nicholas get a ride home on the day he vanished, Chantel says, Jason had "a lot of guilt."

In late 1996, Jason checked into a rehabilitation center and weaned himself from drugs. After he finished the program, he remained at the facility for more than a year, serving as a counselor and working for a landscaping business that the center operated. He was still there when Bourdin turned up, claiming to be his missing brother.

Bourdin wondered why Jason had not met him at the airport and had initially made no effort to see him at Carey's. After a month and a half, Bourdin and family members say, Jason finally came for a visit. Even then, Codey says, "Jason was standoffish." Though Jason gave him a hug in front of the others, Bourdin says, he seemed to eye him warily. After a few minutes, Jason told him to come outside, and held out his hand to Bourdin. A necklace with a gold cross glittered in his palm. Jason said that it was for him. "It was like he had to give it to me," Bourdin says. Jason put it around his neck. Then he said goodbye, and never returned.

Bourdin told me, "It was clear that Jason knew what had happened to Nicholas." For the first time, Bourdin began to wonder who was conning whom.

The authorities, meanwhile, had started to doubt Bourdin's story. Nancy Fisher, who at the time was a veteran FBI agent, had interviewed Bourdin several weeks after he arrived in the United States, in order to document his allegations of being kidnapped on American soil. Immediately, she told me, she "smelled a rat": "His hair was dark but bleached blond and the roots were quite obvious."

Parker knew Fisher and had shared with her his own suspicions. Fisher warned Parker not to interfere with a federal probe, but as they conducted parallel investigations they developed a sense of trust, and Parker passed on any information he obtained. When Fisher made inquiries into who may have abducted Nicholas and sexually abused him, she says, she found Beverly oddly "surly and uncooperative."

Fisher wondered whether Beverly and her family simply wanted to believe that Bourdin was their loved one. Whatever the family's motivations, Fisher's main concern was the mysterious figure who had entered the United States. She knew that it was impossible for him to have altered his eye color. In November, under the pretext of getting Bourdin treatment for his alleged abuse, Fisher took him to see a forensic psychiatrist in Houston, who concluded from his syntax and grammar that he could not be American, and was most likely French or Spanish. The FBI shared the results with Beverly and Carey, Fisher says, but they insisted that he was Nicholas.

Believing that Bourdin was a spy, Fisher says, she contacted the Central Intelligence Agency, explaining the potential threat and asking for help in identifying him. "The CIA wouldn't assist me," she says. "I was told by a CIA agent that until you can prove he's European we can't help you."

Fisher tried to persuade Beverly and Bourdin to give blood samples for a DNA test. Both refused. "Beverly said, 'How dare you say he's not my son,' " Fisher recalls. In the middle of February, four months after Bourdin arrived in the United States, Fisher obtained warrants to force them to cooperate. "I go to her house to get a blood sample, and she lies on the floor and says she's not going to get up," Fisher says. "I said, 'Yes, you are.' "

"Beverly defended me," Bourdin says. "She did her best to stop them."

Along with their blood, Fisher obtained Bourdin's fingerprints, which she sent to the State Department to see if there was a match with Interpol.

Carey, worried about her supposed brother's self-mutilation and instability, was no longer willing to let him stay with her, and he went to live with Beverly in her apartment. By then, Bourdin claims, he looked at the family differently. His mind retraced a series of curious interactions: Beverly's cool greeting at the airport, Jason's delay in visiting him. He says that, although Carey and Bryan had seemed intent on believing that he was Nicholas — ignoring the obvious evidence — Beverly had treated him less like a son than like a "ghost." One time when he was staying with her, Bourdin alleges, she got drunk and screamed, "I know that God punished me by sending you to me. I don't know who the hell you are. Why the fuck are you doing this?" (Beverly does not remember such an incident but says, "He must have got me pissed off.")

On March 5, 1998, with the authorities closing in on Bourdin, Beverly called Parker and said she believed that Bourdin was an impostor. The next morning, Parker took him to a diner. "I raise my pants so he can see I'm not wearing a gun" in his ankle holster, Parker says. "I want him to relax."

They ordered hotcakes. After nearly five months of pretending to be Nicholas Barclay, Bourdin says, he was psychically frayed. According to Parker, when he told "Nicholas" that he had upset his "mother," the young man blurted out, "She's not my mother, and you know it."

"You gonna tell me who you are?"

"I'm Frédéric Bourdin and I'm wanted by Interpol."

After a few minutes, Parker went to the men's room and called Nancy Fisher with the news. She had just received the same information from Interpol. "We're trying to get a warrant right now," she told Parker. "Stall him."

Parker went back to the table and continued to talk to Bourdin. As Bourdin spoke about his itinerant life in Europe, Parker says, he felt some guilt for turning him in. Bourdin, who despises Parker and disputes the details of their conversation, accuses the detective of "pretending" to have solved the case; it was as if Parker had intruded into Bourdin's interior fiction and given himself a starring role. After about an hour, Parker drove Bourdin back to Beverly's apartment. As Parker was pulling away, Fisher and the authorities were already descending on him. He surrendered quietly. "I knew I was Frédéric Bourdin again," he says. Beverly reacted less calmly. She turned and yelled at Fisher, "What took you so long?"

In custody, Bourdin told a story that seemed as fanciful as his tale of being Nicholas Barclay. He alleged that Beverly and Jason may have been complicit in Nicholas's disappearance, and that they had known from the outset that Bourdin was lying. "I'm a good impostor, but I'm not that good," Bourdin told me.

Of course, the authorities could not rely on the account of a known pathological liar. "He tells ninety-nine lies and maybe the one hundredth is the truth, but you don't know," Fisher says. Yet the authorities had their own suspicions. Jack Stick, who was a federal prosecutor at the time and who later served a term in the Texas House of

Representatives, was assigned Bourdin's case. He and Fisher wondered why Beverly had resisted attempts by the FBI to investigate Bourdin's purported kidnapping and, later, to uncover his deception. They also questioned why she had not taken Bourdin back to live with her. According to Fisher, Carey told her that it was because it was "too upsetting" for Beverly, which, at least to Fisher and Stick, seemed strange. "You'd be so happy to have your child back," Fisher says. It was "another red flag."

Fisher and Stick took note of the disturbances in Beverly's house after Nicholas had vanished, and the police report stating that Beverly was screaming at Jason over Nicholas's disappearance. Then there was Jason's claim that he had witnessed Nicholas breaking into the house. No evidence could be found to back up this startling story, and Jason had made the claim at the time that the police had started "sniffing around," as Stick put it. He and Fisher suspected that the story was a ruse meant to reinforce the idea that Nicholas was a runaway.

Stick and Fisher began to edge toward a homicide investigation. "I wanted to know what had happened to that little kid," Stick recalls.

Stick and Fisher gathered more evidence suggesting that Beverly's home was prone to violence. They say that officials at Nicholas's school had expressed concern that Nicholas might be an abused child, owing to bruises on his body, and that just before he disappeared the officials had alerted child-protective services. And neighbors noted that Nicholas had sometimes hit Beverly.

One day, Fisher asked Beverly to take a polygraph. Carey recalls, "I said, 'Mom, do whatever they ask you to do. Go take the lie-detector test. You didn't kill Nicholas.' So she did."

While Beverly was taking the polygraph, Fisher watched the proceedings on a video monitor in a nearby room. The most important question was whether Beverly currently knew the whereabouts of Nicholas. She said no, twice. The polygraph examiner told Fisher that Beverly had seemingly answered truthfully. When Fisher expressed disbelief, the examiner said that if Beverly was lying, she had to be on drugs. After a while, the examiner administered the test again, at which point the effects of any possible narcotics, including methadone, might have worn off. This time, when the examiner asked if Beverly knew Nicholas's whereabouts, Fisher says, the machine went wild, indicating a lie. "She blew the instruments practically off the table," Fisher says. (False positives are not uncommon in polygraphs, and scientists dispute their basic reliability.)

According to Fisher, when the examiner told Beverly that she had failed the exam, and began pressing her with more questions, Beverly yelled, "I don't have to put up with this," then got up and ran out the door. "I catch her," Fisher recalls. "I say, 'Why are you running?' She is furious. She says, 'This is so typical of Nicholas. Look at the hell he's putting me through.' "

Fisher next wanted to interview Jason, but he resisted. When he finally agreed to meet her, several weeks after Bourdin had been arrested, Fisher says, she had to "pull words out of him." They spoke about the fact that he had not gone to see his alleged brother for nearly two months: "I said, 'Here's your brother, long gone, kidnapped, and aren't you eager to see him?' He said, 'Well, no.' I said, 'Did he look like your brother to you?' 'Well, I guess.' " Fisher found his responses grudging, and developed a "very strong suspicion that Jason had participated in the disappearance of his brother." Stick, too, believed that Jason either had been "involved in Nicholas's disappearance or had information that could tell us what had happened." Fisher even suspected that Beverly knew what had happened to Nicholas, and may have helped cover up the crime in order to protect Jason.

After the interview, Stick and Fisher say, Jason refused to speak to the authorities again without a lawyer or unless he was under arrest. But Parker, who as a private investigator was not bound by the same legal restrictions as Stick and Fisher, continued to press Jason. On one occasion, he accused him of murder. "I think you did it," Parker says he told him. "I don't think you meant to do it, but you did." In response, Parker says, "He just looked at me."

Several weeks after Fisher and Parker questioned Jason, Parker was driving through downtown San Antonio and saw Beverly on the sidewalk. He asked her if she wanted a ride. When she got in, she told him that Jason had died of an overdose of cocaine. Parker, who knew that Jason had been off drugs for more than a year, says that he asked if she thought he had taken his life on purpose. She said, "I don't know." Stick, Fisher, and Parker suspect that it was a suicide.

Since the loss of her sons, Beverly has stopped using drugs and moved out to Spring Branch, where she lives in a trailer, helping a woman care for her severely handicapped daughter. Recently, she agreed to talk with me about the authorities' suspicions. At first, Beverly said that I could drive out to meet her, but later she told me that the woman she worked for did not want visitors, so we spoke by phone. One of her vocal cords had recently become paralyzed, deepening her already low and gravelly voice. Parker, who had frequently chatted with her at the doughnut shop, had told me, "I don't know why I liked her, but I did. She had this thousand-yard stare. She looked like someone whose life had taken everything out of her."

Beverly answered my questions forthrightly. At the airport, she said, she had hung back because Bourdin "looked odd." She added, "If I went with my gut, I would have known right away." She admitted that she had taken drugs — "probably" heroin, methadone, and alcohol — before the polygraph exam. "When they accused me, I freaked out," she said. "I worked my ass off to raise my kids. Why would I do something to my kids?" She continued, "I'm not a violent person. They didn't talk to any of my friends or associates. . . . It was just a shot in the dark, to see if I'd admit something." She also said of herself, "I'm the world's worst liar. I can't lie worth crap."

I asked her if Jason had hurt Nicholas. She paused for a moment, then said that she didn't think so. She acknowledged that when Jason did cocaine he became "totally wacko — a completely different person — and it was scary." He even beat up his father once, she said. But she noted that Jason had not been a serious addict until after Nicholas disappeared. She agreed with the authorities on one point: she placed little credence in Jason's reported sighting of Nicholas after he disappeared. "Jason was having problems at that time," she said. "I just don't believe Nicholas came there."

As we spoke, I asked several times how she could have believed for nearly five months that a twenty-three-year-old Frenchman with dyed hair, brown eyes, and a European accent was her son. "We just kept making excuses — that he's different because of all this ugly stuff that had happened," she said. She and Carey wanted it to be him so badly. It was only after he came to live with her that she had doubts. "He just didn't act like my son," Beverly said. "I couldn't bond with him. I just didn't have that feeling. My heart went out for him, but not like a mother's would. The kid's a mess and it's sad, and I wouldn't wish that on anybody."

Beverly's experience, as incredible as it is, does have a precursor — an incident that has been described as one of "the strangest cases in the annals of police history." (It is the basis of a Clint Eastwood movie *Changeling,* which was released in the fall.) On March 10, 1928, a nine-year-old boy named Walter Collins disappeared in Los Angeles. Six months later, after a nationwide manhunt, a boy showed up claiming that he was Walter and insisting that he had been kidnapped. The police were certain that he was Walter, and a family friend testified that "things the boy said and did would convince anybody" that he was the missing child. When Walter's mother, Christine, went to retrieve her son, however, she did not think it was him. Although the authorities and friends persuaded her to take him home, she brought the boy back to a police station after a few days, insisting, "This is not my son." She later testified, "His teeth were different, his voice was different. . . . His ears were smaller." The authorities thought that she must be suffering emotional distress from her son's disappearance, and had her institutionalized in a psychiatric ward. Even then, she refused to budge. As she told a police captain, "One thing a mother ought to know was the identity of her child." Eight days later, she was released. Evidence soon emerged that her son was likely murdered by a serial killer, and the boy claiming to be her son confessed that he was an eleven-year-old runaway from Iowa who, in his words, thought that it was "fun to be somebody you aren't."

Speaking of the Bourdin case, Fisher said that one thing was certain: "Beverly had to know that wasn't her son."

After several months of investigation, Stick determined that there was no evidence to charge anyone with Nicholas's disappearance. There were no witnesses, no DNA. Authorities could not even say whether Nicholas was dead. Stick concluded that Jason's overdose had all but "precluded the possibility" that authorities could determine what had happened to Nicholas.

On September 9, 1998, Frédéric Bourdin stood in a San Antonio courtroom and pleaded guilty to perjury, and to obtaining and possessing false documents. This time, his claim that he was merely seeking love elicited outrage. Carey, who had a nervous breakdown after Bourdin was arrested, testified before his sentencing, saying, "He has lied, and lied, and lied again. And to this day he continues to lie. He bears no remorse." Stick denounced Bourdin as a "flesh-eating bacteria," and the judge compared what Bourdin had done — giving a family the hope that their lost child was alive and then shattering it — to murder.

The only person who seemed to have any sympathy for Bourdin was Beverly. She said at the time, "I feel sorry for him. You know, we got to know him, and this kid has been through hell. He has a lot of nervous habits." She told me, "He did a lot of things that took a lot of guts, if you think about it."

The judge sentenced Bourdin to six years — more than three times what was recommended under the sentencing guidelines. Bourdin told the courtroom, "I apologize to all the people in my past, for what I have done. I wish, I wish that you believe me, but I know it's impossible." Whether he was in jail or not, he added, "I am a prisoner of myself."

When I last saw Bourdin, this spring, his life had undergone perhaps its most dramatic transformation. He had married a Frenchwoman, Isabelle, whom he had met two years earlier. In her late twenties, Isabelle was slim and pretty and soft-spoken. She was studying to be a lawyer. A victim of family abuse, she had seen Bourdin on television, describing his own abuse and his quest for love, and she had been so moved that she eventually tracked him down. "I told him what interests me in his life wasn't the way he bent the truth but why he did that and the things that he looked for," she said.

Bourdin says that when Isabelle first approached him he thought it must be a joke, but they met in Paris and gradually fell in love. He said that he had never been in a relationship before. "I've always been a wall," he said. "A cold wall." On August 8, 2007, after a year of courtship, they got married at the town hall of a village outside Pau.

Bourdin's mother says that Frédéric invited her and his grandfather to the ceremony, but they didn't go. "No one believed him," she says.

When I saw Isabelle, she was nearly eight months pregnant. Hoping to avoid public attention, she and Frédéric had relocated to Le Mans, and they had moved into a small one-bedroom apartment in an old stone building with wood floors and a window that overlooked a prison. "It reminds me of where I've been," Bourdin said. A box containing the pieces of a crib lay on the floor of the sparsely decorated living room. Bourdin's hair was now cropped, and he was dressed without flamboyance, in jeans and a sweatshirt. He told me that he had got a job in telemarketing. Given his skills at persuasion, he was unusually good at it. "Let's just say I'm a natural," he said.

Most of his family believes that all these changes are merely part of another role, one that will end disastrously for his wife and baby. "You can't just invent yourself as a father," his uncle Jean-Luc Drouart said. "You're not a dad for six days or six months. It is not a character — it is a reality." He added, "I fear for that child."

Bourdin's mother, Ghislaine, says that her son is a "liar and will never change."

After so many years of playing an impostor, Bourdin has left his family and many authorities with the conviction that this is who Frédéric Pierre Bourdin really is: he *is* a chameleon. Within months of being released from prison in the United States and deported to France, in October 2003, Bourdin resumed playing a child. He even stole the identity of a fourteen-year-old missing French boy named Léo Balley, who had vanished almost eight years earlier, on a camping trip. This time, police did a DNA test that quickly revealed that Bourdin was lying. A psychiatrist who evaluated him concluded, "The prognosis seems more than worrying. . . . We are very pessimistic about modifying these personality traits." (Bourdin, while in prison in America, began reading psychology texts, and jotted down in his journal the following passage: "When confronted with his misconduct the psychopath has enough false sincerity and apparent remorse that he renews hope and trust among his accusers. However, after several repetitions, his convincing show is finally recognized for what it is — a show.")

Isabelle is sure that Bourdin "can change." She said, "I've seen him now for two years, and he is not that person."

At one point, Bourdin touched Isabelle's stomach. "My baby can have three arms and three legs," he said. "It doesn't matter. I don't need my child to be perfect. All I want is that this child feels love." He did not care what his family thought. "They are my shelter," he said of his wife and soon-to-be child. "No one can take that from me."

A month later, Bourdin called and told me that his wife had given birth. "It's a girl," he said. He and Isabelle had named her Athena, for the Greek goddess. "I'm really a father," he said.

I asked if he had become a new person. For a moment, he fell silent. Then he said, "No, this is who I am."

DENIS JOHNSON

■

Boomtown, Iraq

FROM *Portfolio*

WHEN Ward VanLerberg left Kansas and headed off to the Middle Eastern city of Erbil to build 50 schools, he was careful to tell his family that he was going to the capital of "Kurdistan," and all was well until his daughter Googled his destination and announced to the family that Kurdistan is *in Iraq*. His wife wept, bidding him goodbye, and commenced waiting for him to return home in a coffin.

Three days following Mrs. Van's last farewell, I run into Ward on the elevator at the International Hotel in Erbil, and he asks me if I'd care to join him at the buffet, and what I say is no. Did I fly 7,000 miles from Chicago to talk to a guy from Kansas City? I'm here to get a look at the 1,000-kilometer oil pipeline running from Kirkuk, in northern Iraq, to Ceyhan, Turkey, and this friendly construction contractor is not a pipeline. But then I feel sorry and ask if I can join him after all, and I tell him that when I left home, I bet my wife cried more than his.

This morning, the two deceased husbands sit in the Atrium Coffee Shop at the Erbil International Hotel (known locally as the Sheraton though it isn't one), a 10-story establishment with three additional restaurants, a nightclub, and a buffet to rival any on earth. We eat cornflakes with yogurt and omelets to order. Fresh-squeezed OJ on request. "My family just didn't get it," Ward says. "This place is *happening*. There's no war here in Kurdistan. No war whatsoever."

To be sure, security at the "Sheraton" is tight — first a baggage search at the checkpoint before the gated parking lot, next a metal detector and pat-down at the lobby's entrance, where patrons absolutely have to check their weapons. Since a number of private security contractors stop in for the buffet or take meetings here or even live here in posh quarters — with 24-hour room service and a view, perhaps, of the excavation site from which will rise the future Nishtiman Shopping Mall, one of the largest in the Middle East, or of the American or Italian Villages (little-box, lawless developments for future foreign residents) or a distant view of the yet-unnamed airport's colossal terminal, also under construction — at any given time the desk drawer at the security station rattles with loaded handguns, and here and there in the lobby bulky, physically formidable young Euros sport empty holsters on their hips.

Bloody insurgency and sectarian strife tear at the country of Iraq, but Iraqi Kurdistan — three northern "governorates" under the control of the Kurdistan Regional Government, with its own language, flag, and national anthem, its own parliament and its own army — prospers relatively free of violence. The Kurdistan region is open for business. With the buzz of dealmaking and the ringing cell phones and the smell of oil literally in the air, you get a sense, sitting in the Atrium, of being caught up in this planet's biggest game, of touching the skirts of power and intrigue and life-changing wealth.

The Kurdistan region is Paul Wolfowitz's wet dream: maybe not a beacon of democracy, but certainly a red-hot ember — peaceful, orderly, secular, democratic, wildly capitalist, and sentimentally pro-American — afloat on an ocean of oil.

Very well: We tend to overlook good news because it's generally followed by bad news, and another month from my happy breakfast with Ward VanLerberg, Turkish bombers will run forays in this region's empty northeast corner against the PKK, fugitive Kurd rebels who are at war with neighboring Turkey — little damage, but much booming. And before it gets better, the news will get even worse. By the end of January, the northern Iraqi city of Mosul will see plenty of violence, and U.S. commanders will declare it "Al Qaeda's last urban stronghold." Good news, bad news.

They call it "The Other Iraq," and all of them — the Kurdish representative Qubad Talabany in Washington; Kurdish Regional Government president Masoud Barzani and his nephew, Prime Minister Nechirvan Barzani; head of Foreign Relations Falah Mustafa Bakir;

oil minister Ashti Hawrami; the man in a shop who won't accept money from Americans in exchange for a kilo of apricots — want the news out: This is what Cheney-Bush wanted. That's the news from here. This is free enterprise blooming — not "booming," our driver Hameed insists carefully — in the mountains and desert of northern Iraq.

Hameed is a mustachioed Kurd with a bandit's face who presents himself each morning in well-pressed sports apparel and drives us around in his Land Cruiser, listening to Persian pop tunes on his tape deck. His business card identifies him as a freelance "fixer," but he may also get a paycheck from the Ministry of Foreign Relations and may have some connection with Intelligence. Or maybe not. Susan Meiselas thinks he does. Susan is my photographer on this assignment. Usually I'm half-broke and deliriously off-course from the first day of these journalistic ventures, but this time I get an expense account and a world-class "shooter" — that's what I get to call her. I requested Susan specifically. My impression was that she'd seen a bit of Kurdistan and might know a few folks who could point us to a pipeline.

Our purpose in engaging fixer Hameed is to get us out to look at oil operations of one kind or another. Whichever way we go, we'll find them.

And that's what we do every other day or so, passing first through the relentless checkpoints manned by camo-garbed recruits and then along nicely paved highways among a lot of vehicles going as fast as their drivers can push them, which varies from 30 kph to, let's guess, 150 or maybe more. This calls for some fancy maneuvering on the part of Hameed, who keeps us well in the higher end of that range, leaving behind Erbil, believed by some historians to be the longest continuously inhabited city on earth, then entering the massive plain irrigated from the Tigris River and known as "Iraq's Breadbasket," the very farmland where, archaeologists believe, mankind first practiced agriculture.

On off days we get around Erbil meeting friendly folks and shooting them, and Susan asks about the "situation on the ground" and "future prospects" and shoots the whole city, while I take notes and wonder what happened to the war.

"It's safe here, you can go anywhere" — by which they mean wherever you find yourself in this region the size of Maryland, you'll be safe. But whether you can actually get through the checkpoints without papers from the Ministry of Security, that's quite another matter. With its zealous and largely successful antiterrorist measures and its capitalist fever and as-yet-incomplete system of laws, the country serves up a blend of Orwellian, penitentiary-style security and Wild West laissez-faire: no speed limits, no driver's insurance, no DUI traps — there's very little drinking and apparently zero drug abuse — loose regulations for firearms, and homesteaders' rights to rural land; also — at least while the parliament wrestles with the question of government revenue — no taxes. Of any kind. But to board a plane leaving Erbil, passengers must pass two vehicle checkpoints, four electronic screenings and pat-downs, and a final bag-and-body search planeside. Among the ads on the airport terminal's walls:

> *Khanzad American Village*
> *"Welcome to Luxury"*
> *American Village*
> *The Most Exclusive Villas in Kurdistan*

You can go anywhere if you have the right credentials. Stafford Clarry, a dapper American from Hawaii, formerly a United Nations worker and now the humanitarian-affairs adviser to the Kurdistan Regional Government, spends his every free moment exploring the countryside in his Land Cruiser, sometimes with his 30-year-old son, Arjun. "In Kurdistan, the American effort is a success," he says, then adds, "All right, yes, at least 50,000 have died in central Iraq. Yes, untold destruction, unbelievable mistakes, yes, all of that is true. But what you see around you in Kurdistan is also true. It doesn't justify the destruction, but it has to be recognized as a fact."

And the Kurds love Americans. Love, love. Investors swarm in from all over the globe, and foreigners are common in Erbil, but if you mention tentatively and apologetically that you're American, a shopkeeper or café owner is likely to take you aside and grip your arm and address you with the passionate sincerity of a drunken uncle: "I speak not just for me but all of Kurdish people. Please bring your United States Army here forever. You are welcome, welcome. No, I will not accept your money today, please take these goods as my gift to America."

On Monday, we talk to business folks and some of the government's innumerable ministers. (Actually, the ministers number 43, and five of them are women.) The Kurdish Regional Government is secular, and neither the Kurdish Democratic Party nor its counterpart, the Patriotic Union of Kurdistan, pledges formal allegiance to Islam. The Kurds themselves are overwhelmingly Muslim, however. Younger Kurdish women dress like Europeans, but in smaller towns they retain their scarves, often only covering their shoulders, but also handy for ducking under when a bare head might seem disrespectful to the Prophet. At Erbil's public recreation center, women use the pool at separate hours from men, and unmarried females have nowhere to go to amuse themselves, but that's only until a private 90,000-square-foot women's center that's now under construction opens with its steam bath, Turkish bath, aerobics room, yoga room, workout room, and Internet center.

At Zagros TV, one of Erbil's five television stations, a news producer tells us that he's free to be critical, but only of the government. "If we stray too far politically, we get a phone call. If we decided to criticize the Prophet Muhammad, we'd get a rocket through the roof."

The Board of Investment offers free lots to investors who are ready to build for their businesses. Get it while you can. "I offer it now," says Herish Muhamad, the board chairman, "but in a while, no more."

Twenty miles from town stands a power plant that's expected to be sending 500 megawatts to Erbil by early spring. The project's assistant director, Dliwer Arif, stands atop a 4.5-million-liter diesel tank, 55 feet in the air, and looks over the generators and turbines. A year ago, this was empty desert. Dliwer smiles with one tooth missing and says, "Yes. Because we are in a hurry. All of Kurdistan is in a hurry." The diesel tank is being tested for leaks, the whole thing trembling. Susan points her camera over the 20 acres of buildings and men and machines, I embrace the railing, and Dliwer tests his cell phone. He's very impressed with the reception this high up.

On Tuesday, we head southeast to the town of Taq Taq to watch men grinding and welding 10-meter-deep tanks for Topco, a Turkish oil company, at a field from which they expect to pump 70,000 barrels a day. Afterward, we drive three miles to the site of a future refining facility owned by the Kurdish government and a British oil concern: a stretch of ground leveled and graded in the midst of a vast natural expanse, with a handful of guards who live in trailers and keep it safe and who don't know who the hell these Land Cruising visitors are supposed to be.

The commissioner in charge of the outpost makes it his business to pin down the source of our authority. We tell him the mayor is behind us. He flips his cell phone open, and a round of calls consumes the next hour or so. Between every two calls, the commissioner takes time to address his squad of 13 men, his eyes on fire. Susan prods Hameed to eavesdrop and translate: We've wandered into some kind of political drama here among the mayor, the police chief, and the local head of security, and its climax has arrived. Its climax, in fact, is us.

The commissioner grows so wildly exasperated that hc can ultimately find no expression for his disgust other than to gather up his squad and their equipment, and they resign en masse, quitting their windswept, lonely, pointless outpost — nothing's built here yet anyway — and trudging together toward the town around 15 kilometers across the desert, their faces toward the wind.

We watch them shrink into the distance, and I think, Yes, the magazine will want plenty of that, or a couple of paragraphs anyway, the entertaining Kurds with their fiery eyes — and they're very entertaining — but I don't think I like it. I think I've stumbled onto some news, not entertainment. The war in Iraq is an hour's drive away, and for four years these comical Kurds have actually managed to keep it from coming any closer. Isn't that news?

While Turks and Europeans hopped up on petroleum roll into Erbil to build a new city and become rich, the American Village waits to be filled with teachers, executives, and engineers. The U.S. is waiting for the word from somebody that it's safe, maybe from the same people who told us Saddam Hussein was dangerous. There are Americans around but "fewer than 200 U.S. troops," according to a KRG fact sheet, and if that number is a fact, their whereabouts are only a guess. A few in Mosul, a few in Erbil. Not a one in sight.

Most Americans in Erbil work for the U.S. government, and most governments keep their people here under Baghdad-level security, behind high walls and concertina wire. The U.N. compound looks like a prison, as does both the Blackwater compound on Sabhat Street and the tiny enclosure, not many blocks away, where workers from the U.S. Agency for International Development live. The British diplomats hole up at the high-security Khanzad Hotel with a fleet of armored SUVs, and all these people venture out only under guard.

Even Ross Milosevic, an Australian, one of this city's ample population of high-paid bodyguards, has to sign an insurance waiver just to get out of his hotel and sneak over to the Deutscher Hof Barbecue, which serves really terrible food but also imported beer, for dinner with a friend in the same line. Ross works for Tacforce International, a private outfit, and looks like an ad for bodyguards, clean-cut and earnest, while his friend runs security for the prime minister of Kurdistan and looks like a homeless Rambo with stringy hair to his shoulders but the same sleeve-busting musculature, and he's American — 17 years in the Green Berets, a stint training SWAT teams in New Jersey, and a résumé that grows vague as it approaches the present and from which he himself sort of disappears for a while before materializing at the right hand of the prime minister of Kurdistan with 500 troops to do his bidding. At the public level, he prefers to use an alias and doesn't mind at all if it's Rambo. He's here on an open-ended contract with the KRG to train the prime minister's bodyguards.

This evening, Rambo orders beef stroganoff, therefore so do I, to my considerable regret, and he sips a German beer I should get the name of, but I'm more interested in clocking his consumption, because I wonder if it's possible for this specimen to chug down the calories and still look capable of pinning an elephant in four moves at the age of 47. He drinks only two of them while he and Ross — just one beer for Ross — discuss the world situation. "According to my contacts," Rambo says, "the Israelis have six nuclear-tipped missiles raised from the silos and pointed at Iran and Syria. They launch before Bush leaves office." Who are his contacts? "My brother-in-law."

Ross and Rambo check out a table full of similar-looking men across the candlelit room. "Special-ops team," Rambo guesses. "They sound like Yanks, and their hair is short." Ross isn't so sure. You get the feeling that these guys are in their own movie and will suddenly challenge you to some humiliating physical contest. In his spare time, Rambo has been working to track down a young American girl kidnapped six years ago from a cruise liner off the coast of Venezuela. He's trying to get Ross involved. Ross has spent time in Venezuela, and his wife is Venezuelan, but he says he can't go back there because he's been accused — falsely, he says — of working for the CIA.

Rambo himself seems just the sort to have some connection to the paratrooper-ninja wing of that very organization. "If a guy like me still worked for the U.S., like, for the CIA, he'd only be doing a little kite work now and then," he says.

Kite work? "That's where they can cut the string, and you float away and disappear."

Rambo loves his job. He loves the Kurds as much as the Kurds love Americans, and he feels at home among them in what he calls the Wild West of the Middle East, but he thinks they're pushing too hard to get rich while letting the basics — agriculture, infrastructure, education — fall behind. Here in Erbil, even the head of the prime minister's bodyguards gets electric power from the city only four hours out of 24, and Rambo is missing his daily allotment while he eliminates every morsel from his plate. The rationing should end when the new power plant comes on line, but he still thinks the country's leaping ahead with both feet in the air and no feet on the ground. The shopping center downtown represents three times the investment in the power plant. With their labor force heavily subsidized by make-work government jobs and their agricultural base and infrastructure wiped away by years of Saddam, the Kurds have plenty to do if they want a truly self-sufficient nation.

It's a land definitely on its way, but to what? "Basically," Rambo says, "the model is Dubai, in the United Arab Emirates: oil-rich, almost entirely dependent on imported expertise, imported goods, imported workers. I wish I had a hand clicker to count the number of times each day I heard someone mention that place. That's all you hear about. Dubai, Dubai, Dubai."

Today, mainly security and government workers constitute the American presence in Erbil, but the others will get here. Hunt Oil of Dallas now conducts seismic tests around Kurdistan, and it won't be long before other U.S. oil interests turn up. The oil is here, and we've known it for a long time. Britain knew it in the 1920s, when they drew boundaries on a map that created a British-administered Iraq, making sure it included this region and its petroleum. Kurdistan had actually been promised independence, but no way. "Oil," a Kurdish saying runs, "made Kurdistan Iraqi."

How much oil? Depending on who's counting, Iraq as a whole has anywhere from 115 billion barrels of "proven" reserves down to half that much, which would indicate nothing's really proven. A fifth of that or more lies in the Kurdish region. That puts Kurdistan's reserves well ahead of the U.S.'s total reserves and equal to all of Asia's. George Yacu, a Chaldean Christian Kurd who served as a technical adviser for Iraq's national oil company for nearly 30 years, seems to find the question "how much?" technically interesting but scientifically unanswerable, beyond his saying, "But nobody knows until they drill."

On Wednesday, Susan and I have dinner with George. Since his retirement, he has run his own corporation, Sumer Petroleum Services. His family lives in Chicago these days, and he's applying for U.S. citizenship. They all lived in Baghdad until life there became impossible, and he still has a house in the city, with a library of rare books and manuscripts, "if it still exists." When things calm down, he'll move the collection to his childhood village of Fishkabour, which is here in Kurdistan, just across the Tigris River from Syria.

It's hard to imagine George as some kind of villager. He's in his seventies now, tall and well-dressed, with a large, sad, historic face; formal and gracious in his manner, generous in his conversation, not to say voluble; and with a true kindness emanating from his depths.

In 1975, Saddam gave the largely Christian population of George's village 12 hours to clear out and then let his pilots use it "for bombing practice," George says.

Who are these people? Who goes through this madness and comes out — not exactly laughing; George is certainly no rib-poking joker — but kindly, open, unafraid? And I actually ask him the question, but he only shrugs as if the answer's obvious, or so utterly beyond the experience of anyone who has to ask that he wouldn't even try to respond. His village has been rebuilt, and George keeps a new home there now, but he speaks of its former days as of a paradise: the orchards and the vineyards and the Tigris River going by, all of it gone now but the river and the ruins and the new buildings, and it's hard, without risking rudeness, to steer him back to the subject of petroleum, which is, after all, what makes Kurdistan interesting to America.

We've been involved in the Middle East since 1945, exclusively because it's where the oil is. Although the rhetoric, starting with Truman's in 1946 down to Bush's in today's paper, has been rendered in apocalyptic terms — war between good and evil, the clash of civilizations — if the oil were to move miraculously someday to another point on the globe, so would our involvement. But the oil's under Iraq, and according to George Yacu, 38 percent of it lies in the Kurdish region in natural reservoirs less than 3,000 meters below the surface, some as shallow as 600 meters down — easy to get to and easy to refine, compared with, say, the recent strike off the Brazilian coastline, which is under a mile of ocean and another mile of rock, or most of Canada's reserves, which are mixed with sand.

The Norwegian company DNO recently started three rigs drilling in its new fields near the Turkish border and has been pumping out great gobs of the stuff. DNO and Adox/Genel (a one-rig consortium of Swedes, Turks, and Canadians) have been the first to draw petroleum from Kurdish ground. Plenty of others expect to follow. When I arrived on Sunday, the KRG had so far signed seven foreign companies, Hunt Oil included, to exploration contracts. By the middle of the week, another five had signed on, and by the end of the month, the total was up to 20.

Whatever they've found or expect to find, they're not telling. Before DNO's drill shafts went down, the company listed a public relations person on its website; by November the name had disappeared, and Magne Normann, DNO's vice president, made it clear they weren't entertaining visitors without a lot of vetting first.

So how much oil? For 17 years under Saddam and through one uprising and war after another, Iraq has pumped out only a quarter of its proven petroleum capacity while Saudi Arabia, at full capacity, is now suspected to have peaked and entered the declining phase of its oil-producing history. In any case, commentators as disparate as leftist Noam Chomsky and defense-and-resource expert Michael Klare have called what's under the ground in the Middle East — including Kurdistan — the biggest material prize in human history.

On Thursday, we pay four bucks a gallon for gasoline. Although service stations in recent months started pumping again, the streetside vendors still sell gas and pink diesel from 20-liter jugs stacked by the highways in barricades they can scarcely see over. Hameed prefers to fill his Land Cruiser's tank from a legitimate pump. Whoever you buy it from, it's cash only. The Kurds accept Iraqi money, but they deeply cherish those U.S. Ben Franklin hundreds.

We go north and approach the city of Mosul under a linty-looking haze from its cement plants and brick factories, but we drive around it. "Too many Arabs there," Hameed explains. "They kill you just for fun." We're making excellent time. Susan's a little irked that we didn't give Mosul an even wider berth. "We were told not to go through the Mosul checkpoint," she says.

"No," Hameed answers, "in the morning it's safe."

"But we agreed we'd take the other one. Why did you take this one?"

"Susan, don't you trust me? I'm never going to endanger you, because I'm never going to endanger myself."

"But, Hameed, when we discuss these things, let's stick to the plan."

"Susan, please, I'm sticking to the plan. The plan is to get you to the pipeline." Their delivery is very amiable.

Today, we'll actually reach the Kirkuk-Ceyhan pipeline. There's a metering station in the northwest corner of Kurdish territory, near the Turkish and Syrian borders and also near DNO's new drilling site.

On Friday, a gallon of gas is down 40 cents from the day before. Hameed is philosophical: good news, bad news. Tomorrow could see a rise.

In our two days up near the Turkish border, we hear only two explosions. A Kurdish army recruit says it's just Americans blowing up dud ordnance from previous campaigns. He hasn't actually seen any U.S. soldiers; he's only heard they're around somewhere.

At this metering facility two miles from the Turkish border and three miles from Syria, engineers keep track of the oil flowing north through the 1,000-kilometer Kirkuk-Ceyhan pipeline. In my uninformed imagination, I'd conjured one monstrous, mythic steel artery dominating the desert and shrinking in its journey toward the horizon, but this is all that's visible: a chain-link-fenced enclosure no more colossal than your average Texaco service station, and inside it a 40-inch pipe and a second one 46 inches in diameter, coming up from underground for a distance of 80 feet at a height of maybe six inches, and then diving back under the dirt. There's a checkpoint, a barracks for the guards, and a distant view of Turkish mountains.

Two hundred yards from the facility, DNO supervises two 4.5-million-liter tanks, to which it pumps oil from its strike a few kilometers east. A half-million barrels a day coming from farther south, outside the Kurdish region, pass through the pipelines just a shout across the road, but DNO is forced to send its oil into Turkey on tanker trucks. The pipeline is administered by the central Iraqi government, and they're not ready to recognize the legitimacy of DNO's Kurdish-sanctioned operation. Its pipes are off-limits to DNO and all Kurdish oil. A DNO electrical engineer who won't give his name, a young Frenchman here to look after the big tanks, says the bickering parties will work it all out; the parties always do when there's money to be made. He speaks about the richness of the strike as if it's something to inspire worship; there's that kind of tone in his voice: "I've been around, and I've only seen one bigger." He can't let us visit the drilling site. "You want to see Kurdish oil? Just go a few kilometers to the village of Tawke. You'll see oil."

Safar Mohammed Omer, son of the former mayor and cousin of the current mayor of Tawke, takes us to a region of dun-colored crags and flats to show us black petroleum seeping out of the rocks and trickling down the hillside, and even a small creek that bubbles out of a black spring, two feet across at its widest, but it amounts to an actual slowly trickling black creek of oil. He points to another, and another, and those over there — for a thousand years, Safar says, villagers have been using this oil to start their fires.

He shows us a hand-dug well — a pond, really — about a dozen feet across, bubbling in a desultory fashion. When he was a boy, the villagers had a small distillery set up here and manufactured their own diesel. Thirteen such hand-dug wells, he says, surround the neighborhood, going between 12 and 40 meters into the earth, and on hot summer days an aqua-blue smoke rises from these reservoirs. This morning, the breeze carries a stench like that of an urban roofing operation.

Safar Mohammed dresses in the traditional style known as *Kurmancî*, in a loose oversuit, turban, and wide sash, exactly as he might have if he'd lived hundreds of years ago. The village in which his family is prominent consists of a few dirt streets and concrete buildings, skinny chickens wandering around. Sewage trickling along hand-gouged gutters. Oil bubbling up 100 yards from the place.

What does Safar see coming from all this? Is he going to live in a mansion with his chickens and mess with the heads of all the cultured folks, like the Clampetts on *The Beverly Hillbillies*?

Hameed seems to have trouble translating the question. "These villagers," Hameed says, "they don't think like that. He just thinks about today."

But come on, this man is the Jed Clampett of Kurdistan. How does he think the DNO oil strike will change his future?

"It won't."

Safar may be the Jed Clampett of Kurdistan, but the fortunes of the village don't quite compare. Safar says that the farmers hereabouts agreed to rent their land to DNO for roughly $300 an acre annually, but the tenant is casual about payment, and when all is said and done, the locals get about $13 a month. This oil may buy a mansion, but somebody else will live in it.

On the way back to Erbil, we pass the Harir Flats and the runway built for Saddam's air force — the first runway used by the coalition forces in the latest war. Money from the new Kurdish construction projects has found its way out into the desert: Already the heights overlooking the old runway bristle with the castles of the newly rich, the tender beginnings of a Middle Eastern Beverly Hills.

Susan has kept it something of a secret, but here in Kurdistan she's famous, thanks to her book *Kurdistan: In the Shadow of History,* a compendium of documents and photos weighing in at five pounds, and we've been invited to rendezvous with some of her admiring friends. We're going to be "guested," is the term Susan uses, and I detect a kind of apology in the way she says it, and a tiny hint of hopelessness I don't understand any more than a child understands when the nurse says it's time for "a little hypodermic."

In the town of Zakhu, on the Turkish border, at a compound of impressive stone buildings called KDP location No. 8, the Kurdish Democratic Party is giving away 80 red-and-black wheelchairs manufactured in Port Washington, New York, brand-new and shining in the afternoon sun. These gifts from Masoud Barzani, the Kurdish president, are conveyed one at a time by the president's second cousin Karwan Barzani, who sits in the courtyard in an easy chair behind a big desk, among a number of officials seated on couches. A man with a microphone calls out names, and through the course of the afternoon recipients with every manner of paralysis, incompleteness, or demobilizing disfiguration of their frames come forward with great ceremony: little children and old ladies and legless war veterans, each carried by two or three relatives toward the shiny new conveyances and each putting an ink thumbprint on a registry page and another on a large certificate, which is theirs to keep as proof of ownership.

Zakhu is a Turkish border crossing. Beside its main highway, cargo trucks wait in a line four kilometers long to pass back empty into Turkey, having unloaded everything from chicken feed, fresh produce, and canned goods to appliances, construction materials, and machines — almost everything, in fact, that the Kurds spend their money on. With $5 billion a year in goods and construction contracts coming south into Kurdistan, nobody's worried that the Turkish army massed on the other side will actually invade this country and put a glitch in all that commerce just to spank a few rebels. Even when the bombing raids against the PKK begin, the pilots steer clear of the highways and the pipeline.

After the ceremony, we adjourn with a couple dozen of Karwan Barzani's friends and relatives to a big hall, where we sit in chairs against the walls and sip chai, a double shot glass of tea with an inch of sugar at the bottom, and I'm introduced to the smooth young Karwan and his jolly uncle Dara, both of them great friends of Susan's and now, I gather, great friends of mine too. We have the tea and some fruit and some talk, and mainly we talk about dinner, where it's going to be, what are the alternatives — these guys are Barzanis, members of the family currently in power, and dinner can be whatever we want wherever in Kurdistan we want it — and that takes a while, and no decision is made, but we're all starving, so let's go, man, and we and an entourage of a dozen or more people form our vehicles into a convoy, and we go.

These, I repeat, are Barzanis, family to the legendary leader Mullah Mustafa Barzani, who fought for Kurdish independence for decades against the British and then against Saddam and whose portrait hangs on the wall of every Kurdish government office. These are the cousins of the current Kurdish president, Masoud Barzani, who in 1991 held off a division of Saddam's troops, helicopters, and tanks in the Kore Valley with just 150 of his bodyguards, known as *pesh-merga* ("those who face death"). Three days ago, Rambo, the prime minister's security man, asked me, "Have you ever dealt with the Barzanis?" and did not expect an answer. In the 1980s, in order to deal with these Barzanis once and for all, Saddam Hussein began construction of a power dam intended to flood the entire Barzan Valley and all its villages, submerging and erasing, in a biblical style of retribution, the very origins of his enemies.

We are dealing with the Barzanis, which right now means traveling at homicidal speed behind their big, black Hummer (pronounced

"Hammer" hereabouts) from Zakhu to the mountain city of Dahuk, still discussing the dinner possibilities by cell phone. I can hear Karwan's stereo through Susan's earpiece playing something with a lot of bass. "The Hammer will never lose me," Hameed promises, and in his voice I hear the tribal Kurd beneath the city Kurd, and I know he means not even death, not all our bloody deaths, will separate him from the Hummer.

We have dinner at the Shandakha Hotel in Dahuk, in a private room with a 23-inch TV playing. As we enter, we find the owner and entire staff lined up to greet us. The place has an opulent five-star atmosphere. The johns have automatic-sensor towel dispensers.

I'm too busy with dinner to take notes, chomping resolutely, anxious to make a good showing in what feels more than a little like a pie-eating contest because I'm sitting next to portly, ravenous Uncle Dara, who preaches gluttony: more of these olives, more hummus and baba ghanoush, one more hubcap-size piece of the best flatbread in all of Kurdistan, and now some beef kebab — never pork — and turkey and chicken in a large bowl of broth with an equally large bowl of rice. Dara cries, "Free-range turkey! And the chicken is free-range!" I've seen chickens ranging free in some alarmingly squalid corners the past few days, but this is delicious. Meanwhile, there's a lot of discussion about what to watch on the satellite TV. Hameed wants *Tom and Jerry* cartoons, but he's only a fixer, so we watch the news in Arabic. For these Kurds, the news is good. The times are good.

Today's a lucky day, and these Kurds know what to do with it. We go to Dream City, once the site of a military barracks under Saddam, now a 25-acre amusement park with all the usual attractions: the Crazy Disco tilt-a-whirl and the bumper cars and the Ferris wheel, but also billiards and bowling, a swimming pool, an arcade, and a "4-D" movie theater. That means a 3-D establishment with extra effects, a floor that tilts and lurches and a wind that blows past as the film rushes you along tracks through a spooky labyrinth called *The Tomb of the Mummy* and a mist that wets your face as you come out beside a cataract, never actually moving except as the platform shifts the seats. Our hosts and their friends and bodyguards, in their expensive suits, with their holstered sidearms and yellow 3-D glasses, can't get enough of this one. Karwan buys everyone tickets to a second show, *The Death Mine of Solomon.*

Followed by billiards, followed by bowling. The billiards don't quite amuse: The balls won't go in the holes. It turns out we're mainly here for the bowling anyway; it's catching on all over the Kurdish region, and in this early phase, if you care to, you can witness its practitioners using familiar equipment in the development of an entirely new sport, keeping no score, nobody caring whose turn it is, whirling and grabbing the very next ball on the server — no need to wait for your own, any ball will do — and then an approach best called "the charge of the Kurds" and a kind of almost baseball-mound-worthy windup and a delivery somewhere between that of discus and shot put, the evident objective being to keep the ball airborne for as far as possible in its journey, its lonely flight, downlane.

And then to the Dream City "supermarket," the first department store in Kurdistan, erected in 2003, about half the size of a Wal-Mart and offering a little of everything. The two escalators are running tonight, both the up and the down. In the daytime they're switched off, to save power. The Barzanis and friends move around the place languidly, handling and discussing every item for sale and buying presents for everyone they've ever known. Then we all gather out front for the loading of the many purchases and for a small conference. They've had us now for about 10 hours, but the discussion seems to center on our plans for tomorrow, the people we must meet, the beautiful mountains we must visit, our breakfast, our lunch, our dinner.

And I'm thinking, Yes, this is the climax of the piece right here, affluent Kurds clowning around, the magazine's going to love this entertaining stuff, so why does that make me feel like a pimp in a burgundy velvet suit? Who are these people who keep Al Qaeda from infiltrating their homeland while the U.S. Army scratches its head and watches the rest of Iraq fall to pieces? And why haven't the *New York Times* and CNN taken notice? Here's a guess, just one possibility: because journalists are pimps for war, my friends, in burgundy velvet suits. And that's the news from here.

We all stay at the Dilshad Palace Hotel, the most wonderful hotel in Dahuk, surely five-star, with plastic trees out front covered with plastic blossoms; newly built, and open tonight for the first time in history. We sit together in the lobby for chai and chai and animated small talk and chai before I resolve to commit the rudeness of saying good night. Good night takes a while. You have to circle in slowly on the concept — about 30 minutes.

The bellboy assures me that we're the first customers of the Dilshad Palace. I have to teach him how to operate my door's card lock. The next day, Dara tells me that after I left, I missed some fun: An elevator jammed and caught him between floors. "I was just about to fire my pistol a few times when it started to move again. They have to work these things out!" He seems disappointed, but I can't tell whether it's because the hotel's equipment failed him or because he didn't get to fire his gun in an elevator.

TOM KACZYNSKI

■

Million Year Boom

FROM *MOME*

MILLION YEAR BOOM

BY TOM KACZYŃSKI

PAINFULLY, MY EARS FAILED TO POP AFTER THE LANDING.

EVERYTHING SOUNDED MUTED AND DISTANT. I FELT LIKE A DEEP SEA DIVER DESCENDING INTO A BOTTOMLESS OCEANIC TRENCH.

MY CAB WAS A BATHYSPHERE STUMBLING UPON SOME ANCIENT SUBMERGED CIVILIZATION.

THE SILENCE OF MY DESCENT WAS INTERRUPTED ONLY BY THE TAXI'S RADIO, WHICH, DURING COMMERCIAL BREAKS BECAME ALMOST AUDIBLE.

THE DESPERATE PITCH OF THE ADS MADE THEM SOUND LIKE CRYPTIC WARNINGS FROM AN INCREASINGLY DISTANT SURFACE WORLD.

WAS I BEING RECALLED TO THE SURFACE?

MY UNDERWATER REVERIE WAS INTERRUPTED BY MY ARRIVAL AT **THE WILDERNESS ESTATES.** THIS WAS A GATED CORPORATE HOUSING COMPLEX AND IT WAS GOING TO BE MY HOME FOR THE NEXT SEVERAL WEEKS.

BUILDING 2, SECOND FLOOR, APARTMENT 26.

WHAT? OH... THANKS

THE NAME OF THE PLACE SEEMED A BIT OFF. PERHAPS **WILDERNESS** SIMPLY DENOTED THE ABSENCE OF A CIVILIZING METROPOLIS? WHAT KIND OF **SAVAGES** INHABITED ULTRA-MODERNIST MACHINES FOR LIVING?

OOOF...

MY NEW EMPLOYER LEFT ME A STRANGE NOTE...

...A GREAT TRIP. PLEASE TAKE ADVANTAGE OF ALL THE AMENITIES TO CLEANSE YOUR BODY & SOUL. YOU WILL NEED ALL YOUR STRENGTH TO JOIN US ON THIS EXTRAORDINARY JOURNEY! –R. RAFFERTY, PHD.

OW! WHY WON'T THEY POP?

... WHO'S DR. RAFFERTY?

DECIDED TO FOLLOW THE DOCTORS ADVICE.

NOW ... WHO'S THAT?

MY EARS FINALLY POPPED WHEN I HIT THE WATER.

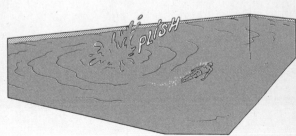

PLISH

THE COMPANY WAS A HOT START-UP TRYING TO MAKE ITS MARK ON THE NEW GREEN ECONOMY. THEIR BUSINESS WAS DIFFICULT TO DEFINE, AS THEY SEEMED TO HAVE THEIR TENTACLES IN A WIDE VARIETY OF INDUSTRIES.

IT WAS LOCATED IN THE FORMER HEADQUARTERS OF A ONCE INVINCIBLE INTERNET GIANT. BUT, THE COMPANY'S GLOBAL AMBITIONS, EMBODIED IN THE HUGE CAMPUS, WERE MARRED BY A LACK OF CLEAR CORPORATE IDENTITY.

ESSENTIALLY, THE COMPANY WAS A GROUP OF HIPPY SCIENTISTS, LAWYERS AND MANAGERS, DROWNING IN INVESTOR CAPITAL, OPERATING UNDER THE BANNER OF A CLIP-ART SQUID.

I'M HERE TO SEE MR. LUBBOCK.

HE'S IN CONFERENCE ROOM 23.

THE COMPANY WAS ABOUT TO GO PUBLIC AND NEEDED A NEW IMAGE, A NEW BRAND TO CHARM THE DEMONIC MARKET FORCES IN THEIR FAVOUR.

I WAS HIRED AS PART OF A SMALL TEAM OF BRAND EXPERTS. IT TOOK ME A LONG TIME TO COME UP WITH A REASON TO SIGN UP...

KNOCK KNOCK

LIKE ALMOST EVERYONE HERE I DIDN'T WANT TO LEAVE A COMFORTABLE COSMOPOLITAN CITY LIFE FOR THIS UNCERTAIN SUBURBAN ENTERPRISE. I CAN'T SPEAK FOR THE OTHERS...

... A GRAPHIC SOLUTION TO THE BEGINNING OF A NEW AEON ...

LOOK WHO FINALLY DECIDED TO JOIN US!

... BUT IN THE END I COULDN'T RESIST HAVING A HAND IN THE CREATION OF THE MYTHOLOGY OF THE NEXT GREAT GLOBAL CORPORATION...

HI GUYS!

...THE END OF MY FIRST DAY, LUBBOCK [GA]VE ME A TOUR OF THE COMPANY COMPLEX.

...THE GROUNDS ARE SOME OF THE MOST ENVIRONMENTALLY ADVANCED IN THE COUNTRY. THIS ISN'T YOUR TYPICAL CORPORATE HQ SITTING ON THE ECOLOGICAL EQUIVALENT OF A **GOLF COURSE**!

LUBBOCK SLIPPED INTO THE ROLE OF A TOUR GUIDE EFFORTLESSLY AND WITH THE CONVICTION OF A NATIVE. HIS EASY FAMILIARITY WITH THE ANCIENT HISTORY OF THE AREA GAVE HIM THE AURA OF A **STONE AGE** WISE MAN.

THE LAWN, IF YOU CAN CALL IT THAT, IS A CLOSE RECONSTRUCTION OF THE MIX OF PLANTS THAT GREW IN THE AREA UNTIL THEY WERE DISPLACED BY THE ADVENT OF AGRICULTURE...

UH, HUH

OVER HERE IS A FRAGMENT OF THE **ABORIGINAL** DECIDUOUS FOREST. WE WANT IT TO GROW FURTHER! WE'RE ALL TREE HUGGERS HERE!

BUT THEY SERVE A VALUABLE FUNCTION AS WELL. THE TREES ARE A REFUGE FOR SEVERAL ENDANGERED SPECIES. THEY COME HERE TO FIND SHELTER FROM HUMANS AND **EXTREME WEATHER**... IN A WAY WE'RE NOT SO DIFFERENT FROM THEM.

WE'VE BUILT UP QUITE A PLEASANT MICRO-CLIMATE HERE... OH...

LOOK HERE!

HUH?

THIS IS **ERUCA INGENIUM**! ONE OF THE RAREST AND MOST VALUABLE FLORA! IT'S NEARLY EXTINCT...

HUH?! WHY'D YOU PICK IT?

TSK! NO WORRIES! THERE IT'S SAFELY BACK IN THE GROUND... IT WOULDN'T BE WORTH **ANYTHING** IF WE DIDN'T EVER PICK IT... THAT'S WHY WE'RE HERE, TO INJECT SOME ECONOMIC VALUE INTO ALL THIS **WILD SPLENDOR**!

AAAHHHHHHH...CHOO

PAT PAT PAT

GESUNDHEIT...

AND OVER HERE IS THE...

WHAT'S WITH THE **STONE CIRCLES**?

SNIFF

THE PACE OF WORK WAS INTENSE. LATE NIGHTS AND WEEKEND WORK WERE STANDARD. THE ENORMITY OF THE COMPANY'S PROJECT BECAME QUICKLY APPARENT.

...SNIFF... WE NEED A SYMBOLIC CONTAINER THAT CAN HOLD BOTH... ARCHAIC HERITAGE AND...SNIFF... THE LIMITLESS POSSIBILITIES OF THE FUTURE...

UGH... I THINK I'M GETTING A COLD...

IN SHORT THE COMPANY WAS ATTEMPTING TO MAP THE ENTIRE PRODUCTIVITY OF THE PLANET'S BIOSPHERE INTO DOLLAR TERMS... EVENTUALLY THIS WOULD LEAD TO THE CREATION OF A NEW GLOBAL **BIO-CURRENCY** ...

... SO EVEN A BLADE OF GRASS WOULD HAVE, SNIFF, **EXCHANGE VALUE** ?

TO GET A MORE ACCURATE MEASURE OF THE PERFORMANCE OF THE GLOBAL BIO-ECONOMY, THE COMPANY WAS RETROACTIVELY PROJECTING CONTEMPORARY MARKET ECONOMICS INTO A MILLION YEARS OF PLANETARY HISTORY.

MY COLD IS GETTING WORSE.

SNIFF

KLACK KLACK

IT WAS ENOUGH TO MAKE ANYONE'S HEAD SPIN... AND I WAS ALREADY DIZZY FROM WHAT SEEMED LIKE A NASTY SINUS INFECTION.

SMOKE BREAK?

SNIFF... SURE!

... YOU HAVEN'T COME TO ANY OF THE SPECIAL CREATIVITY SESSIONS YET...

AAHH-CHOO

GESUNDHEIT

YOU OK?

YEAH... I JUST HAVE THIS PERPETUAL CONGESTION... IT'S PROBABLY JUST A COLD OR SOMETHING ...

MHMM...

SNIFF

... I HAD SOMETHING SIMILAR WHEN I STARTED HERE ... TURNED OUT TO BE A RARE ALLERGY CAUSED BY AN ENDANGERED PLANT... I GUESS IT'S HAPPENED TO OTHERS TOO...

REALLY?

YEAH... YOU SHOULD SEE DOCTOR RAFFERTY ABOUT IT.

SNIFF, I DON'T LIKE DOCTORS ... I'VE NEVER BEEN ALLERGIC TO ANYTHING BEFORE... BESIDES ISN'T HE A SHRINK?

I HADN'T MET DOCTOR RAFFERTY YET, BUT I NOTICED HOW HIS NAME WAS ALWAYS INVOKED WITH A HUSHED AWE...

YEAH HE'S A SHRINK... BUT HE'S ALSO MUCH MORE THAN THAT... GO SEE HIM.

I'M SURE I'LL GET BETTER SOON ...

OVER THE NEXT FEW DAYS I WAS REMINDED OF MY INITIAL MISGIVINGS ABOUT LEAVING THE RELATIVE SAFETY OF THE BIG CITY.

UGH... THESE MEDS AREN'T HELPING MUCH ... MAYBE THIS **IS** SOME KIND OF WEIRD ALLERGY...?

THE CORPORATE HOUSING COMPLEX ACTED AS A KIND OF STERILE DEPRIVATION CHAMBER IN CONTRAST TO THE SENSORY RICHNESS OF THE ECOLOGICAL EDEN SURROUNDING THE COMPANY CAMPUS.

THAT LAMP GIVES ME THE CREEPS...

THE COCKTAIL OF SUBURBAN ISOLATION AND **NON-DROWSY** COLD MEDICATION WAS DEADLY. I WAS SLOWLY GOING OUT OF MY MIND.

WHO WOULD EVER NAME THIS PLACE THE WILDERNESS ESTATES...!?

THE ONLY ANTIDOTE AGAINST CRUSHING BOREDOM WAS PHYSICAL EXERTION. I BECAME OBSESSED WITH SWIMMING.

I WOULD SWIM UNTIL COMPLETE EXHAUSTION ... THEN, DRAINED I WOULD FLOAT, **SUSPENDED** PRECARIOUSLY IN THE MIDDLE OF A GENTLE TUG OF WAR BETWEEN GRAVITY AND WATER ... THE FAINT, CHEMICAL ODOR OF CHLORINE KEEPING MY CONGESTION AT BAY...

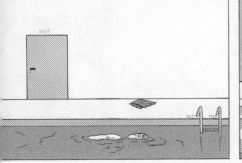

MY ONLY SPECTATOR WAS A BEAUTIFUL WOMAN WHO REGARDED MY PRESENCE WITH THE KIND OF ATTENTION USUALLY RESERVED FOR DRIFTWOOD.

WHAT'S HER STORY?

STILL SUFFERING?

SNIFF... YEAH... UM... I THINK YOU MIGHT BE RIGHT.

LISTEN, HERE'S WHAT RAFFERTY GAVE ME FOR THIS ALLERGY. I HAVE A COUPLE OF PILLS LEFT. YOU SHOULD TRY THEM.

BUT DON'T YOU NEED THEM?

I CAN ALWAYS GET MORE.

YOU WON'T REGRET IT! AND GO SEE THE DOCTOR!

THANKS

COUPLE OF HOURS LATER THE MEDICATION KICKED IN. ALL SYMPTOMS VANISHED.

...ODD, MY FINGERS ARE TINGLING...

KLACK KLACK KLACK

MORE THAN THAT, ONCE THE SINUS HAZE CLEARED, MY BODY WENT INTO SENSORY OVERDRIVE.

I THINK I'M GETTING HIGH FROM THESE DRY ERASE MARKERS

SQUEEEEK

HA HA HA

SIMPLE ACTIVITIES LIKE EATING ACQUIRED NEW IMPORTANCE. I CHEWED WITH DETERMINATION.

TASTES LIKE SHIT... BUT I CAN TASTE IT...

CHEW CHEW

VMMMMM...

VMMMMM

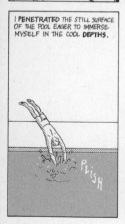

I PENETRATED THE STILL SURFACE OF THE POOL EAGER TO IMMERSE MYSELF IN THE COOL DEPTHS.

PLISH

MY LIMBS FLAILED WITH WILD ABANDON IN AN ATTEMPT TO AGITATE NOT ONLY THE STAGNANT WATER BUT ALSO MY INERT AUDIENCE.

BUT SHE WAS UNMOVED BY MY PHYSICAL DISPLAYS. WHAT WOULD IT TAKE TO DISTURB HER UN-BREAKABLE POISE?

I WOKE UP TIRED AND DRAINED. THE ALLERGY SYMPTOMS RETURNED.

I HAVE TO GET MORE OF THAT MEDICATION

SNIFF

SCRITCH SCRITCH

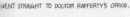

...WENT STRAIGHT TO DOCTOR RAFFERTY'S OFFICE.

WHAT WAS IN THOSE MEDS?

IT'S ODD THAT I WASN'T TOLD ABOUT THIS ALLERGY WHEN I WAS STARTING HERE... WHY IS IT SUCH A SECRET?

HMM... WHAT'S THAT?

OUT OF THE CORNER OF MY EYE...

...I SAW SOMETHING...

HEY!

!!! I CAN'T BELIEVE SOMEONE TOOK A SHIT OUT IN THE OPEN LIKE THAT... MAYBE I SHOULD MENTION THIS TO SECURITY...?

SNIFF

A FEW MINUTES LATER I WAS AT RAFFERTY'S OFFICE AND THE SCATOLOGICAL INCIDENT RECEDED INTO MEMORY. I TOLD HIM ABOUT MY ALLERGY.

HMM...

I'M GLAD YOU CAME TO SEE ME...

YOU'RE NOT THE FIRST PERSON TO DEVELOP THIS CONDITION... THOUGH TECHNICALLY IT'S NOT AN ALLERGY... IT'S PARTIALLY CAUSED BY A RARE PLANT THAT GROWS ON THE GROUNDS.

TAP TAP TAP

THE RETURN OF WILDERNESS HAS SOME SURPRISES FOR US. WE'VE SPENT TOO MUCH TIME IN COMFORTABLE AIR-CONDITIONED CELLS. WE'VE LOST OUR IMMUNITY TO COUNTLESS SPECIES OF FLORA... AN UNIMAGINABLE ECONOMIC LOSS... BUT ALSO A GREAT OPPORTUNITY!... BY THE WAY, HOW IS THE BRANDING PROJECT COMING ALONG?

UH FINE...

GOOD, GOOD... THE IPO IS APPROACHING... I THINK YOU'RE ON A GOOD TEAM... BUT THE CEO IS WORRIED... LUBBOCK APPRECIATES THE COMPANY'S VISION... BUT HE IS TOO COMFORTABLE IN HIS BOURGEOIS SKIN, HE'S TOO MUCH OF A HIPPIE... NOT ENOUGH OF A WILD MAN...

ER...

THE **FUTURE** IS NOT ABOUT WEARING SANDALS, GREEN TIE-DYE T-SHIRTS AND FEELING ALL WARM AND FUZZY INSIDE... IN SOME WAYS THE GREEN ECONOMY MAY TURN OUT TO BE FAR MORE **SAVAGE** THAN WE IMAGINE... CAN THE **ANTIDOTE** BE WORSE THAN THE POISON? HAVE YOU STUMBLED ON ANY **ANIMAL TRACKS** LATELY?

UH WHAT?

?

NEVER MIND... I HAVE ANOTHER APPOINTMENT NOW... I WILL GET YOU YOUR MEDICATION NOW...

SNIFF, THANKS...

MY REVITALIZED SENSES DRAGGED ME OUT OF THE FILTERED AIR OF THE CUBICLES.

WHAT DID HE MEAN BY "TECHNICALLY IT'S NOT AN ALLERGY...?

KLAEK KLAEK KLAEK

I DECIDED TO FAMILIARIZE MYSELF WITH THE GROUNDS. DURING BREAKS I EXPLORED THE OLD FOREST. I BECAME CONVINCED THE SOLUTION TO THE COMPANY'S BRAND LAY SOMEWHERE IN ITS DENSE THICKET.

MAYBE I'LL FIND THOSE TRACKS...

I CAME UPON MORE FECES. WERE VAGRANTS AMONG THE ENDANGERED SPECIES SHELTERED BY THE TREES? DID THE COMPANY HAVE A SECURITY PROBLEM?

DEFINITELY HUMAN, SIMILAR ODOR AS BEFORE.

MY NEW MOBILITY ALLOWED ME TO TAKE PART IN OUTDOOR CREATIVITY AND TEAM BUILDING EXERCISES. APPARENTLY THEY WERE ONE OF RAFFERTY'S MANY MANAGERIAL INNOVATIONS.

THE STONE CIRCLES MYSTERY SOLVED!

OOF!

PERHAPS WE SHOULD TRY **CAVE PAINTING** INSTEAD?

WHEN THE STONE CIRCLE WAS FINISHED, I RESTED. MY ELEVATED HEARTBEAT REMINDED ME OF RAFFERTY'S TAPPING FINGER... FOR THE FIRST TIME I BEGAN TO UNDERSTAND THE FUTURE THE COMPANY WAS ENGINEERING.

AT HOME I SPENT MORE AND MORE TIME IN THE POOL. I WAS DRAWN TO ITS AUSTERE EMPTINESS, A MODERNIST WOMB. MY BODY DISSOLVED IN ITS AMNIOTIC FLUID INTO AN ALCHEMY OF AMINO ACIDS.

THIS IS HOW I IMAGINED THE PRIMORDIAL SOUP OF LIFE... A CHEMICAL CONSCIOUSNESS, UNFORMED, UNBURDENED BY EVOLUTION, NOT YET READY TO SEIZE THE OFFERINGS OF THE COSMOS, BUT ALREADY FLUSH WITH GENETIC DESIRE.

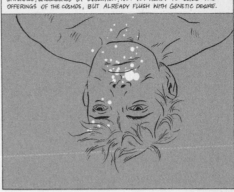

INSIDE I WOULD UNDERGO A DAILY IN VITRO MORPHOGENESIS... A SERIES OF MUTATIONS...THE GENETIC EQUIVALENT OF RAPID PROTOTYPING. I LEARNED TO BREATHE UNDERWATER. MY VISION ADJUSTED TO FLUID DISTORTIONS.

RELUCTANTLY I WOULD RETURN TO THE SURFACE. I KNEW THAT EVENTUALLY I WOULD HAVE TO RE-LEARN TO WALK ON LAND... NOT BECAUSE I LOST THAT ABILITY, BUT BECAUSE THE LAND WILL HAVE TRANSFORMED TOO...

DID I IMAGINE HER?

A FEW DAYS LATER RAFFERTY CALLED A MEETING. THE EMAIL INVITE ENDED WITH A QUOTE BY SIGMUND FREUD: "ANATOMY IS DESTINY." I SUSPECTED THIS WAS A NOT SO VEILED ATTEMPT TO RALLY THE STRUGGLING BRAND TEAM.

THE DOCTOR TRANSFORMED ON STAGE...

SUCCESS. VISION. ENERGY. ASK YOURSELVES THIS : WHO ARE YOUR **ANCESTORS**? GENERAL ELECTRIC, FORD, IBM, APPLE, SONY, MICROSOFT GOOGLE ? NO! YOUR ANCESTORS ARE THE **HUNTER-GATHERERS** OF THE PALEOLITHIC WHO INVENTED LANGUAGE, MUSIC AND ART!

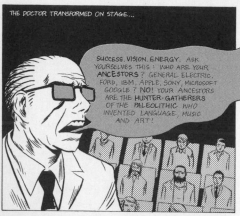

THE AUDIENCE WAS MESMERIZED BY THE PERFORMANCE. I BECAME AWARE OF FAINT DRUMMING.

WE'RE ON THE VERGE OF THE GREATEST COMMERCIAL **OPPORTUNITY** IN HUMAN HISTORY. CARBON TRADE, BIO-FUELS, SOLAR ENERGY, THESE ARE ALL INSIGNIFICANT PUDDLES COMPARED TO THE VAST OCEANS OF **PROFITS** TO BE **EXTRACTED** FROM THIS PLANET...

WAS I HEARING A RECORDED SOUNDTRACK OR THE **THROBBING BLOOD** IN RAFFERTY'S VEINS ?

THE COMING AGE OF CLIMATE DISASTERS WILL TEST THE INGENUITY OF THE SPECIES. WILL WE ACCEPT EXTINCTION LIKE THE NEANDERTHALS?

AT SOME POINT I STOPPED LISTENING. I ALREADY KNEW WHAT RAFFERTY WAS GOING TO SAY, I HEARD IT BEFORE... IN THE POOL... WHEN THE WATERS FLOODED MY EARS WITH **KNOWING WHISPERS.**

INVEST IN EVOLUTION REVERSE THE GENETIC CREDIT CRUNCH COMPOUND THE INTEREST OF BIODIVERSITY

...RE-WILD THE HUMAN MIND, GET PAST THIS **DOMESTICATED** CREATIVITY ... NO MORE iPODS, iPHONES, iHUMANS ... WE NEED TO REINVENT **FIRE!** IGNITE YOUR SAVAGE INTELLIGENCE ... PREPARE FOR THE MILLION YEAR PROFIT CYCLES...

THE APPLAUSE RESEMBLED A **STAMPEDE** OF NORTH AMERICAN BISON. I ALMOST PEED MY PANTS.

CLAP CLAP CLAP CLAP CLAP CLAP CLAP CLAP CLAP CLAP CLAP CLAP CLAP CLAP CLAP CLAP CLAP CLAP

YOU'RE WELCOME...

WHAT'S YOUR BATHROOM LIKE? DO YOU LET IT GO... ALLOWING LAYERS OF GRIME AND SCENT TO ACCUMULATE UNTIL YOU'RE FORCED TO CAMOUFLAGE THEM WITH A CHEMICAL APPROXIMATION OF SPRING?

CONSIDER THE MODERN BATHROOM. WHAT LIES BEHIND THIS INJUNCTION TO CLEAN? HOW DID THIS ANTISEPTIC ROOM WHERE EXCREMENT MAGICALLY DISAPPEARS COME TO BE?

WHAT DO WE GAIN BY SEVERING THE CONNECTION BETWEEN OUR BOWELS AND THE FERTILITY CYCLES OF THE SOIL?

THE HUMAN GASTROINTESTINAL TRACT IS A MARVEL OF EVOLUTIONARY ENGINEERING. BEST OF ALL IT'S **COPYRIGHT** FREE... IMAGINE THAT!

HAVE YOU FOUND WHERE THE TRAIL LEADS? I THINK YOU ALREADY KNOW... I TRUST YOU'VE BEEN TAKING YOUR MEDICATION?

SLAM

I STOOD THERE FOR A LONG TIME UNABLE TO GO...

SHIT!

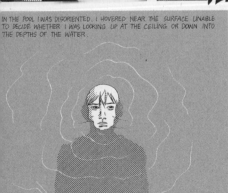

IN THE POOL I WAS DISORIENTED. I HOVERED NEAR THE SURFACE UNABLE TO DECIDE WHETHER I WAS LOOKING UP AT THE CEILING OR DOWN INTO THE DEPTHS OF THE WATER.

I WAS NO LONGER SURE THAT THE WOMAN EXISTED IN THE SAME SPACE-TIME CONTINUUM AS ME. COMMUNICATION BETWEEN US WOULD BE IMPOSSIBLE WITHOUT SOME KIND OF INTER-DIMENSIONAL LEAP OF FAITH.

WHAT AM I WAITING FOR?

YOUR PARTICIPATION IS NEEDED ON AN OFFSITE PROJECT...

WE WERE ACCOMPANIED BY A COUPLE OF MEMBERS OF THE BRANDING TEAM, AND A PERSON I DIDN'T KNOW. LUBBOCK WAS CONSPICUOUSLY ABSENT.

WE ARRIVED AT ANOTHER CORPORATE CAMPUS AND ENTERED THE PREMISES SOMEWHAT OBLIQUELY. AT THIS POINT MY RECOLLECTION OF THE EVENTS THAT FOLLOWED BECOMES HAZY AT BEST...

GO, GO!

IT REEKS OF ARTIFICIAL FERTILIZER...

APPARENTLY THE PLACE BELONGED TO A FIRM THAT WAS RESISTING A TAKEOVER ATTEMPT BY OUR COMPANY.

MEET KURZWEIL YOUR CEO.

UH, HI ... SIR ...

NO TITLES!

WE'RE HERE TO STAKE OUR LEGITIMATE CLAIM ... THE TAKEOVER HAS ALREADY HAPPENED, THEY JUST DON'T KNOW IT YET... THERE IS NO RESISTANCE TO **HISTORICAL INEVITABILITY** ...

MMH MMHMMHM...

TONIGHT WE MAKE AN **INVESTMENT** TO **FACILITATE** THE **RESTRUCTURING** OF ANTIQUATED **BUSINESS MODELS**... WE COME TO FERTILIZE THIS BARREN SOIL WITH THE SEEDS OF OUR CORPORATE DNA ...

ACTION PLAN: SHED YOUR CIVILIZED INHIBITIONS! **DELIVERABLE**: GARDEN OF PURE **PROFIT**... **GOING FORWARD**, COME THE PARADIGM SHIFT, EVOLUTIONARY SYNERGIES WILL **COMPOUND**...

AND THEN WE'LL RETURN TO REAP THE HARVEST...

KURZWEIL MADE THE FIRST DEPOSIT... I REALIZED WHY THE BRANDING TEAM WAS CREATIVELY BLOCKED... CONSTIPATED BY OUTDATED MARKETING ASSUMPTIONS.

I WATCHED A SMALL GOLDEN STREAM FORM ON THE CONCRETE FLOWING AROUND MY FEET... I WAS THE HEADWATERS OF THE NILE... HERACLITUS IN THE EVERCHANGING RIVER...

A FAINT HUM OF ELECTRICAL ENGINE...

...SECURITY GUARD ON A SEGWAY ...

YOU FU--

SPARK OF CREATION ...

THUD

DOVE EAGERLY INTO THE DEPTHS. AT THE BOTTOM HE WAS WAITING FOR ME...THE CHANNEL WAS FINALLY WIDE OPEN...

I COULDN'T HAVE BEEN OUT FOR LONG.

WE COMMUNICATED NON-VERBALLY, LIKE TWO CELLS ENGAGING IN OSMOTIC FLUID EXCHANGE...

THE GUARD MUST HAVE GONE TO FIND THE OTHERS...

MY MOUTH WAS RAPIDLY FILLING WITH BLOOD.

I THINK HE BROKE A COUPLE OF TEETH...

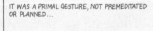

THE RIGHT SIDE OF MY FACE PULSED WITH PAIN. I DREW A DEEP BREATH.

IT WAS A PRIMAL GESTURE, NOT PREMEDITATED OR PLANNED...

I STOOD THERE FOR A LONG TIME WATCHING MY BLOOD CONGEAL INTO THE LOGO OF THE NEXT GREAT GLOBAL CORPORATION.

END

AMELIA KAHANEY

■

The Temp

FROM *Crazyhorse*

Monday

WHEN WE FIRST MET THE TEMP, we didn't give her a second thought. Sure, there were things you noticed about her: she had a chain-smoking anchorwoman's voice, midwestern and deep, and she had a clomping little walk that reminded us of certain ponies we'd ridden as children. It took us a minute to put it together when she introduced herself as *Karen from the agency*. What agency, we thought, CIA? Then we remembered that the boss had ordered a temp and we relaxed. She waited patiently while we decided where to put her.

We dragged a chair over to the broken-down desk behind the copy machine, the one with nine hundred leftover sugar packets stuffed into the drawers, and waved her over.

This is where you'll sit for the week, we said. Good thing you're small, you'll almost fit! The temp was slim and tanned — some kind of Asian.

This is the database, we said, pointing at the computer. And here are the numbers. We showed her the rows of three-ring binders where we kept the raw data.

All you have to do, we said, is make sure the database matches the numbers. We backed away from the temp with big smiles, hoping she wouldn't open the binders and run to the bathroom hyperventilating the way we all did when we first started here. Just do your best, we added. Our cheeks were starting to hurt from smiling so hard. She nodded, and her voice rang out with an odd confidence: *No problem!*

The truth was, we had all sullied the database. When we first started here, we didn't know what we were doing. And it was so boring! Sometimes, if we were planning to do data entry, we would come to work drunk. We got sloppy. We were not careful.

At ten o'clock, the boss came out of his office and shook the temp's hand. Garbage in, garbage out, he said, jabbing his finger in the direction of the computer. Garbage in, garbage out, was one of the six things he liked to say. We didn't know what it meant, and we didn't think he did either.

If you have a question, come in and ask me. Come straight to me, he said in a loud whisper, looking at us over the top of his glasses as if we were the dried-up remnants of a cold-cut platter. He was the only man in our department, which made him that much easier to despise.

The temp was a glamorous smoker. On our first cigarette break together, she pulled out an antique mother-of-pearl lighter we instantly wanted.

Your boss has difficult energy, she said. She talked and French-inhaled simultaneously, and it made her look smart. He shouldn't have been given a position of leadership.

We laughed when she said that — big horsy guffaws. That was when we started thinking we liked her. As a person, not just as help.

So, Karen, what's your story, we asked.

It turned out the temp was writing a novel! It was going to be the Filipino version of *One Hundred Years of Solitude*. She was stuck on a particular chapter, and she was here, she said, to put her novel on the back burner of her mind and fill the front burner with easily accomplished tasks.

Well, we thought, that's certainly unusual. We had never considered our tasks easy to accomplish. We had always found them virtually impossible to accomplish. But we nodded sagely, like we got it.

We were practically speechless when, by the end of the day, the temp had the computer spitting out piles of good data. You just had it tied up in these crazy knots, she said. It was like she had some kind of bird's-eye view of all of us, of our petty difficulties. Like she could undo every mistake we'd ever made.

Tuesday

The temp did our charts! She brought in a computer program that calculated everything based on our birthdays. In minutes, we were each given printouts that Karen said were *road maps to our destinies.* She told us about our Venus in the fourth house, our Saturn return. And it turned out that four of us — two thirds of us — had Cancer moons! The odds of that, the temp said, were extremely low. It was obviously why we had an emotional, watery office instead of a decisive, fiery office where things got done. Only a watery office like ours could have made such a mess of the database.

You — she pointed at Kirsten — should absolutely not be working here. You were made for the theater!

She was? we said.

Without a doubt, she said. This woman needs to express herself. Her body is her instrument. And *you* — she said to Erica — *you* are someone who needs to make a lot of money. What in god's name are you doing here?

She said Michelle would sleep with hundreds of men.

We gasped. *Hundreds?*

She's already up to forty, Deena said, and we all laughed.

None of you belong here, she said. She'd looked at our charts. She'd done the calculations. You're all so talented, she said. You're wasting valuable time in this place.

Yes, we thought. This was just what we'd always suspected.

We talked to the temp all day after that. As if it wasn't enough to be writing a novel, the temp was also starting her own company! Every night after work she went to an office in TriBeCa and worked on her business plan with her partners. It was going to be huge.

We were on the edge of our seats: *What is it?*

I can't really talk about it, she said. Legal reasons. But let's just say it's a product we've all needed for a long time.

Our heads swam with ideas. We pictured molded plastic in beautiful colors, a curving, can-opener-shaped object that would save us all. We thought it might have an ingenious sort of hinge, a new way of folding that would emit a satisfying sound. A click. A snap.

In our beds that night, we thought of the temp. She wasn't unattractive. Her beauty wasn't showy or obnoxious, and it wasn't the kind you'd notice if it passed by on the other side of the street, but she had an expensive-looking haircut with all kinds of spiky layers in it, and she had an eggplant-shaped mole on the right side of her nose that looked good on her. Not everyone could pull off something like that, we thought. She offset the mole with very good shoes, shoes we had never seen before, soft kidskin half-boots.

We used to think that if we knew anything at all, it was a thing or two about shoes, but the temp made us realize that there was a whole world of shoes we were ignorant of. We wondered fretfully what else we didn't know.

Wednesday

The next day, we arrived at nine sharp. We wore our best outfits, clothes we normally wore for a night out. The temp was dressed impeccably, as usual. The fabric of her clothes was delicate and textured, as if it had been harvested from tropical hardwood pulp and the skins of endangered species. Her normal outfits could eat our special outfits for lunch.

Midmorning was when the influx from the eighteenth floor started. One of us — and we had a good idea who — had been talking about our temp with the people on the eighteenth floor! They wanted their charts done too. They wanted to know why their bosses were incompetent, what careers they should be pursuing instead of the horrible careers they were in now. You couldn't blame them, really, for wanting their destinies explained. It wasn't their fault they had to work on the eighteenth floor.

They came up one by one, asking for ludicrous items. Do you have industrial staples? Coffee filters? The annual report from 1996? No, we said. No.

They looked at us, then they looked at our temp, then they looked back at us.

This is our temp, Karen, we said, because they forced us into it. Then they had their opening: Hi Karen, I hear you know a lot about astrology!

You had to hand it to her — she was amiable. Our temp had time for everyone, even Stephanie from accounting who you could see just by looking at her didn't have any destiny at all.

We seethed inwardly at the interlopers until finally our boss came out of his lair to put a stop to it. Enough, enough, he said. Karen is doing valuable work on our database — let's allow her to get to it!

We loved the boss right then. He was just misunderstood, we thought, and should not have been given a position of leadership.

After lunch at our desks that day, the temp pulled out a big bag of tamarind candy. We had never tasted anything like it before. It was sweet and sour both, and tasted faintly of wet dirt. We chewed pieces of it all afternoon until there was tamarind paste stuck in every crevice of our teeth and we had to dig it out with the floss Joanna kept in her desk drawer. We smiled brown smiles at the temp. You're rotting our teeth out, we said. You're turning us into savages.

I know, she said, and you love it. The temp always had a flirtatious retort ready for us. She made us feel like better people than we actually were. We were surprised at how easy it was to be witty and pleasant, and we wondered why we couldn't sustain it, what it was that had made us so coiled and mean.

That evening, we imagined the temp in her big bed, lying next to her ghostly boyfriend, who was practically an albino, she'd said, a long thin noodle of a man. We pictured them postcoital, the temp lying there in just a lacy wisp of something, a red pen in her mouth, her manuscript beside her, presentation posters of her company's mysterious product scattered on the floor below.

We lingered on our temp. We stretched her out on thousand-thread-count sheets, lit her up in flattering soft-focus. We let her lie there not doing a thing, imagined her waiting patiently while her boyfriend fetched delicacies from the fridge — a fermented bean cake, something involving unripe papaya.

Thursday

At nine-thirty, the boss called the temp in to join our department meeting.

The database is really coming along, Karen, he said. You've been such a help. Maybe you could share with us your outsider's perspective of our team — maybe you have some ideas about how we can be more efficient?

His head swiveled around and he looked at each of us like we were fossilized tea bags stuck to the bottom of dirty mugs.

Sure, Martin, she said. But why was she calling him Martin? She hadn't learned that from us — we called him boss or sir or nothing at all. Was our temp spending intimate time with the boss? Something wasn't right, and we felt our shoulders starting to tense up, one after the other, all around the conference table.

Well, she said. She took a deep breath, as if she'd prepared a long list of bullet-pointed grievances that she was about to whip out and pass around to the group. Then she launched into it.

Everyone here hoards information, she said. There is an atmosphere of mistrust in the office, Martin. People here cling to the few tasks they're able to accomplish, and even those they work on half-heartedly because there's a sense that none of it matters . . .

We gnawed at our cuticles while she talked. We stared out the window at the white crust of pigeon droppings on the building across the street. We looked like we weren't paying attention, but we were. We had never felt so betrayed, not since the time Eddie from the Executive Office had started a vicious rumor that pitted us against one another at the Christmas party. We had made Eddie very sorry he'd done that. Now when we saw him in the lobby he ran — ran! — to open the door for us before we could do it ourselves. He frequently broke out into a sweat when we passed him in the hall, and that's the way we liked it, because we were not to be trifled with.

Finally, the temp shut her mouth.

The boss was impressed. Thank you Karen, he said, you've given us a lot of food for thought. Hasn't she, ladies?

Oh yeah, we said. Tons.

The boss's vacant blue eyes matched his shirt. He had a weak chin with the kind of neck skin you wanted to reach your hand out and flick. Judging by what came out of the printer, he had spent most of the day pricing personal electronic devices. We weren't the only ones who were inefficient.

We were going to be bitchy to the temp for the rest of the day, but when she pulled out her pearl-inlaid lighter and shook her pack of cigarettes at us, we couldn't help ourselves.

Fine, we said icily. Let's go.

Of course I didn't mean any of that, she said. She leaned back against the wall of the stairwell and arched her head upward. The light from the air shaft dotted her cheek with spots of sun. You know that, right? I just told him what he wanted to hear.

Oh, we said. Well, it sounded like you meant it. We leaned against the wall next to her and looked at the watery gray opening five stories up. We listened to the slow dripping of the pipes and tried not to think about how close we were standing to the temp or how badly we wanted her to put her arms around us.

He's just a sad little man, the temp said.

We had to forgive her when she said that. She probably thought we were all sad little people, and she might have been right. Before we went inside, just for good measure, one of us blew smoke into her hair when she wasn't looking. And all day while we ate the tamarind candy we looked at each other behind the temp's back and rolled our eyes, mouthing the word *traitor*. But we didn't mean it.

Friday

For the first time ever, we didn't want the week to end. We had learned so much about our temp, and more importantly, so much about ourselves! We had big ideas now about our careers, dreams the temp believed could be realized in the not-too-distant future. She knew we could make a valuable contribution to the tapestry of human life if only we tapped into our real gifts, which were being wasted in this office, in this visionless field.

When we hugged the temp goodbye on Friday afternoon, some of us had to discreetly wipe tears from our eyes. She was shorter than we'd imagined when we'd fantasized about hugging her, and her hair tickled our necks.

How will we get in touch with you? we asked. We didn't want to seem like stalkers, but that's how we felt. Even the boss slithered out of his office and said Karen, perhaps you could leave your phone number in case we have any questions about the database. A rush of color swelled in his cheeks then, because he too was in love with the temp. We understood perfectly. We didn't begrudge him this.

Sure, she said. She whipped out business cards for each of us. They were printed on beautiful cream paper, and we held them carefully by their edges as though they might dissolve at any moment. After the boss signed her time card, she flashed us a glittering smile and swished out the door in her fabulous coat and hat.

Right about then, something in us clicked on. Wait, we said. We looked at the little desk in the corner, at the neat piles of data she'd laid across it like an offering. Wait, wait, Karen! We heard the door to the elevator ding open.

We ran after her.

She was stepping into the elevator, holding her purse to her chest. Wait, we yelled. We rushed down the hall.

What, she said. She wasn't smiling. Her hat was tilted on her head just so. We felt our hearts thumping.

We forgot —

We need —

Don't go! Jennifer finally got the words out. We want to buy you a drink, Karen. For everything you've done.

Oh, that's so *sweet*, she said, taking her hand away from the elevator door, but I'm actually late for this *thing* I have to get to.

Can we go with you?

Oh, girls, I'm sorry, it's sort of an intimate thing.

But Karen, we said. We were moving in a group. The elevator door was closing and we had to stop it, so we got in.

Karen, we said. We'll miss you. Then someone reached out and touched her lapel, and then someone else joined in. And then, for some reason, she began to scream.

And then something cracked open, and her purse went flying. Dozens of our office pens fell out and landed on the elevator floor, along with hundreds of jumbo paperclips, two notepads, three spools of correction tape still in their packaging, and some of our best high-lighters.

Some of us — we didn't know who, could never definitively say in a court of law — clawed at the temp's chest in an attempt to quiet her down, inadvertantly popping a button off her cashmere cardigan. There were so many arms and hands and legs and hips, it was hard to know what was going on. The elevator, still open, went *ding ding ding ding ding ding ding.*

Shhhh, we said. Let's get this cleaned up.

Some of us bent down and began scooping our brand-new of-fice supplies back into her purse, while others of us just looked on, stricken.

Just leave me alone, the temp was saying, her voice high and shaky. Just go away! But we couldn't. Shhhh, we said. Almost done.

Then someone's foot made contact with a small shiny object. It skittered across the elevator floor and onto the carpet. We saw it was the antique mother-of-pearl lighter, and we all leapt for it.

There was a pile-up in the hallway then: thrashing limbs, fistfuls of hair ripped out of heads, heels grinding into flesh. It felt good — necessary, even — to fight hard. To cry out, to hit and kick and scratch, to make ourselves known to one another like this. It seemed to go on for a long time.

When we finally looked up, Bethany was standing off to the side with her fist closed around the lighter, saying *I got it, I got it* and the elevator door had dinged shut with Karen and her purse inside. We stared at each other, our faces slowly untwisting, returning to nor-mal.

That was weird, Deena said.

We smoothed out the wrinkles in our clothes, picked carpet lint out of our hair. Yeah, we said. Huh.

Then we went inside and shut down our computers.

Suddenly, we were very tired.

One by one, we would quit for other jobs, for pharmacology school or extended trips to Ecuador. Sometimes we would wonder about the temp. Had she even existed? When we got other temps, they were so ordinary: nervous women with weak handshakes, men with concave chests under colorless shirts.

It would only be a matter of time before our department lost a big account, and then another, which meant those of us who remained would be let go. And we would notice we felt strangely good about it, buoyant and full of possibility.

It's time, we would say. We're ready.

REBECCA MAKKAI

■

The Briefcase

FROM *New England Review*

HE THOUGHT HOW STRANGE that a political prisoner, marched through town in a line, chained to the man behind and chained to the man ahead, should take comfort in the fact that this had all happened before. He thought of other chains of men on other islands of the Earth, and he thought how since there have been men there have been prisoners. He thought of mankind as a line of miserable monkeys chained at the wrist, dragging each other back into the ground.

In the early morning of December first, the sun was finally warming them all, enough to walk faster. With his left hand, he adjusted the loop of steel that cuffed his right hand to the line of doomed men. His hand was starved, his wrist was thin, his body was cold: the cuff slipped off. In one beat of the heart he looked back to the man behind him and forward to the man limping ahead, and knew that neither saw his naked, red wrist; each saw only his own mother weeping in a kitchen, his own love lying on a bed in white sheets and sunlight.

He walked in step with them to the end of the block.

Before the war this man had been a chef, and his one crime was feeding the people who sat at his tables in small clouds of smoke and talked politics. He served them the wine that fueled their underground newspaper, their aborted revolution. And after the night his restaurant disappeared in fire, he had run and hidden and gone without food — he who had roasted ducks until the meat jumped from the bone, he who had evaporated three bottles of wine into one pot of cream soup, he who had peeled the skin from small pumpkins with a twist of his hand.

And here was his hand, twisted free of the chain, and here he was running and crawling, until he was through a doorway. It was a building of empty classrooms — part of the university he had never attended. He watched from the bottom corner of a second-story window as the young soldiers stopped the line, counted 199 men, shouted to each other, shouted at the men in the panicked voices of children who barely filled the shoulders of their uniforms. One soldier, a bigger one, a louder one, stopped a man walking by. A man in a suit, with a briefcase, a beard — some sort of professor. The soldiers stripped him of his coat, his shirt, his leather case, cuffed him to the chain. They marched again. And as soon as they were past — no, not that soon; many minutes later, when he had the stomach — the chef ran down to the street and collected the man's briefcase, coat, and shirt.

In the alley, the chef sat against a wall and buttoned the professor's shirt over his own ribs. When he opened the briefcase, papers flew out, a thousand doves flailing against the walls of the alley. The chef ran after them all, stopped them with his feet and arms, herded them back into the case. Pages of numbers, of arrows and notes and hand-drawn star maps. Here were business cards: a professor of physics. Envelopes showed his name and address — information that might have been useful in some other lifetime, one where the chef could ring the bell of this man's house and explain to his wife about empty chains, empty wrists, empty classrooms. Here were graded papers, a fall syllabus, the typed draft of an exam. The question at the end, a good one: "Using modern astronomical data, construct, to the best of your ability, a proof that the Sun revolves around the Earth."

The chef knew nothing of physics. He understood chemistry only insofar as it related to the baking time of bread at various elevations or the evaporation rate of alcohol. His knowledge of biology was limited to the deboning of chickens and the behavior of *Saccharomyces cerevisiae*, common bread yeast. And what did he know at all of moving bodies and gravity? He knew this: he had moved from his line of men, creating a vacuum — one that had sucked the good professor in to fill the void.

The chef sat on his bed in the widow K——'s basement and felt, in the cool leather of the briefcase, a second vacuum: here was a vacated life. Here were salary receipts, travel records, train tickets, a small address book. And these belonged to a man whose name was not blackened like his own, a man whose life was not hunted. If he wanted to live through the next year, the chef would have to learn this life and fill it — and oddly, this felt not like a robbery but an apology, a way to put the world back in balance. The professor would not die, because he himself would become the professor, and he would live.

Surely he could not teach at the university; surely he could not slip into the man's bed unnoticed. But what was in this leather case, it seemed, had been left for him to use. These addresses of friends; this card of identification; this riddle about the inversion of the universe.

Five cities east, he now gave his name as the professor's, and grew out his beard so it would match the photograph on the card he now carried in his pocket. They did not, anymore, look entirely dissimilar. To the first man in the address book, the chef had written a typed letter: "Am in trouble and have fled the city . . . Tell my dear wife I am safe, but for her safety do not tell her where I am . . . If you are able to help a poor old man, send money to the following postbox . . . I hope to remain your friend, Professor T——."

He had to write this about the wife; how could he ask these men for money if she held a funeral? And what of it, if she kept her happiness another few months, another year?

The next twenty-six letters were similar in nature, and money arrived now in brown envelopes and white ones. The bills came wrapped in notes — Was his life in danger? Did he have his health? — and with the money he paid another widow for another basement, and he bought weak cigarettes. He sat on café chairs and drew pictures of the universe, showed stars and planets looping each other in light. He felt, perhaps, that if he used the other papers in the brief-case, he must also make use of this question. Or perhaps he felt that if he could answer it, he could put the universe back together. Or perhaps it was something to do with his empty days.

He wrote in his small notebook: "The light of my cigarette is a fire like the Sun. From where I sit, all the universe is equidistant from my cigarette. Ergo, my cigarette is the center of the universe. My cigarette is on Earth. Ergo, the Earth is the center of the universe. If all heavenly bodies move, they must therefore move in relation to the Earth, and in relation to my cigarette."

His hand ached; these words were the most he had written since school, which had ended for him at age sixteen. He had been a smart boy, even talented in languages and mathematics, but his mother knew these were no way to make a living. He was not blessed, like the professor, with years of scholarship and quiet offices and leather books. He was blessed instead with chicken stocks and herbs and sherry. Thirty years had passed since his last day of school, and his hand was accustomed now to wooden spoon, mandoline, peeling knife, rolling pin.

Today, his hands smelled of ink, when for thirty years they had smelled of leeks. They were the hands of the professor; ergo, he was now the professor.

He had written to friends A through L, and now he saved the rest and wrote instead to students. Here in the briefcase's outermost pocket were class rosters from the past two years; letters addressed to those young men care of the university were sure to reach them. The amounts they sent were smaller, the notes that accompanied them more inquisitive. What exactly had transpired? Could they come to the city and meet him?

The post box, of course, was in a different city than the one where he stayed. He arrived at the post office just before closing, and came only once every two or three weeks. He always looked through the window first to check that the lobby was empty. If it was not, he would leave and come again another day. Surely one of these days, a friend of the professor would be waiting there for him. He prepared a story, that he was the honored professor's assistant, that he could not reveal the man's location but would certainly pass on your kindest regards, sir.

If the Earth moved, all it would take for a man to travel its distance would be a strong balloon. Rise twenty feet above, and wait for the Earth to turn under you; you would be home again in a day. But this was not true, and a man could not escape his spot on the Earth but to run along the surface. Ergo, the Earth was still. Ergo, the Sun was the moving body of the two.

No, he did not believe it. He wanted only to know who this professor was, this man who would, instead of teaching his students the laws of the universe, ask them to prove as true what was false.

On the wall of the café: plate-sized canvas, delicate oils of an apple, half-peeled. Signed, below, by a girl he had known in school. The price was more than three weeks of groceries, and so he did not buy it, but for weeks he read his news under the apple and drank his coffee. Staining his fingers in cheap black ink were the signal fires of the world, the distress sirens, the dispatches from the trenches and hospitals and abattoirs of the war; but here, on the wall, a sign from another world. He had known this girl as well as any other: had spoken with her every day, but had not made love to her; had gone to her home one winter holiday, but knew nothing of her life since then. And here, a clue, perfect and round and unfathomable. After all this time: apple.

After he finished the news, he worked at the proof and saw in the coil of green-edged skin some model of spiraling, of expansion. The stars were at one time part of the Earth, until the hand of God peeled them away, leaving us in the dark. They do not revolve around us: they escape in widening circles. The Milky Way is the edge of this peel.

After eight months in the new city, the chef stopped buying his newspapers on the street by the café and began instead to read the year-old news the widow gave him for his fires. Here, fourteen months ago: Minister P—— of the Interior predicts war. One day he found that in a box near the widow's furnace were papers three, four, five years old.

Pages were missing, edges eaten. He took his fragments of yellowed paper to the café and read the beginnings and ends of opinions and letters. He read reports from what used to be his country's borders.

When he had finished the last paper of the box, he began to read the widow's history books. The Americas, before Columbus; the oceans, before the British; the Romans, before their fall.

History was safer than the news, because there was no question of how it would end.

He took a lover in the city and told her he was a professor of physics. He showed her the stars in the sky and explained that they circled the Earth, along with the Sun.

That's not true at all, she said. You tease me because you think I'm a silly girl.

No, he said and touched her neck. You are the only one who might understand. The universe has been folded inside out.

A full year had passed, and he paid the widow in coins. He wrote to friends M through Z. I have been in hiding for a year, he wrote. Tell my dear wife I have my health. May time and history forgive us all.

A year had passed, but so had many years passed for many men. And after all what was a year, if the Earth did not circle the Sun?

The Earth does not circle the Sun, he wrote. Ergo, the years do not pass. The Earth, being stationary, does not erase the past nor escape toward the future. Rather, the years pile on like blankets, existing at once. The year is 1848; the year is 1789; the year is 1956.

If the Earth hangs still in space, does it spin? If the Earth were to spin, the space I occupy I will therefore vacate in an instant. This city will leave its spot, and the city to the west will usurp its place. Ergo, this city is all cities at all times. This is Kabul; this is Dresden; this is Johannesburg.

I run by standing still.

At the post office, he collects his envelopes of money. He has learned from the notes of concerned colleagues and students and friends that the professor suffered from infections of the inner ear that often threw his balance. He has learned of the professor's wife, A——, whose father died the year they married. He has learned that he has a young son. Rather, the professor has a son.

At each visit to the post office, he fears he will forget the combination. It is an old lock, and complicated: F1, clockwise to B3, back to A6, forward again to J3. He must shake the little latch before it opens. More than forgetting, perhaps what he fears is that he will be denied access — that the little box will one day recognize him behind his thick and convincing beard, will decide he has no right of entry.

One night, asleep with his head on his lover's leg, he dreams that a letter has arrived from the professor himself. They freed me at the end of the march, it says, and I crawled my way home. My hands are bloody and my knees are worn through, and I want my briefcase back.

In his dream, the chef takes the case and runs west. If the professor takes it back, there will be no name left for the chef, no place on the Earth. The moment his fingers leave the leather loop of the handle, he will fall off the planet.

He sits in a wooden chair on the lawn behind the widow's house. He hears her washing dishes inside. In exchange for the room, he cooks all her meals. It is March, and the cold makes the hairs rise from his arms, but the sun warms the arm beneath them. He thinks, The tragedy of a moving Sun is that it leaves us each day. Hence the Aztec sacrifices, the ancient rites of the eclipse. If the Sun so willingly leaves us, each morning it returns is a stay of execution, an undeserved gift.

Whereas: If it is we who turn, how can we so flagrantly leave behind that which has warmed us and given us light? If we are moving, then each turn is a turn away. Each revolution a revolt.

The money comes less often, and even old friends who used to write monthly now send only rare, apologetic notes, a few small bills. Things are more difficult now, their letters say. No one understood when he first ran away, but now it is clear: After they finished with the artists, the journalists, the fighters, they came for the professors. How wise he was to leave when he did. Some letters come back unopened, with a black stamp.

Life is harder here, too. Half the shops are closed. His lover has left him. The little café is filled with soldiers.

One afternoon, he enters the post office two minutes before closing. The lobby is empty but for the postman and his broom.

The mailbox is empty as well, and he turns to leave but hears the voice of the postman behind him. You are the good Professor T——, no? I have something for you in the back.

Yes, he says, I am the professor. And it feels as if this is true, and he will have no guilt over the professor's signature when the box is brought out. He is even wearing the professor's shirt, as loose again over his hungry ribs as it was the day he slipped it on in the alley.

From behind the counter, the postman brings no box, but a woman in a long gray dress, a white handkerchief in her fingers.

She moves toward him, looks at his hands and his shoes and his face. Forgive me for coming, she says, and the postman pulls the cover down over his window and disappears. She says, No one would tell me anything, only that my husband had his health. And then a student gave me the number of the box and the name of the city. He begins to say, You are the widow. But why would he say this? What proof is there that the professor is dead? Only that it must be; that it follows logically.

She says, I don't understand what has happened.

He begins to say, I am the good professor's assistant, madam — but then what next? She would ask questions he had no way to answer.

I don't understand, she says again.

All he can say is, This is his shirt. He holds out an arm so she can see the gaping sleeve.

She says, What have you done with him? She has a calm voice and wet, brown eyes. He feels he has seen her before, in the streets of the old city. Perhaps he served her a meal, a bottle of wine. Perhaps, in another lifetime, she was the center of his universe.

This is his beard, he says.

She begins to cry into the handkerchief. She says, Then he is dead. He sees now from the quiet of her voice that she must have known this long ago. She has come here only to confirm.

He feels the floor of the post office move beneath him, and he tries to turn his eyes from her, to ground his gaze in something solid: postbox, ceiling tile, window. He finds he cannot turn away. She is a force of gravity in her long gray dress.

No, he says. No, no, no, no, no, I am right here.

No, he does not believe it, but he knows that if he had time, he could prove it. And he must, because he is the only piece of the professor left alive. The woman does not see how she is murdering her husband, right here in the post office lobby. He whispers to her: Let me go home with you. I'll be a father to your son, and I'll warm your bed, and I'll keep you safe.

He wraps his hands around her small, cold wrists, but she pulls loose. She might be the most beautiful woman he has ever seen.

As if from far away, he hears her call to the postmaster to send for the police.

His head is light, and he feels he might float away from the post office forever. It is an act of will not to fly off, to hold tight to the Earth and wait. If the police aren't too busy to come, he feels confident he can prove to them that he is the professor. He has the papers, after all, and in the havoc of war, what else will they have the time to look for?

She is backing away from him on steady feet, and he feels it like a peeling off of skin.

If not the police, perhaps he'll convince a city judge. The witnesses who would denounce him are mostly gone or killed, and the others would fear to come before the law. If the city judge will not listen, he can prove it to the high court. One day he might try to convince the professor's own child. He feels certain that somewhere down the line, someone will believe him.

YANNICK MURPHY

■

The Good Word

FROM *One Story*

ON VACATION WE MET A GERMAN. He wanted to go south to the ocean for two nights. He invited us along. There will be many buses to take, he said. In the end we would stay in a place he knew on the beach. He had stayed there once before. His name was Jurgen. We said okay while eating dinner in the dining room of the boarding house. We were tired of the food they served us. We were tired of the same old tablecloth that was never washed. We ate with our plate rims shadowing stains from our breakfasts of black beans spilled days before. We could use a few days' vacation from our vacation.

He explained a German word for which there was no translation in English. It means a good feeling people have when they are together, he said, and then he said the word. We could not pronounce the word. Iris said how trying to say the word hurt her throat. She took a drink of her water, she touched her pale skin at her small Adam's apple.

We left the next morning. There were many buses. Each time we boarded a new bus we noticed how the people all looked like they had been on the last bus and the chickens on their laps looked the same as the chickens who had been on the last bus.

After the buses, there was a small boat. We had to wait for it to come. We waited at a bar that was outside. The roof was made of dry grass and we ordered ceviche along with our beers and Jurgen said we had best squeeze as much lime juice as we could on the ceviche so that we wouldn't become sick.

Jurgen's cheeks were always red and we told him we imagined

him as a boy wearing lederhosen and standing on a mountaintop covered with snow. He told us we imagined right.

When we boarded the boat, the people who had been on the buses, and their chickens, boarded too and so all the while crossing the river, we heard the chickens cluck and it was louder than the chug of the outboard motor.

When we reached the shore, Jurgen led us a down a road. We walked for a while, and then we cut in to the beach. We were on the ocean side and the waves were big. The house we stopped at had a porch and there was an old man sitting on the porch, smoking a pipe. Jurgen waved to him.

Here we are, Jurgen said. We set our backpacks down on the porch. The old man said hello and sucked in on his pipe.

You've got a nice view, Iris said, and the old man nodded and looked Iris up and down.

I'm dying to swim, Iris said.

Iris and I changed in our room. There were only two cots in the room. There was no other furniture. The window had no glass. It was just an opening cut into the wall. A large branch from a tree growing outside reached into the room. A few of its leaves had fallen to the floor.

We went into the hall wearing our bikinis with our towels wrapped around our waists and saw Jurgen come out of his room wearing his bathing trunks. As he came out of it, I saw into Jurgen's room and noticed there was just a cot there too, only there was no window at all.

The old man went into the water with us. He stood in the shallows still smoking his pipe. The water came up to his knees, but then when a wave came the water rose higher, above his waist.

Iris went deep. She yelled for me to come join her. She liked riding waves. Jurgen swam to her and I watched them a while. Iris always rode farther in on her waves than Jurgen. The old man laughed.

Didn't you learn to swim in Germany? he called out to Jurgen.

I was standing in a bad place. The old man's pipe smoke traveled to me. The waves broke right where I was standing, hitting me down low. I kept losing balance. I swam out to Iris in the deep. It took me a while. I had to duck my head and swim into tall oncoming waves. Something brushed against my leg. I thought it was Jurgen, horsing around, pretending to be a monster from the sea. But when I turned to look for him swimming around me in the water, he wasn't there. He had ridden a wave all the way in. He was on the beach now, shaking his head back and forth, drying his hair the way a dog would dry his coat.

I rode the next wave in. It was small, without much push. When I stood up I was near the old man. So far as I can tell, he said, only one of you knows how to swim.

Iris was catching another wave, disappearing for a long time before she finally came up.

Later we lay on our towels on the beach and Jurgen, since he did not have a towel, lay on the sand. The old man did not have a towel either and so Iris sat up and patted one side of her towel. Share with me, she said and he sat down next to her.

The old man was not so old. He was sixty or so, he said. He could not quite remember since he had been living here so long he had not celebrated birthdays. He did not know the date. His pipe was no longer lit, but still he sucked on it. Iris asked about a wife, about children. Jurgen slept, his chest turning red where his ribs poked out, the part of him closest to the sun.

The old man once had a wife. He had left her in an apartment in a city with a river that turned to ice in the winter and that she would walk on with her toy dogs, schnauzers or Shih Tzus, he could not remember which. She threw them balls and it was something to watch the dogs skitter and skate across the ice in pursuit of the balls. The old man shook his head, remembering. There was a son who came to visit once. It was he who had helped build the porch and the back rooms where we slept, our room with the window without glass. Now the son built bridges. I call him the Connector, the old man said.

What does he call you? Iris wanted to know.

Old Man, the old man said.

We were all hungry, but it wasn't quite dinner yet. The old man said he had beers, but we would have to pay for them. Of course, we said. We drank them on the porch. All of Jurgen had turned red now, from the sun and from the beer. Even his eyes were red and he said it was from the salt. He said he always kept his eyes open when swimming underwater, just in case there was something to see.

Then the old man said it again. He said, As far as I can tell there is only one of you here who knows how to swim.

I can swim, Jurgen said. Germany has pools. Everyone is expected to know how to swim.

You all sink though, what with all that bread and beer, the old man said.

What is it you've got against Germany? Jurgen said.

The old man shook his head. Not much, he said. Maybe I just have something against Germans.

Iris laughed. Where is there to eat around here? she said.

There is only one place, the old man said. I always have whatever fish they have caught that day. You'll like it, he said to Iris.

We went to change out of our bathing suits and when I walked past the old man's bedroom I saw that he had left the door open and in there he too had a cot and a window, but his window had glass and the glass needed cleaning. It was yellow with what must have been pipe smoke and it was hard to imagine how much light it let in.

We walked with our beers on the beach to the one place that served food. Ordering was fast, the same all around of what the only meal was, blind river dolphin. We touched the necks of our beers together in a toast. To our vacation from our vacation, Jurgen said.

You won't like the blind river dolphin, the old man said to Jurgen, it doesn't come with heavy bread and a slab of butter.

Maybe I won't like it because it's blind, Jurgen answered. We laughed. The old man nodded.

How did someone like you get to know these two lovely women? the old man asked, looking at Iris while he spoke.

It's German, Jurgen said, to be friendly to everyone while on vacation. It's sort of an unwritten rule, when a German goes on vacation, he goes to meet people, and not just to take in the sights.

Tell me, the old man said, you weren't taking in the sights when you spotted these two girls.

The food came. Iris and I ate small bits of the blind river dolphin, but mostly we drank beer. The old man ate very little too, and he kept ordering more beer for Iris and me, but he told Jurgen he could pay for himself.

All right, Jurgen said and he took big mouthfuls of his blind river dolphin.

Then, when Jurgen had finished a few beers, he patted the old man on the back and said the word in German again, the word he called the good word that meant the good feeling between people in a group, the word that hurt Iris's throat to say.

Can you say the good word? Jurgen said to the old man. The old man shook his head.

I can't, he said.

Try, Jurgen said. The old man stood up. In one hand he held his beer, with the other hand he pushed on Jurgen's shoulder, sending him backward onto the floor where there lay scattered sand that had blown from the beach in the breeze through the open doorway or had come in on the bottoms of our shoes. One of the legs on Jurgen's wooden chair was now split. He got up and righted the chair. He sat back down on it and while he did I could hear the sound of the wood splintering, splitting some more. He would fall again soon. Jurgen reached up and smoothed down his hair.

I'll pretend that didn't happen, he said.

The old man did not sit back down. He stood by the table as if waiting for the check to come or for us to leave.

We must all be tired from the sun, Iris said. Jurgen, you're burnt, she said.

Vinegar can help, I said. Iris nodded.

Yes, vinegar, she said.

It's a good word to know. Everyone should know it, Jurgen said. Germans, Americans, everyone, because it's about everyone getting along.

The old man hooked his foot around Jurgen's chair leg, and he pulled. Jurgen fell off. He stayed on the floor this time and did not bother to try and sit back down again in the chair whose leg was now completely broken. He crossed his legs there on the floor. He reached up and found his fork and took another bite of his blind river dolphin without being able to see what portion the tines of his fork had pierced.

I can eat like this. Who needs a chair? he said.

We should leave, Iris said.

No, the old man said. More beer, he said. He called to the waiter. Just for the girls, he said.

Iris stood up and went to an empty table and found another chair. She brought it behind Jurgen.

Take a seat, she said, and he did. Then Iris sat back down in her own chair.

Tell us more about your son, Iris said to the old man. When will he come next? she said.

The Connector? the old man said and shrugged. Hell if I know, he said.

Do you miss the city? I asked the old man.

Only the river that turns to ice in the winter, the old man said. Then he smiled and laughed. Oh those little fucking dogs, he said. You should have seen them slide.

Iris was drunk now. She stood up to use the restroom and she teetered as if the floor beneath us had shifted. The old man went to her and took her by the arm and helped her find her way.

Let's go, Jurgen said to me.

Go? I said.

They won't miss us, he said. That old man's off his rocker. Let's swim, he said.

I looked out at the ocean. The sky was so dark I could barely see the water; I just had the sense that it was there.

You go on, I said. I'll wait for her. Sometimes her shoulder gets loose and she needs me, I said.

Loose? Jurgen said.

Mmm, I said. When she drinks like this sometimes it goes and then I have to push it back in. I have to stand her up against a wall and push with all my might, until she tells me it's back in.

In Germany there's a simple operation for that, Jurgen said.

Yeah, well, we have it in the States too, only difficult part is paying for it. Costs money, I said.

You're American, you're rich. You can pay for it, Jurgen said.

Oh, sure, I said. Go on and swim, I said. I moved my head in the direction of the ocean I could barely see.

All right, but then come join me later, won't you? Jurgen said.

Sure, I said. He left and he was drunk too; again the floor beneath us seemed to shift as he walked across it, like a man aboard a ship rolling in the waves.

They did not come back. I waited a while. I looked down at my plate and I could see the blind river dolphin, which was cooked in a white sauce, starting to turn brown. I went in search of Iris. I opened the bathroom door and both Iris and the old man were in there. He had Iris up against the wall and was pushing on her hard. Her eyes were closed because of the pain. When he got her shoulder back in she smiled and opened her eyes. All better, she said and reached for her bottle of beer that had been set on the porcelain sink and she took a long drink.

Back at the table she said, Where'd our German go?

He said for a swim, I said.

A swim, doesn't that sound like fun? Iris said to the old man.

The old man said he would enjoy that, watching her swim.

No, all of us, let's swim, Iris said. She started walking out the door, hitting the doorjamb accidentally and then laughing and saying "Oh, excuse me" to the doorjamb.

The old man paid while I followed Iris out onto the sand. The top layer of the sand at first was still warm from the sun, but then after a second it felt cold as my feet sunk down beneath the top layer, hitting wet sand.

Jurgen! Iris yelled. There was no answer from the black ocean water.

Iris bent over and pushed her bottle of beer upright in the sand so it would not tip over and then she took off her clothes.

The old man came and helped her with her shirt. Watch that shoulder, he said.

Naked, Iris's thin body glowed and then she ran and dove in and disappeared.

I wish I were young, the old man said to me, watching the place where Iris disappeared.

All along the shore the wet sand shone with bits of something phosphorescent.

Looks like snow, I said. I kicked it up.

It was Jurgen who came out, as if Iris had turned into him beneath the water and it was he who walked toward us now naked and shaking the water from his hair.

Come on in, Jurgen said to me.

I shook my head.

I'll help you, Jurgen said. He went to lift up my shirt but I held my shirt down.

Where's Iris? I said.

I don't know. Where is she? Jurgen said. Then he looked down and saw Iris's beer planted in the sand and he picked it up and drank the rest of it down.

The old man yelled for her. He ran into the ocean. He dove down and then came up and then dove down again.

The current had carried her. She came out of the water farther down the beach than where she had gone in. She walked back toward us while the old man was still looking for her in the water, yelling out her name.

He'll give himself a heart attack, Jurgen said.

I ran in after him. She's here, I yelled, but he was yelling so loud and diving back down so often, he could not hear me.

I stepped on him. I think it was his back I stepped on. He must have been down low, on the bottom's surface, reaching and digging for where she might be. I went under and pulled him up. We found her, I told him. He gasped.

Thank God, he said.

We went back to the old man's place. He wouldn't let Jurgen in until he was dry. He told him to stay on the porch and let the wind dry him. Meanwhile the old man himself was very wet. The shirt and shorts he wore dripped on the floor in his hallway as he made his way to the closet and brought towels for Iris.

Two's enough, she said, and handed me one. He had brought her four.

Well, thanks for the dinner, Iris said to the old man, and then Iris and I went into our room and shut the door.

Before I fell asleep I could hear the old man lock the front door and then I heard him go into his bedroom and shut the door.

I'm wide awake, Iris said while she lay on her cot, but then a second later I could hear her softly snoring.

I woke up later to Jurgen climbing down the large branch that came in through the open window of our room.

More leaves fell because of him climbing on it and the sound they made reminded me of rain.

Bastard locked me out, Jurgen said, jumping down onto the end of my cot. My body bounced up on the cot's mattress when he did it.

Jurgen didn't leave. He stayed sitting on the end of my cot that was now covered with leaves, leaning his back against the wall.

He asked about America. He wanted to know where I lived. I described for him the building and the heating duct in the building that ran through all the floors and how it was easy to hear what the neighbors upstairs or downstairs were talking about because the sound carried, up and down the duct. I told him it wasn't that good German feeling thing, either. I didn't like hearing other people talk. I didn't like knowing they were so close by. He wanted to know if I had a boyfriend. I told him I didn't think I did when I left, but I might when I get back.

Americans don't talk straight, he said. Germans do. Ask me a question, he said. Any question and I'll answer it.

I didn't want Jurgen at the foot of my cot any longer. I couldn't stretch out my legs and lie down. I wanted to sleep.

All right, one question, I said. I tried to think of what to ask him. I didn't know. I pictured him at the restaurant, how he got back on the chair again with the broken leg after the first time he fell.

All right, I said. If Hitler were around again today, would you join him? I asked.

Jurgen shook his head. Hitler, Nazi Germany, that's all foreigners seem to remember about Germany.

Not true, I said. I remembered how they ate heavy bread and drank beer.

Do you think when Hitler and all of them decided to go after the Jews together that they had that feeling, the German word you know I can't say? I said.

Jurgen said the word.

Yes, that. Did they have it? I asked.

Yes, no, maybe, Jurgen said.

That's not a straight answer, you're answering like an American now, I said.

Yes, they had it, Jurgen said.

I shook my head. That's funny, I said, to think they had the best feeling of all to do the worst thing.

Then Iris said it. She said the word. She must have been listening. When she said it, it sounded like she was German, like she was Jurgen saying it.

Jurgen jumped off my cot, trailing some of the leaves with him, sending them to the floor. Perfect, Iris. You said it perfectly, he said, going over to her.

It didn't hurt my throat this time, Iris said. I'm getting the hang of it, she said and then she closed her eyes and started softly snoring again.

The next day, the old man knocked on our door. He had breakfast on a tray for Iris. He said he had walked to the restaurant early in the morning and had asked them to fix it for her. But Iris was sick from drinking too much. Ugh, she said when the old man brought the tray close to her, lifting a napkin covering a plate, showing her fried eggs and fried silver sardines, still with their heads and their eyes, their mouths partly open, showing small sharp teeth.

The old man started to walk away with the tray and back himself out the door, but then Iris said, Not the coffee, leave the coffee, and the old man lifted the coffee for her and held it to her mouth so she could drink.

Iris did not leave the room. The sun outside was too strong for her eyes. The old man, every so often, would open up the door and look in on Iris, and then he would close the door and tiptoe through his house. I think he even stopped smoking his pipe, so as not to let the smell bother her. Jurgen and I sat on the porch and Jurgen talked. The old man came out and told us to keep it down, to let Iris sleep. Jurgen would keep his voice down for a while. Then, forgetting, he would raise it again. The old man was telling Jurgen to keep it down again when the Connector walked up the beach. At first, of course, we did not know it was the Connector, but later we learned.

Old Man, he said to the old man, I wrote to you. I told you I was coming.

I never received the letter, the old man said to his son. The Connector shook his head. He went into the old man's room. When he came out, he was holding up a piece of paper.

It was on your desk, he said to the old man. The old man took the paper and he read it.

This is the first I've seen of this letter, the old man said.

The Connector laughed. Oh, Old Man, he said and then he put an arm across his father, and brought him close, a kind of half-hug.

Later, when the old man went to check on Iris, the Connector and Jurgen and I sat outside on the porch and the Connector said he had been worried about his father here all alone. Did we notice anything peculiar about his behavior? he asked.

Yes, Jurgen said.

No, I said. We don't know him, how could we guess what was peculiar and what wasn't? I said.

He's a nut job, Jurgen said. He tried to fight with me.

I'm thinking, the Connector said, that I can't leave him here alone much longer. He'll have to come back with me. I can get care for him at home, he said.

When Iris finally came out of her room, the Connector smiled.

How do you do? the Connector said and he stood tall and straight and shook Iris's hand for a long time, as if Iris were famous and he was so glad to finally meet her.

The old man hurried onto the porch behind Iris. Don't listen to a damn thing he says, the old man said, looking at Iris. He's all his mother, the old man said.

I'm you too. What about our thumbs? the Connector said. He held up his thumb and made his father hold up his too. See, look — the Connector showed Iris — we have the same thumbs.

And they did. Except for the Connector's thumb being paler, not darkly weathered by this country's sun, their thumbs could be the same.

We all laughed. Drinks, we need drinks, Jurgen said, and for once the old man agreed with Jurgen and sent Jurgen into the house to get beer from the cooler.

Iris wanted to know where he was from. Did the Connector live in that city, the one with the river that froze in winter?

The Connector said he did. He told Iris how she would have to come and visit. He would show her the river, it was beautiful and the water turned pale green when it froze. The Connector said he would take her to restaurants in buildings reaching high above the city's skyline.

Iris smiled. How nice, she said. She looked out at the ocean, and then she said, Anybody up for a swim? I think it'll clear my head, she said.

The Connector was the first to say yes, then the old man said yes. Jurgen said he was going to stay and take a nap. He was tired from drinking beer in the afternoon and that in Germany, that's how they did it, they sometimes drank in the afternoon and then took a nap and later they could embrace the night.

The Connector could swim. He and Iris went far out. The old man stood in the shallows watching. They did not ride the waves in. They stayed in the deep, floating, treading water, talking, I could tell. I went up to my waist. I rode the small waves that lacked push. Once in a while I could catch a bit of what they were saying. The Connector talked about bridges and his projects and how he sometimes stood on the supports and girders and felt the wind off the river trying to knock him down.

At the restaurant that night, the Connector had us play a game. Guess what I'm thinking of, he said. We guessed and guessed, using questions requiring yes or no answers. Oh, come on, the Connector said, ask better questions.

We don't want to play this game, the old man said. We're not in school, he said.

It's all right, I can guess this, Iris said and she did. She guessed anchor. She was right. The Connector said, Bravo! And because she won, she had to drink a shot of tequila.

She guessed correctly often. She drank a lot of shots. Then again, after our meal, she wanted to go swimming.

Come this time, Jurgen said to me. So I did.

We were all in the water. The old man had come out with us. He had left his pipe behind. Race me, the old man said to his son. The

Connector looked out across the water, to the deep where his father was facing.

To where? he said.

Afraid? the old man said. I'll beat you, he said. Come on, he said. On the count of three, he said. One, two, three. Then he swam hard. He swam and soon the sound of his kicking in the water and his arms splashing became distant. The Connector did not race.

Come on back, Old Man, the Connector said. Old Man? he called. The Connector went out after his father; Iris and Jurgen and I went back to shore. We put on our clothes.

He builds bridges, Iris said. Quite remarkable, she said.

It's not like he builds them with his hands, he just draws them on paper, Jurgen said.

The Connector and the old man came back, but the old man would not walk back with us to the house. The old man walked ahead, almost running. Come on, can't you keep up? he said over his shoulder to his son.

On the walk back to the house Jurgen said we should get to bed early, we planned to leave the next day to catch the boat and the many buses back to the boarding house where we had started our vacation. I agreed with him and we left Iris and the Connector and the old man on the porch, still drinking what was left of the beers. Jurgen went to his bedroom and I went to mine.

When I woke up Iris was loose, her shoulder was out of its socket and she was standing by my bed, waking me up, moaning with pain.

Please, put it back in, she said. I got out of bed and stood her up against the wall. I began to push on her shoulder hard. When I did it I heard something coming from the hallway. It was the sound of fist-fighting. I heard grunts and I heard the old man saying Stop, stop. Still, I hadn't put Iris's shoulder back in yet, so I did not go and see what was the matter. I tried to push as hard as the sound of the fists hitting. It was more like slamming is what I was doing. I did it in time with the hits. I think it helped. I slammed into Iris hard. I threw my weight into her.

There, it's in, she said. But I still kept slamming. Maybe I kept slamming her and hurting her because I kept thinking how if it hadn't been for Iris, no one would be fighting now. If Iris wasn't so nice to everyone, not everyone would want her. If she hadn't patted her beach towel asking the old man to sit down next to her and making him feel good, then maybe he never would have fallen for her. Maybe if she hadn't played along with the Connector at his guessing game, he wouldn't have fallen for her either. I thought how Iris was like the good word itself, she was what the word meant, only she didn't know it. She was the good word walking, the good word living and breathing. The good word talking. It wasn't until she cried Stop, that I stopped.

I helped Iris to her cot and then I looked into the hallway. The old man was down and the Connector was standing over him, holding a wet cloth and wiping his father's brow.

When the Connector saw me he said, more to himself than to me, I really think it's time I took him home.

When we left in the morning neither the old man nor the Connector was awake. We went walking with our backpacks down the beach, heading for the boat on the river side that would take us to the buses.

On the first bus back home to the boarding house, we again sat with more people and chickens. It was hot and Iris said what she would not give for a drink. An old woman beside her understood, and she pulled out a bottle that looked old, that looked like it had spent years lost at sea. The liquid in the bottle looked old too, it was pale yellow and reminded me of the color of the window glass in the old man's room. She passed Iris the bottle and Iris drank and drank. The old woman smiled and nodded her head and lifted her hand in a gesture letting Iris know she could drink more. When Iris was finished, she said the word, the German word, to Jurgen and me and then she taught the old woman how to say the word and the old woman learned how to say it too. Then the entire bus wanted to learn the word. They all said it. All the men and women with chickens on their laps practiced saying the good word. Jurgen stood up in the aisle saying the word so they could repeat it after him. He lifted his arms, palms up, getting everyone to say it louder, and they did. Everyone was saying it, even the chickens seemed to be saying it, their clucks really the good word and not clucks at all.

MATTHEW POWER

■

Mississippi Drift

FROM *Harper's Magazine*

FOR SEVERAL YEARS, beginning when I was six or seven, I played a hobo for Halloween. It was easy enough to put together. Oversize boots, a moth-eaten tweed jacket, and my dad's busted felt hunting hat, which smelled of deer lure; finish it up with a beard scuffed on with a charcoal briquette, a handkerchief bindle tied to a hockey stick, an old empty bottle. I imagined a hobo's life would be a fine thing. I would sleep in haystacks and do exactly what I wanted all the time.

Since then, I've had occasional fantasies of dropping out, and have even made some brief furtive bids at secession: a stint as a squatter in a crumbling South Bronx building, a stolen ride through Canada on a freight train. A handful of times I got myself arrested, the charges ranging from trespassing to disorderly conduct to minor drug possession. But I wasn't a very good criminal, or nomad, and invariably I would return to the comforting banalities of ordinary life. I never disliked civilization intensely enough to endure the hardships of abandoning it, but periodically I would tire of routine, of feeling "cramped up and sivilized," as Huck Finn put it, and I would light out for another diversion in the Territory.

It was on one such outing, a hitchhike up the West Coast in the summer of 1999, that I met Matt Bullard in a palm-fringed city park in Arcata, California. A dumpster-diving, train-hopping, animal-rights-crusading anarchist and tramp, with little money and less of a home, Matt was almost exactly my age, and from that first time we talked I admired his raconteurial zest and scammer's panache. He considered shoplifting a political act and dumpstering a civil right.

As we sat on a park bench in the sunshine, Matt reached into his backpack and pulled out what he called a "magic dollar," an ordinary bill save for its twelve-inch tail of cellophane packing tape. He would dip it into a vending machine, select the cheapest item available, collect his purchase and change, and pull his dollar back out by the tail. An unguarded machine could be relieved of all its coins and every last one of its snacks in the space of an hour. It was a very impressive trick.

Matt was convinced that there was something deeply wrong with most Americans: they were bored and unfulfilled, their freedom relinquished for the security of a steady paycheck and a ninety-minute commute, their imagination anesthetized by TV addiction and celebrity worship. He had decided to organize his life against this fate. He utterly refused to serve; he lived exactly as he desired. Matt's was the kind of amoral genius that I had always longed to possess. He not only had quit society altogether but was gaming it for all it was worth, like some dirtbag P. T. Barnum. I, meanwhile, would soon be returning to a temp job in a Manhattan cubicle. Matt couldn't understand why I needed to go back, and I couldn't really myself, but I went back anyway, tugged by the gravity of expectations. In the ensuing years, I got occasional emails documenting Matt's drift, describing days on grain cars passing through Minnesota blizzards, nights in palm-thatched squats on Hawaiian islands: dispatches from a realm of total freedom beyond the frontiers of ordinary life.

Two summers ago, Matt sent an invitation that I could not ignore. He was in Minneapolis, building a homemade raft, and had put out a call for a crew of "boat punks" to help him pilot the vessel the entire length of the Mississippi River, all the way to New Orleans. They would dig through the trash for sustenance. They would commune with the national mythos. They would be twenty-first-century incarnations of the river rats, hoboes, and drifters of the Mississippi's history, the sort who in Mark Twain's time would have met their ends tarred, feathered, and run out of town on a rail. Catfish rose in my mind; ripples expanded outward and scattered any doubts. I wrote back straightaway and asked to join up.

I met Matt on a scorching July afternoon and followed him through leafy, upper-middle-class residential streets toward Minneapolis's

West River Park. The industrious hum of weed-whackers and leaf-blowers filled the air, and helmeted children tricycled along a path, their watchful parents casting a suspicious eye at us. But through a small hole in the foliage by the edge of the bike path, we instantly stepped out of the middle-American idyll, scrambling down a narrow path through the tangled undergrowth, through cleared patches in the woods littered with malt-liquor cans and fast-food wrappers, hobo camps with the musty wild smell of an animal's den. I clutched at the roots of saplings to keep from tumbling down the slope. The sounds of civilization receded to white noise. We stumbled out of the trees onto a sandy spit, and I suddenly saw the river before me, narrow and amber-colored, flowing silently south, lined on both banks with forested bluffs.

Matt's raft was moored to the bank next to a storm sewer outflow pipe. My first impression was of the Unabomber's cabin set afloat. A brief description of the vessel: ten feet in the beam, twenty-four feet stem to stern, its decks had been laid down over three rows of fifty-five-gallon drums, twenty-three in all. "I got them from a dumpster behind a chemical plant," Matt told me. "Some of them still had stuff sloshing around inside." The barrels had been framed out with lumber, mostly 2x4s swiped from construction sites, and a deck of marine plywood set on top. On this platform Matt had built a cabin, about ten by fourteen feet, leaving a small motor deck aft and a front porch fore. The porch connected to the cabin through a pair of French doors, and a screen door exited the rear. The cleats, railroad spikes welded to diamond plate, were "punk as fuck," said Matt, admiring his amateur blacksmithing. On the roof was bolted a large solar panel of larcenous provenance, as well as a small sleeping quarters and a worn-out armchair from which the boat could be steered. A wheel salvaged from a sunken houseboat was connected by an ingenious series of pulleys and wires to the outboard motor on the back deck, a thirty-three-horsepower, two-stroke Johnson, which was showroom-new during the Johnson Administration. It was one of the few purchased items on the boat, bought by me as a gesture of my commitment to the mission. Several workbenches lined the cabin, and there was a galley with a propane stove, a chest of drawers, and a rusty high school gym locker for storage. Matt had brought everything he had scrounged that could possibly be of use: old fishing anchors, tied-up lengths of rope, lawn furniture, a folding card table. Three bicycles. Several five-gallon gas tanks. A stereo speaker system with subwoofers made of paint cans, hooked up to a motorcycle battery. A collection of practice heads from the dumpster of a beauty college. In keeping with the rustic theme, the boat's front had a porch swing made of shipping pallets and a pair of plastic pink flamingos, "liberated from some lawn," screwed to its posts.

Matt's six-foot-two frame had bulked up since I'd last seen him, and his hair had grown into a waist-length mullet of dreadlocks hanging behind a battered black baseball cap. He wore a goatee, and his round face squeezed his eyes to mischievous slits when he smiled. He had added to his tattoo collection to form a sort of identity-politics résumé: NOT REALLY VEGAN ANYMORE advertised an amended dietary philosophy on his wrist; a piece on the back of his hand showed crossed railroad spikes and the free-associative motto WANDERLUST ADVENTURE TRAMP; on his left biceps was a black-masked figure standing behind a dog, above the phrase ANIMAL LIBERATION.

Matt hadn't held a steady job since a brief stint at Kinko's in the late nineties. One time in court, he said, a judge had admonished him: "You can't be homeless the rest of your life. You have to work." He laughed as he recalled this. "I fucking hate work," he said. "If I could see some result from it, besides money, maybe I'd do it. I went into the welfare office to apply for food stamps, and they took one look at me and said, 'Clearly, you're unemployable.'" He saw no shame in this, and he looked at food stamps as a way of getting back the taxes he paid when he was at Kinko's. From the hundreds of hours he had put into the boat, it was evident that what he hated was not doing work per se but rather trading his time for money. Matt had been working on the boat for over a year and had spent almost nothing on it. What wasn't donated or dumpstered was procured by extralegal means. "Half this boat is stolen," he chuckled, with unmistakable pride in his handiwork and resourcefulness.

The neo-hobo lifestyle, such as it was, often blurred the boundary between ingenuity and criminality. On the legal side, there were the old standbys: "spanging" (bumming spare change), "flying signs" (asking for money with a cardboard sign), and the governmental largesse of food stamps. Matt was also a big proponent of pharmaceutical studies, which gave out nice lump-sum payments as well as free food. In one study, he said, he had taken the largest dose of ibuprofen ever administered to a human being. In that instance, the result of being a human lab rat was only diarrhea, though he hadn't landed a new study in a while. "I had plans to buy a house with drug studies," he said wistfully. The only semi-legitimate work Matt was willing to pursue was seasonal farm labor, particularly the sugar-beet harvest in North Dakota, which has become something of an annual pilgrimage for the punk traveler community. From three weeks of driving forklifts or sorting beets on a conveyor belt, enough money could be earned to fund months of travel.

On the illegal side of gainful unemployment, there were many techniques of varying complexity. The digital revolution in retailing had led to gift-card cloning (copying the magnetic strip on an unused gift card, returning it to the store display, and then waiting until it is activated) and bar-code swapping (either printing up low-price bar codes on stickers or switching them from one item to another). Various lower-tech shoplifting methods could be employed anywhere, from the primitive "wahoo" (wherein the shoplifter walks into a convenience store, takes a case of beer, screams *Wahoo!* and runs out the door) to "left-handing" (paying for an item with your right hand while walking through the checkout with another item in your left) and "kangarooing" (the more theatrical use of a dummy arm and a pair of overalls with a large hidden pouch). One of the most lucrative scams was called "taking a flight" and involved having an accomplice steal one's luggage from an airport baggage carousel, which, with enough persistent calls to customer service, could result in a $3,000 payday from the airline. Matt and his friends saw stealing as a form of revolt, a means of surviving while they chipped away at the monstrous walls of the capitalist fortress.

For Matt, the river trip was to be a sort of last great adventure before he left the United States for good. As long as he stayed, he felt the ultimate unfreedom of jail lurking around every corner. For years he was heavily involved with the animal-liberation movement and

logged weeks of jail time in three different states for protests at an-
imal-testing facilities. He claims to be on a domestic-terrorist watch
list. "When I get my ID run by the cops, it comes up 'Suspected
member of Animal Liberation Front. Do not arrest.'" A recent home-
coming for Matt in LAX resulted in a five-hour interview with Homeland Security. He related all these stories with thinly veiled pride, the
way a parent might describe a child's performance in a Little League
game.

After the river journey, he was moving to Berlin, a squatter's paradise he had visited once and found far more livable than anywhere in
the United States. "I hate America," he said, without the menace of a
McVeigh or a Zarqawi but nevertheless with feeling. I asked what he
would do with the raft once we reached New Orleans and he left for
Germany. "Only one thing to do," he said. "Torch it. I'm gonna give
this motherfucker a Viking burial."

To inaugurate the voyage, Matt had planned a launch party a mile
downstream, at a beach on the river's edge. With a few more arriv-
als, our little crew swelled to five: me and Matt, plus Cody Dorn-
busch, a compact, bearded twenty-four-year-old from South Dakota;
Chris Broderdorp, a twenty-one-year-old bicyclist and master dumpster-diver from Minneapolis, rail-thin with a half-shaved mop of
curls and a high-pitched laugh; and Kristina Brown, a fetching, lev-
elheaded twenty-five-year-old from Seattle, who among them had the
most schooling and seemed most to be play-acting at the pirate life.
I was the only crew member without a pierced septum. The general
mood among my boatmates was upbeat: the overflowing dumpsters
of Middle America would be more than enough to sustain our bodies, and adventure would nourish our spirits. Matt fired up the ancient engine, and in a haze of blue exhaust smoke we chugged slowly
out into the current, which had the color and foaminess of Coca-
Cola, and headed downstream, hidden from the city by the limestone
bluffs. The abandoned mills around the Falls of Saint Anthony — the
falls that had brought the city here — had been converted into mil-
lion-dollar condominiums. The Minneapolis–St. Paul metroplex, tidy
and forward-looking, seemed to have turned its back on the river that
birthed it.

The party, advertised among the local punk scene through word of mouth and printed flyers, commenced at sundown. The raft was hung with Christmas lights, and a driftwood bonfire blazed on the sand. Kids drank 40s of malt liquor and climbed over and over again onto the roof of the raft, jumping, diving, and cannonballing in various states of undress into the muddy brown river water. The night was humid and sultry, tinged with menace, and a thick darkness pressed down upon the river. Amid all the wild shouting and splashing, the dirt-smudged faces lit up by flames and colored Christmas lights, it seemed as though the raft had run aground on some cargo cult's island, the natives working themselves into a frenzy as they decided whether to worship us or eat us or escort us to the edge of the volcano at spearpoint. Someone stumbled into me in the dark, dripping, and grabbed me by the shirt, smelling of sweat and booze and the river, his voice slurred. "Hey! You're the writer. From New York." I reluctantly confirmed this. "Well, your fuckin' story better be about *solutions*." (He dragged out the word for emphasis.) "Otherwise it's bullshit. Solutions!" His grip tightened. He attempted to fix his gaze to mine and failed. He shouted "Solutions!" once more for good measure before shambling away and jumping into the river again.

In the morning, with the ashes of the bonfire still smoldering and a half-dozen half-dressed casualties of the bacchanal sprawled on the beach, we pulled the lines in and pushed the raft's barrels off the sand bar, drifting out and spinning like a compass needle until the boat nosed at long last into the flow of the river. With the Lyndon Johnson (the nickname I had given the forty-year-old engine) at half-throttle, the raft meandered with the current, the green wall of trees slipping by at walking pace. The five-gallon gas tank was draining disturbingly fast. I sat on the front-porch swing, rereading a dog-eared newspaper. Chris idly strummed a guitar as Cody and Kristina sat up top with Matt, who was steering from the captain's chair. "You know, you're going to be reading that fucking July 16th *New York Times* for the next month," Cody told me, sticking his head over the edge. I put the paper down. A Hmong family fished from a railroad embankment, waving excitedly as we passed, perhaps remembering the long-tail boats of their far-off Mekong. Eagles wheeled and dove into the river, which unscrolled before us as we rounded each bend.

It was high summer, blue skies and sunny, about as auspicious as one could hope for the start of a two-thousand-mile journey. We had hung up ragged pirate flags, and now they fluttered behind us in the breeze, the grinning skulls wearing a look of bemused delight.

Our first obstacle was Lock and Dam #1. To maintain a navigable channel on the upper Mississippi, which would otherwise be too low in the summer for commercial traffic, the U.S. Army Corps of Engineers built a system of twenty-nine locks and dams between Minneapolis and St. Louis. These serve as a stairway for ships to survive the Mississippi's 420-foot drop during its 673-mile journey to St. Louis; below that, the river (joined by the Missouri and then the Ohio) is sufficiently deep not to require locks, and there the Corps built levees instead. This engineering work has altered the natural flow of the Mississippi, allowing millions of acres of former flood plains and wetlands to be converted into intensively cultivated industrial farmland, which in turn sends fertilizer- and pollutant-rich runoff from thirty-one states coursing back into the channel and downstream. Floods are held back by levees, and the resulting pressure, like that of a thumb pressed over the nozzle of a hose, erodes 15,000 acres of wetlands a year from the Delta, creating an oxygen-starved "dead zone" the size of New Jersey each summer in the Gulf of Mexico. The Mississippi is one of the most managed, and mismanaged, river systems in the world.

The upper river may be restrained by dams, but it is not without its hazards, both natural and man-made. I flipped through our photocopied set of charts of the upper river, on the cover of which there was a hand-drawn picture of a squarish boat, seen from above as it travels in a circle, about to plow over a stick figure flailing in the water. Underneath was written: CIRCLE OF DEATH.* Each page of the

---

* Matt explained this rather gruesome nautical term: when a speedboat operator stands up and catches the throttle, he can be tossed overboard, yanking the tiller to one side. The unmanned boat, at full throttle, will then trace a wide circle and return to the same spot where its pilot was sent overboard, running him down and causing death by hideous propeller wounds. Although the two-mile-an-hour cruising speed of our vessel made such a scenario unlikely, the crew decided to christen our raft the SS *Circle of Death*.

charts covered ten miles of river, and each enumerated a frightening array of obstacles. "Wing dams," long jetties of rocks that jut out
into the river to direct flow toward the channel, lurked just inches below the surface, waiting to tear our barrels from under us. "Stump
fields," the remnants of clear-cut forest lands that had been drowned
by the river, appeared as cross-hatched forbidden zones that would
strand us in an enormous watery graveyard. But of the many things
we had been warned about, barges were by far the most dangerous.
Seventy-five million tons of wheat, soybeans, fertilizer, coal — the
bulk produce of mining and industrial agriculture — are shipped by
barge along the upper river every year. A standard fifteen-barge tow,
three hundred yards in length, can carry the freight equivalent of 870
semi trucks. They are as large as a high-rise building laid on its side,
and about as easy to steer. A tow plying the river under full steam
can take as long as a mile and a half to slide to a stop, plowing over
anything in its path. The Lyndon Johnson sputtering out in the nav-
igation channel while a tow bore down on us was not something I
wished to contemplate.

As if reading my thoughts, just yards from the mouth of the lock
chamber, the motor coughed a few times and then quit. We spun in
place, and Matt flew down the ladder from the top deck to try to get
the engine started. "Shit, shit, shit!" he yelled. "I forgot to mix the oil
in with the gas!" The old two-stroke lubricated itself with an oil-gas
mix, and we had very nearly blown the engine by running straight
gas through it. Matt popped open a bottle of oil and sloshed it into
the gas, measuring by eye. The rest of the crew scrambled for our
canoe paddles, hacking at the water futilely to try to guide the raft
into the lock. Matt barked orders that no one heeded, and the general
response of the crew (myself included) to our first emergency was
unrestrained panic. Finally, after loud cursing and many wheezing
turns of the starter, the engine roared to life, leaving an oily rainbow
on the water and a cloud of blue smoke in its wake.

"That's fucking great," said Matt. "Dead fish and dead Iraqis."

The lock loomed ahead of us, and we slid into its chamber, cutting the engine and bumping up against the concrete retaining wall.
A lock worker walked along the wall to us and threw down ropes to
keep the raft in place. I had hoped he'd be excited at our arrival, or

at least amused, but he had the world-weary countenance of a man who had seen all things that float, and our jerry-built vessel of scrap lumber and barrels was insufficient to impress him. I asked him what other strange things had passed through his lock. A guy came through rowing a raft of lashed-together logs just last year, he said. I realized that we were just the latest in a long line of fools, and not even the most hard-core.

Behind us, the door to the chamber swung silently shut, and like a rubber duck in a draining bathtub we began sliding down along the algae-slick wall as millions of gallons of water drained into the next stage of the river. Within a few minutes we had dropped thirty feet, and the top of the chamber glowed distantly as if we were at the bottom of a well. With the majesty of great cathedral doors swinging open, a crack appeared between the gates of the lock, and the murky green waters of the chamber joined the still waters of the lower river, glinting in the sunlight. Matt whooped, to no one in particular. New Orleans, here we come.

The first night, still in St. Paul, we pulled up to a hobo jungle, a fire-pit-pocked stand of trees below a rusting railroad bridge where in the past both Matt and Cody had waited to catch freight trains. The jungle sits on land that floods out yearly. Wrack and trash were scattered about; it looked like the desolate set of a horror movie. Chris rode his bike off to search dumpsters, and the rest of us carried the gas cans ashore to fill them up. Having covered barely ten miles in about the time it would take to walk that distance, we had already used up an enormous amount of gas. While the Lyndon Johnson got slightly better mileage than, say, an Abrams tank, it was nowhere near as fuel-efficient as a Hummer. This appalling carbon footprint aside, at three dollars a gallon our meager gas budget would be eaten up before we got out of the Twin Cities. My back-of-the-envelope calculation suggested that it would take somewhere near $5,000 worth of gas to make it the whole length of the river. Matt, however, felt no guilt about this use of fossil fuels. "I figure since I never use gas the rest of the year, it all balances out. We'll make it. We're gonna bust our asses, get some work somewhere, do some scams, look for a Wal-Mart."

Wal-Mart was frequently invoked by Matt as a source of almost limitless material bounty, a natural resource as rich as the midwestern prairies its parking lots had buried. Enormous and ubiquitous, the mega-stores offered almost everything we needed to survive. Aside from outright theft (the most straightforward procurement strategy), there were the wonders of Wal-Mart dumpsters, overflowing with inventory that was slightly damaged or barely past its expiration date. There were also a wide variety of "return scams" as elaborate as anything the Duke and the Dauphin could have pulled over on the rubes. "Receipt diving" involved plucking a crumpled receipt from an ashtray by the exit, entering the store, selecting the same object off the shelves, and promptly returning it, receipt in hand, for store credit. Another ruse involved finding goods in the trash (a bag of chips, perhaps), to which a PAID sticker had been affixed. This sticker was removed and placed on a small, expensive object, which was then returned for store credit; and since many of the larger Wal-Marts in the Midwest had their own gas stations, a half-eaten bag of chips could thereby be converted into a large supply of free gasoline. Or so my crewmates told me. We paid retail for our new load of gas, hauling the heavy jerricans a mile through the woods to where the raft was moored. I was beginning to realize that there was a considerable amount of heavy lifting involved in dropping out.

Chris returned with a garbage bag full of cold pepperoni pizza slices, a new staple of our shipboard diet, removed from under the heat lamps of a convenience store and discarded only hours before. We all dug into the congealing bounty. Chris's dumpstering was a good supplement to our ship's stores, which were stacked against a wall in stolen milk crates, a depressing harvest from community food banks: government-commodity-labeled cans of cheese soup, string beans, creamed corn; bags of generic Froot Loops, some Kool-Aid powder to fend off scurvy. The crew's dietary ethos was what is commonly referred to as "freeganism," wherein foodstuffs that are about to be thrown away are rescued from the waste stream and thereby ethically cleansed. An estimated $75 billion worth of food is thrown out yearly in America, and it doesn't take a great leap of logic to connect the desire to live sustainably with the almost limitless supply of free food that overflows the nation's dumpsters. Thus the opportunivore can forage either overtly or covertly, by asking up front or diving out back.

"We're going to dumpster everything we can," Matt told me. "Plus food shelves, donations, and you should apply for food stamps the first chance you get downriver." I'll eat out of the trash as happily as the next guy, I told him, but I didn't feel right applying for food stamps; this set Matt off on a series of gibes about my "so-called journalistic ethics." Matt was happy enough to sustain himself on the detritus of a world he saw as careening toward self-destruction, and equally happy to scam a government he despised. "I'm glad everyone's so wasteful," he told me. "It supports my lifestyle."

In the middle of a watery expanse of grain elevators and moored barges to the south of St. Paul, our engine emitted a tubercular hack and died again. There was a stiff headwind, and the ungainly raft acted as a sail, dragging us against the current and back upriver. We paddled and poled ourselves to shore and tied up just before the skies opened up with a thunderstorm, and we huddled inside the cabin, soaked, as the robot voice on the weather radio warned of dime-size hail carpet bombing the Twin Cities. Matt stomped around the boat, dripping and furious, yelling at the disorder in the galley and the general uselessness of the crew. Most orders were monosyllabic, the commonest being "Move!" Rain hissed on the plywood cabin roof, thunder rattled the windows, lightning tore the air. The flashes burned photonegatives of the landscape onto my vision. The river had removed its bucolic mask to show a darker, wilder aspect.

The mood was grim. Cody stared off into the distance every time he heard a train whistle in the nearby yard, freights being his preferred mode of transport. We spent two nights tied up along the rocky, wave-swept shoreline, the roof leaking in half a dozen places, with every pot in the galley set out to catch the water. The cabin became increasingly claustrophobic, smelling of sweat and mildew and cigarette smoke and rotting produce. I waded ashore and walked through a shuttered suburb in the pouring rain to buy spark plugs. In the hardware store I overheard the two tellers discussing a care package to be sent to their coworker, now a roof gunner in Iraq. Would the pudding separate in the heat? Would applesauce be better? Our drifting life felt mean and meaningless in comparison. I walked back down to the river in the rain. We changed the fouled plugs and limped on again under bleak gray skies.

Matt had arrived at a magic solution to the fuel dilemma, a way to absolve ourselves of complicity in the Iraq war and reduce the *Circle of Death*'s carbon footprint. We were going to drift to New Orleans, taking advantage of the gravitational pull of a quarter-mile drop over the 2,000 miles of river. I pointed out the folly of this. There were twenty-eight dams still in front of us, slowing the river down. A breath of headwind would hold the raft in place as if we had dropped anchor. He dismissed my doubts with a sneer. Matt was even harder on Chris, upbraiding the young biker for his lackadaisical work ethic and enormous appetite. As a dumpster-diver, Chris had proven to be overeager, and our galley was perpetually full of overripe fruit and moldering doughnuts. And he was always eating, even during crises: he would have been grazing the buffet on the sinking *Titanic*. Matt barked orders at him constantly and generally considered him to be an oogle.*

Twain, writing in *Life on the Mississippi* of his days as a cub pilot, describes a certain Pilot Brown: a "horse-faced, ignorant, stingy, malicious, snarling, fault-hunting, mote-magnifying tyrant." In a section unsubtly headed "I Want to Kill Brown," Twain deals with his hatred of his superior by lying in his bunk and imagining dispatching the tyrant "not in old, stale, commonplace ways, but in new and picturesque ones, — ways that were sometimes surprising for freshness of design and ghastliness of situation and environment." At night, swarmed by mosquitoes on the beached raft, I entertained some of the same fantasies that sustained a young Sam Clemens, feeling the fellowship of oppression through all the years that had passed down the river. There is a long record of psychotic sea captains in literature, and Matt, by historic standards, was somewhat less formidable than Bligh, or Queeg, or Ahab. He was a bit hard to take seriously, even when he launched into a tirade. But he was still profoundly unpleasant to live with and sail under on a ten-by-twenty-four-foot floating

---

* A poser; a street rat without street smarts; the lowest caste in the nominally non-hierarchical gutterpunk social hierarchy.

platform. I became increasingly of the opinion that Matt resembled a romantic anarcho-buccaneer less than a narcissistic sociopath. Perhaps he had traveled alone too often, depending on no one but himself, to be a leader of others. And this, I had come to realize, was what a functioning crew — even of anarchists — demanded.

We passed at long last beyond the Twin Cities, below the flaring stacks of an oil refinery that looked like a postapocalyptic fortress, a column of orange flame swaying in the night sky. Matt cut the engine and drifted whenever the wind allowed, and our pace slowed to a crawl. We averaged a handful of miles a day. A drop of water from the Mississippi's source at Lake Itasca will flow down along the river's length to the Gulf of Mexico in ninety days. In 2002, an overweight and lanolin-slathered Slovenian named Martin Strel swam the entire length in just over two months. It would have taken us at least nine months at the rate we were drifting. I made a game of watching dog walkers on the shore outpace us. Bloated catfish floated past belly-up, bound to reach New Orleans long before we would. Hundreds of spiderwebs garlanded the raft; they draped across the curved necks of the lawn flamingos and between the spokes of the ship's wheel. I spent hours on the front-porch swing, chain-smoking like a mental patient at the dayroom window. I learned quickly not to bring up the glacial pace of our progress toward the Gulf.

"This is my boat, and my trip, and nobody is going to tell me what to do," Matt snapped. "If it takes two years, it takes two years. I won't be rushed." The paradox of Matt's position had become clear to all but him: by building a raft to escape the strictures of society, he had made himself a property owner, and subject to the same impulses of possessiveness and control as any suburban homeowner with a mortgage and a hedge trimmer. He was as much a slave to civilization as the locked and dammed river on which we drifted, and far less likely to break loose.

Meanwhile, a shipboard romance had blossomed between Matt and Kristina. None of us talked about it, though it was hard not to notice, as every movement of their accouplements in the captain's quarters was telegraphed through the entire raft in minute detail. Although Matt showed her more deference than he extended to anyone else, he still condescended to her, barked orders at her, got jealous over phantoms. She told me she was having fun and wanted to stay on the river as long as she could stand to be with him. I pointed out that it wasn't a particularly healthy way to have a relationship, and she laughed. "It's kind of ironic that he's so big on animal liberation and can't stand people," she said. "It's because animals can't contradict him."

As if to augur my own psychological dissolution, the raft itself was falling apart. The heavy oak transom to which the 200-pound engine had been bolted was pulling out from the raft's wooden frame. A little more torque from the engine and it would rip itself right off, sinking to the bottom of the channel like an anvil. Thrown up against the shore by wakes, we tied up to a tree outside the town of Hastings, Minnesota, where Matt told us we would need to stay for several days to fix the broken frame. He ordered me to find a Wal-Mart and return with a little electric trolling motor, which could help steer the drifting raft or pull it out of the way of a tow. I walked up through Hastings, down the main street of curio shops and antiques stores, past the end of the town sidewalks, and out along the highway.

One can bemoan the death of the American downtown at the hands of exurban big-box stores, but to truly understand the phenomenon, try reaching one without a car. It was a triple-digit day, the heat shimmering up from the softened blacktop, the breeze hot as a hair dryer. I tried to hitchhike, sticking my thumb out as I stumbled backward down the road. Cars flew by, their drivers craning to look or studiously avoiding eye contact. I wasn't a very appealing passenger: I hadn't showered or shaved in the week since we'd left Minneapolis, and had worn the same clothes throughout. I had a permanent "dirt tan," a thick layer of grime that no amount of swimming in the river could fully remove. My black T-shirt had been torn by brambles and faded by the sun, and a camouflage trucker's hat covered my matted hair as I trudged for miles along the grassy shoulder. Shame eroded; I didn't mind if I was seen peering into dumpsters behind convenience stores, looking for cardboard to make a hitchhiking sign. But still no one stopped.

After walking for almost an hour, I reached the edge of a wide sea of blacktop, and walked across to the vast shed of a building that wavered on its edge like a mirage. Enormous doors slid open, and arctic air engulfed me, pulling me into the glorious air-conditioned acreage of the largest Wal-Mart I had ever seen. I pushed a cart through the aisles, picking out a trolling motor and a deep-cycle marine battery to run it. No one paid me much mind, not the too-young couples arguing in Housewares, not the carbuncular stock boys tallying inventory on the vast shelves. As I rolled up to the counter, the checkout girl offered some scripted pleasantries, asked if I had a club card. She rang up the trolling motor, a large oblong box sticking out of the cart, but didn't notice the $70 battery lying under it.

All I had to do was keep smiling and push the cart straight out the door, across the parking lot, back to the river, and the battery would be mine. Who would miss it — my seventy dollars, from Wal-Mart's billions? Matt would have walked out proudly, or bluffed his way out if confronted by security. He would certainly have called me a coward for passing up the chance. I told the girl about the battery, and she rang it up, and I struggled back across the sea of asphalt in the blazing sun.

When I returned to the raft, which was tied up amid bleached driftwood and plastic flotsam on the shoreline, I found Matt waist-deep in the water, rebuilding the transom, and Cody, drunk on malt liquor, busying himself by stuffing his gear into his backpack. I asked him where he was going.

"I don't really feel like going half a mile an hour along the river with people I don't really get along with. I'd rather go fast as hell on the train. Go work the beet harvest, make four grand, and go to India with my girlfriend." On the far side of the raft, Matt said nothing, only scowled and hammered on the boat. "Matt's a fascist," he whispered to me. "If I stay on the boat, I won't be able to be his friend anymore." The raft, which for Huck and Jim supplied the only space where they could be friends, had wrought quite the opposite effect on our crew.

With no goodbyes, Cody threw his skateboard and pack to the shore and jumped after them, walking off in the direction of the railroad trestle that spanned the river downstream. Half an hour later, a pair of Burlington Northern engines pulling a mixed string of grainers and boxcars rattled over the bridge, bound for Minneapolis, and I wondered, with envy, whether Cody had clambered aboard.

On the far shore from the bluffs of Red Wing, across the broad bend of the river, an old man waved us over. In a cloud of blue exhaust smoke we cut across the channel and pulled up to a weathered boat dock on which a plywood hut was built. The old man had close-cropped hair and a white beard and bore a striking resemblance to a toothless Hemingway in his last years. He extended his hand to me as I stepped onto the shore, and in a moment of uncanny recognition, as close to Stanley meets Livingstone as I had ever experienced, I knew his name before he introduced himself.

"Hello, I'm Poppa Neutrino."

Poppa Neutrino, for the uninitiated, was to the world of raft punks and river rats what Yoda is to tyro Jedis. He was the great predecessor and innovator of the form, a seventy-two-year-old wanderer who had traveled the world for decades, constructing and sailing rafts of scavenged junk up and down the East Coast and clear across the ocean to Ireland. He built his rafts out of found objects: old docks, scrap lumber, soda bottles, Styrofoam blocks, cobbling them together and building them into enormous floating trash-art sculptures. The last I had heard of him, he had built an enormous raft on the Sea of Cortez and had vanished south, with a plan to cross the Pacific Ocean alone to China. There is a book about his life, by Alec Wilkinson, called *The Happiest Man in the World*. He was living evidence that the nomadic life could be more than just an escapist fantasy: he had dedicated his life toward proving that possibility. Finding Neutrino here on the banks of the Mississippi came very near to making me believe the river gods existed.

Neutrino (his real name is David Pearlman, but he adopted Neutrino two decades ago to symbolize his status as a wandering particle in the universe) had abandoned his last raft on a beach in Mexico, along with a brand-new fifty-horsepower outboard, a fact that made our entire crew cringe with envy, imagining how fast the *Circle of Death* could go with a decent engine. He had come up from New Orleans with a pair of suntanned college-age acolytes, June and Eric, and a load of lumber — salvaged from the wreckage of the Lower 9th Ward — strapped to the roof of a beat-up Volvo. They were building a new raft, Neutrino's fourteenth, out of a huge floating dock donated by a local restaurant owner. Neutrino planned to sail it down the river, through New Orleans, across the Gulf of Mexico, and depending on its seaworthiness either through the Panama Canal or around Cape Horn, and thence across the Pacific to China. It was refreshing to meet someone crazier than us.

They had been there three weeks and were proceeding very slowly, building a flimsy shack on the raft, which they planned to pull behind a dinghy with a tiny outboard. Neutrino stepped into the water and clambered aboard the *Circle of Death*. He drank a glass of water, slowly, and sat in the shade of the galley and admires Matt's workmanship and attention to detail. "It's a beautiful vessel," he said, "and a good thing you've done. Congratulations for being on the river. It's a free life and a great life." I told him about some of our technical difficulties, and what slow going it had been, averaging a few miles a day. His advice, drawn out in his gravelly voice, was to accept the pace of the river, calm down and develop what he called "essential timing." To wit: "Once you break this linear timing, your nervous system opens up to all sorts of new timing. On a two-dimensional plane back and forth from job to school, you have to isolate yourself from all kinds of impulses. When you first get into circular timing, essential timing, you think you're going to lose your mind when you make the transfer. You think 'I've never been so bored in my life.' You have to have things to keep you amused. The triad I have is necessity, boredom and creativity. That's what you're dealing with, to take care of the necessities, to take care of the boredom, and to be creative."

June and Eric, both of whom quit school to join up with Neutrino, listened with rapt attention as Neutrino held forth about the need to do chores three times as slow, to completely give oneself over to the pace at which the world offers things up. They nodded simultaneously in total agreement. Neutrino's philosophy had something to do (and this is where I lost the thread) with the various hydrogen ions produced by the different shakras. Matt was surprisingly deferential and polite to Neutrino, but I could see his eyes narrowing into a skeptical smirk.

Neutrino wanted us to stay on with him while he built his raft, but Matt told him it was time for us to head on. There was an anarchists' gathering a few days down the river in Winona, and he wanted to make it in time for the cream corn wrestling on Saturday. It was the first time I had ever heard him put a timeframe on the journey, and I could tell he didn't want to hang out with Neutrino any longer than he had to. We fired up the engine and took our leave, Neutrino standing on the shore waving as we pulled out into the channel. Out of earshot, Matt shook his head and laughed. "I give him credit for what he's done, but they'll never make it. It was like he was trying to get us to join some blissed-out cult."

He had a point. I was sure if Twain were present he would have found plenty of evidence of the humbug and the huckster in this toothless old man with a crazy dream. Matt may have trafficked in goods, stolen or scavenged, but Neutrino trafficked in souls. In another age he could have easily been a tent revival preacher; a little tetched, but quite convincing when it comes to the laying on of hands. Perhaps he'd have dabbled in mesmerism or phrenology, a snake oil racket at every tent meeting on the river. I didn't know if Neutrino was a guru or a fraud, but he had certainly chosen to live life exactly as he saw fit, and possessed something I found myself wanting to believe in, despite my more cynical instincts. Maybe he did hold the key to total happiness. Maybe my doubts were because I couldn't give myself over to Neutrino's sense of time and patience with the river, and so couldn't really understand the enlightenment that comes when one releases their grasp on the world and drifts.

Not that I'm not drifting. Days on the river passed in a haze, time expanding to fill the spaces between words and events. Even reading was difficult, a sentence scanned a half-dozen times before the meaning was absorbed, and as quickly forgotten. None of us talked much, and Matt played music up top while I sat smoking on the front deck, feeling sad and restless. Despite what Neutrino preached about transcending boredom to a new enlightenment, the weight of passing hours created an acute pain, just below my rib cage. Day after day I studied the charts and traced our snail's progress. Each marked buoy passed like a minute hand making its way across the face of a schoolroom clock. The time, the date, all the measures of normal life were stripped of meaning.

But just when boredom threatened to overwhelm the senses, the river would offer up some bit of unimpeachable beauty. Bald eagles circled overhead and landed in snags to watch us with wide yellow eyes. Deer startled from the shore, crashed into the understory, white tails flashing. Opalescent sunsets silhouetted herons at dusk. The great birds paced their own glassy reflections before pulling up like brushstrokes to stand in the shallows of the far shore.

Late one night we motored along a stretch of the dark river and pulled up at Latsch Island, a houseboat community in Winona, Minnesota. Several hundred young anarchists from around the country had train-hopped and hitchhiked there to attend the annual event known as the CrimethInc Convergence. CrimethInc is more a mindset than an actual organization, but its stated credo is essentially anticapitalist and antiauthoritarian, serving as a catchall for a host of other social and political viewpoints, from post-left anarchism to situationism to violent insurrection against the state. A large group gathered on the darkened beach when we arrived, and cheered the raft, strung with Christmas lights, as we beached it at full throttle.

I wandered around the encampment the next day. Grimy and feral-looking, the CrimethInc kids squatted in small groups around a clearing. The campsite was overgrown with poison ivy, and many legs were covered with weeping red blisters. It was the first time in weeks I hadn't felt self-conscious about being filthy, but now I felt self-conscious about not being punk enough, and I worried I was being eyed with suspicion. Almost none of the kids were older than twenty-five, as if there were a sell-by date on radical social philosophy, a legal age limit after which one must surrender lofty ideals and shave off all dreadlocks. CrimethInc's core function is the creation of propaganda, mainly in the form of books and zines, and they held a swap of such anarcho-classics as *Days of War, Nights of Love*; *Evasion*; and *Fighting for Our Lives*. One of my favorite free pamphlets was "Wasted Indeed: Anarchy & Alcohol," a searing indictment of the revolution-sapping properties of the demon drink, which offered potent slogans: "Sedition not Sedation!" "No cocktail but the Molotov cocktail!" "Let us brew nothing but trouble!"

The CrimethInc kids were in the middle of several days of self-organized workshops, seminars, and discussions ranging from the mutualist banking theories of the nineteenth-century anarchist philosopher Pierre-Joseph Proudhon, to an introductory practicum on lock-picking, to a class on making one's own menstrual pads. One well-attended discussion was on consent ("Not the absence of no, but the presence of yes!"), and it seemed to underscore the CrimethInc goal of reevaluating the rules and customs of society and creating new ones. Consent was central to the idea of functioning anarchism, which they believed to be the purest and most direct form of democracy. Everyone ate as a group, and a huge cauldron of dumpster-dived gruel bubbled over a campfire, tended by a grubby-handed group of chefs dicing potatoes and onions on a piece of cardboard on the ground. Huck may have been right that a "barrel of odds and ends" where the "juice kind of swaps around" makes for better victuals, but it occurred to me that the revolution may well get dysentery.

Anarchism has not made much of a mark on American politics since 1901, when Leon Czolgosz assassinated President McKinley; but neither has it entirely vanished, and running through the American ideal of the rugged individualist is a deep vein of sympathy for the dream of unmediated liberty. What would happen, I had often wondered, if their anarchist revolution ever got its chance? If everyone just up and quit, and did exactly as he or she pleased in an orgy of liberated desire? Who would keep the lights on? Who would make the ciprofloxacin or, for that matter, the calamine lotion? What kind of world would the sun rise on after that victory?

But the revolution hadn't happened, and it probably never would. The kids were naive fantasists, but I could see their basic point: there was a huge amount wrong with America and the world, from impending environmental collapse to widespread sectarian warfare to a real lack of social justice and equality. CrimethInc's adherents had come together there because they wanted to live their lives as some sort of solution. They saw "the revolution" not as a final product but as an ongoing process; they wanted not just to destroy the capitalist system but to create something livable in its place. I didn't want to smash the state, but I realized that in my adulthood I had faced those same dispiriting questions: How should we live in a world so full of waste and destruction and suffering? What *were* the "solutions" that the inebriated oracle insisted I find, that first dark night on the riverbank? I didn't know if I had ever been one of these kids or if I had just been play-acting, wishing I were an idealist and acting as if it were so. There were solutions, I felt sure. But they were not to be found there, adrift, disconnected from the world.

We floated ever southward, through rolling farmland and beneath chalky bluffs, past tiny towns clinging to the riverbank, the raft bobbing like a cork in the wakes of tow barges and jet skis. We were averaging about seven miles of drifting a day, and there were still more than 1,600 miles of river between us and the Gulf. Sometimes I'd look up from a book after twenty minutes to see we hadn't moved. Matt became more aggressive and bossy as the days passed, exploding over tiny things: an open dish-soap cap, a pot of leftovers uncovered, an empty matchbook not thrown out. A week after Cody left, Chris had unloaded his bicycle from the top deck and in a single afternoon pedaled back the mere fifty miles we had come from Minneapolis; and with both of them gone, the brunt of the abuse fell on me. We got into an argument about money one night, as I had financed pretty much every purchase of un-dumpsterable or otherwise freely procurable necessity for the past several weeks. Matt had seventeen dollars to his name and wanted money to tide him over until he took a break from the river and went to the beet harvest. I told him I didn't want to be his banker, and that he was clearly resourceful enough to figure things out just fine.

After that, Matt refused to talk to me at all. He and Kristina spent their days playing cards and dominoes, and I either took shifts at the steering wheel or sat on the porch, trying to read. We drifted in a heavy silence for two days, passing Victory, Wisconsin, and at last making it out of Minnesota and into Iowa, the river unraveling before us into a swampy waste of braided channels and black backwaters, widening out at times into half-submerged fields of rotting stumps.

We tied up for a night at a dock above the Black Hawk Bridge, and the tires of tractor-trailers moaned on its steel grating, ghost-like as they flew over the river. I walked up the hill above the river to use a pay phone at a smoky bar, the regulars hunched over their stools like heartbroken gargoyles. When I came outside I saw Matt and Kristina surrounded by local police next to a convenience-store dumpster, framed in a circle of streetlight. They had been fishing out some food, and the manager had called the cops on them. But after checking their ID's, the police let them go. Matt walked back to the boat, and Kristina and I went for a drink at the bar before returning to the same dumpster, filling a bag with cold cheeseburgers and pizza slices. The petty authoritarianism of the police had been confounded, but it didn't feel like much of a victory. Walking back to the river past the neat lamplit lawns of Lansing, Iowa, I felt weary of being a stranger. I told Kristina I had to leave.

As much as I had wanted to see the raft down the entire river, to possess the strength to quit everything and live on river time, to see Hannibal and Cairo and Memphis and New Madrid, I couldn't do it. I woke up at sunrise, packed my bag, and sat on the dock in the dawn glow. Matt and Kristina were asleep inside his quarters. Mist rose off the river, which wound south past dark banks hung with wisps of fog. I heard Matt stir; he squinted and grimaced as he stepped out onto the porch and saw me sitting on my pack on the dock. We seemed to understand each other.

We exchanged goodbyes, good lucks. Kristina undid the lines from the cleats, and Matt pushed away from the dock. With a wave they motored out into the middle of the channel and then cut the engine, catching the current and drifting along to wherever the river would bear them. I sat watching for what seemed like hours before the *Circle of Death* rounded a far bend and vanished. I shouldered my pack, walked up to the bridge, and began hitchhiking east toward home, borne along by kindly strangers. Waiting for a lift at sunset, I found myself on a stretch of blacktop rolling to the horizon through a landscape of wheat fields and grain silos. Swarms of grasshoppers flitted around me, flashing golden in the fading light, leaping out of the fields at the highway's edge. Alone in the middle of the country, far from home but heading there, I felt more free than I had since leaving Minneapolis, since I'd first set eyes on the Mississippi. But the ground still seemed to rock below my feet, as though a ghost of the river rolled beneath me.

Kristina sent me occasional updates, but soon she left the raft herself and went off traveling on her own. Two months later I got an email from Matt. With astonishing persistence, he had made it all the way to St. Louis, through the entire lock-and-dam system, nearly seven hundred miles down to the wild reaches of the lower river, where the current, freed at last from its restraints, flowed unhindered to the Gulf. Drifting through St. Louis, the raft had been hemmed in between a moored barge and a pair of tugboats. A third tug had pulled through, creating a huge bow wash that sent water rushing sidelong into the cabin. Inundated, the *Circle of Death* had keeled over and sunk, almost immediately, to the bottom of the Mississippi. Matt, barefoot in only shorts and a T-shirt, had narrowly escaped drowning by swimming to the barge and climbing out. All his clothing, his journals, photographs, identification — everything but his life had been lost, and he found himself in a place he had often been: broke and homeless, coming ashore in a strange city. The river, of course, continued on without him.

K. G. SCHNEIDER

■

The Outlaw Bride

FROM *Ninth Letter*

WE CAROMED INTO MARRIAGE in less than a month, beetling into
San Francisco on the Friday of a chill, grey Valentine's Day weekend
in 2004 on the heels of the news — *It had to be a joke! No, it wasn't a
joke! Dinah and Gail had married! Other people had married! We could
marry!* — that gay people were being married at City Hall.

We raced out of the garage and toward Civic Center, and there they
were, shuffling two by two around the block and up the wide, wet
steps of City Hall and through the gilt-and-glass doors, a solid, happy
mass swaddled in rain gear or in some cases black plastic trash bags,
heads tilted back with smiles and laughter even as the cold rain beat
their faces; and everyone cheered and clapped every time newlyweds
burst outside waving their marriage licenses; and the statue of Abe
Lincoln held a hand-lettered sign that said *Everyone deserves the right to
marry* and his long face frowned like he meant it; and we would have
stood in line ourselves under the damp sagging sky but *we hab bad
head colds we doad wand to bake it worse*; and so with our eyes dazzled
by the miracle before us we promised ourselves we would come back
as soon as our health permitted, assuming They had not stopped the
weddings, as indeed They were already threatening to do.

All week City Hall cranked out married couples with the speed,
precision, and urgency of a wartime munitions plant while politicians railed, florists and restaurateurs rejoiced, reporters shoved mi-
crophones in the faces of shouting protesters, and granite-faced lawyers duked it out in the state courthouse. Sandy repeatedly e-mailed
me the *Chronicle* photo of two men walking out of City Hall hand

in hand with twin baby girls in Snugglies on their chests, and each time I opened that message I would cry and laugh and honk into tissue (Sandy loves it when I am not such a toughy), and every night we fell asleep, cats snuggled on our heads as we dreamed of becoming brides at last.

Toward the end of that week, the city Fathers and Mothers imposed some order on the nuptial chaos by announcing that couples could make appointments to get married, so we again sped into the city, this time to spend an afternoon shuffling forward in the basement of City Hall with hundreds of other homophile marrieds-to-be, trading newspapers and stories of how we met as we waited to sign up for an appointment to marry as if we were signing up for a driving test, except no one at the DMV smiles, while at City Hall everyone, would-be spouses and paper-pushers alike, wore foolish won-the-lottery grins. By nightfall we had an appointment for two weeks hence, and I shifted into bridal overdrive to marshal up family, friends, a reception luncheon, and a cake topped with two wee brides.

On the morning of our marriage appointment I dragged us into San Francisco three hours early and we proceeded to walk in circles around Civic Center, effervescent with excitement and love, but also damp with fear that any minute Someone from Sacramento would make the weddings stop (as indeed happened the following week). When it was finally our time, we snuck around the back of City Hall to avoid walking past the shouting protesters and the guy with the sign that said *I Want to Marry This Tree*, and we pushed through the door to find the City Hall rotunda spread out proudly before us like a prize rose unfurling its petals. Bunting and banners twirled around creamy Georgian columns; young men with spit-polished shoes and ruffly white boutonnières strolled hand in hand, their faces pink with excitement; the shining stone floor reflected back the mounds of beribboned bouquets sent by well-wishers from around the country; and Sandy and I in our knee-length lavender dresses contributed our own gorgeousness, Sandy's nails tipped with matching polish she had bought that very morning at a Civic Center drugstore along with a skein of purple yarn.

So on our shaking legs we stood on the stairs in front of friends and family and a few astonished Japanese tourists, everyone weeping, and we clasped together our moist, trembling hands, and with our faces alight from the sparkling of a thousand camera flashes and the veins in our neck pulsing, Sandy and I, in front of God, our sobbing friends and family, the blubbering tourists clinging to one another, and the august and munificent environs of the City and County of San Francisco, were pronounced Spouses for Life.

Or at least for 159 days.

I am a woman betrothed to order and structure. But on August 12, 2004, I became an outlaw, after a deluge of e-mails from concerned friends and relatives informed us that the State of California had just invalidated our marriage. It is not like me to be an outlaw. It is not simply that I am a librarian, and therefore I ardently love, honor and obey taxonomies and ontologies and the Five Laws of Librarianship, which I can recite on command. It is no mere vocational sensibility, this love of order, but who I am. I vote in every election and vote for every office, no matter how small, and nag others to do the same. I follow recipes slavishly, and have been known to drive around town on a Thanksgiving morning in search of an open grocery store because *it's not pumpkin pie without clove*. Though Sandy, my one-time wife of 159 days, is a Congregational minister, I remain an Episcopalian, committed to a religion that has more unbending rules for its liturgy than the space shuttle has for its launches. I park my car between the lines, and if one wheel strays, I back the car up and move again; and I am not above leaving notes on people's windshields advising them that SUVs do not belong in parking spots marked "Compact." I am always crushed not to be selected for jury duty, which probably happens because I look far too eager to serve. I am the best person to call when something needs assembling, because not only will I follow directions and find every part, but I bring a special bossy joie de vivre to assembling stereo cabinets and bookshelves and computers that allows my friends and family to order pizza or simply sit and chat while I happily impose order where none was before, molding structure from the clay of life.

But on August 12, 2004, something in me shifted. I did not realize this immediately. I did not feel angry (though I pretended to be angry, for Sandy's sake, nodding and rocking on the couch as she paced the living room shouting about Justice while the cats stared at her, tails straight up). I did not feel sad, because sorrow is an emotion with its own powerful downward pull. Reading the *San Francisco Chronicle*, I noted the man who said, "I consider myself still married," but did not understand what he meant, or what he felt. Sitting in the living room as our laptops chimed from messages pouring into our e-mail boxes, I simply felt nothing at all.

Except, weeks later, the next time I had to fill out an official form in some green office — a doctor's, perhaps, or maybe it was the DMV — I hesitated. *Married or single?* asked the form. I sat with a clipboard in my lap, feeling something unwind inside me, uncurling its disobedient little self. *Married*, I checked off the little gray box. Then looked around. And turned in the form. And felt a little angry, and a little sad, but also hotly defiant; and that thing in me, that small protesting voice buried under the goodnik, became a little louder, and became articulate, and began to speak. For the first time since August 12, I was feeling something about the marriage-that-was-no-more. "I consider myself still married," I repeated to myself as I left the scene of my civil disobedience, and felt a deliciously rebellious frisson streak up my newly outlaw spine.

It wasn't just that I was filling out an official form with a statement that in the eyes of officialdom was not true. Driving home along quiet, orderly streets — in a city that nonetheless had never held its own gay marriages — I realized that I also disagreed with the State. In my head, the State could not invalidate our marriage. It was not simply a political disagreement; it was a disagreement of fact.

For over a decade of our lives together, I had conformed with the idea that Sandy and I could not marry. It was an assumption invisibly circling our lives: we could be many things, but not married. We went to friends' weddings, bearing lovely gifts, and we smiled and applauded, and we drank champagne and ate cake, and we went home, but we did not say, "Hey, let's do this!" Because "this," the marriage, was not doable. We bought gleaming gold "commitment bands," and we celebrated the day we met and the day we moved in together and even the days our cats joined our household; but it was understood that marriage was not on our landscape. We talked about having a ceremony of sorts, the kind you read about in the Style section of the Sunday *New York Times* in which *Jennifer Craftwomyn and Susan Roosevelt, who clerked together under Supreme Court Justice Antonin Scalia, celebrated their partnership — yes, that kind of partnership — with a special service at the Central Park Boathouse performed by Unitarian minister Alfred Thatcher*, but neither of us felt terribly enthusiastic about a faux wedding, even though, as I pointed out, it would involve gifts, and that's always nice.

Even our humor had been underscored with the assumption that marriage was not possible. Once, a few years ago, Sandy and I woke up at 3 A.M., victims of a transient insomnia brought on by too much coffee and cheap wine. Lying in the dark as car headlights skimmed traces of light across our ceiling, surrounded by humming cats, we had a meandering conversation that eventually wound around to the issue of our last names. If we could get married, we asked — a ridiculous idea, we knew, but *what if* — what would we do about our last names? But the idea that we could be married was so outlandish that seriously discussing the issue seemed pointless, so we unseriously planned to send out engraved announcements that we had changed our last names to Oatmeal, and that in the future we wish to be addressed as Mrs. and Mrs. Oatmeal. This scheme struck us as terribly funny, if cruel, as we knew our well-meaning straight friends and family members would earnestly and unquestioningly abide by our wishes in order to appear fully accepting and nonjudgmental, and that our gay friends would just roll their eyes. Though we never carried through with our plans — they were just the stuff of late-night conversation — to this day we sometimes call one another Mrs. Oatmeal. (My sister says it makes her think of a children's picture-book series: *Meet Mrs. and Mrs. Oatmeal; Mrs. and Mrs. Oatmeal Go to the Overpriced Grocery Store; Mrs. and Mrs. Oatmeal Replace Their Water Heater . . .*)

But after we were married, and then not married, I saw that the humor of our practical joke rested on how preposterous it was to us, a decade ago, to imagine that we could legally wed. We had been obedient in a heartbreaking manner, buying into the cultural assumption that we were unfit to marry, and even making that fundamental unfitness the fulcrum of a joke under which lay a pallid wistfulness: an unspoken yearning to be preoccupied with engraved invitations, discussions about last names, what to wear and whom to invite — those little chores of marriage we suddenly found ourselves happily plunging into during that amazing time when we could and would be married.

I became uneasy with my former self, even a little angry, and wondered if anyone else thought our joke was so transparently pathetic. "We completely bought into the state of affairs that made our relationship unfit to be honored in the eyes of the government," I pointed out to Sandy one agonized evening, my elbows dug into the dining room table and my face in my hands while Sandy crocheted on the couch. She smiled. She set down her needlework, walked across the room, and kissed me on the head. It is good to live with a pastor: I dwell in a household with infinite forgiveness and extravagant love. I saw that my anger was part of the process of awakening, a sharp lungful of awareness oxygenating my formerly accommodating mind. Our marriage could be invalidated, but the mischief had been done: I no longer saw us as people who could not or should not marry. If we ever changed our last names, it would be lawful and real.

(In fact, investigating our marriage license, we would need to take extra steps to become Mrs. and Mrs. Oatmeal; nowhere on the embossed, bar-coded, pink and black Certified Copy of Vital Records stamped by Diane Cirrincione, Assessor, does it indicate that *First Applicant* and *Second Applicant* automatically change their *Current [Last] Names*.)

My slow but sure political awakening only sharpened my newfound tendencies toward civil disobedience — though my actions remained focused on my declared marital status, I rush to add; I will continue to park between the lines until the Rapture. As the weeks went by, I found other forms on which to say, "I consider myself still married": a change of address for a grocery-store savings card; an emergency contact form; some software I purchased. It turns out an awful lot of people — or at least the forms they create — ask if you're married. Yet to date, no one has called me to grill me on my marital status. (Just try registering a car in California without a smog certificate. But apparently it is taken on faith by many agencies that people do not lie about their marital status.)

Other sensations marched to the forefront, assembling themselves into a tight warp and woof of pent-up lesbian fury over a dream deferred, and a poutish middle-class ire over my second-class status as a first-class taxpayer. My anger at my lack of civil rights did not so much ratchet up and down in intensity as simply tighten its focus. I was no longer raging at that large, vague world with its discriminatory rules; I became specifically angry at clear targets, even when the expression of my anger was slightly askew. I found myself having lengthy arguments with the governor of California — debates silent and unrequited, but nonetheless eloquent, at least on my part. "Der people hast shpoken," he had told gay-rights supporters in 2005 when he refused to sign the marriage law passed by the California Assembly; but that was not correct, I argued to myself, because I was still speaking. I even became angry at Maria Shriver, in part for her silence on gay marriage, not that we could expect much on that issue from a Republican First Lady, but also for assuming the mantle of politician's wife and in doing so wasting a perfectly good Kennedy.

I felt my patience begin to buckle and shrink. I had to live with the facts of life, but I did not have to live with them quietly. The man in front of City Hall still waving that, I WANT TO MARRY THIS TREE sign? "Somebody call up a justice and arrange for a ceremony," I told my friends, as the anger bubbled and stewed in my brain while I checked off "Married" on yet another form. Barney Frank didn't think it was "time" for gay marriage in San Francisco? He objected to "the San Francisco thing"? Then to hell with him! "Yes, to hell with him!" Sandy repeated, indulging me in a cozy domestic moment of Two Minutes' Hate. She was unraveling an afghan so she could reuse the yarn, and our tabby cat sat on the shoulder of the armchair, batting the skein as Sandy built it up. "Deconstruction," Sandy calls it. I have learned not to become too attached to any one of her afghans, given that any minute it might be unraveled so its yarn can be rewoven into a thick new blanket of capacious proportions and unique color combinations. Go away for a week on a business trip, and on my return I find that there are exactly the same number of afghans, and Sandy is sitting where she was when I left, with at least one happy cat perched on her chair, waving a paw at the yarn skittering from the unwinding skein; but on closer inspection, the afghans have rearranged themselves in an exciting new postmodern tableau Derrida himself would admire. It is order, but reordered; it is a minute shift in our domestic landscape, satisfying in both its change (things are not what they were) and its stability (things have changed in ways we understand and appreciate). "Look," Sandy will breathe, holding up the new afghan, and I will say, as always, with great truth, "It's beautiful."

My eccentric one-woman campaign to prevaricate about my marital status was also a sort of unraveling. After all, no one noticed or cared; it took me a surprisingly long time to realize that anyone reviewing the forms I so defiantly lied on would assume I was married to a man. For that matter, our other de facto married friends had not been led to civil disobedience. Gail and Dinah were annoyed but did not simmer or steep over the invalidation of their marriage; they pressed on, getting ready for the fall church concert, buying a new car, planning trips. Other friends seemed equally sanguine. "Oh yes," said one. "We were married, too. Wasn't that nice? So good of Gavin" (every gay person in North America now being on a first-name basis with the mayor of San Francisco).

It was Sandy's response that stirred the most doubt in me about my outlaw behavior. After her initial anger, she too returned to life as usual, a life of work and preaching and laundry and crochet and thick biographies from the library and persimmons from the neighbor's tree and trying to decide if it was cold enough yet for the first fire of the season, a life where an entire Saturday can dissolve in a series of tiny errands as we progress down sleepy suburban streets from Costco to the farmers' market to Albertsons to the hardware store and then back to Costco for the thing we forgot, our car windows rolled down so we can hear the brown leaves of autumn crunching under the wheels of our car, hours luxuriously drifting by as we talk and talk, talking about nothing, talking about everything, occasionally patting one another on the knee as if to say, Mrs. Oatmeal, I am glad you exist.

The simple observation, the very obvious lesson learned, is that of course we are married. Marriage is not a simple square of fabric, a one-time event to hang on the wall, but a process slowly knitting lives together, a gradual weaving, row by row, that begins when we are able to set aside enough of ourselves to create a third entity from the union of two: *I* becomes the warp, and *we* becomes the woof.

Where you go I will go, and where you stay I will stay; and under the comfort of one garment, we will be redeemed. By that standard, Sandy pointed out on a winter evening, deconstructing a dark green afghan while a fire crackled, we have been married for well over a decade. We do not know the exact date, but there are many moments that could serve us well: the afternoon I took the PATH train from Manhattan to New Jersey, a cat hidden in my gym bag, to move into Sandy's home; the time we chose not to live in Michigan; the time we toasted one another with stiff shots of vodka in the garage before Thanksgiving dinner to fortify ourselves in advance of my mother's political diatribes; the many times we have forgiven one another for the sulks and storms and minor transgressions of any relationship. I could continue to be angry that our legal marriage had been invalidated, and I could enjoy the brisk salt air of the realization that we were worthy of this social contract; yet I could not deny we were married.

But a jacquard pattern lay on top of all this consciousness, a raised figure in the fabric that was a new and unavoidable design. In reviewing the steps leading up to our hasty madcap wedding, I realized that most of the impetus for the marriage came from me; I called it "our" wedding, but it was a project with my peculiar stamp on it. I had pulled Sandy to City Hall, I had pushed for a wedding date, I had insisted we stand in line for hours, I had organized the attendees and the lunch afterwards; I was the one who packaged up the chocolate from the top of our cake and put it in our freezer to eat a year hence, I had not even asked Sandy if she wanted to be *First Applicant* on our Certificate of Vital Records, unthinkingly shouldering up to the counter at City Hall to take the top listing. And I was the one most visibly crushed when our marriage was voided, and most invested in a rebellious if somewhat awry response. Sandy had followed my lead uncomplainingly, had cried as we repeated our vows, had been angry at the turn of events; but I had brought a loony urgency not only to my response to the wedding and its aftermath, but also to its very origins, which were seated more deeply in our lives than I wanted to admit.

In probing the motives behind my lavishly uxorious efforts, there was first the matter of my minor infidelities. Not infidelities in the

grossest, most unkind sense of the word — the crossed line of cor-
poreal transgressions — but the minor cheats of married life. There
was my habit of taking the larger steak off the platter without asking
Sandy if she wanted it, knowing she would not challenge me. There
was my little quirk of ignoring Sandy's phone calls from her office of
an evening, when I wasn't quite finished reading a juicy magazine
story and did not want the narrative experience of *The New Yorker* or
the *Atlantic* — or, I admit it, *People* — disturbed by spousal demands.
I even felt a twinge of penitence for the little pockets of hidden space
I quietly carve for myself inside our marriage, such as those times
when I find myself leaving a meeting or class early and instead of
calling Sandy will take a longer route home in order to enjoy the brief
delusion of a life untrammeled by light bulbs that need changing,
cat boxes that need cleaning, or lengthy discussions about condomin-
ium insurance.

But all long-term relationships have selfish moments and grand
fantasies — dreams of carefree liberation which in my case usually
evaporate on the third night of a business trip, when solitary meals
and cold beds become intolerably bleak, and I yearn to be back in the
yoke of domestic chores, fixing Sandy's computer or baking a pie for
a church dinner. My infidelities, I knew, were not the real source of
my angst, but those images of solitude — the empty bed, the single
plate — pulled me to the source of the disturbance.

I began to see that behind the fog and friction of cakes, dresses, invitations, licenses, and other relics lurked a decade-old crisis, a harsh
divagation from the generally calm narrative of our lives. Sandy's di-
agnosis: cancer. Hurried consultations. Surgery. The antiseptic odor
of hospital hallways. The breathlessness of constant fear. Sleeping in
the corner of a hospital "family room," my coat a makeshift blanket.
The frightening lack of control, the crazy out-of-kilter events scatter-
ing disorder through our lives, threatening us with pain, disfigure-
ment, death, and unbearable loneliness. The cousin who always referred to me as Sandy's "special friend" pulling me aside while Sandy
lay sleeping to warn me, as we stood under a harsh white hospital
light, that "everyone in Sandy's family died early" — in other words,
that whatever I wanted from this relationship needed to be cashed in

at the end of every day, hour, minute, a statement that when repeated to Sandy caused her to laugh but also to turn away.

In remembering this time, I saw that the State and I, for all our disagreements, agreed on one thing: weddings are powerfully numinous ceremonies, crude talismans to defiantly shake in the face of Thanatos. Perhaps it is not so coincidental that weddings are so weirdly similar to funerals — the elaborate, stylized preparations, the high formality, the priest incanting blessings, the gathered family, the tears, even the sense of something present, immortal, but not seen: in one case, a marriage; in the other, a soul. The narrative of the wedding is beautiful, but it is also one of life's heartbreaking fictions, a dreamscape worthy of Hypnos, this insistence on a permanent union for two lives, a union that will nevertheless be sundered by death. I cannot agree with the State's assessment of my worth, but I can almost admire its cruel acuity in using one of life's most mystical, primitive events as a citadel separating the sanctioned from the unacknowledged. If you must deprive people of their rights, do it in a way that also robs them of our culture's most totemic yet most useless stand against mortality.

A decade earlier, we had been allowed to resume our own gentle fictions. Our crisis gradually subsided, beginning with the grace of a surgeon's measured words: cautious optimism, things to heed, markers to observe. Then the slow watching and waiting. One year. Five years. Ten years. Relieved, yes we were, yet also conscious that the crisis had wound a clock that now ticked through our lives, forcing us — or allowing us — to experience life stitch by stitch, thread by thread, our foibles and eccentricities and nutty projects and shotgun weddings, all our unravelings and reweavings, knit together in a thickly textured narrative, fact and fiction, that sheltered us from the future—not shelter enough to protect us forever, for, like Penelope, eventually we would be stopped; but almost enough shelter for the moments we have been given, we two outlaw brides, we who with our hands clasped together are walking toward an unseen land.

MICHELLE SEATON

■

How to Work a Locker Room

FROM *The Pinch*

DON'T LOOK DOWN. Look up instead, toward the tops of the lockers, because that's where you'll find the players' names. Some, the starters, have theirs engraved on the Formica blocks. The scrubs just up from minor leagues have pieces of tape marked with block letters in ballpoint.

Don't talk to the stars — the high scorers, the French-Canadian goalies, the Eastern European wingers, or any rookie with a multi-million-dollar signing bonus. No one governs their behavior. No one reprimands them. No one even warns them. And on some days, who knows when, cruelty becomes sport. Talk to the captain, because he has to be nice to reporters. Talk to the goon — the guy hired for his fists, the guy whose job it is to beat opposing players while thousands cheer — because goons are plainspoken and often funny. Nobody knows why, but they are. Perhaps human nature compels them to wrap an ugly skill in a charming package. And talk to the guy who went to Harvard. There's one on every team. These guys are never big stars, but they give nice, long answers, philosophical answers, in which most of the nouns and verbs agree. Those quotes can be handy if the story runs short.

Don't tell anyone that you don't know anything about hockey, that you've never sat through an entire game, that you don't know any of the players' names, or that you had to call for directions to the practice facility. Act like you've been here before. The beat writers who are here every day have it down. They sigh heavily while gazing into the middle distance. They keep their coats on and check their watches frequently, as though they're late for an important meeting. They cultivate tics of boredom: tapping their notebooks against an open palm, rolling their shoulders to get at some ancient kink. They nod briskly to each other and say, "How's it goin'?" Nobody ever answers this question.

Don't flinch at the smell, or the media guy will smirk at you and know you for what you are, a girl on an assignment that nobody else wanted, a girl who might need babysitting. Then he will say, "You have to walk up to them, you know. They're never going to walk up to you." It is important to hide any searing disdain for the media guy as you thank him for his inane advice.

The stench is not just the body odor of thirty men trapped in an airless, windowless cave. Sweaty men with bad diets have been undressing in this room for decades. The sour molecules have seeped into the fluorescent lighting above, into the wooden stalls that serve as lockers, and into the tattered industrial carpeting below. Steam pours into the room from the open-air shower at one end of the room. A half-dozen showerheads run in a constant low hiss, and as a result, even the paint on the walls has acquired a sheen. And yet no one notices the heat, the clammy air, or the closeness of too many bodies.

Practice deference always. Remember that the lowliest man in this room makes $5,000 a week. Name players earn ten times that. This week, for this story, you will make $350.

Know when you've been sent on a fool's errand, when you've been asked to interview a professional hockey player about the years of sexual abuse he suffered while playing junior league hockey in Canada. The player, who was fourteen at the time the abuse started, endured it — along with years away from his family, years out of formal schooling, and years on a punishing road schedule of games — because playing junior hockey was his only chance to become a pro. Six months ago the player turned in his former coach, pressed charges, and aided prosecutors through the trial and conviction. It is the biggest story a young reporter could hope to cover. The trouble is that the story broke a month ago. It has been smothered by every major news outlet. Everyone has already done this story. Say this to the assigning producer, and he will respond, *We haven't done it.* When you ask, *What if the player refuses to talk?* he will say, *Do your best.*

By the time the players trudge into the locker room, they've already removed their gloves, their helmets, and their skates. They scratch their sweaty heads with red and swollen hands and pad around in bare feet. Someone will tell you later that hockey players never wear socks. They wear skates that are two sizes smaller than their street shoes. Their skates are molded so tightly to their feet that the seams leave long indentations in the skin. Each foot bears two lines of little red circles marking the eyeholes of the laces.

Ignore the media guy when he says, "Sheldon isn't doing interviews about that anymore." Wait until he walks away and then turn your 60-watt smile on the nearest, least naked scrub and ask, "Which one is Sheldon?" Walk up to Sheldon and say his name softly, gently, because your heart is pounding in your ears. When he turns, hesitant, say quietly, "Do you have a minute?"

Use time wisely. Luckily, the players wear a lot of equipment. Before he can shower, each player must tug off his sodden nylon jersey and drop it on the floor at his feet. An old man pushing a cart through the room will pick it up later. The player then peels off his elbow pads before sitting down to work the shin guards off. Then he unlaces and shrugs off his shoulder pads. Next he stands and unbuckles his pants, which look kind of like knickers, except that they're filled with pads to protect the kidneys, thighs, and tailbone. Under this a player will wear compression pants, really a nylon girdle that keeps his thigh muscles warm between shifts. The older guys wear jockstraps under their compression pants. By this point you'd better be done with your questions because there really is no nice, carefree way to interview a bored twenty-two-year-old millionaire who is naked.

Ignore the media guy again when he runs at you, shouting, "No! I told you no!" so loudly that everyone turns to look. Turn pleadingly to Sheldon and wait for the nod. "You don't have to," the media guy says to him.

"No. It's okay," says Sheldon. Thank him silently.

Trail Sheldon across the room, while the players do what they do. They fart, gossip, tell jokes, whip each other with wet towels, make golf plans while buttoning their flannel shirts and tucking them into their jeans. Sheldon, who is down to his compression pants and shower shoes, walks to a laundry bin and rifles through it. He picks out a ragged olive T-shirt, maybe his, and pulls it over his head. You wait. Is there going to be an interview or not? "Come on," he says, and leads you out of the locker room toward the ice. At rink-side he gestures to the bottom row of the stands. You both sit. Thank him again while you paw through the bag holding the Marantz recorder and microphone, your notebook scribbled through with notes on other sports you know little about, from other awkward interviews with other athletes, less famous, less wealthy, but less intimidating too. Fumble for the record button, while he waits. Lift the headphones to your ear and check for sound, while he waits. Formulate a likely first question, while he waits.

Know what you're supposed to do. You're supposed to walk him up the ladder of pain, like all the talk-show hosts do. It seems so easy. When did he first molest you? What happened? And how did you feel about that? The producer of the evening drive-time news wants details, especially about how hard it must be for him to get on in that tough hockey culture. *Be sure to ask him how the other players treat him now,* said the producer, and then he said, *I imagine a cone of silence around him.*

In the weeks following the coach's conviction, Sheldon Kennedy's cone of silence has included interviews with hundreds of reporters who have followed him to and from the rink, to and from the shower, to and from his car. Every day he receives several letters from men who were themselves molested as children. He carries these letters in a separate suitcase on the road. He says he intends to answer them all. Then he says he wants to start a charity for abused kids. Each one of these revelations sets off a new round of stories.

He stares at the floor, at the space of concrete between his bare feet. A likely first question seems to be, "How are you doing?"

"Okay," he says, still looking down.

A likely next question seems to be, "Do you have a therapist?"

Here he flashes his gaze at you. "Yeah," he says. "You know, a guy I can call twice a week. I'll go see him after the season is over."

Strangle the urge to say, "That's no good." Instead, nod enthusiastically and say, "Good. Great."

What you really want to know is how. Not how did he survive? Amateur psychologists ask that. Survival is actually a kind of inertia. Sometimes adolescence is a controlled fall down a steep hill. You tuck and roll. The question of survival is pertinent once you reach the bottom of the hill and find that whole chunks of your character have been scraped away. Stuff you might need later to make friends and love someone. That's where Sheldon sits, at the bottom of that hill, in the middle of a career that's not turning out the way he'd like. He has been lit by the kind of media glare unheard of even in sports celebrity, his name linked inextricably to the worst thing that has ever happened to him. Here he sits on a bench in a chilled arena and hunches his back to make himself smaller. He trembles and smells of smoke. He rocks and works the muscles on his forearms. You want to shake him and say, *I know*. I know your food tastes like mud. I know why you drink. I know you wake up every morning with a headache because you've been gritting your teeth in your sleep. You want to shake him and demand to know, *How are you planning to survive this year?*

But nobody wants to hear the answer to that question.

You want to ask how. How did you do it? How did you walk into a police station and turn him in? How did you sit through police interviews? How did you face him in court, while the coach said, "I didn't do anything"? And then when he said, "I was in love"?

That's what they all say. They say, "I didn't do it." And then they say, "I couldn't help it." Or sometimes they say, "You made me." How do you listen to that and not collapse?

Only certain people would want the answer to that question.

What you ask instead is how. "How is your wife dealing with all of this?"

That brings his head up. "My wife?" he says. He seems annoyed.

Scramble and improvise. "Some people," you say, "some people say that, you know, telling a spouse is the hardest part."

He nods at the floor, and then it's safe to watch him while he talks. "She was the first person I told," he says, and then he talks fast, too fast, about that night and how she listened and how she understood and how she encouraged him to come forward.

Ignore the pang of emotion this confession raises. Check the needle on the recorder.

Hold the microphone close enough to his face to get clear sound.

This is good. You can use this. Never mind that it is truly touching, truly private and, as such, is a kind of violation. That's the deal, trading privacy for fame. You know this, and so does he. Doesn't he?

Don't talk about yourself. Remember what these guys do. They collect cars, watches, wives, addictions, stockbrokers, and mischief. They have depth at the nanny position. They have depth at the girlfriend position. They don't care about your childhood, your ambitions, or how hard it is to be you. So, shut up about all of it. You're not here to make friends.

On the other side of the arena, the Zamboni fires up. The engine roars, and the needle on your aging Marantz recorder pegs accordingly. Sheldon keeps talking about his wife, his decision to step forward, his struggle with the image of a tough hockey player against the reality of being an abused kid. Every bit of it has been drowned out by the Zamboni as it spreads a thin layer of water over the ice, covering the blade marks in preparation for afternoon skating lessons or high school hockey practices. Let him talk anyway.

Don't face him. These questions are too intimate. They are more intimate than even he knows. Direct your questions to the ice, and let him study your face while you talk. Then look at him while he answers. He has learned already not to look at people when he talks about his past. Too often they show their shock and disgust. He looks at the floor, at that same piece of concrete between his shower shoes, or he looks toward the ice, now glassy and smooth and exhaling steam as the new layer of moisture dries. The conversation takes on a rhythm, with each of you looking at the other without being seen. He can flinch at the questions if he wants without feeling shame, and you can flinch at the answers.

Don't talk too long, or there won't be anyone left in the locker room to interview.

Your last question is about his daughter. Will he tell her?

Here comes a sad smile. He talks about taking her on long drives into the country and about how she is the only person to whom he can confess everything that was done to him and every irrational fear about his own insanity. "She's only five months old," he says. "She can't judge me."

Wonder at the two halves of your brain working at once. One side says, *Don't use this; it's too personal.* The other side says, *Use this at all costs; it's so personal.*

Shake his hand at the end and say again, thank you for your time. "You listened," he says. "Most of them don't." Nod sagely. Let him walk to the locker room alone, then follow. Interview the captain, who is nice because he has to be, and the goon, who is wide-eyed with admiration for Sheldon's bravery. The Harvard guy has already gone home.

Go home and cry as you log tape and as you write. Hate the story but turn it in anyway. Feel dismay when others say they love it, especially the quote about the baby.

Afterward, when another sportswriter asks about the interview, confess that you wanted to soothe Sheldon and offer advice but held back. Listen to this writer when he says, "Good. That's not your job." It's not professional to offer comfort, not in a newsroom, and certainly not in a locker room. At some point, every reporter wishes to shed the role of public informant to become a person, to be recognized as a caring or interesting individual to one of these men. Remember that individuals do not get invited into locker rooms. Individuals do not get paid to ask personal questions of celebrities. Only reporters do.

A month later accept another assignment to report on the team's historic losing streak. Go back to the same stinky room filled with the same sweaty guys. Ask stupid questions like: How does it feel to lose thirteen games in a row? How do you think the fans feel? Are you guys going to be able to turn this around?

Ignore Sheldon. It's the least you can do. Finally, he has stopped giving interviews. He laughs and jokes and sets tee times even though his stats are horrible, his ice time has dwindled. He has a towel wrapped around his waist when he walks by you, and then he turns, pointing one index finger. He squints as he looks at your face. "You interviewed me," he says.

Say, "Yes. Thank you. I appreciated that."

Don't say, "Everyone in North America interviewed you." Don't say that.

Accept his outstretched hand and shake it.

"I remember you," he says.

Mumble something nonsensical about your assignment. Feel fully the urge to say more. Thank him again for his time, and don't watch him walk away.

Forget the dreams in which you hug him and tell him he's going to be okay. Suppress the daydreams in which you admonish him not to try to be the perfect victim, in which you insist that he fire that stupid long-distance therapist and hire somebody real. Tell yourself over and over again to stop thinking about him.

Later, accept another assignment about the team's now-historic plunge to the very bottom of the NHL standings. *Dead last place*, you are told to ask, *how does that feel?* And so you find yourself in front of the Harvard guy who is wearing only a jockstrap, saying, "Do you think fans are frustrated?" The look on his face suggests that he could punch you.

Wander back out to the arena, where the coach lines up pucks to shoot them into the net. Everyone knows he will be fired tomorrow after the final game of the season. He seems relieved.

Walk past Sheldon, who is standing outside the ice, still wearing all his gear. He holds his hockey stick upright like a staff and chats with someone in the stands. Still, he turns to you when you pass. "I know you," he says.

"Yes."

"You interviewed me," he says.

Say "Yes" again, stupidly. "Thank you. I appreciate it. How are you?"

"Okay," he says, and his gaze flicks away and then back.

Next month he will be traded away. He will return to Canada and to the minor leagues until an injury ends his career. In Canada, he will launch a national campaign to raise money for other survivors of sexual abuse. Then he will take a regular job and sequester himself away from reporters like you.

He tucks his right glove under his left arm, removes his hand, and extends it. Take it. Feel the heat and the sweat in his palm. Know that this is the moment you will regret forever. This is the moment to say, "I know about this, and you're going to be okay. One day you will smile and trade small talk, and it won't seem like everyone else lives at the other end of a long tube." This is the chance to say, "Forgive yourself for attracting his notice. Forgive yourself for your complicit acts, for your own dogged silence. It's the only way."

Don't say anything like that. Don't say any of the caring things that decent people say after a shared confidence. Don't even say something meaningless, like, "Hang in there." Smile coolly instead, and say the only thing a reporter ever says to an athlete after an interview. Say, "Thank you for your time."

NICK ST. JOHN

■

Further Notes on My Unfortunate Condition

FROM a self-published mini-comic

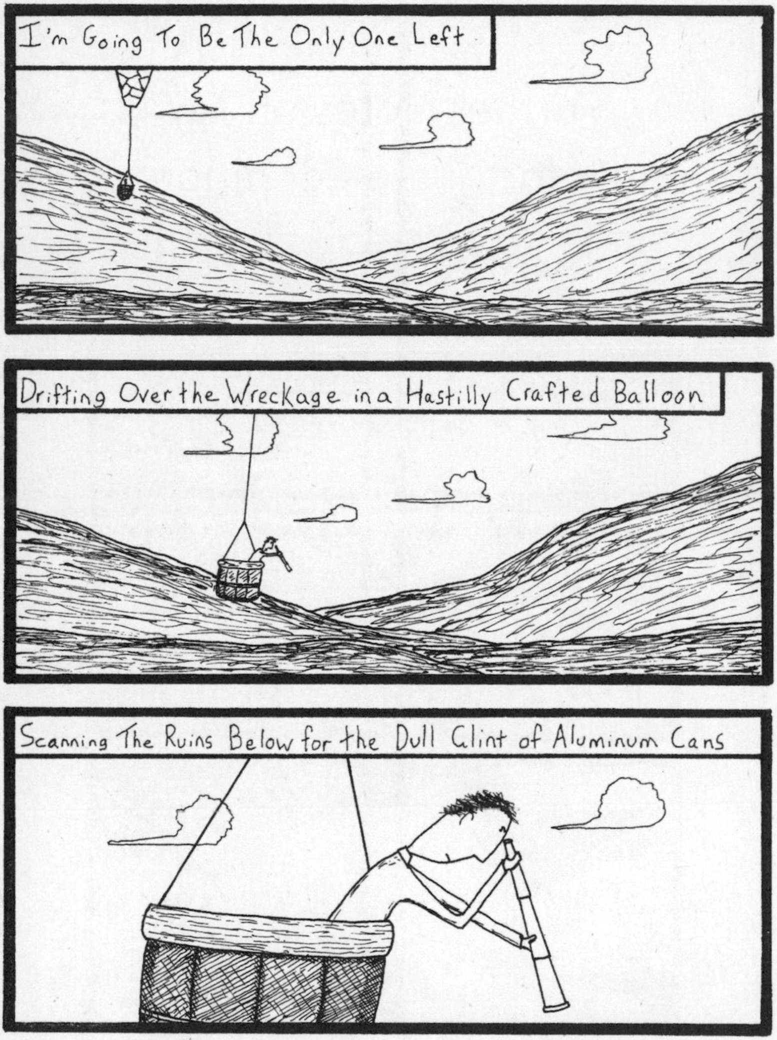
I'm Going To Be The Only One Left
Drifting Over the Wreckage in a Hastilly Crafted Balloon
Scanning The Ruins Below for the Dull Glint of Aluminum Cans

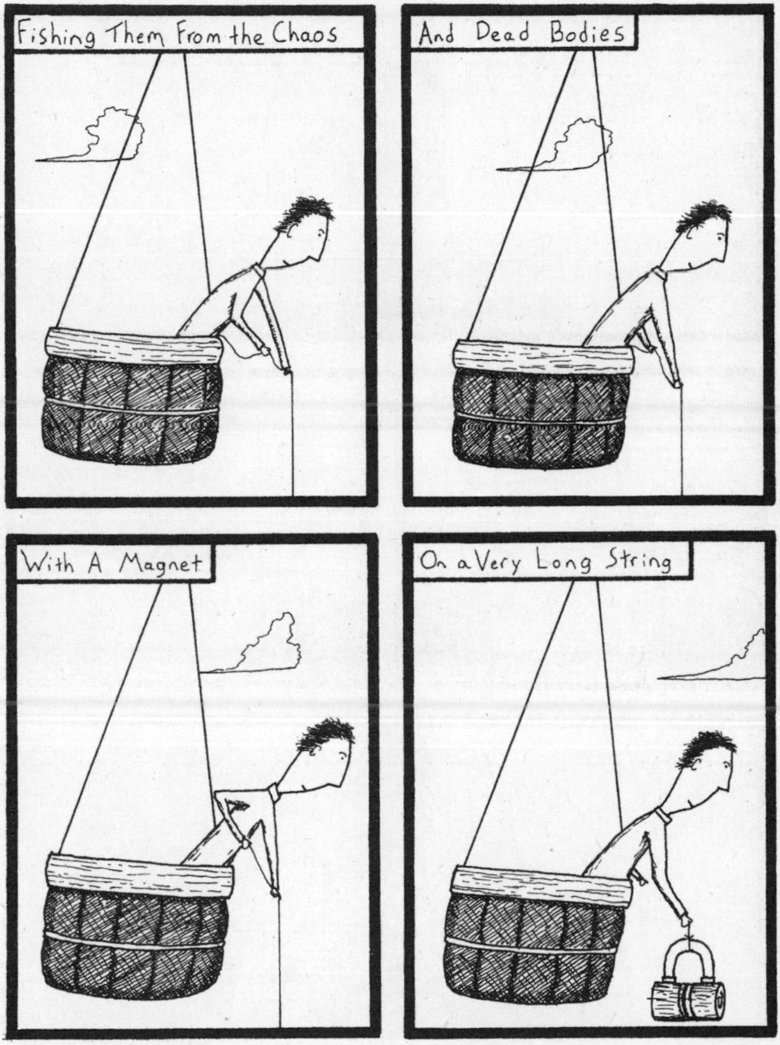
Fishing Them From the Chaos
And Dead Bodies
With A Magnet
On a Very Long String

Of Course The Labels Will Have Burned Off
Opening Each Can Will Yield A Surprise
Like Unwrapping A Birthday Present
I'm Going To Be So Happy

Dear Claire,

  Yesterday Someone Asked Me What The Most Formative Experience of My Childhood Was.

I Remembered One Night When We Were Small and I Lay Sleeping In My Bed.

In the Middle of the Night You Crept In

Creak!

And You Said To Me, Get Up. We Have To Do Something.

And You Were Perfect and Infallible, So I Followed Without Asking Questions.

We Went To the Shed and Got Two of Dad's Shovels.

The Heads Rusted and the Wooden Handles Worn Smooth by His Hands.

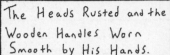

We Carried Them Across the Field and Into the Orchard.

Where You Told Me We Were Going To Dig For the Lost Corpse of Our Great Uncle Xavier.

I Still Remember How Dark the Shadows Were Beneath the Trees

And How Unafraid I Was.

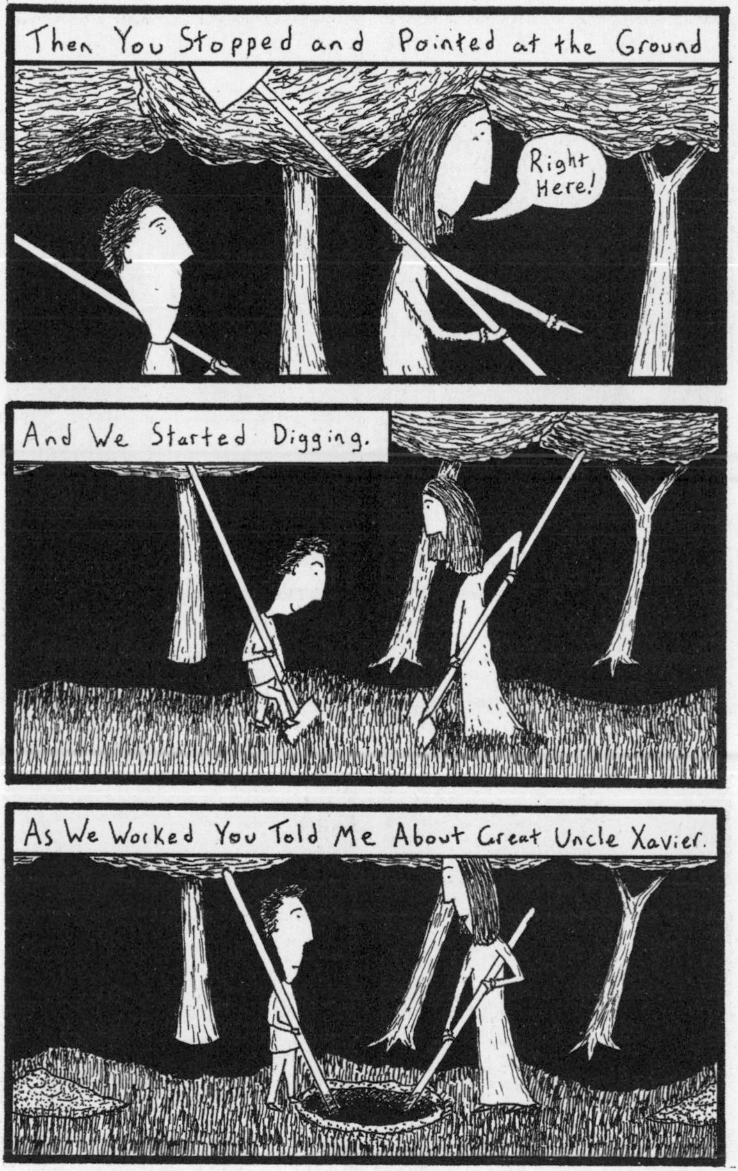
Then You Stopped and Pointed at the Ground
Right Here!
And We Started Digging.
As We Worked You Told Me About Great Uncle Xavier.

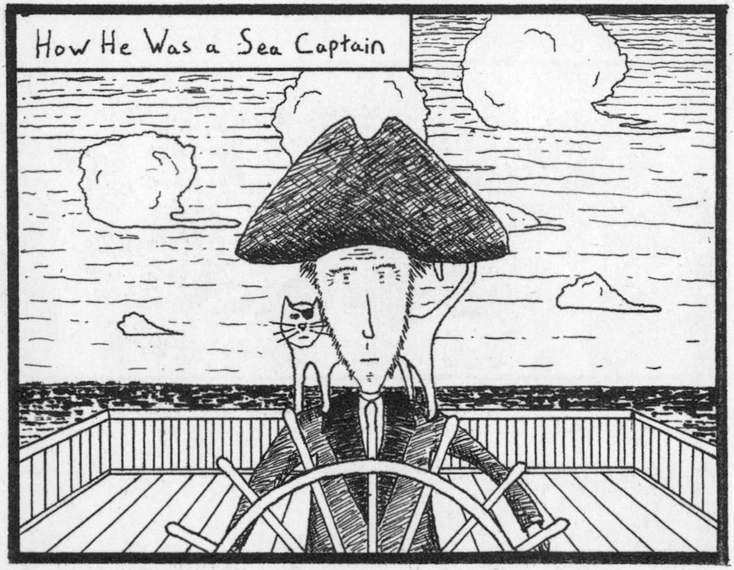
How He Was a Sea Captain

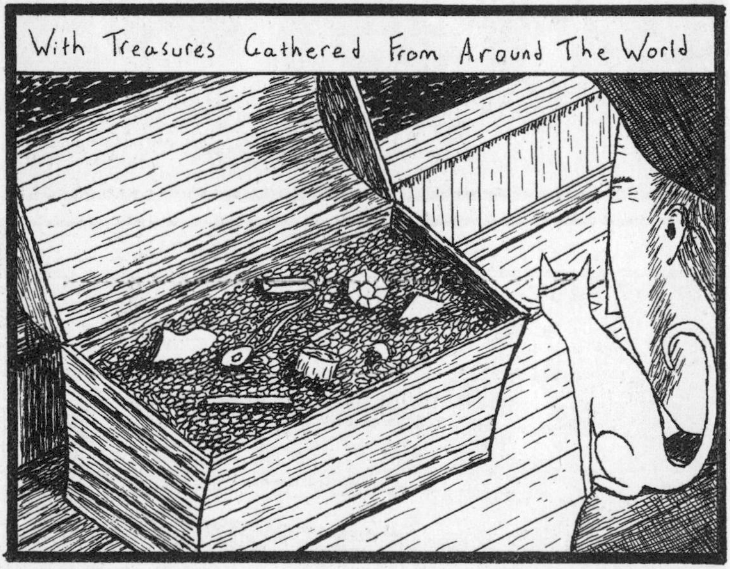
With Treasures Gathered From Around The World

How He Buried These Treasures in a Secret Place
And Later, With The Only Map Still in His Pocket,
Was Himself Buried

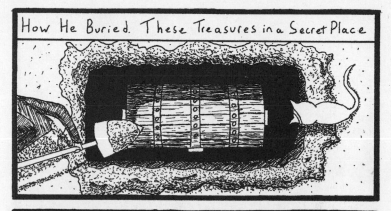

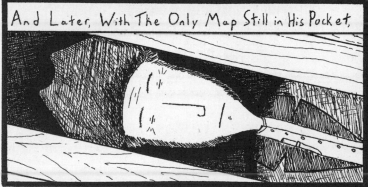

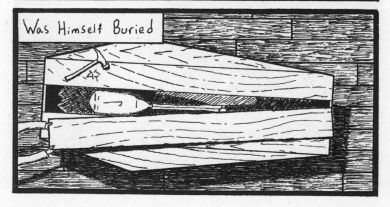

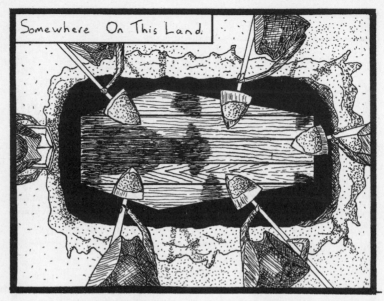

Somewhere On This Land.

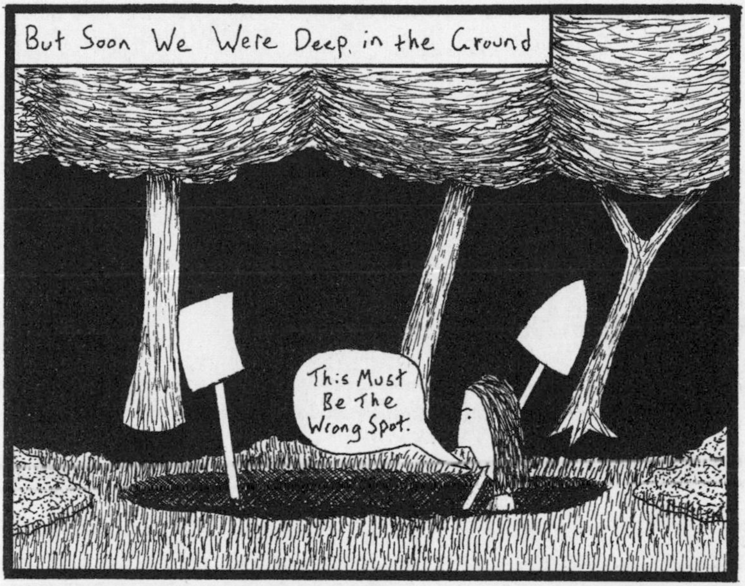
But Soon We Were Deep in the Ground
This Must Be The Wrong Spot.

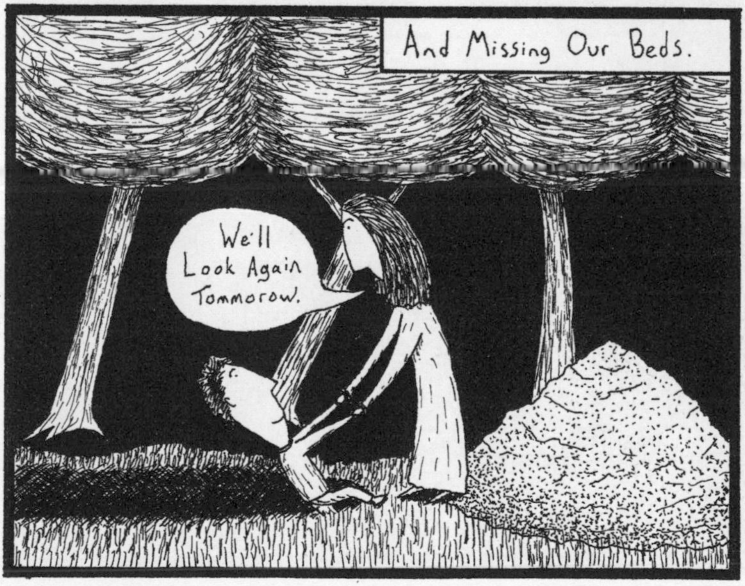
And Missing Our Beds.
We'll Look Again Tommorow.

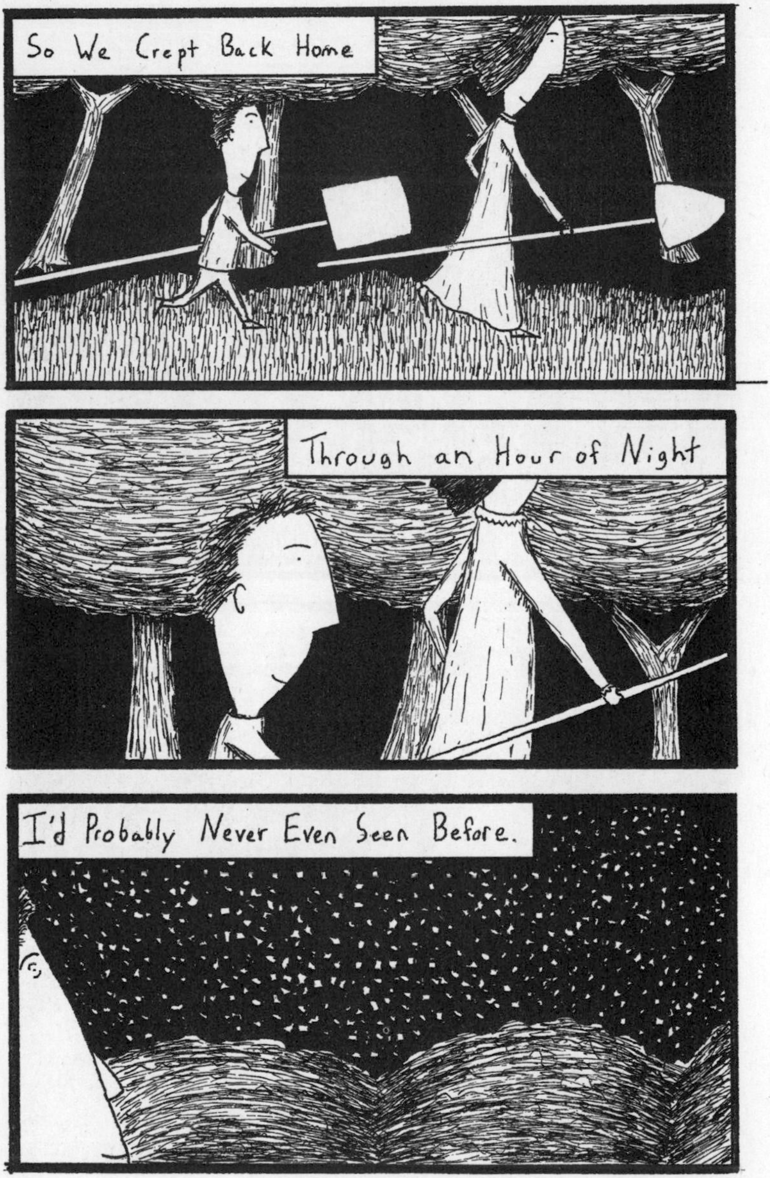
So We Crept Back Home
Through an Hour of Night
I'd Probably Never Even Seen Before.

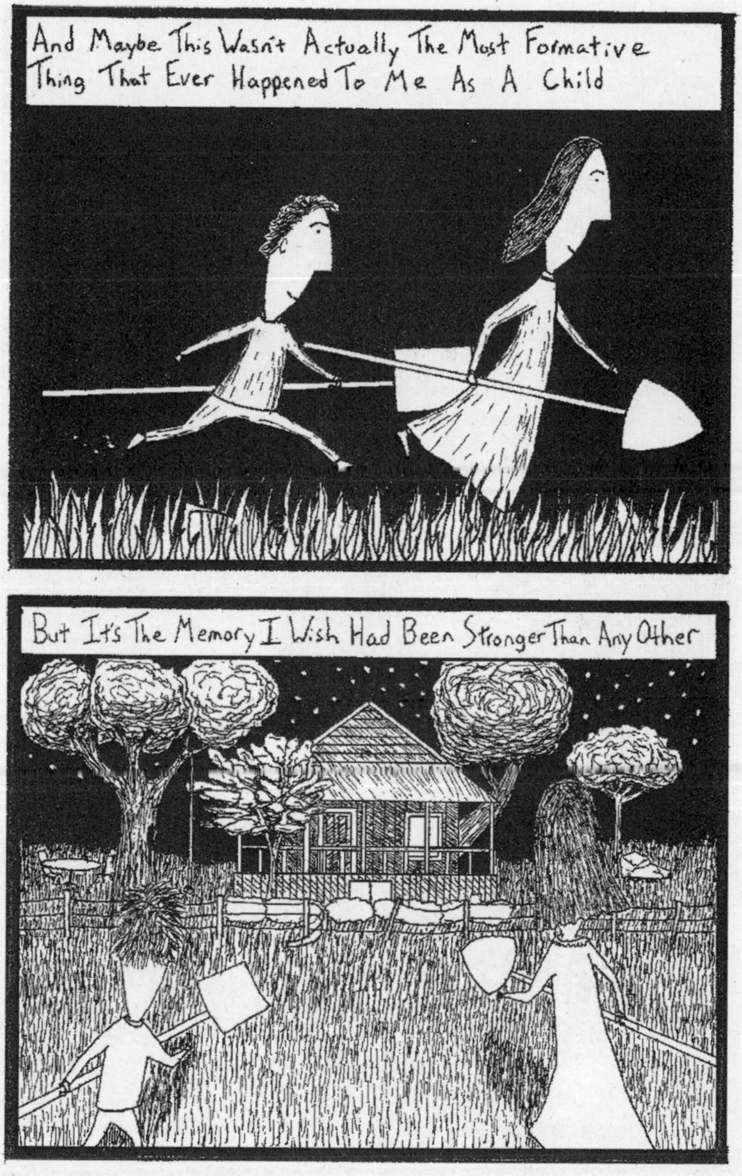
And Maybe This Wasn't Actually The Most Formative Thing That Ever Happened To Me As A Child
But It's The Memory I Wish Had Been Stronger Than Any Other

The Event To Which I Trace All of the Best Parts of Myself.

Tell Me Again Why I Can't Be a Mantaray

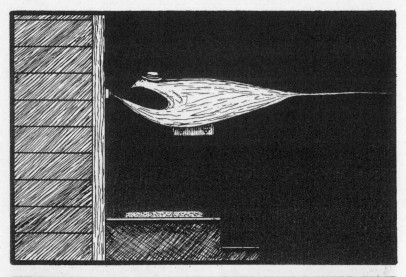

Everyone is So God Damned Happy To See Me

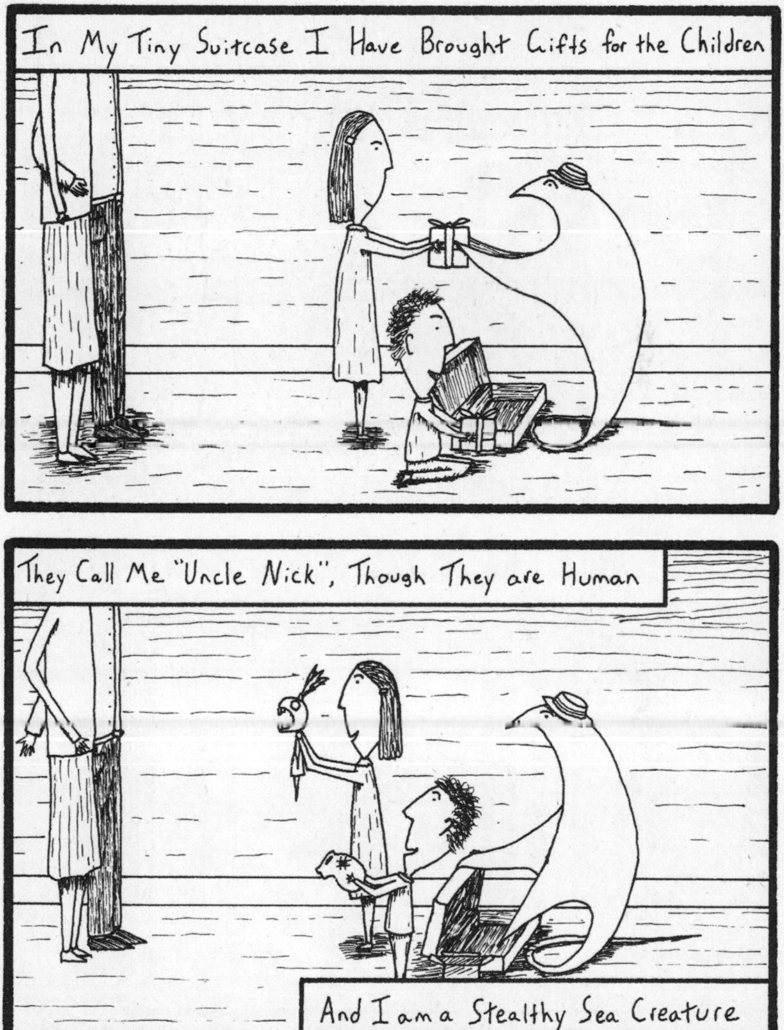
In My Tiny Suitcase I Have Brought Gifts for the Children
They Call Me "Uncle Nick", Though They are Human
And I am a Stealthy Sea Creature

Beside the Fire I Tell Them Stories of the Places I've Been

Glad for a Moments Respite From the Cold Outside

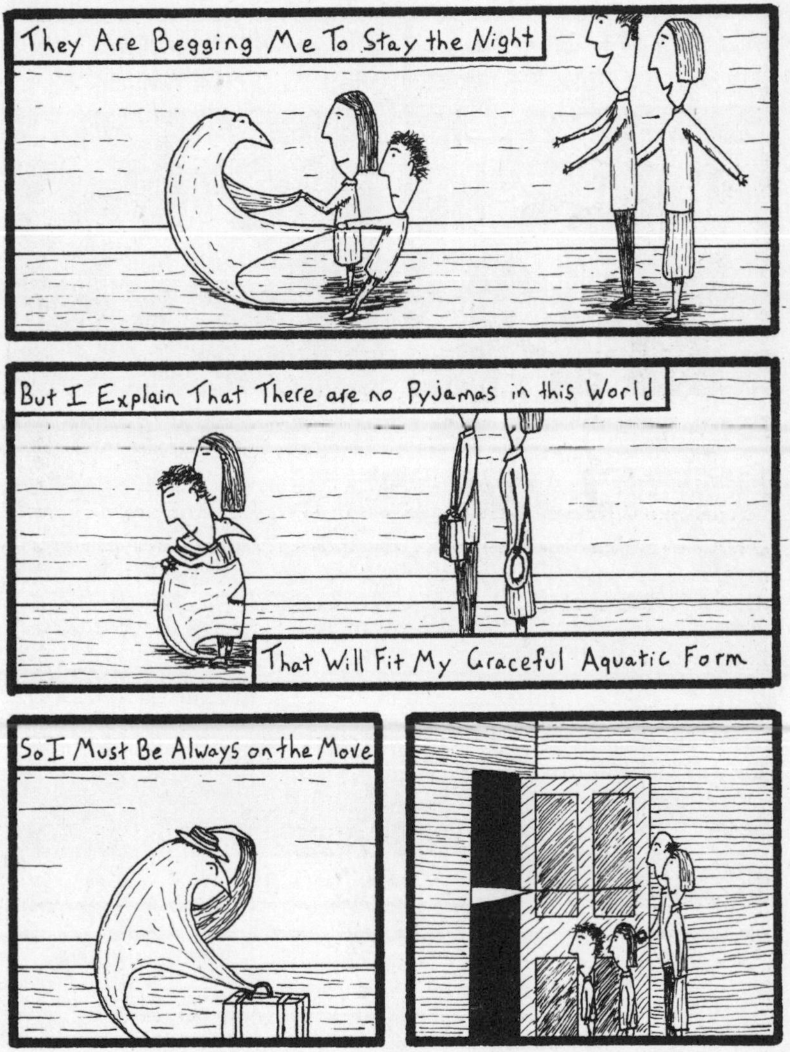
They Are Begging Me To Stay the Night
But I Explain That There are no Pyjamas in this World
That Will Fit My Graceful Aquatic Form
So I Must Be Always on the Move

Tell Me Just One More Time

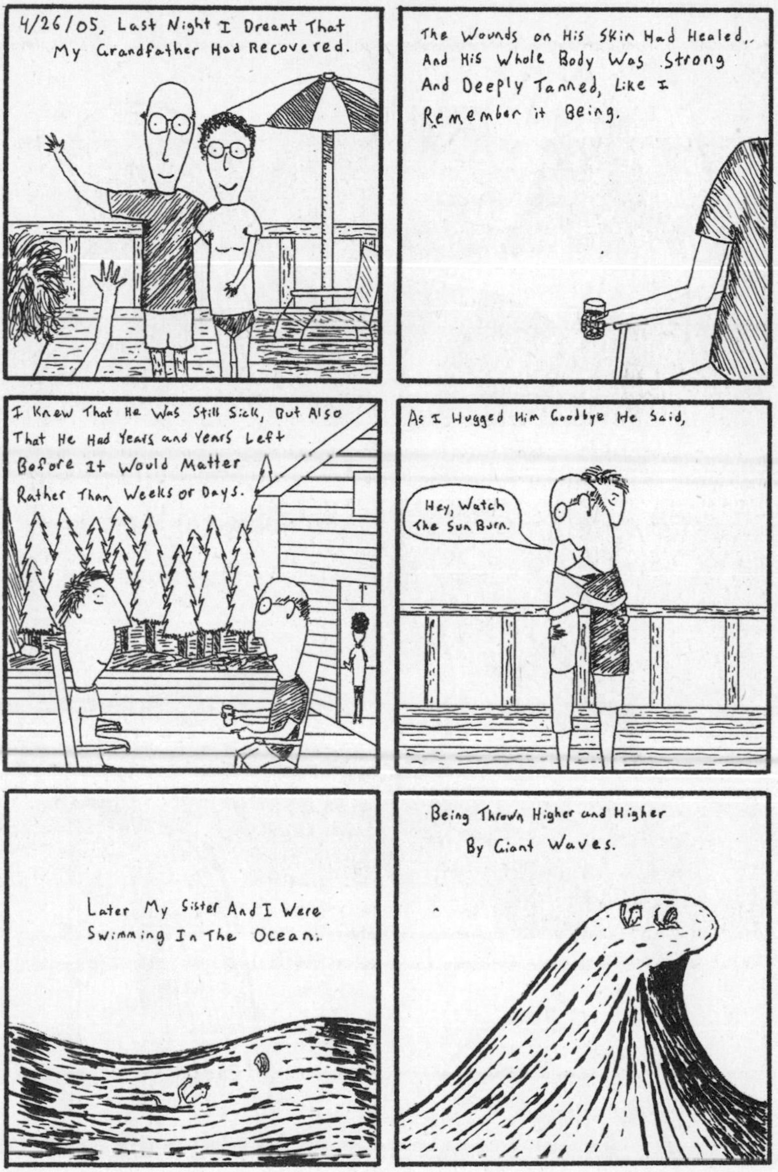
4/26/05, Last Night I Dreamt That My Grandfather Had Recovered.
The Wounds on His Skin Had Healed, And His Whole Body Was Strong And Deeply Tanned, Like I Remember it Being.
I Knew That He Was Still Sick, But Also That He Had Years and Years Left Before It Would Matter Rather Than Weeks or Days.
As I Hugged Him Goodbye He Said,
Hey, Watch The Sun Burn.
Later My Sister And I Were Swimming In The Ocean.
Being Thrown Higher and Higher By Giant Waves.

If We Caught Them Right They Would Surge Upward, Carrying Us Thousands of Feet In To The Sky.

Then Fall Away.

Leaving Us To Plummet Like Skydivers

And Crash Back In To The Ocean.

We Swam Straight In To The Tallest Wave We'd Ever Seen and Rode It Upward Until The Buildings Below Looked Like Tiny Specks.

At the Very Top We Caught Hold of a Giant Chairlift Pole Towering Inexplicably Over the Ocean, Attached To Nothing.

But When We Looked Down
The Ocean Was Gone.
The tide must have pulled it away.
So We Hung There Over The Dry Sand, Somehow Calm, Though Knowing We'd Eventually Have To Fall.
I'm Really Going to Miss My Grandfather.

CONTRIBUTORS' NOTES

Banksy is a graffiti artist from Bristol, England. His work has appeared recently on the wall between Israel and the West Bank, in the Lower Ninth Ward of New Orleans, and in an exhibit on Seventh Avenue in New York City.

Stories and nonfiction by **Rebecca Bengal** have been published in *The Believer, The Washington Post Magazine, Southwest Review, New York, Oxford American,* and elsewhere. She is at work on a novel, *June Gloom,* and a collection of stories.

Eula Biss is the author of *The Balloonists* and *Notes from No Man's Land: American Essays,* winner of the 2008 Graywolf Press Nonfiction Prize. She teaches nonfiction writing at Northwestern University and is coeditor of Essay Press, a small press dedicated to innovative nonfiction. Her essays have recently appeared in *The Best Creative Nonfiction* and the *Touchstone Anthology of Contemporary Nonfiction* as well as in *The Believer, Ninth Letter, The Iowa Review,* and *Harper's Magazine.*

Émile Bravo was born in Paris in 1964. In 1995 he founded the Vosges Studio along with David B., Christophe Blain, Joann Sfar, Emmanuel Guibert, and Frédéric Boilet. He is best known for the multivolume album series *Les Épatantes Aventures de Jules* (*The Thrilling Adventures of Jules*), published by Dargaud, for which he won the Goscinny Outstanding New Writer Award at the 2002 Angoulême Festival.

Susan Breen's first novel, *The Fiction Class*, was published by Plume in 2008. Her short stories have appeared in a number of journals, among them *American Literary Review* and *North Dakota Quarterly*. She teaches creative writing in the Gotham Writers' Workshop in New York.

Philip Connors is writing a book about being a fire lookout, to be published by Ecco. He lives in New Mexico.

Nathan Englander is the author of the story collection *For the Relief of Unbearable Urges* (Knopf, 1999) and the novel *The Ministry of Special Cases* (Knopf, 2007). His fiction and essays have been published in *The New Yorker*, *The New York Times*, *The Atlantic Monthly*, *The Washington Post*, and anthologized in *The O. Henry Prize Anthology* and numerous editions of *The Best American Short Stories*. Englander was selected as one of "20 Writers for the 21st Century" by *The New Yorker*, received a Guggenheim fellowship, a PEN/Malamud Award, and the Sue Kaufman Prize from the American Academy of Arts and Letters. He is currently at work on a novel.

Summarily dismissed from every restaurant he ever tried to work in, **Nick Flynn** ended up working as a ship's captain, an electrician, and a caseworker for homeless adults. His books of poetry and nonfiction include *Some Ether*, *Another Bullshit Night in Suck City*, and *The Ticking Is the Bomb*. Film credits include artistic collaborator on the feature documentary *Darwin's Nightmare*, which was nominated for an Academy Award in 2006. Each spring he teaches at the University of Houston, and then he spends the rest of the year in Brooklyn.

Castle Freeman, Jr., is a novelist, short story writer, and essayist living in southern Vermont.

Jonathan Franzen is the author of *The Twenty-Seventh City, Strong Motion, The Corrections, How to Be Alone,* and, most recently, *The Discomfort Zone.* He lives in New York City and Santa Cruz, California.

Rebekah Frumkin is a resident of Chicago, Illinois. Her stories have appeared in *Grimm Magazine, The Common Review,* and *Scrivener Creative Review,* among other places.

Rivka Ricky Galchen answers to many names, but most lovingly to "Rufus." She is the author of the novel *Atmospheric Disturbances.*

J. Malcolm Garcia's work has appeared in a variety of magazines and newspapers and has been included in *The Best American Travel Writing* and *The Best American Nonrequired Reading.* His memoir, *The Khaarijee: A Chronicle of Friendship and War in Kabul* (Beacon Press) will be released in fall 2009.

Anne Gisleson teaches writing at the New Orleans Center for Creative Arts, Louisiana's arts conservatory for high school students. She has published poetry, fiction, and nonfiction in various places. She also helps run Press Street, a nonprofit which promotes art and literature in the community through events, publications, and art education.

David Grann is a staff writer at *The New Yorker* and the author of the *New York Times* bestseller *The Lost City of Z: A Tale of Deadly Obsession in the Amazon.* An anthology of his stories will be published by Doubleday next year.

For the past four years, **Daniel Heyman** has concentrated his art on making images about the war in Iraq, specifically the abuse and torture of innocent Iraqis at Abu Ghraib and other prisons. For the work in this book, Heyman traveled to Jordan and Turkey, where he has talked face-to-face with over forty-five former detainees, painting their portraits and taking down their own versions of what happened to them at the hands of their American captors. Three of these detainees have since been killed in the war. He has also met and drawn the portraits of survivors of the September 16, 2007, Blackwater attacks at Nasoor Square in Baghdad. Many museums and libraries have acquired portfolios of Heyman's work, including the Library of Congress, the New York Public Library, the Yale University Art Gallery, the Baltimore Museum of Art, and the Minneapolis Institute of Arts. Heyman was awarded a 2009 Pew Fellowship in the Arts and holds degrees from Dartmouth College and the University of Pennsylvania. He currently teaches at Swarthmore and the Rhode Island School of Design.

Denis Johnson is a poet, short story writer, and novelist. He was born in 1929 in Munich, and his novel *Tree of Smoke* (2007) won the National Book Award. He lives in Arizona and Idaho.

Tom Kaczynski learned English by reading American capitalist comics in communist Poland. He studied art and architecture as preparation for becoming a cartoonist. His comics have appeared in *MOME, Punk Planet, The Drama,* and the *Backwards City Review.* Even though he's lived in Minneapolis (with his girlfriend, Nikki, and two black cats) for two years, many people still think he lives in New York. Tom also writes a blog (www.transatlantis.net), but that's not a distinguishing characteristic.

Amelia Kahaney's short stories have appeared in *Crazyhorse* and *One Story,* among other publications. She earned her MFA in fiction from Brooklyn College, where she now teaches creative writing and composition. She lives in a lopsided apartment with her son and her husband, the writer Gabriel Sanders, and is at work on a novel and more stories.

Rebecca Makkai's fiction has appeared in *The Best American Short Stories 2009* and *2008,* and in various journals, including *The Three-penny Review, Shenandoah,* and *The Iowa Review.* She also has a story in the forthcoming *Best American Fantasy 3* (Underland Press). She lives north of Chicago with her husband and daughter, and teaches at a Montessori school.

Yannick Murphy's latest novel is *Signed, Mata Hari* and her most recent collection of stories is *In a Bear's Eye.*

The artwork of **Tucker Nichols** has been featured in exhibitions and publications around the world. He is represented by ZieherSmith Gallery in New York. He lives near San Francisco.

Matthew Power has reported from post-tsunami Thailand and post-Taliban Afghanistan, documented the lives of dump scavengers in Manila, ridden motorcycles through the Kashmir Himalaya and the Bolivian Andes, and hopped freight trains across Canada and Mexico. Power is a contributing editor at *Harper's Magazine* and *National Geographic Adventure*, and his writing has appeared in *The New York Times*, *Men's Journal*, *Wired*, *GQ*, *Discover*, *The Virginia Quarterly Review*, *Granta*, *Slate*, *The Best American Spiritual Writing 2006*, and *The Best American Travel Writing 2007*. He grew up in Vermont and lives in Brooklyn.

Marjane Satrapi is a graphic novelist, illustrator, and animator. She was born in Iran and is the author of *Persepolis* and *Chicken with Plums*. Her work has been published on the op-ed page of *The New York Times*.

K. G. Schneider is a librarian and a writer who, in 2006, relocated from Northern California to Florida with her partner, two cats, a frightening number of books, and an invalid marriage license. She has an MFA from the University of San Francisco and has been published in *White Crane*, *Nerve*, *Gastronomica*, *The Best Creative Nonfiction, Volume 2*, and *Powder: Writing from Women in the Ranks*.

Olivier Schrauwen studied animation at the Academy of Art in Gent, and comics at the Saint Luc in Brussels. He has contributed to publications such as *Hic Sunt Leones*, *Beeldstorm*, *Demo*, *INK*, *Zone5300*, and *Spirou*. He contributes regularly to the Fantagraphics anthology *MOME*. He lives in Berlin.

Michelle Seaton has been a frequent contributor to the NPR sports show *Only a Game* for fourteen years, covering everything from competitive bird watching to the National Hockey League. She created the curriculum (and is the lead instructor) for Boston's Memoir Project, a program that offers free writing classes to senior citizens in Boston city neighborhoods. The project's two anthologies are *Born Before Plastic* and *My Legacy Is Simply This*. She teaches memoir writing and other mischief at Grub Street, Inc., and is the coauthor of several books, including *The Way of Boys: Raising Healthy Boys in a Challenging and Complex World* (William Morrow, 2009).

Nick St. John lives in San Francisco, where he is currently working on several comic projects and a novel. *Further Notes on My Unfortunate Condition* is his first published work.

Nick Twemlow was a Fulbright fellow in New Zealand, where he is researching the life of his great-aunt, who was a novelist. His poems have appeared in *A Public Space, Court Green, Fence, Sentence*, and *Volt*. He is married to the poet Robyn Schiff.

THE *BEST AMERICAN*
NONREQUIRED READING
COMMITTEE

THIS YEAR, the student committee in San Francisco was joined from afar by a group of intrepid Michigan high schoolers. Based at 826 Michigan (in Ann Arbor) and under the guidance of Jared Hawkley, this contingent of the *Best American Nonrequired Reading* committee — like the students in San Francisco — dug up articles and stories, read them, argued over their merits and flaws, and helped with the massive task of assembling this book.

 Fiona Armour graduated from the Creative Writing department at the San Francisco School of the Arts. This picture of her was taken just outside McSweeney's HQ on a blustery spring day. She has wanted a dog forever and feels that this year is the year. She's from San Francisco.

Adrianne Batiste is from Oakland and she is now a freshman at the University of San Francisco studying finance and business. She is also exploring her artistic aspirations of becoming a poet and/or a lyricist. She loves chocolate. She also loves experiencing different cultures. She has traveled to Japan, Ecuador, the Galápagos Islands, and Mexico, and hopes to continue her travels while embracing many walks of life. Adrianne would prefer that you direct fan mail to her secretary, Virginia Urzua.

Molly Bolten is a senior at Castileja School. She lives in Atherton, California. Likes include talking, eating, writing, driving, and painting things that are not paper (and also things that are paper). Dislikes include cough medicine and writing bibliographies. Her favorite character in *The Lion King* is Scar. A person in China recently told her that she was a "cool type" and that she looked like Tibby from *The Sisterhood of the Traveling Pants*. Molly has yet to respond to this comment.

Julia Butz is currently a junior at Greenhills School in Ann Arbor, Michigan. She likes to play soccer and field hockey and writes a fashion column for her school newspaper. Waterskiing with friends and listening to music is her idea of a wonderful day. She thinks that family dinners are awe- some, and she would jump at the opportunity to travel almost anywhere. Julia has really enjoyed working on this edition of the book and hopes to be involved with the next one too.

 Adam and Eva Colás are, respectively, an Ann Arbor high school junior (prospective filmmaker) and a graduate (prospective Eastern Michigan University student/writer). They are siblings. That is to say that they are brother and sister (respectively). They have mutually been at 826michigan for over three years. If Adam were a vegetable he would be celery. If Eva were a type of mythical creature she would be a dwarf(ette). He makes movies and she makes stories. Respectively.

Joseph Cotsirilos has been a part of 826 Valencia since its beginning. He lives in Berkeley. He did not kill Karl. In his spare time, Joseph enjoys browsing comic book shops, working on his zine, and playing the acoustic bass. He also listens to horribly repetitive music, draws naked people on Saturday mornings (he tells his parents they're figure drawing classes), and attends bizarre functions on Saturday nights thrown in very questionable locations. He comes back on Sunday mornings with stories that both amaze and disgust his friends and family. He keeps a very detailed log of his adventures and reads it aloud to his cats. They don't care. They're cats. They never liked Karl anyway. *[Editor's note: Karl was a beloved pufferfish, mascot of 826 Valencia. Ten-year-old Joseph stuck his finger in the tank and Karl, mistak-*

ing it for lunch, bit down hard. Responding to the pain evoked by Karl's parrot-like-beak, Joseph pulled his finger quickly out of the tank with Karl still firmly attached. Karl flew through the air in a perfect arc, landing on the floor ten feet away from the tank. Although promptly replaced back into his aquatic environment, Karl died two days later. May Karl rest in peace.]

Elizabeth Deatrick is currently enjoying a gap year in Ann Arbor, Michigan, between homeschool and Wesleyan University. A published writer, Elizabeth thinks *Best American Nonrequired Reading* is the best thing since sliced bread, and quite possibly since unsliced bread. She's passionate about her volunteer work at the Toledo Zoo, her family's farm, writing, birds of prey (both the animals and the Klingon starships), and obscure British sci-fi TV shows.

Carlina Duan is a junior at Pioneer High School in Ann Arbor, Michigan. She has a passion for bright colors, and also craves the spoken word. She is a staff writer for her school paper and wants to pursue a career in journalism.

Sam Freund is a graduate of Ypsilanti High School in Michigan and proudly represents the Y-Town. He has hopes of becoming a published writer and is most likely working on that now. If not, then he is probably studying at whatever college he currently goes to. He is an avid comic book reader and being able to write one (*Deadpool*) for a living is his dream. Or being a rapper. He'd be cool with that too.

Will Gray is a senior at Crystal Springs High School. He's from San Mateo, California. Will does not like to discuss dead cats. In his free time he enjoys reading, eating ramen, and playing Ultimate Frisbee. He is also very pale, or so his friends claim.

Yael Green is from San Francisco. She graduated from School of the Arts in San Francisco, where she studied creative writing, and is now a freshman at NYU. She misses Tuesday nights at McSweeney's and all the wonderful people she met there.

Michelle Grifka is a junior at Community High School in Ann Arbor, Michigan. While she loves sarcasm and humor, she is incapable of writing a witty bio. She writes fantasy, draws, sings, and dances, as well as casually speaks Spanish in front of her French-speaking friends. She intends to be a doctor. However, in a perfect, salary-free world, she would be a voice actress/formalwear designer.

 Sophia Hussain is a freshman at Wesleyan University. While on the committee she lived in Greenbrae, California. She aspires to be the next Woodward or Bernstein. She enjoys getting the *New York Times* on Sunday mornings and she likes everything except math.

Bora Lee is from Berkeley, California. This fall she is attending Brown University. She is excited to experience actual seasons. Bora enjoys four-part harmony and iambic pentameter. She appreciates neither hyperbolic statements nor too much color.

 Graham Liddell grew up in Livonia, Michigan. He lived the suburban life: neighborhood lemonade stands to bike tag to basketball to skateboarding. Finally he settled on music. Music tried to explain the aspects of life that no one really understood. And this questioning of life and life's responses led him to find a deep love for literature and the arts. Graham is a member of the band Knockturne and is a freshman in college. He aspires to create songs, stories, or movies for a living.

Charley Locke is a senior at Berkeley High School, where she enjoys writing faux-Republican opinion articles for the school newspaper and studying languages, dead or alive. She has acted in many plays and she specializes in playing little sisters. She lives in Oz.

 Tanea Lunsford, currently a freshman at Columbia University in New York City, is an eighteen-year-old San Francisco native. She enjoys learning new things of all kinds, advocating for the righting of wrongs, and traveling. She has completed a senior thesis and graduated from San

Francisco School of the Arts. She is as excited as one can get about college and life thereafter.

Roxie Perkins, a native of Albany, California, attended Albany High School during her time working on *Best American Nonrequired Reading*. By the time you read this, she will be a proud freshman at UCLA. Apart from reading and talking about stories, she enjoys writing plays, reading 'zines, and talking. She has been paralyzingly afraid of deep sea creatures since the age of eight, and has been writing since the age of seven; both fascinations contribute equally in her determination to lead a land-dwelling, literary life.

 Barnaby Thomas Root is an accidentalist philosopher currently finishing his senior year at Community High School in Ann Arbor, Michigan. Barnaby has been with 826 Michigan on and off for about two years. He loves cardboard, making pterodactyl noises, and freaking out when anyone mentions the name Karen O. He has also been a radio host at WCBN-FM for a little over a year. So there.

Rachel Shevrin is a high school junior in Ann Arbor, Michigan. She has enjoyed working on this project very much because of the funny-weird people she got to meet, but also, of course, for all the great short stories she got to read and discuss with these odd people. When Rachel Shevrin is not reading, she is often at school, at dance, or outside in the sun.

 Virginia Urzua is from Oakland, where she is a senior at Oakland Unity High School. She enjoys soldering transistors, LEDs, and capacitors. She enjoys creating art while listening to foreign music. Virginia would prefer you direct fan mail to her secretary, Adrianne Batiste.

Chloe Villegas is a junior at International High School. She writes short stories about lions and keeps fit by struggling with a variety of instruments daily. The famous Chloe hat is indeed a "cat hat," but on occasion a "wolf hat," too. She lives in San Francisco.

Marley Walker is a junior at San Francisco's School for the Arts. She is currently left-handed, is a vegetarian, and enjoys squeaking, playing the bass guitar, and eating mangoes. She took on writing because her friends told her there was no future in squeaking.

Eli Wolfe is an eighteen-year-old writer and a freshman at University of California, Santa Cruz. He is from San Francisco. He graduated from San Francisco School of the Arts. Eli has gotten a haircut since this photo was taken. He wishes you weren't so concerned with looks.

Shelley Zhang is a junior at Pioneer High School in Ann Arbor, Michigan. She loves pasta, sunshine, mango-melon flavored Starbursts, reading prose and policy debate. Shelley cherishes her bucket list and before she dies, she's going to visit Switzerland, be vegetarian, drive a zamboni, and intentionally forget Daylight Savings Day for a week. Shelley hopes to graduate from college soon and aspires to freewrite as a hobby along with her undecided career.

Special thanks to assistant (to the) managing editor **Jared Hawkley**, and to editorial assistants **Lauren Walbridge** and **Michael Zelenko**. Thanks also to the following people and organizations: 826 Valencia, 826 Michigan, 826 Seattle, Houghton Mifflin Harcourt, Adrienne Mahar, Jaclyn Bordelon, Sandy Nathan, Brian McMullen, Eli Horowitz, Andrew Leland, Jordan Bass, Juliet Litman, Christopher Benz, Darren Franich, Graham Weatherly, Report McNally, Angela Petrella, Heidi Meredith, Mimi Lok, Chris Ying, Eliana Stein, Michelle Quint, Greg Larson, Laura Howard, Lauren Hall, Eugenie Howard Johnston, Jory John, Cherylle Taylor, Ninive Caligari, Leigh Lehman, Justin Carder, Yvonne Wang, Marisa Gedney, Emilie Coulson, Connor Timmons, Angi Stevens, Lauren Koski, Amy Sumerton, Amanda Uhle, Stephanie Long, Lauren LoPrete, Bruce Robertson, Ibarra Brothers, and Golden Gate Copy Service.

NOTABLE
NONREQUIRED READING
OF 2008

CHRIS ABANI
   Coming to America, *Tarpaulin Sky*
JON ADAMS
   Truth Serum, *City Cyclops*
DANIEL ALARCÓN
   The Idiot President, *The New Yorker*
DAWSEN WRIGHT ALBERTSEN
   Chris Stops the Boys, *Post Road*
WOODY ALLEN
   A Little Face Work Never Hurt, *Zoetrope: All-Story*
SCOTT ALAN ANDERSON
   Saints Alive, *Glimmer Train*
RAMONA AUSUBEL
   Welcome to Your Life and Congratulations, *Green Mountains Review*
   Safe Passage, *One Story*

NICHOLSON BAKER
   The Charms of Wikipedia, *The New York Review of Books*
JESSE BALL
   Archon LLC, *The Paris Review*
AMY BARSKY
   Rosary, *Raritan*

CHARLES BAXTER
The Chaos Machine, *The Believer*

JOSHUAH BEARMAN
The Legend of Master Legend, *Rolling Stone*

WENDELL BERRY
Fly Away, Breath, *Threepenny Review*

TOM BISSELL
Punishment, *The Normal School*

ROBIN BLACK
Harriet Elliot, *One Story*

JASON BOOG
The Military-Toy-Industrial Complex, *The Believer*

RACHEL BORMANN and NATE POWELL
Cakewalk, Self-published mini-comic

JOHN BRANDON
The Whim of the Client, *Duck and Herring*

LONNIE BUSCH
Alley Fighter, *Portland Review*

JEREMIAH CHAMBERLIN
Missionaries, *Michigan Quarterly Review*

DAN CHAON
What Happened to Sheila, *The Rumpus*

MARILYN CHIN
Fables, *Prairie Schooner*

MARTHA CLARKSON
Brittle Complications of Love, *The Smoking Poet*

DANIEL CLOWES
Mister Wonderful, *The New York Times Magazine*

JONAS MADDEN-CONNER
Ochre Ellipse, Self-published mini-comic

AIMEE CURL
Separated at Busey, *Seattle Weekly*

JOSHUA DAVIS
High Tech Cowboys of the Deep Seas, *Wired*

MATTHEW DERBY
January in December, *Guernica*
EMMA DONOGHUE
Man and Boy, *Granta*
HALINA DURAJ
Tenants, *Third Coast*
STUART DYBEK
Cordoba, *Alaska Quarterly Review*

MATTHEW ECK
Ward No. 6?, *Mid-American Review*
ROB EHLE
Thanksgiving, *Epoch*
STEPHEN ELLIOT
F*#@ Pop Culture, *The Rumpus*
JOSH EMMONS
Humphrey Dempsey, *Five Chapters*

RAY FENWICK
The Five Oracles of Gossip, *MOME*
GARY FINCKE
A Room of Rain, *The Journal*
MAX FRASER
The House Folds, *The Nation*
RODRIGO FRESÁN
The Sorcerer's Apprentice, *Habitus*

AARON GARRETSON
The Winner, *Opium*
JANE GILLETTE
Divine Afflatus, *Michigan Quarterly Review*
PATRICIA GRACE
Pa Wars, *Harvard Review*
KARL TARO GREENFELD
NowTrends, *American Short Fiction*

John Griswold
Three Graces, *Brevity*
Lauren Groff
Sir Fleeting, *One Story*

Daniel Handler
Why I'm Pro Life, *Anderson Valley Advertiser*
Josh Harkinson
Tar Wars, *Mother Jones*
Baird Harper
Two-Twenty-Two, *Mid-American Review*
Scott Hutchins
Thirty Thousand Dollars, *Five Chapters*
Samantha Hunt
The House Began to Pitch, *Five Chapters*

Shelley Jackson
Mars, Marred, Married, *Fence*
Muzamil Jaleel
A Kashmiri in America: The Lucky Shade of Brown, *dispatches*
Drew Johnson
The Last Dead, *The Virginia Quarterly Review*

Jeff Kass
On the Case, *Writecorner*
Dawna Kemper
Say the Word, *The Idaho Review*
Chuck Klosterman
Bending Spoons with Britney Spears, *Esquire*
Andrew Kozma
Prayers to Those Who Wait, *The Iowa Review*
David Kranes
The Weight-Loss Performance Artist, *Isotope*
Sana Krasikov
Debt, *A Public Space*

DAVID NAIMON
The Golem of Orla Shalom, *Zyzzyva*

CAITLIN NEWCOMER
Only This Torn Room Forever Sleeps, *Hayden's Ferry Review*

MAUD NEWTON
Conversations You Have at Twenty, *Narrative*

JASON OCKERT
Insectuality, *Ecotone*

STEPHEN O'CONNOR
Man in the Moon, *Conjunctions*

ZZ PACKER
A Finished Revolution?, *Oxford American*

JEFF PARKER
Our Cause, *Indiana Review*

ADAM PETERSON
Department of Calamitous Events, *CutBank*

CARL PETERSON AND MICHAEL MARTONE
I Am Michael Martone, *Notre Dame Review*

MATTHEW PITT
Wanted: Rebel Song, *Oxford American*

AIMEE POKWATKA
The Glass Mountain, *The Greensboro Review*

NATHANIEL POPPER
The Novelist and the Murderers, *The Nation*

ROLF POTTS
The Henry Ford of Literature, *The Believer*

GLEN POURCIAU
Claim, *The Paris Review*

KIRSTIN VALDEZ QUADE
Den Mother, *Colorado Review*

SETH RAAB
Heart Failures, *Lumina*

TRICIA READY
United States of Anxiety, *The Stranger*

MICHELLE RICHMOND
A Life in Pods, *The Kenyon Review*

MARY RUEFLE
My Search Among the Birds, *The Iowa Review*

PREETA SAMARASAN
Birch Memorial, *A Public Space*

LUC SANTE
Words and Pictures from the Pinakothek Web Log, *Yeti*

JANET SARBANES
The Adventures of the President's Daughter, *Black Clock*

THEO SCHELL-LAMBERT
A Certain Kind of Murder, *The Believer*

MATTATHIAS SCHWARTZ
The Trolls Among Us, *The New York Times Magazine*

DAVID SEDARIS
April & Paris, *The New Yorker*

REBECCA SOLNIT
Iceland's Polite Dystopia, *Harper's Magazine*

BENJAMIN SOLOMON
Yeoman on the Front Lines, *Boneshaker*

RYAN STONE
Catching Earl, *Natural Bridge*

EVA TALMADGE
The Cranes, *New York Tyrant*

FRANK TEMPONE
Everlasting, *Upstream*

AMELIA THOMSON-DEVEAUX
Night People, *The Nassau Literary Review*

WELLS TOWER
Leopard, *The New Yorker*

ALEXEI TSVETKOV
Leaving Prague, *Poetry Foundation*

STEPHEN TUTTLE
　Amanuensis, *Hayden's Ferry Review*

DEB OLIN UNFERTH
　Natural Citizens, *New York Tyrant*

JULIA WHITTY
　March of the Tourists, *Mother Jones*
KEVIN WILSON
　Days at the Beach, *Mid-American Review*
ANNE-E WOOD
　The Beast, *Agni Online*
TONY WOODLIEF
　Name, *Image*

REBEKAH YEAGER
　The Couch, *Potomac Review*

JOHN ZAKLIKOWSKI
　Expletive Deleted, *Santa Monica Review*

ABOUT 826 NATIONAL

Proceeds from this book benefit youth literacy

A LARGE PERCENTAGE of the cover price of this book goes to 826 National, a network of youth tutoring, writing, and publishing centers in seven cities around the country.

Since the birth of 826 National in 2002, our goal has been to assist students ages six through eighteen with their writing skills while helping teachers get their classes passionate about writing. We do this with a vast army of volunteers who donate their time so we can give as much one-on-one attention as possible to the students whose writing needs it. Our mission is based on the understanding that great leaps in learning can happen with one-on-one attention, and that strong writing skills are fundamental to future success.

Through volunteer support, each of the seven 826 chapters — in San Francisco, New York, Los Angeles, Ann Arbor, Chicago, Seattle, and Boston — provides after-school tutoring, class field trips, writing workshops, and in-school programs, all free of charge, for students, classes, and schools. 826 centers are especially committed to supporting teachers, offering services and resources for English Language Learners, and publishing student work. Each of the 826 chapters works to produce professional-quality publications written entirely by young people, to forge relationships with teachers in order to create innovative workshops and lesson plans, to inspire students to write and appreciate the written word, and to rally thousands of enthusiastic volunteers to make it all happen. By offering all of our programming for free, we aim to serve families who cannot afford to pay for the level of personalized instruction their children receive through 826 chapters.

The demand for 826 National's services is tremendous. Last year we worked with more than 4,000 volunteers and close to 18,000 students nationally, hosted 385 field trips, completed 147 major in-schools projects, offered 307 evening and weekend workshops, welcomed over 188 students per day for after-school tutoring, and produced over 600 student publications. At many of our centers, our field trips are fully booked almost a year in advance, teacher requests for in-school tutor support continue to rise, and the majority of our evening and weekend workshops have waitlists.

826 National volunteers are local community residents, professional writers, teachers, artists, college students, parents, bankers, lawyers, and retirees from a wide range of professions. These passionate individuals can be found at all of our centers after school, sitting side by side with our students, providing one-on-one attention. They can be found running our field trips, or helping an entire classroom of local students learn how to write a story, or assisting student writers during one of our Young Authors' Book Programs.

All day and in a variety of ways, our volunteers are actively connecting with youth from the communities we serve.

To learn more or get involved, please visit:

826 National: www.826national.org
826 in San Francisco: www.826valencia.org
826 in New York: www.826nyc.org
826 in Los Angeles: www.826la.org
826 in Chicago: www.826chi.org
826 in Ann Arbor: www.826michigan.org
826 in Seattle: www.826seattle.org
826 in Boston: www.826boston.org